"Matt Braun

—Elmer Kelton

"Matt Braun is one of the best!"
        —Don Coldsmith, author of The Spanish Bit series

"He tells it straight—and he tells it well."
        —Jory Sherman, author of *Grass Kingdom*

"Matt Braun has a genius for taking real characters out of
the Old West and giving them flesh-and-blood immediacy."
    —Dee Brown, author of *Bury My Heart at Wounded Knee*

"Braun blends historical fact and ingenious fiction . . . A top-
drawer Western novelist!"
        —Robert L. Gale, Western Biographer

DEADWOOD

Matt Braun

St. Martin's Paperbacks

MANHUNTER / DEADWOOD

Manhunter copyright © 1981 by Matthew Braun.
Deadwood copyright © 1981 by Matthew Braun. Published by arrangement with Pocket Books.

Cover photo © Creatas/Inmagine.

ISBN: 0-312-94604-X
EAN: 978-0-312-94604-3

Printed in the United States of America

Manhunter Sphere Books Ltd edition / 1982
St. Martin's Paperbacks edition / March 2003

Deadwood Pocket Books edition / December 1981
St. Martin's Paperbacks edition / August 2003

St. Martin's Paperbacks are published by St. Martin's Press, 175 Fifth Avenue, New York, NY 10010.

10 9 8 7 6 5 4 3 2 1

To
My Folks
on Their
Golden Wedding
Anniversary

Author's Note

Deadwood was one of the richest gold camps in the Old West. The lure of overnight wealth proved a lodestone for prospectors and miners, grifters and outlaws, and a wide assortment of characters who inhabited the vice district. Vast amounts of money exchanged hands, and as a result, violence was commonplace. The town was tough and dangerous, no place for the faint of heart. Only the strong survived in Deadwood.

Yet the untold story had nothing to do with gold. Until now a footnote to history, it was the politics of Dakota Territory that deserved the greater infamy. Corruption and graft were rampant, and the stakes far exceeded the transitory riches of a mining camp. Power brokers and the vested interests, during the early 1880s, were involved in a systematic looting of the territory itself. The chief conspirator was the governor, and few public officials were untouched by the web of intrigue and shady practices. Dakota Territory was a textbook example of the system gone wrong, and the ultimate price was staggering. Ambition proved the deadliest killer of all.

Deadwood is for the most part a true account. Some license has been taken with time and date and place. The historical characters, however, are represented as they actually were, with no apology and no attempt at whitewash. Within the framework of the story, Butch Cassidy and Hole-in-the-Wall are also depicted with true-to-life authenticity. The tall tales surrounding Hole-in-the-Wall, like so many Old West myths, were fostered by outlaws and widely exaggerated by the press. On the other hand, the lawmen central to the story required no literary invention. Nat Boswell and Seth Bullock *were* legend in their own time.

Luke Starbuck represents yet another breed of lawman. A detective and an undercover operative, he was a master of disguise. His fame as a manhunter was unsurpassed, and his reputation as a mankiller was known throughout the Old West. His assignment in *Deadwood* deals more with truth than fiction. What he unearths during the course of his investigation is based on documented fact. He saw it happen exactly the way it's told.

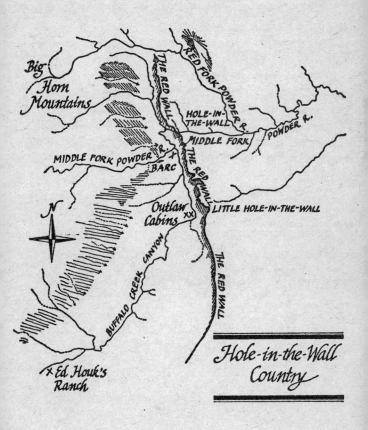

Hole-in-the-Wall
Country

DEADWOOD

Chapter One

Starbuck checked the loads in his old Colt. Then he lowered the hammer on an empty chamber and stuffed the sixgun into a crossdraw holster. His suit jacket concealed the rig with no telltale bulge.

On the way out the door, he jammed a Stetson on his head and paused to inspect himself in the foyer mirror. His suit was conservative, as befitted a man in his profession, and he wore a four-in-hand tie that was equally sober. His appointment today at the Denver Club required that he look the part, create a certain impression. He thought he would pass muster.

In the hallway, he bypassed the newly installed elevator. His suite in the Brown Palace was located on the top floor, but he still preferred the stairs. Along with a daily regimen of exercise, the hike up and down four flights of stairs kept him in reasonable shape. He emerged into the lobby some minutes later and walked directly to the street door. Outside, he turned uptown beneath a warm noonday sun.

Springtime was to Starbuck the best of all seasons. Off in the distance, the Rockies were still blanketed with snow, towering skyward into the clouds. Yet by late May the city itself was slowly recovering from the onslaughts of winter. The air was clear and exhilarating, and with the mud season at an end, the streets were baked hard as stone. Passersby seemed somehow uplifted in spirit, and even the clang of trolley cars took on a merry ring. Starbuck's mood was no less buoyant. The weather, combined with one of his swift-felt hunches, gave him a sense of promise. It looked to be a good day.

Once through the business district, Starbuck continued along Larimer Street. His immediate destination was the Tenderloin. There, within a few square blocks, every vice known to man was available for a price. Saloons and gaming dives catered to the sporting crowd, and variety theaters featured headline acts from the vaudeville circuit. The racy blend of fun and games attracted high rollers from all across the West.

One block over, on Holladay Street, was Denver's infamous red-light district. Known locally as the Row, it was a lusty fleshpot, with a veritable crush of dollar cribs. Girls waited in doorways, soliciting customers, available by the trick or by the hour. Yet, while these hook shops dominated, there was no scarcity of parlor houses on the Row. Essentially a high-class bagnio, the parlor house offered younger girls and a greater variety, all at steeper prices. Something over a thousand soiled doves plied their trade on Holladay Street, and each in her own way was a civic benefactress. The revenues generated by their license fees were the only thing that kept the city treasury afloat.

For those with a taste for the bizarre, there was Hop Alley. A narrow passageway running between Larimer and Holladay, it was Denver's version of Lotus Land. Chinese fan-tan parlors vied with the faint, sweet odor of opium dens, and those addicted to the Orient's heady delights beat a steady path to this back-street world of pipe dreams. To a select clientele, young China dolls were for sale as well.

Still, it was not gambling or girls that brought Starbuck to the Tenderloin. Whenever he was in town, he made a practice of dropping by Murphy's Exchange, otherwise known as the Slaughterhouse. A watering hole for the underworld, it was home away from home to thimbleriggers, bunco artists, and a wide assortment of shady characters. Moreover, it was the chief source of gossip, not to mention a message drop, for those who lived on the fringes of the law. To a private detective, that made it a lode of hard intelligence. One to be mined at regular intervals.

Starbuck was known to those who frequented Murphy's Exchange. His reputation as a manhunter— some called him a mankiller—was widely celebrated throughout the West. Only last month he had been instrumental in the death of Jesse James, and previous cases had pitted him against such notorious gunmen as Wyatt Earp and Billy the Kid. Over the years he'd been retained by banks and train companies, and he was reputed to have killed at least twenty outlaws. Yet, for all his renown with a gun, it was his skill as a detective that kept his services in constant demand. He always got results, and it was no secret that he enjoyed his work. He was a hunter of men who seemed born to the job.

Upon entering the saloon, Starbuck walked to a vacant spot at the end of the bar. The noontime crowd, after a quick glance in his direction, suddenly got busy minding their own business. Apart from his reputation with a gun, he was also noted as a man who brooked no familiarity. A strapping six-footer, he was lean and tough, full-spanned through the shoulders. His features were ruggedly forceful, with a square jaw and wide brow, and a thatch of light chestnut hair. But it was his eyes—smoky blue and impersonal—that gave other men pause. His gaze was detached, not so much cold as stoic. A look of one who makes alliances but not friends. The look of a loner, and someone best left alone.

Jack Murphy, the proprietor, moved forward to greet him. Their relationship was one of quid pro quo—a favor here for a favor there—and it had proved mutually profitable in the past. A squat fat man, with a greasy moonlike face and a larcenous disposition, Murphy had only one redeeming quality. He was Starbuck's principal informant in the Denver underworld.

"Afternoon, Luke." Murphy wiped the counter with a dirty bar rag. "Buy you a drink?"

Starbuck wagged his head. "Guess I'll pass."

"What can I do for you, then?"

"Wondered what you've heard on the grapevine."

"Nothing special." Murphy stared back at him with round, guileless eyes. "Things are pretty quiet."

"Things are never that quiet," Starbuck said pointedly. "Try me and see."

"Well, lemme think." Murphy furrowed his brow. "Couple of weeks ago Frank Loving got it down in Trinidad. A saloonkeeper by the name of Allen put his lights out."

"Cockeyed Frank Loving?" Starbuck inquired. "The gambler?"

"Some folks said it wasn't gambling, not the way he dealt."

"Anything else?"

"You remember Jim Courtright?" When Starbuck

nodded, he went on. "A pair of toughnuts tried to rob an ore shipment he was guarding. He shot 'em deader'n hell."

"Whereabouts?"

"New Mexico Territory."

"Nothing closer to home?"

"Like I said," Murphy reminded him, "things are slow."

Starbuck gave him a stony look. "I don't suppose you've heard anything about William Dexter, the lawyer?"

"Not a peep." Murphy fidgeted uncomfortably. "Why do you ask?"

"I've got my reasons."

"Take some advice, Luke." Murphy cleared his throat, leaned closer. "Don't get crosswise of Dexter. He runs with the uptown crowd, and they play rough."

"Yeah?" Starbuck's eyebrows narrowed in a quick characteristic squint of mockery. "I always heard that bunch prided themselves on being upstanding Christians."

"That's what I mean!" Murphy grunted. "God's on their side—leastways to hear them tell it—and that makes them double-damn dangerous."

"I'll keep it in mind." Starbuck consulted his pocket watch. "Guess I'd better move along, Jack. Wouldn't do to be late for an appointment."

"Hope to hell it's not with Dexter!"

"You really don't want to know . . . do you?"

"Not me!" Murphy's lips peeled back in a weak smile. "I just got a sudden case of deaf."

Starbuck flipped him a salute. "See you around."

"Take care, Luke."

"I always do."

Outside, Starbuck turned from the Tenderloin and headed back uptown. He thought to himself the saloonkeeper's advice was worth the trip. He would indeed take care.

The Denver Club was the sanctum sanctorum of the city's upper crust. Only recently constructed, it was an imposing stone building, four stories high and occupying nearly half a block. Like some medieval fortress, it commanded the intersection of Seventeenth Street and Glenarm.

Crossing the street, Starbuck was reminded that the club was a symbol of Denver's power structure. Membership was restricted to those of wealth and position, the elite of the business world. Gentlemen met there to socialize and discuss deals, and the pacts they struck often produced a ripple effect throughout the whole of Colorado. Their numbers included bankers and merchant princes, railroad barons and mine owners, financiers and lawyers. As a group, their influence was incalculable, and their political connections extended to the state house itself. They were, in every sense of the word, the aristocracy of Denver's social order.

For his part, Starbuck held the power brokers in mild contempt. His own origins were humble; but like many of Denver's upper class, he too was a self-made man. A cowhand turned range detective, he'd grown and prospered, slowly developing a reputation as the leading private investigator in the West. His investment portfolio—which included municipal bonds, real estate, and various mining stocks—now exceeded a quarter million dollars. Yet success and personal wealth had not gone to his head. At bottom, he was still a man of simple tastes, no sophisticate. Nor was he under any great compulsion to curry favor with those who ruled Denver. His opinion of himself was what counted, nothing more.

A similar attitude extended to his professional life. He worked by choice—rather than necessity—for the simplest of reasons. He took pride in his craft, and derived a certain emotional sustenance from danger. High stakes were the lodestone, and in his view, a manhunt was the ultimate wager. Financal independence, of course, allowed him to pick and choose from the many assignments offered. He accepted a case because of the degree of risk entailed, the challenge. To win, there must exist a chance to lose. And each time out, he bet his life.

The interior of the Denver Club was scarcely less than Starbuck had expected. The ceilings were high, and the staircase facing the entrance rose upward like an aerial corridor. Dark paneling predominated, with a massive chandelier suspended overhead and lush Persian carpet underfoot. An attendant escorted him into a room immediately off the central hallway. The decor was opulent, with velvet drapes and damask wallpaper, all heightened by a black marble fireplace and luxuriant leather furniture. An immense oil painting of the Colorado Rockies hung resplendent over the fireplace.

A man in his late forties turned from a sunlit window. He was attired in a black broadcloth coat and gray-striped trousers, with a pearl stickpin nestled in an elegant silk cravat. His voice was well modulated and his manners impeccable. He walked forward, extending his hand.

"How nice of you to come, Mr. Starbuck."

"Pleasure's all mine, Mr. Dexter."

"Won't you have a seat?" Dexter let go of his hand, motioned him into the room. "May I offer you something to drink?"

"No, thanks." Starbuck settled into an overstuffed chair. "I never mix liquor with business."

"An admirable trait." Dexter dismissed the attendant with a faint nod. He took a chair opposite Starbuck and crossed his legs. "I do appreciate your promptness, Mr. Starbuck."

"Your note indicated it was a matter of some urgency."

"And so it is."

William Dexter, like everyone else in Denver, was aware of Starbuck's reputation. He knew the detective was admired for his cool judgment and nervy quickness in tight situations. So now, assessing the man and the moment, he wasted no time on preliminaries. He went straight to the point.

"I asked you here on behalf of a client, Mr. Starbuck. I have been empowered to offer you a . . . commission."

"Commission." Starbuck repeated the word without inflection. "Would you care to spell that out?"

"Of course," Dexter replied genially. "My client owns a rather substantial copper mine in Butte, Montana. Day before yesterday, the paymaster was brutally beaten and robbed. My client wants the payroll returned."

"How much money's involved?"

"Forty-seven hundred dollars."

"Hardly seems worth the effort."

"On the contrary," Dexter said with exaggerated

gravity. "My client is willing to pay you five thousand dollars now and five thousand dollars upon completion."

Starbuck's mouth curled in a sardonic smile. "Why do I get the impression we just stopped talking about the payroll?"

"Very discerning, Mr. Starbuck." Dexter examined him with a kind of bemused curiosity. "Actually, my client's principal concern is justice. He wants an object lesson made of the robber. A warning, as it were, to anyone with similar ideas."

The message was familiar. Couched in discreet terms, it was one Starbuck had heard many times before. He was being asked to dispense summary justice, kill an outlaw. His expression revealed nothing.

"Why not let the law handle it?"

Dexter slowly shook his head. "I regret to say that avenue has been foreclosed. The sheriff in Butte identified the robber—a ruffian by the name of Mike Cassidy—but he declined to carry it further. Valor, it seems, has its limits."

Starbuck studied him with a thoughtful frown. "Are you saying the sheriff lost his nerve?"

"I am indeed!" Dexter announced. "Not without reason, however. Perhaps you've heard of a place called Hole-in-the-Wall?"

There was a long silence. Hole-in-the-Wall, located in the wilds of Wyoming, was considered an inaccessible outlaw sanctuary. To Starbuck's knowledge, no lawman had ever ventured into the remote mountain fastness and returned alive. The assignment, until now a seemingly mundane affair, suddenly piqued his interest. At length, his tone matter-of-fact, he nodded.

"Let's say I've heard of it. So what?"

"Quite simply," Dexter observed, "the robber has taken refuge in Hole-in-the-Wall. So far as we can determine, no peace officer will go near the place. We thought you might be the man for the job."

"In other words"—Starbuck kept his gaze level and cool—"you want me to locate Mike Cassidy and kill him. Is that the gist of it?"

"I didn't say that," Dexter remarked stiffly. "Of course, by entering Hole-in-the-Wall, I should imagine you'd have no choice. I understand those desperadoes refuse to be taken alive."

Starbuck regarded him with great calmness. "Who's your client?"

"Ira Lloyd," Dexter informed him. "Owner of the Grubstake Mining Company. And, I hasten to add, one of the wealthiest men in Butte."

"Why use a go-between? Why didn't he contact me himself?"

"For one thing, he rarely travels to Denver. For another, a man in his position prefers anonymity in such matters. All things considered, an intermediary seems very much in order. Don't you agree, Mr. Starbuck?"

A moment elapsed while the two men stared at each other. Then Starbuck's mouth twisted in a gallows grin. "Well, it's tidy, Mr. Dexter. And I do admire tidy arrangements."

"Then you'll take the case?"

Starbuck uncoiled from his chair and stood. "I'll let you know."

"Let me know?" Dexter echoed blankly. "When?"

"When I make up my mind."

Starbuck turned and walked from the room. William Dexter watched him out the door, then eased back in his chair and gazed up at the panoramic painting over the fireplace. A slow, foxy smile creased the corners of his mouth.

Chapter Two

Starbuck walked directly from the Denver Club to his office. The building was around the corner from the Windsor Hotel, centrally located to the business district. His agency, which consisted of a two-room suite, was on the second floor. He seldom went there.

For several years Starbuck's office had been under his hat. During the period he'd worked as a range detective, there had been no need for a permanent location. With time, however, the nature of his business had undergone a gradual change. From chasing horse thieves and cattle rustlers, it had slowly evolved into investigative work of greater complexity. Wells Fargo was his first major client, and within a span of three years his reputation rivaled that of the Pinkertons. By 1882, he was regarded as the foremost detective west of the Mississippi. His list of clients read like a directory of railroads, banks, and stagecoach lines.

Upon locating in Denver, he had established a modest office. A one-room cubbyhole, and quite spartan by normal standards, it had served as a clearinghouse for correspondence. Since he was usually off on a case, there was need for little more than a secretary and an address. Only recently had he decided to expand his headquarters. An adjoining room had been leased, and he'd had a connecting door installed. A desk and a chair gave it some semblance of a private office, but he used it for an altogether different purpose. There, locked in a massive safe, he maintained a repository of hard intelligence on the criminal element. It was, in effect, a rogues' gallery of western outlaws.

Upstairs, Starbuck entered the office and pegged his Stetson on a hat rack. Verna Phelps, his secretary, glanced up from an accounting ledger. She was a spinster, on the sundown side of thirty, and prim as a missionary. She wore her hair in a tight chignon, and pince-nez eyeglasses were clipped onto the end of her nose. She looked every inch the old maid.

"Good afternoon." She greeted him with starch civility. "How was your meeting?"

"I haven't decided yet."

"Pardon me?"

"It's a queer setup," Starbuck told her. "Dexter's only the front man. Turns out he's representing some mine owner up in Butte."

Verna lifted an eyebrow in question. "Why should that bother you?"

"Don't know," Starbuck admitted. "Guess I get a little leery when a man won't do business face to face."

"Some people would consider it routine practice. After all, a lawyer often has power of attorney to act in his client's behalf."

"Maybe." Starbuck hesitated, then shrugged. "Or maybe it's Dexter that worries me. I never did trust a man who's got nothing to hide. And he comes across like every word's sworn testimony."

"Humph!" Verna sniffed and looked away. "Your cynicism never ceases to amaze me."

Starbuck grinned. "So far, it's kept me fogging a mirror. Which isn't exactly no small feat, considering the company I keep."

Verna Phelps conceded the point. She appreciated the danger involved in Starbuck's work, and understood the need for expedient methods. She even took a certain macabre pride in the number of men he'd killed. Yet she thought him too cynical for his own good, and secretly worried it would lead to some darker alienation of the spirit. She abruptly switched topics.

"Speaking of company," she observed, squinting querulously over her glasses, "Miss Montana sent a street urchin by with a message."

"Urchin?"

"That's correct!" Verna said with frosty disapproval. "No doubt some poor orphan she and her associates have corrupted with handouts."

"The girls at the Alcazar would be mighty pleased to know you've elevated them to 'associates.' "

"A charitable term," Verna noted with a feisty scowl. "Would you care to hear my real opinion?"

"I'd sooner not." Starbuck warded her off with upraised palms. "Let's just stick to the message."

"Miss Montana," Verna said sharply, "requests the pleasure of your company at tonight's performance. I have the distinct impression she feels you've been neglecting her."

Starbuck's expression was one of amiable tolerance. "What do you think, Verna? Should I give her a break or not?"

"I'm sure I don't care one way or the other."

By no means monogamous, Starbuck entertained any number of women in his hotel suite. Yet his affair with Lola Montana—a headliner at the Alcazar Variety Theater—appeared to be a thing of some permanence. Her disclaimer aside, Verna had mixed emotions on that score. She applauded his constancy to one woman, which was a singular departure from his normal behavior. Still, she thought the woman—who shamelessly flaunted herself onstage—was little more than a common strumpet. It was all very perturbing, and Starbuck himself did nothing to alleviate her anxiety. His overall attitude was that of a boar grizzly in rutting season. He took his women where he found them.

Verna considered it not only scandalous, but thoroughly reprehensible. And more than a little titillating. She often wondered how Lola Montana felt, locked naked in the intimacy of Starbuck's embrace. The mere thought prompted a vicarious sensation that gave her naughty dreams, and vivid awakenings. Even now, she felt a tingling warmth along her loins, and her face suddenly reddened to the hairline. She took hold of herself, ruthlessly purged the thought.

"You have your message," she said in a waspish tone. "Now, perhaps we can return to business. You were telling me about Mr. Dexter."

"Nothing more to tell," Starbuck said equably. "He just struck me as a man with secrets . . . lots of secrets."

"Then you intend to refuse the case?"

"Nooo," Starbuck said slowly. "Tell you the truth, I'm tempted to have a crack at it."

"Oh?" Verna gave him a quizzical glance. "Something unusual?"

"Out of the ordinary," Starbuck affirmed. "He wants me to track down a payroll robber—last reported at Hole-in-the-Wall."

"Hole-in-the-Wall!" Verna suddenly appeared apprehensive. "I understood Hole-in-the-Wall was certain death to lawmen!"

"Yeah." Starbuck chuckled, and lowered one eyelid in a conspiratorial wink. "A place where angels fear to tread. Sounds like just my speed, doesn't it?"

"It sounds like you could get yourself killed."

"What the hell!" Starbuck deadpanned. "Nobody lives forever."

"On the other hand," Verna said, a hint of reproach in her voice, "why leap at a challenge simply because it's there?"

"Always look before I leap," Starbuck noted wryly. "Suppose you dig out your directory on mining companies? I'd like to know if there's a Grubstake Mining Company in Butte."

"Anything else?"

"Dexter told me the owner's name is Ira Lloyd. Check that, too."

Verna rummaged around in the bottom drawer of her desk and pulled out a directory published by the Denver Stock Exchange. Starbuck left her flipping pages and moved into the inner office. He walked to a large double-door safe standing against the far wall. He spun a sequence on the combination lock, then turned the handle and swung open one door. On an inside shelf were stacked four loose-leaf ledgers, each of them bound in dark leather. He removed the top ledger, which was stenciled A–F on the cover, and crossed the room to his desk. He sat down and opened the ledger to the section flagged with the letter C.

Not quite a year ago, Starbuck had begun organizing his personal rogues' gallery. As a first step, he subscribed to dozens of newspapers throughout the states and territories that constituted the western United States. He next circulated his name throughout the law-enforcement community and got himself on the mailing list for wanted posters; the dodgers on fugitives included across-the-board felonious crime, from horse stealing to murder. Finally, he undertook a program of correspondence with various peace officers and U.S. marshals across the frontier. The response was far more productive than anything he'd imagined. The post office began delivering his mail in a sack.

Quite soon, Verna inherited the project. She read the newspapers, clipping out all articles dealing with criminal activity. She sorted through the wanted posters, cataloguing them by name and locale. And she attended to the correspondence with lawmen, cleverly forging Starbuck's signature whenever he was out of town. The final step, bringing all the intelligence together, involved the four leather-bound ledgers. A page was assigned to each wanted man, and therein were detailed his physical description, his habits and associations, and every known fact regarding his crimes and method of operation. Whenever possible, a tintype or photo was acquired and added to the file. The result was a complete and rather meticulous dossier on nearly three hundred western outlaws. A *Who's Who* of desperate men and desperadoes.

The page on Mike Cassidy was revealing. There was no photo, but listed there were the salient, and somewhat surprising, details. Cassidy was age thirty-eight, with dark hair and brown eyes, and a pronounced scar on his left jawbone. He was five feet ten inches in height, of muscular build, and considered extremely dangerous. A former cowhand, he had turned to rustling in 1879, operating principally in Utah and western Colorado. He was wanted on four counts of cattle rustling, three counts of horse stealing, and one count of murder. The murder victim, a Utah rancher, had been killed attempting to halt a livestock raid. Following the homicide, barely two months past, Cassidy had vanished. His associates were not identified by name, and his only known haunt was the Robbers Roost country of southeastern Utah. There were no further reports on his activities since the murder. He was thought to have skipped Utah, present whereabouts unknown.

Starbuck fished a pack of cigarettes from his coat pocket. He shook one out and struck a match on his thumbnail. After lighting up, he took a deep drag, exhaling little spurts of smoke. He studied the fiery tip of the cigarette a moment, his expression abstracted. Then his eyes went back to the page and stopped. His gaze centered on two words—Robbers Roost.

Several years past, peace officers had discovered the existence of an Outlaw Trail. Extending from northern Arizona to the Canadian border, it traversed the western territories, with three principal hideouts along the route. The first stop, commonly called a station, was Robbers Roost. Bounded by mountains, the desolate wasteland was a maze of canyons and windswept mesas. With only three entrances and a few isolated water holes, the Roost was hazardous country for anyone unfamiliar with its layout. On several occasions, lawmen had penetrated the Roost in pursuit of outlaws. Those who returned told hair-raising stories of being lost and near death before stumbling upon a hidden water hole. Outlaws enjoyed every advantage in the deadly game of hide-and-seek within Robbers Roost.

Farther north, the second station on the trail was Brown's Hole. Located in the northwest corner of Colorado, parts of the Hole extended across the eastern boundary of Utah and the southern boundary of Wyoming. Roughly three hundred miles from Robbers Roost, the Hole was a narrow valley surrounded by mountains. There were only two known entrances into the valley; both of them were down steep and precarious paths from mountain rims to the north and south. Few law officers dared the treacherous passageways, and those who did were confronted by a baffling legal problem. Their quarry eluded capture by skipping back and forth across a patchwork of territorial boundaries. Brown's Hole was a jurisdictional nightmare, where outlaws forever held the edge. Fugitives drifted in and out of the valley almost at will.

The last station on the Outlaw Trail lay some two hundred miles to the northeast. Known simply as Hole-in-the-Wall, it was considered the most formidable of all the hideouts. Located in the barrens of upper Wyoming, the refuge was centered in the foothills of the Big Horn Mountains. According to legend, there was only one entrance, which wound through a narrow gorge into a remote valley. Steeped in mystery, the mountain stronghold was reportedly impregnable. The entrance, by all accounts, could be defended by a mere handful of men. At any given

time, it was believed that upward of a hundred outlaws found sanctuary at Hole-in-the-Wall. Lawmen
never ventured there, and for all practical purposes it
was sacrosanct to the outside world. A true no-man's-
land where death awaited any stranger.

Starbuck took a last drag on his cigarette and
stubbed out the butt in an ashtray. He pulled at his
earlobe, lost in thought. With time and hard-won experience, he had developed the trick of putting himself in the wanted man's boots. All he'd gleaned from
the file—added to that hunter's sixth sense—led to
an obvious conclusion. Mike Cassidy, like most western badmen, was familiar with the hideouts along the
Outlaw Trail. Intelligence reports indicated that rustlers and horse thieves regularly worked the route,
disposing of stolen livestock outside their own homeground. It was reasonable to assume Cassidy had quit
Utah following the murder and journeyed northward
to avoid the hangman's rope. The logical hideout, and
by far the safest, was the last station on the trail. Hole-
in-the-Wall.

One thought led to another, and Starbuck found
himself pondering an unknown. Cassidy was a horse
thief and rustler—no robber—a fact clearly documented in his dossier. Yet he was now charged with
payroll robbery, which seemed somehow out of character. Outlaws generally stuck to one line of work,
and their crimes almost always followed a pattern.
But, of course, the only inviolable rule was that there
were exceptions to the rule. Perhaps, after shifting his
base of operations to Hole-in-the-Wall, Cassidy had
decided on a shift in occupation as well. Even the
lowliest horse thief could aspire to greater things, and
robbery was definitely the more lucrative profession.

All of which would account for the payroll job and dovetail neatly as well with Cassidy's disappearance from Utah. It was, moreover, a matter of proximity. Butte, and the Grubstake Mining Company, were only a few days' ride over the Wyoming line. A quick hit-and-run, within easy striking distance from Hole-in-the-Wall.

Starbuck silently repeated the name to himself. *Hole-in-the-Wall.* There was a foreboding ring to it, and he wondered if all the stories were actually true. In his experience, anything shrouded in mystery and legend generally weighed out to about twelve ounces of bat crap to the pound. The fact that lawmen accepted the stories at face value merely intrigued him all the more. He thought it might be worth the ride just to have a look-see for himself.

Verna appeared in the doorway. She walked to the desk and laid the mining company directory before him. Then she stepped back, hands clasped at her waist.

"You can read it for yourself," she advised him. "But the information you received is essentially correct."

"Tell me about it."

"The Grubstake Mining Company," she recited in a singsong voice, "was organized in August, 1874. The original owners of record were Thomas Benson and Fred Wells. The mine has been in continuous operation, and its principal business is copper. All stock certificates were transferred to Ira Lloyd on July 12, 1879. No current production figures are available."

"About three years," Starbuck mused out loud. "Any indication of the mine's value?"

"None," Verna said briskly. "The company is wholly owned, and no shares are currently listed with the exchange."

"How about Lloyd?" Starbuck persisted. "Anything on him personally?"

"Only his name," Verna remarked. "His mailing address is the same as that of the company."

An instant of weighing and calculation slipped past. Then Starbuck leaned forward and took a sheet of foolscap from the desk drawer. He dipped a pen in the inkwell and hastily scribbled a note. He signed it with a flourish and handed it to Verna.

"Stick that in an envelope and get it over to William Dexter."

"Am I to surmise you've taken the case?"

"Have a gander and see for yourself."

The frown lines around Verna's mouth deepened. She adjusted her pince-nez and held the paper at arm's length. Then she quickly scanned the note.

Assignment accepted. Will depart upon receipt of your check.

Luke Starbuck

"You're really going, then?"

Starbuck smiled. "You might say that."

"Might?" Verna fixed him with a stern look. "I don't understand."

"Neither will the boys at Hole-in-the-Wall."

Chapter Three

Some while later Starbuck left the office. He caught a crosstown trolley and hopped off at Blake Street. Dodging a carriage, he walked to the corner and proceeded along a block of business establishments. He turned into a small shop flanked by a pool hall on one side and a hardware store on the other. The sign on the window was faded and peeling, barely legible.

DANIEL CAMERON
GUNSMITH
PISTOLS—RIFLES—SHOTGUNS

A bell jangled as Starbuck moved through the door. He passed a rack of long guns and walked toward a glass showcase at the rear of the shop. Beyond the showcase was a workbench, and off to one side there was an entrance leading to a back room. A small gray-haired man hurried out, wiping his hands on an oily cloth. He was stooped and wiry, with a face like ancient ivory and a humorous expression suggesting incisive wisdom. His features creased with a wide smile.

"Well, well, who have we here?"

"Afternoon, Daniel."

Starbuck pulled the Colt and thumbed it to half-cock. Though the pistol was in excellent condition, the bluing was worn and the barrel showed signs of wear from years of contact with the holster. He opened the loading gate and slowly spun the cylinder. One at a time, five cartridges spilled out on the counter. With practiced ease, he closed the loading gate and deftly lowered the hammer. Then he laid the pistol before Cameron.

"Time to trade," he said crisply. "I leave tomorrow."

"How were you so sure I'd have the new one finished?"

"Just on a hunch"—Starbuck eyed him keenly—"I'd lay odds you had it ready last week."

Cameron gave him a bewildered look. "Now you're a mind reader!"

"You're an open book, Daniel."

"Am I, now?"

"I've got twenty dollars that says I'm right."

"So tell me, Mr. Detective! What makes you so certain?"

"Simple," Starbuck said confidently. "You won't let go of a gun until someone comes and takes it away from you. You've always got to tinker with it just one day more."

There was no arguing the point. Daniel Cameron was a master gunsmith and a superb craftsman. The inner workings of a firearm were to him like the movement of a fine timepiece. To men who knew weapons, his work bore an invisible, albeit unmistakable, signature. The smoothness of operation and overall functional reliability were hallmarks of his skill. Yet he was a congenital perfectionist; no matter how flawless his work, he was convinced one more day would make it still better. As Starbuck had noted, he surrendered a gun only under duress. The artisan in him simply would not let go.

Cameron laughed, spread his hands. "You know me too well, Luke! Not that it couldn't stand a bit more—"

"Spare me the sermon!" Starbuck interjected. "Trot it on out and let me be the judge."

Cameron muttered something to himself, then turned to the workbench. He opened a drawer and removed a bundle wrapped in dark blue velvet. He crossed back to the counter and placed the bundle on the glass top. Gingerly, like a jeweler displaying a gemstone, he peeled away the velvet folds. His gaze shifted quickly to Starbuck.

The pistol was a Colt's Peacemaker. Chambered for .45 caliber, it had a 4¾-inch barrel with standard sights. The finish was lustrous indigo blue and the grips were gutta-percha, custom-made and deep brown in color.

Apart from its handsome appearance, the gun had been stripped and completely overhauled inside. The sear, as well as the half-cock and full-cock notches on the hammer, had been honed with a fine stone. The result was a trigger pull of slightly more than three pounds, which required only a feathered touch of the trigger finger. The mainspring had also received expert attention, for in a gunfight it was vital that the hammer could be cocked swiftly and with ease. A specially tempered mainspring had been fitted to the gun, thereby enabling the hammer to be eared back with a flick of the thumb. Yet it would still strike the primer with sufficient force to ignite the cartridge.

After a final polishing, all the parts had been rehardened to guarantee strength and prevent excessive wear. The end product was a weapon of incomparable quality. The action was silky smooth, and operation, even under the most adverse conditions, was utterly reliable. The Colt mirrored the artistry of Daniel Cameron.

Starbuck hefted the pistol. His eyes narrowed, and a smile appeared at the corners of his mouth as he tested it for balance. After assuring himself it was unloaded, he thumbed the hammer and touched off the trigger. Then his hand seemed to open and close in rapid succession—working hammer and trigger—and the cylinder made an entire revolution within the span of a few heartbeats. At last, with a look of muted wonder, he turned back to Cameron.

"A helluva job," he said softly. "Your best yet, Daniel."

"Yes, it's special," Cameron said with quiet pride. "I hate to see it go."

"Don't worry." Starbuck chuckled. "I'll put it to good use."

"I never doubted it for a moment, Luke."

Starbuck swiftly loaded the Colt. The cartridges he scooped off the counter were Cameron's handiwork as well. In effect, the slug had been turned upside down and loaded backward in the casing. The base of the slug, which was blunt and truncated, was now seated in the forward position. Upon impact, the slug would mushroom and expand to roughly half again its normal size. It was an instant manstopper, and a deadly killer.

Holstering the Colt, Starbuck stuck out his hand. "I'm obliged, Daniel."

"Wear it in good health, Luke."

"I'll sure do my damnedest!"

With a wave, Starbuck turned and walked from the shop. Cameron waited until the door closed, then picked up the old Colt. He studied the gun at length, wondering how many men it had sent to the grave. Only Starbuck knew the true number, and he never talked. Which in the end was perhaps the best policy.

A mankiller, Cameron told himself, was entitled to silence.

Starbuck trusted Daniel Cameron as much as he trusted any man. Yet he would never entrust his life to another man's judgment. Nor would he accept on faith alone the workmanship of any gunsmith. Not without performing his own rigorous test.

Across town, he stopped by the hotel and collected a box of cartridges. His next stop was a saloon, where he came away with a bag of empty bottles. From there, he walked to the banks of the Platte River. No one was anywhere in sight and he was reasonably certain of privacy. He emptied the bag on the ground and selected five bottles. One at a time, with a high overhead toss, he pitched them far upstream. The bottles bobbed to the surface and floated toward him.

Starbuck's hand snaked inside his jacket and came out with the Colt. At such times, his mind closed down and his nerves went dead. He willed out all thought and reverted to some trancelike state where he operated on reflex and instinct. Time fragmented into split seconds, and yet there was an icy deliberation suspended within each moment. He simply saw and reacted. There was the gun and the thing

he was shooting at and an overwhelming sense of
calm. Nothing else.

His arm leveled and the Colt bucked in his hand.
The first bottle erupted in a geyser of water and glass.
With controlled speed, he swung the Colt in an arc
and locked onto the next bottle. His eyes shifted
along the barrel—caught within that frozen instant of
deliberation—and he feathered the trigger. The second bottle in line exploded. Then the next and the
next, and finally the last as the current swept it some
yards below his position. From the time he pulled the
gun until the moment he lowered his arm, less than
five seconds had elapsed. The Colt was quick and
smooth, and it shot where he pointed. He was impressed.

Timing himself, Starbuck shucked the empty
shells and reloaded. On a measured count of ten, he
snapped the loading gate closed and lowered the hammer. His hand moved, and all in a motion he holstered
the Colt.

Then he selected five more bottles.

A pale sickle moon lighted the sky. Somewhere in the
distance a tower clock struck one as the carriage
rolled to a halt before the Brown Palace. The driver
jumped down and opened the door. He doffed his hat
in an eloquent bow.

Starbuck stepped from the coach. He extended his
hand and assisted Lola Montana down. Her eyes were
radiant, and in the silty light the mass of golden curls
piled atop her head seemed to sparkle with moon-
beams. She was attired in a long lavender cape and a
full-length gown. For an instant, as she raised her skirts
to descend the coach step, a delicate ankle was visible.

She noted his appreciative glance and squeezed his hand. He chuckled lightly, depositing her on the curb. Then he tipped the driver a ten-spot and they turned toward the entrance.

Together, arm in arm, Starbuck and the girl swept into the hotel lobby. The night clerk spotted them and hastily set aside the latest issue of the *Police Gazette*. The sight of Starbuck entering the hotel with a woman on his arm was by now commonplace. Yet the clerk was an ardent admirer of Lola Montana, and he secretly burned with envy that she shared the bed of the hotel's most notorious resident. He quickly moved to a position behind the front desk. No word was spoken, but he met Starbuck's sideways glance with a conspiratorial look. He dipped his head in a slow nod.

Starbuck acknowledged the signal with a faint smile. He crossed the lobby, with Lola clinging to his arm, and entered the elevator. A sleepy bellman waited until they were inside, then closed the gate. The elevator shuddered, responding as the bellman rotated the control lever, and lumbered upward. When they disappeared from view, the night clerk sighed and walked back to his chair. He resumed leafing through the *Police Gazette*, but with dampened interest. He wondered to himself why some men had all the luck.

Upstairs, the elevator rumbled to a halt and the bellman opened the gate. Starbuck bid him goodnight, then led the girl down the hall and unlocked the door to his suite. She preceded him through the foyer and stopped just inside the sitting room. A low table, positioned before the sofa, was laid with fine linen and gleaming silverware. Candles were lighted, and in the

center of the table a single yellow rose arched from
a stemlike vase. Serving dishes, artfully arranged
around the vase, contained a light supper of cold roast
squab, brandied pears, and marinated artichoke hearts.
A chilled bottle of champagne stood glistening in an
ice bucket.

"Ooo Luke!" Lola slipped out of her cape and
dropped it on a chair. "All this for me?"

"Nobody else."

Starbuck hung his hat in the foyer and moved into
the sitting room. She turned, her expression animated
with a sudden verve. Her arms circled his neck and
she kissed him soundly on the mouth. Then she pulled
back, searching his face with a knowing smile.

"I thought something was up! You and that desk
clerk both looked like you had a mouthful of feathers!"

"Don't miss a trick, do you?"

"Not where you're concerned."

"Well, you can thank Joe, the clerk. He's the one
who arranged it."

Lola vamped him with a look. "I'd rather thank
you."

"You're missing a bet," Starbuck said in a jesting
tone. "Joe's sweet on you ... regular case of puppy
love."

"Honey, half the men in Denver are sweet on
me!"

Her statement was no idle boast. Lola Montana
was the star attraction at the Alcazar Theater, and the
toast of Denver's night life. A singer, she was small
but nicely put together, with a body like mortal sin.
Her jutting breasts tapered to a slim waist and were
offset by perfectly rounded hips. Her features were

exquisite, with creamy skin and a lush coral mouth that accentuated her high cheekbones. Onstage or off, she was a vision of loveliness, a bawdy nymph bursting with vitality. She was every man's fantasy, and Starbuck's woman.

Yet she was not Starbuck's only woman. She accepted the fact with a certain resignation, and cleverly concealed jealousy. She possessed the wisdom and experience to understand their affair would end if ever she attempted to clip his wings. He slept with other women, but she prudently overlooked those minor lapses; he always returned and she was confident he always would. He was an emotional nomad, wanting no strings and asking none in return. All the same, to the extent he was any woman's man, he was hers. A bond had developed between them, and he let her know in small ways that the attachment was an important part of his life. She cherished the thought.

The champagne and supper were one of those small gestures. Earlier that evening he had appeared at the theater and waited until she finished her midnight performance. Then, without explanation, he'd come backstage and rushed her into changing clothes. At the time, he had been very mysterious, and evaded her questions with a charm normally hidden beneath layers of reserve. Now, suddenly, she understood. The candlelight and rose, all the little added touches, were by way of an affectionate goodbye. He would be gone when she awoke in the morning.

"You sly devil!" Her voice was light and mocking. "You're taking off on a case—aren't you?"

"Damn!" Starbuck watched her with an indulgent smile. "I thought I had you fooled."

"Fat chance!" Lola gave him a bright, theatrical

smile. "Would it do me any good to ask where you're headed?"

"I never fib to ladies"—Starbuck smiled gently—"unless I've got no choice."

Lola wrinkled her nose. "Any idea how long you'll be gone?"

"No longer than it takes."

"Well, don't take too long, lover. I'm liable to start drinking alone, or biting my nails."

"No cause for worry," Starbuck said lightly. "I generally get it done one way or the other."

All of which was true. Lola was concerned but not overly alarmed by the nature of his work. She knew every inch of his body, and she'd personally satisfied herself that it was unmarred by bullet or knife wounds. Added to the number of men he'd killed, it revealed much about his ability to survive. She believed him immune to harm.

"Let's forget I asked." Her lips curved in a teasing smile. "I'll know you're back when I see you. How's that?"

"Sounds fair." Starbuck met her gaze, found something merry lurking there. "How about some champagne? I had this spread laid out special."

"Not now." A vixen look touched her eyes. "Later."

She stretched voluptuously and held out her arms. Her low-cut gown dipped lower, exposing the swell of her breasts. Her laughter was musical and her expression suddenly gleamed with mischief.

"I want my dessert first."

Starbuck marveled again at her almost total lack of inhibition. Her passion was wild and atavistic, and her a sexual appetite was easily a match for his own.

He lifted her in his arms and carried her toward the bedroom. She playfully nibbled his earlobe, laughed a low throaty laugh.

A spill of light from the door flooded the darkened room. He lowered her onto the bed and within a few moments they were naked. She snuggled close in his embrace, her lips moist and inviting. Her hands cupped his face, caressing the hard line of his jaw, and a strange thing happened. She trembled, staring intently into his eyes, and almost spoke. Then she shuddered and her fingernails pierced his back like talons. She pulled him to her.

Their tongues met and dueled. His hand covered one of her breasts, and the nipple swelled instantly. Then his fingers drifted downward, probed the curly delta where her thighs forked. She was damp and yielding, and she uttered a low moan, thrusting against him. Her hand went to his manhood, grasped that hard questing part of him, and stroked it eagerly. For several moments they kissed and fondled, until finally, aroused and aching, she could wait no longer. Her mouth opened in a gasping cry of urgency.

"Ohhh Luke! Now! *Now!*"

Chapter Four

Starbuck left the hotel shortly before sunrise. He took the backstairs and made his way unseen to the basement furnace room. There he exited through a rear door into the alley.

The purpose of his secrecy was twofold. By leaving the hotel unobserved, his departure from Denver would go unnoticed. Only after he'd been gone a few days would he be missed. There was, additionally, an even more critical factor. He was traveling in disguise.

Overall, his appearance was that of an easterner. He was attired in a sedate, expensively tailored tweed suit, topped off by a fashionable beige fedora. He wore spectacles, with heavy wire frames and lenses of plain glass. His shoes were kid leather, polished to a high gloss, and specially constructed. The instep of the left shoe had been built up slightly more than an inch, which had the immediate effect of shortening his left leg. The result was a pronounced limp and a somewhat halting gait. All in all, he looked like a bookish intellectual with a mild deformity.

The publicity surrounding many of his past cases had robbed Starbuck of anonymity. His photo, which had appeared in newspapers throughout the West, made his face known wherever he traveled. Working undercover, it thereby became imperative that he operate in disguise. Early on, when he'd begun his career as a range detective, he had discovered a certain gift for subterfuge and guile. He possessed a streak of the actor, and over the years he had played a wide variety of roles. By turn, he'd posed as a whoremonger and grifter, Bible salesman and drummer, and an assortment of outlaws ranging from horse thief to bank robber. Every assignment offered a unique challenge, and his natural flair for disguise enabled him to create a character suitable to the occasion. He was, in a very real sense, a one-man stock company.

Not unlike a sleight-of-hand artist, Starbuck used misdirection to great effect. The externals—outward appearance and physical quirks—created an illusion. What people saw was the superficial, the obvious; their eye was misdirected from the reality underneath. The deception was then rounded out with mannerisms and speech patterns peculiar to the character he portrayed. A general rule was the simpler the better, with just a touch of the bizarre. Added to the disguise, a credible cover story provided the final twist. His survival rested on the skill of his performance, and once he'd assumed a role, Luke Starbuck simply ceased to exist. He submerged himself, mentally and physically, within the character of the moment.

To enhance security, Starbuck followed still another cardinal rule. He never divulged professional secrets to anyone, whether client or friend. His disguise, the cover story, even the alias he employed, was a matter of strictest confidence. Verna Phelps, whose loyalty was unquestionable, knew only the broad outlines of his assignment. Lola Montana and Daniel Cameron, while trustworthy, were told nothing. What they didn't know couldn't be repeated; the most innocent remark, whether about the case itself or his destination, would find a ready audience in Denver's Tenderloin. From there, the word would spread by moccasin telegraph to every corner of the underworld. The upshot would jeopardize not only the assignment, but perhaps his life as well. He operated on the principle that a secret, once shared, was no longer a secret.

Nor was he any less closemouthed with clients. He operated on his own terms, take it or leave it. Once he'd accepted a case, there was seldom any further communication. He submitted no reports, and revealed nothing with regard to his methods or his strategy. To the extent possible, he kept the client in the dark until the assignment was concluded. He was paid to get results, and when the final tally was taken, the results spoke for themselves. How he went about it was his own business.

The assignment undertaken today was no different. Beyond Starbuck's terse note, there had been no further communication with William Dexter. The lawyer had doubtless notified Ira Lloyd, the mine owner in Butte, as to the disposition of the case. That seemed reasonable to assume since Dexter's check for five thousand dollars had arrived at the office late yesterday afternoon. Yet, from this point onward, the lawyer would know nothing. He might surmise Starbuck had departed for Wyoming, and in that he would be correct. Anything else would remain privileged information.

The morning train for Cheyenne was scheduled to depart at six o'clock. A cautious man, Starbuck allowed himself an hour's leeway. Upon emerging

from the alleyway, he crossed the street and walked
west from the hotel. He spent the next thirty minutes
circling and doubling back, constantly looking over
his shoulder. There was no reason to believe he was
being followed; but the practice was by now a deeply
ingrained habit. He never took anything for granted,
and unless unavoidable, he never left anything to
chance. Today was no exception.

By sunup, he felt confident he wasn't being
tailed. He reversed course as an orange ball of fire
crested the horizon. The city was slowly coming to
life, and street traffic increased markedly as he hurried
toward Union Station. Less than three minutes before
train time, he moved through the depot and walked
directly to the passenger platform. The locomotive
was chuffing steam, and late arrivals were rushing to
scramble aboard. He'd cut it close, but he knew there
would be no problem purchasing a ticket from the
conductor. Stepping onto the last coach, he stowed
his valise in an overhead rack and took a window
seat. The train got under way within a matter of moments.

Starbuck had the seat to himself, and he sat for a
while watching the mountains. Always a spectacular
sight at sunrise, the Rockies seemed to mirror every
color in the spectrum. There was a stately grandeur
to the scene that never failed to impress him. Still, as
the train chugged northward out of Denver, his
thoughts slowly turned to the task ahead. He pulled
the fedora down over his eyes and pretended to
snooze. Yet his mind was very much on Cheyenne.
And the Wyoming Stock Growers Association.

The plan formulated by Starbuck was necessarily
sketchy. Mike Cassidy, the outlaw he'd been hired to

track down, was almost a cipher. With no photo, and no positive means of identification, the assignment definitely posed a challenge. The problem was compounded by still another unknown, Hole-in-the-Wall. All of which meant Starbuck was operating largely in the blind. Yet he was by no means at a loss for a place to start. His investigation would begin with Nathaniel Boswell.

A mankiller of some repute, Nat Boswell was widely respected throughout Wyoming. His service as a peace officer began in 1868, when the Union Pacific was laying track west and Cheyenne was a lawless hellhole. Boswell aroused the citizenry and organized a vigilante committee, which was responsible for ridding the town of outlaws and troublemakers. Shortly thereafter, the territorial governor appointed him sheriff of Albany County. With the commission, he became the chief lawman of a vast region stretching from Colorado to Montana. After several terms in office, he went on to become a detective and undercover operative for the Union Pacific. Only recently, he had been appointed director of the Wyoming Stock Growers Association. Under his command was a force of five range detectives, and he was charged with routing bands of rustlers who preyed on association herds. He was, according to all reports, eminently good at the job. The number of cow thieves killed or hanged had risen dramatically in the last few months. His detectives were not noted for bringing wanted men in alive.

Over the past year, Starbuck had carried on extensive correspondence with Boswell. In organizing his rogues' gallery, he had contacted the Wyoming lawman and requested assistance. Boswell readily cooperated, and in the intervening months, he had become an invaluable source of hard intelligence. The information he forwarded to Denver was concise and timely, and indicated a deep insight into the mentality of outlaws. Though they had never met, Starbuck considered him a top-notch detective. He was, moreover, a legend on the High Plains. No one purposely crossed paths with Nat Boswell.

Starbuck's plan was simple, though somewhat devious. Without revealing his identity, or the nature of his assignment, he intended to pump the stock detective dry of information. His cover story was a corker, and he thought it would play well in Cheyenne. All the more important, he believed it would appeal to Nat Boswell's sense of personal esteem.

And thereby open the door to Hole-in-the-Wall.

Cheyenne was a bustling plains metropolis. The capital of Wyoming Territory, with a population of nearly twenty thousand, it was a major railhead and center of commerce. As a stopover for those en route to the Dakota gold camps, it was also a beehive of trade. On the southside, bordering the railroad tracks, gambling dens and dance halls, variety theaters and bawdy-houses comprised a thriving vice district. Farther uptown, the business district was packed with stores and hotels, restaurants and saloons, several banks, and the territory's leading newspaper. For good reason, Cheyenne had been dubbed the Magic City of the Plains.

Starbuck went directly from the depot to one of the uptown hotels. There he engaged a room for the night and left his valise with the bellman. Then he inquired the location of the Wyoming Stock Growers Association. The desk clerk obligingly pointed him in the right direction. On the street again, he walked toward the town's main intersection.

Some minutes later he went past a bank and rounded the corner. An outside staircase led to an office on the second floor. Upstairs, he entered and found himself in a room with the plain look of a monk's cell. There was a single desk, a couple of file cabinets, and several wooden armchairs. On one wall was a large map of Wyoming Territory. Seated behind the desk was a man who seemed fitted to the sparse accommodations.

Somewhere in his early forties, Nat Boswell was lynx-eyed and whipcord lean. He had gnarled hands, a straight, razored mouth, and features the color of ancient saddle leather. He assessed Starbuck in a single glance. The eastern clothes were duly noted, and his gaze lingered a moment on the gimpy leg. Then, without expression, he looked up and waited.

"Hello there!" Starbuck fixed his face in a jaunty smile and limped across the room. "By any chance, would you be Mr. Nathaniel K. Boswell?"

"Who's asking?"

"Edward Farnum." Starbuck beamed. "I'm with the *Police Gazette.*"

"A reporter?"

"Chief correspondent and associate editor."

Boswell seemed to thaw a little. "What can I do for you?"

"You're Mr. Boswell!" Starbuck grabbed his hand and pumped vigorously. "It's an honor and a pleasure, Mr. Boswell. I simply can't tell you how delighted I am!"

"That a fact?" Boswell waved him to a chair. "What brings you to Cheyenne?"

"Why, you do, Mr. Boswell I'm writing a series of articles on western lawmen, and the paper sent me here expressly to interview you."

"Do tell." Boswell sounded flattered. "What sort of series?"

"The crème de la crème!" Starbuck struck a dramatic pose. "Bill Tilghman of Dodge City. Heck Thomas in Indian Territory. John Armstrong of the Texas Rangers. And Nat Boswell—the Wyoming Avenger!"

"Wyoming Avenger, huh?" Boswell grinned, clearly pleased with the ring of it. "You've got me traveling in pretty fancy company."

"Not at all!" Starbuck observed grandly. "You are too modest by far, Mr. Boswell. In the East your name is legend—without peer!"

"Well—" Boswell tried for humility. "I'm just doing my job, that's all."

"Indeed you are! And that is precisely the angle I wish to explore in the article. A man of noble purpose battling the western Visigoths!"

"Who?"

"Marauders!" Starbuck explained. "Cattle rustlers and horse thieves and gunmen. The outlaw element!"

Boswell nodded wisely. "Wyoming's got its share, no two ways about it."

"Well, now!" Starbuck pulled out a pad and pencil. "Perhaps we could get down to cases. Would you say, Mr. Boswell, that cattle rustlers are Wyoming's principal problem at the moment?"

"I would," Boswell affirmed. "That's why the big ranchers got together and formed the Stock Growers Association."

"A classic citizens' action"—Starbuck scribbled furiously—"when organized law enforcement fails to mete out justice. And might I assume your results to date are encouraging?"

"I reckon you could say that."

"Perhaps some figures," Starbuck said with an expansive gesture. "How many have you hanged or killed in gun battles? Our readers do love the blood and gore of western expediency."

Boswell eyed him warily. "I'd like to accommodate you, Mr. Farnum. But there's certain things the association don't want bandied about. Might give folks the wrong idea."

"A pity." Starbuck feigned disappointment. "However, in general, it would be fair to say you have depleted their ranks. Is that correct?"

"Mostly." Boswell wrestled with himself a moment, then shrugged. "Course, you no sooner weed out one bunch and another crop springs up. It's a job that never gets done."

Starbuck paused, thoughtfully tapped the pencil on his notepad. "Perhaps we could draw an illustration between today and how it was when you were appointed director. In your own words, how would you characterize the situation, Mr. Boswell?"

"Under control," Boswell said firmly. "We've got 'em on the run and that's the way we aim to keep it. Where there's cows, there'll always be rustling, and nobody's gonna stop it cold. But we do a damnsight better job than most."

"Bully!" Starbuck chortled, writing it all down. "I can see it now! A bold headline! Boswell Routs Wyoming Rustlers! Capital stuff, Mr. Boswell. Really first-rate!"

"Hmmm." Boswell studied him with mock gravity. "Well, don't go overboard, Mr. Farnum. Like I said, we've still got our work cut out for us."

"Now that you mention it," Starbuck inquired innocently, "we've heard some rather strange reports about a place—I believe I have the name correct—Hole-in-the-Wall?"

Boswell studied him with some surprise. "What about it?"

"I'm asking you!" Starbuck appeared bemused. His gaze was inquisitive, oddly perplexed. "Are the rumors true? Is it a haven for outlaws and desperadoes?"

"Yes and no." Boswell regarded him dourly. "We get 'em when they come out of Hole-in-the-Wall. Once they're in there, we bide our time and play a waiting game."

"Are you saying"—Starbuck peered over his glasses with owlish scrutiny—"you never follow them into Hole-in-the-Wall?"

"Yeah." Boswell's frown deepened. "That's about the size of it."

Starbuck looked thoroughly mystified. "May I ask why not?"

" 'Cause there's only one way in and one way out. And there's men guarding the entrance night and day. It'd take an army to get through, and even then they'd be cut to ribbons."

"So the reports are correct?" Starbuck asked. "It's a stronghold, some sort of mountain fortress?"

"Close enough," Boswell grated. "What you've got is a valley surrounded by mountains. The mountains are impassable and there's only a narrow canyon leading into the valley. Call it whatever you will, it's a tough nut to crack."

"How perfectly astounding!" Starbuck marveled. "You've seen it for yourself, then?"

Boswell blinked, sat erect. "No, not just exactly."

"I don't mean the valley," Starbuck added hastily. "I was referring to the canyon . . . the Hole-in-the-Wall itself."

"Answer's still the same," Boswell said flatly. "I never looked it over personal."

"*Never?*" Starbuck repeated incredulously. "Why on earth not?"

Boswell pulled in his neck and stared across the desk with a bulldog scowl. "Mister, I don't care much for your tone. You're just a mite too goddamn pushy for my taste."

"Pleeeze!" Starbuck fluttered weakly. "I wasn't questioning your courage, Mr. Boswell. Good Lord, no! I was merely asking why you've never gone there . . . just taken a peek?"

"Suicide's not my game."

"I beg your pardon?"

"Tell you a little story." Boswell's voice dropped. "Back in the summer of '78 a couple of Union Pacific detectives trailed some robbers into Hole-in-the-Wall. They never been heard from since. The same thing happened to a deputy sheriff who was long on grit and short on brains. You get my drift?"

"Indeed I do!" Starbuck looked properly impressed. "You're saying those who tried sacrificed their lives in the effort. So, as a result, peace officers very prudently avoid it altogether."

"I think you got the picture, Mr. Farnum."

"Out of curiosity"—Starbuck glanced at the large wall map—"exactly where is Hole-in-the-Wall?"

Boswell rose and moved around his desk to the

map. He traced a route north to Fort Laramie, then indicated a stretch along the Oregon Trail, and finally stopped at the foothills of the Big Horn Mountains. He rapped a spot on the map.

"That'll give you a rough idea."

"Good heavens," Starbuck breathed softly. "It really is godforsaken, isn't it?"

"Smack-dab in the middle of nowhere, and that's a fact."

"What about ranchers?" Starbuck scanned the map. "Or homesteaders? Has anyone dared settle up there?"

"Oh, there's some," Boswell allowed. "The closest one to Hole-in-the-Wall is a fellow named Ed Houk. He's got a fair-sized spread on Buffalo Creek. That's just south of the canyon I told you about."

Starbuck made a mental note of the name. Then, playing to Boswell's touchy pride, he went on with the interview. He jotted down every word in copious detail, acting the part of a journalist hot on the trail of a story. At last, with much handshaking and profuse thanks, he took his leave. On the way out the door, he had to suppress a smile. His hunch had proved dead on the money. Lawmen, solely for their own devices, had joined fact and fable in an unholy alliance.

Nobody knew beans about Hole-in-the-Wall.

Chapter Five

Early next morning Starbuck emerged from the hotel. He was still attired in the tweed suit and fedora, and he stood for a monet surveying the street. Then he turned and walked toward the train depot.

Cheyenne was a sprawling hodgepodge of buildings. Hammered together on the windswept plains, it was a curious admixture of cowtown and citified elegance. The Union Pacific had transformed it into a hub of trade and commerce, with an ever expanding business district. As the territorial capital, the city had slowly assumed an aura of respectability and cultivation. Yet it was also the major railhead for Wyoming's vast cattle industry.

Every summer herds were trailed into Cheyenne from ranches all across the High Plains. After being sold to cattle brokers, the cows were shipped east for slaughter. A great deal of money exchanged hands, and in the process, the town prospered. However progressive, the political bigwigs and local merchants catered to cattlemen for the best of reasons. Cows were big business, the mainstay of Cheyenne's economic growth.

Centered around the train depot were various enterprises related to the cattle trade. The vice district, where a carnival atmosphere prevailed during trailing

season, was devoted exclusively to the rough tastes
of cowhands. Nearby were holding pens and loading
yards, along with several livestock dealers. Horses,
usually trailed overland from Texas, were yet another
flourishing business in Cheyenne. Wyoming cattlemen found it easier to buy than breed, and thereby
created a market. Good saddle mounts were in constant demand.

Starbuck chose one of the larger livestock dealers. He entered the office, and was greeted by a
paunchy, whey-faced man with muttonchop whiskers.
The dealer gave his eastern clothes a slow once-over,
but asked no questions. A sale was a sale, and he
expressed no curiosity as to why a greenhorn wanted
a saddle horse. He led the way to a large stock pen
outside.

Something more than a hundred horses stood
munching hay scattered on the ground. Starbuck circled the fence, checking conformation and general
condition. After several minutes, he selected a blood
bay, with black mane and tail. A gelding, the animal
was barrel-chested, standing fifteen hands high and
weighing well over a thousand pounds. His hide glistened in the sun like dark blood on polished redwood,
and he looked built for stamina.

A stablehand roped the bay and led him from the
pen. Starbuck inspected his hooves and teeth, then
asked to have him saddled. Stepping aboard, he rode
the horse to the edge of town and brougt him back at
a full gallop. The bay was spirited, though not high-
strung, and exhibited an even disposition. He possessed speed and catlike agility, and plenty of bottom
for endurance over a long haul. Starbuck decided to
look no further.

"Nice pick." The dealer nodded sagely. "You got an eye for horseflesh."

"Thank you." Starbuck took out a handkerchief and began wiping dust from his glasses. "What price are you asking?"

The dealer quoted a figure nearly double the going rate. Starbuck acted gullible, but dickered awhile merely for effect. At last, when the dealer offered to throw in a saddle, he allowed himself to be cheated by some fifty dollars. He paid in cash, and rented a stall in the dealer's livery stable. With a bill of sale in his pocket, he headed back uptown. The dealer looked pleased as punch.

Starbuck's next stop was a store frequented by cowhands. He'd already worked out a disguise and a plausible cover story for Hole-in-the-Wall. Now he needed a wardrobe to fit the part. Since outlaws traveled light, he planned nothing elaborate in the way of camp gear. His purpose was to create yet another illusion—a man on the run.

The store was on the order of a general emporium. Apart from clothing, the stock included saddles and tinned goods and a wide assortment of firearms. The interior smelled of leather and gun oil and musty woolens. A clerk bustled forward, eyeballing Starbuck's eastern getup with a quizzical look. He gave the impression he was biting his tongue. Yet, like the livestock dealer, he asked no questions.

With some care, Starbuck selected an outfit. He stuck to serviceable range duds, nothing fancy. To a linsey shirt and whipcord trousers, he added a mackinaw, plain high-topped boots, and a dun-colored Stetson. Then he picked out a blanket and bedroll tarp, along with the bare essentials in camp gear. A supply of tobacco and some victuals completed his shopping list.

The clothing was new and looked fresh off the shelves. Still, he saw that as no insurmountable problem. By necessity, he'd long ago perfected the knack of aging clothing so that it had a worn appearance. Then, too, he would be several days on the trail, and sleeping on the ground. By the time he arrived at Hole-in-the-Wall, the problem would have resolved itself. His clothes would look as rank as he smelled.

On impulse, he bought a belt studded with silver conchas and a leather vest. The combination added a showy touch, suitable to the character he had in mind. Then, turning toward the counter, his eye fell on a rack of long guns. He abruptly recalled one last item.

"I'll need a rifle," he said, motioning to the clerk. "Let me see something with a little range to it . . . no carbines."

"Oh, you're a hunter!" the clerk said brightly. "I wondered what you were outfitting yourself for."

"You guessed it." Starbuck smiled. "Thought I'd try my hand at some big game."

"Well, now, I might have something that'll interest you! Yessir, I surely might!"

"Winchester?"

"No, sir." The clerk pulled a rifle from the rack and held it out. "A Colt Lightning! It's new, not even in production yet. The factory released a few prototype models—just to test the market."

"I thought Colt was strictly pistols."

"Apparently they're after some of Winchester's business. Here, try it on for size! I guarantee you, it's a humdinger!"

Starbuck hefted the rifle. The balance and workmanship were superb. A pump-action repeater, the stock and foregrip were dark-grained walnut, and the octagon barrel was twenty-six inches long. A tubular cartridge magazine extended beneath the barrel; a backward stroke of the foregrip ejected the spent shell and a forward stroke chambered a fresh round. The sights were quick to the eye, with a buckhorn rear sight and a gold-beaded front sight.

Stepping away from the counter, Starbuck tested the sights and found the pickup amazingly swift. He jacked the slide-action several times, and discovered operation was a shade faster than a lever-action. He swung the rifle in an arc—sighting on a tin of peaches—and squeezed the trigger. The let-off was crisp and light to the touch. He smiled, and turned back to the clerk.

"Got a nice feel."

"My sentiments exactly." The clerk lowered his voice. "Most of our customers were weaned on lever-actions, and won't even take a second look. I can see you're a man who's not stuck in a rut."

Starbuck inspected the rifle closer. "What caliber?"

".50-95!" The clerk grinned as though sharing a secret. "It packs a real wallop!"

"I'd say so," Starbuck observed quietly. "How many rounds does it hold?"

"Ten."

The clerk took a box of cartridges off the shelf. He opened it and held up a shell. The massive fifty-caliber slug was seated in a brass casing almost as long as his finger. He slowly shook his head.

"I'd hate to get hit with that."

"You and me both," Starbuck agreed. "How is it on accuracy?"

"According to the factory, it's a sizzler clean out to five hundred yards."

"I suppose that's far enough."

"Yessir, it's a rare shot at that range!"

Starbuck laid the rifle on the counter. "I'll take it."

"I believe you've made a wise choice, Mr.—?"

"Farnum," Starbuck replied. "How are you fixed for cartridges?"

"We have three boxes in stock."

"I'll take those, too. And a saddle boot for the rifle."

"Very well, Mr. Farnum," the clerk said pleasantly. "Now, could I interest you in a pistol? We have an excellent selection."

"With that rifle"—Starbuck mugged, hands outstretched—"who needs a pistol?"

"Who indeed, Mr. Farnum? Yessir, who indeed!"

Starbuck again paid in cash. Then he asked the clerk to package everything and have it delivered to the hotel. On his way out the door he checked his watch and saw it was approaching the noon hour. Outside, he turned upstreet and went looking for a café.

To Starbuck, food in itself was unimportant. He appreciated—and distinguished between—good cooking and poor cooking. He much preferred tender beefsteak, properly juicy and rare, to a piece of meat charred rawhide tough. Yet, in the overall scheme of things, the culinary fixings were of no great consequence. For him, eating was simply a bodily function, much like a bowel movement. He ate because his body demanded sustenance, and no elaborate ritual was attached to the eating. A minute after shoving his plate away, the meal was forgotten. Good, bad, or indifferent . . . food was food.

Halfway up the block Starbuck spotted a greasy spoon. Walking toward it, he suddenly pulled up short when the bat-wing doors of a saloon burst open. A cowhand lurched outside and stepped directly into his path. The man was tall and burly, dressed in faded range clothes, and to all appearances stumbling drunk. His features were set in a quarrelsome scowl.

Before Starbuck could step aside, the cowhand bulled into him. The force of the collision knocked him upside the wall of the saloon. With a violent oath, the cowhand turned on him.

"Who you shovin'?"

"Sorry." Starbuck wanted no trouble, and tried to ease past. "No harm intended."

"The hell you say! Think you own the gawddamn sidewalk?"

"Look, friend—"

"Friend!" the cowhand bellowed. "Who you callin' friend, you pansy sonovabitch!"

"I only—"

The cowhand launched a looping roundhouse. Starbuck's countermove was one of sheer reflex. He slipped inside the haymaker and exploded a left hook to the jaw. The punch rocked the cowhand and he reeled backward off the boardwalk. A streetside hitch rack saved him from falling, and he seemed to shake off the effects of the blow. Then, too quick for the eye, a gun appeared from inside his jacket. He snapped off a lightning shot.

Starbuck got lucky. He was a beat behind, but the

cowhand hurried the shot. The slug tore through the sleeve of Starbuck's coat and thunked into the wall. He pulled the Colt, thumbing the hammer in the same motion, and fired. A bright red dot blossomed on the cowhand's shirtfront. The impact of the blunt-nosed slug slammed him into the hitch rack. He hung there a moment, then his legs buckled and his sphincter voided in death. He slumped to the ground without a sound.

A wisp of smoke curled from the barrel of Starbuck's pistol. He was aware of voices and people crowding the street. Yet his gaze was on the dead man, and in some dim corner of his mind a question slowly took shape. The man was uncommonly sudden with a gun, too sudden.

He wondered how a ragtail cowhand got so fast.

"You say you never saw him before?"

"Never."

"So he jumped you out of the clear blue?"

"It would appear that way."

Amos Rodman, town marshal of Cheyenne, sat across the desk from Starbuck. Summoned to the scene of the shooting, he had questioned several eye-witnesses and ordered the body removed to a funeral parlor. Then he'd taken Starbuck into custody and marched him back to the city jail. Now, with a cigar wedged in the corner of his mouth, he tilted back in his chair. His expression was one of puzzlement.

"Why would he do that—jump a stranger?"

Starbuck warned himself to go slow. The interrogation was something more than mere formality. He was still posing as an easterner, and that fact clearly troubled the marshal. He lifted his hands in a shrug.

"The man was drunk and belligerent. I can only surmise he was spoiling for a fight."

"Funny thing," Rodman said lazily. "The barkeep in that saloon said he never even had a drink. Walked in off the street, and a couple of minutes later he walks right out again. How do you explain that?"

"I wouldn't try." Starbuck gave him a weak smile. "Who knows what prompts men to violence?"

"Good question," Rodman remarked. "Suppose you tell me. If it wasn't liquor . . . what was it?"

"I'm afraid I have no answer to that, Marshal."

Rodman lowered his chair and leaned forward. He took Starbuck's Colt off the desktop and slowly examined it. His brow wrinkled in a frown.

"That's a mighty fancy gun for a pilgrim."

Starbuck played dumb. "Pilgrim?"

"You told me you're a reporter."

"That's correct."

"An *eastern* reporter!"

"I fail to see the connection."

"Do you?" Rodman scoffed. "You've got a hair-trigger pistol and a slicker'n-grease crossdraw holster. Wouldn't you say that's a pretty peculiar rig for a reporter?"

"Not necessarily." Starbuck hesitated, chose his words with care. "A man versed in weapons should carry the best."

"You're versed, all right!" Rodman growled. "Too damn versed! Unless maybe you're not what you claim."

Starbuck looked bewildered. "I beg your pardon?"

"Maybe you're a gambler or a bunco artist. You could've gigged that fellow in some other trail town and he just accidentally happened across you today. It's got all the earmarks of somebody settlin' a personal score."

"That's ridiculous!"

"Folks don't generally go around pullin' guns on a stranger."

"Well, I assure you he was a stranger to me."

"Yeah?" Rodman inquired skeptically. "Then how come he tied into you so fast?"

"I have no idea," Starbuck said lamely. "After all, he picked the fight . . . not me."

"You ended it, though! That's what we're talkin' about here."

"I merely defended myself, Marshal."

"So you keep sayin'."

"Good Lord!" Starbuck said indignantly. "Any number of people substantiated my story! You have eyewitness accounts of everything that transpired. What more do you want?"

"For one thing," Rodman countered, "I want to know considerable more about you."

"Then I suggest you check with Nathaniel Boswell. I came here to interview him, and he found my credentials perfectly satisfactory. I'm quite confident Mr. Boswell will vouch for me."

"Oh, I'll check around." Rodman paused, gave him a dull stare. "Meantime, I wouldn't want you to plan on leavin' town."

"May I ask why?"

"Suppose we just say something smells fishy."

"How long will I be detained?"

"All depends," Rodman said evasively. "I'll let you know."

"Very well." Starbuck rose, stood fidgeting with

a hangdog look. "Since I'm not under arrest, I would appreciate the return of my gun."

"Help yourself," Rodman said, motioning toward the pistol. "Course, I ought to warn you. We've got a city ordinance against carryin' concealed weapons."

"Someone should have informed the dead man."

"I'm informing you and that's enough!"

"And in the event he has some friends who also ignore your ordinance? What would you suggest then, Marshal?"

"I'd suggest you stick to your hotel room."

"How comforting."

Starbuck holstered the Colt and walked to the door. With his hand on the knob, he turned and looked back over his shoulder. "One last question."

"Shoot."

"The deceased—" Starbuck made an empty gesture. "Were you able to identify him?"

"Nope," Rodman said without inflection. "There were no papers on the body, and no one recalled seein' him before today."

"Perhaps he worked for one of the cattle outfits."

"Possible," Rodman conceded. "Or he could've been a drifter."

"In which case, we'll never know."

"I wouldn't bet it either way, Mr. Farnum."

The comment gave Starbuck all the clue he needed. Outside, walking toward the hotel, he told himself the bet was a lead-pipe cinch. Marshal Amos Rodman would have a wire off to the *Police Gazette* within the hour. Then he would start nosing around town, asking questions. By tomorrow, maybe sooner, he would discover that an easterner wearing glasses had bought a horse, along with outdoors gear and a rifle. All that, added to a reply from the *Police Gazette*, would lead to more questions. Questions Starbuck couldn't afford to have asked, or answered. Which meant nightfall was the deadline.

By then, he had to be long gone from Cheyenne.

Chapter Six

Starbuck rode north toward Fort Laramie. He used the stars for a compass and he rode straight through the night. He left behind nothing of Edward Farnum.

Earlier, in his hotel room, Starbuck had laid the reporter to rest. The glasses and eastern clothing, along with the specially built shoes, were stowed in his valise. His new disguise was less elaborate, but no less effective. From the valise, he took a masterwork of dental handicraft. On the order of a false tooth, it was actually an enameled sleeve, colored a dark nut brown. Custom-fitted, it slipped over his left front tooth and was secured much like a partial bridge. To all appearances a dead tooth, it was yet another exercise in misdirection, and an immediate eye-stopper. People saw the blackened tooth and were distracted from the man.

The balance of his disguise relied on clothing and whiskery stubble. His beard, which grew rapidly, would alter the set of his features. By the time he arrived at Hole-in-the-Wall, he would have sprouted a mustache and a full growth along his chin and jawline. The conchas belt, added to the range clothes and vest, would complete the transformation. A dead tooth, nestled in a coppery beard, would erase any vestige of Luke Starbuck. What emerged would be a

whiskery, rough-garbed hardcase. An outlaw who
called himself Arapahoe Smith.

Starbuck's departure from Cheyenne had gone
smoothly. Shortly after dark, he left money on the
washstand for his hotel bill. Then he knotted bed-
sheets into a rope and went out the window of his
second-floor room. The valise, which contained the
remnants of Edward Farnum, was dumped in an alley
trash heap. Sticking to back streets, he then made his
way to the livery stable. The blood bay gelding was
saddled without awakening the night hostler. All his
gear was crammed into saddlebags; then the rifle
scabbard and bedroll were lashed down securely.
Once outside, he mounted and circled west of town.
There, he fixed on the North Star and booted the horse
into a steady lope. No trace of him or the direction
he rode remained behind. He vanished, unseen, into
the night.

By sundown of the second day Starbuck sighted
Fort Laramie. The army post was situated at the juncture of the Laramie and North Platte rivers. Originally
built by fur traders, it was taken over by the military
when emigrant trains began the westward migration.
Thereafter it served as a shakedown point for those
traveling the Oregon Trail. The Bozeman Trail,
mapped out when gold was discovered in Montana,
also passed through Fort Laramie. Stretching north
and west, a chain of forts was then constructed to
combat the Sioux and other hostile tribes. Yet, for all
their number, these forts were merely outposts in the
wilderness. Fort Laramie remained the crossroads of
the western plains.

Avoiding the fort, Starbuck rode on a few miles
and pitched camp. The next morning he struck out

along the Oregon Trail, which followed the North
Platte in a westerly direction. He would have made
better time overland, for the trail twisted and turned
in concert with the winding river. But he was on unfamiliar ground, and dared not overshoot a vital landmark, known generally as the Upper Crossing. There,
on a dogleg in the river, the Oregon Trail intersected
the old Bridger Trail. Little traveled, the trail had been
blazed many years before by the mountain man and
scout Jim Bridger. Angling northwest from the river,
it meandered through the Big Horn Basin and ultimately linked up with the Bozeman Trail. Along the
way, it also skirted the only known entrance to Hole-
in-the-Wall.

Three days out of Fort Laramie, Starbuck turned
onto the Bridger Trail. Ahead lay the foothills of the
Big Horn Range and an ocean of grassland. The basin, with distant mountains on either side, stretched
endlessly to the horizon. The landscape evoked a
sense of something lost forever. Nothing moved as
far as the eye could see, and hardly a bush or a tree
was visible in the vast emptiness sweeping northward.
Earth and sky were mixed with deafening silence, almost as though, in some ancient age, the plains had
frozen motionless for all time. A gentle breeze, like
the wispy breath of a ghost, rippled over the tall grass,
disturbing nothing. It was a land of sun and solitude,
a lonesome land. A land where man somehow seemed
the intruder.

Only a few years ago it had been the land of the
Sioux. From the North Platte in Wyoming to the
Rosebud in Montana, a swath of grassland over a hundred miles long teemed with buffalo. The vast seas
of bluestem and needlegrass were the natural range-

land of a herd numbering in the millions. Then, in quick succession, gold and the lure of free land brought a flood tide of emigrants. Not far behind were the hide hunters, openly encouraged by the army, whose leaders sanctioned the slaughter. Within a decade, the great buffalo herds—the Indians' commissary—were no more. Nor were the Sioux themselves any longer in evidence. Custer's defeat at the Little Big Horn proved a pyrrhic victory for the red man. By early 1877 the Sioux and Cheyenne had been removed to reservations. Not quite a year past, Sitting Bull and his band had returned from their exile in Canada and surrendered to the army. The last of the hostiles were pacified, and the land itself opened to settlement. Most homesteaders, however, continued to pass through on their way to Oregon. The solitude and distance of the High Plains were somehow ominous. A place where few cared to try their luck.

Late the next afternoon, Starbuck topped a rise overlooking the South Fork of the Powder River. The earth shimmered under the brassy dome of the sky, and the sun seemed fixed forever on the horizon. Off in the distance the Big Horns thrust awesomely from the basin floor. A day's ride due north, deep in the foothills, lay Buffalo Creek. And somewhere beyond that, his destination. Hole-in-the-Wall.

Starbuck reined to a halt. He sat for a moment studying on the last leg of his journey. According to Nat Boswell, the ranch of Ed Houk was south of Buffalo Creek Canyon. He had no idea whether Houk was an honest man or in league with the outlaws. Either way, the rancher most certainly possessed knowledge about Hole-in-the-Wall. Any man who lived that close to the stronghold—and survived—

was a man worth knowing. A man who might be persuaded to talk. The approach would require discretion and craft; otherwise Starbuck would risk tipping his hand before he got started. Yet the odds dictated he try, for one likelihood stood out above all else. The secrets of Hole-in-the-Wall were no secret to Ed Houk.

The bay gelding suddenly alerted. He stood, nostrils flared, like an ebony statue bronzed by the sun. His hide rippled, and he nervously stamped the ground as he tested the wind. His eyes were fixed on a stand of trees bordering the river.

A visceral instinct told Starbuck to move. He never questioned such instincts; he obeyed. Too many times before some intermittent sixth sense had warned him of danger, and thereby allowed him to live awhile longer. All thought suspended, he jerked his rifle and swung down out of the saddle. A shot cracked, and in the same instant a slug fried the air around his ears. He saw a puff of smoke billow from a thicket on the riverbank.

A second slug kicked dirt at his feet as he dropped to one knee. The rifle butt slammed into his shoulder and he centered the sights on the thicket. Working the slide-action, he chambered a round and fired. Then, with no more than a pulsebeat between shots, he pumped five quick rounds into the dense undergrowth. The last report still rang in his ears when a man stumbled out of the thicket and wobbled drunkenly along the riverbank. Starbuck took careful aim and squeezed off a shot. The man's head exploded in a gory mist of brains and bone matter. He went down as though struck by a thunderbolt.

Starbuck waited several moments, scanning the

treeline. At last, satisfied the man was alone, he rose
and walked down the slope. Off to one side, screened
by the undergrowth, he saw a horse tied to a tree. The
rifle cocked and ready, he drifted closer, approaching
slowly. On the riverbank, he stopped, watchful a moment longer. He spotted a Winchester carbine on the
ground behind the thicket, and grunted softly to himself. Then his gaze shifted to the body.

The man lay head down in the shallows. He was
dressed in grungy range clothes and smelled of death.
One of the fifty-caliber slugs had drilled him clean
through, just below the breastbone. The back of his
shirt, where the slug had exited, was soaked with
blood. His features were no longer recognizable. The
last shot had blown out his skull directly above the
browline.

Starbuck searched the dead man and found no
identification. Then, for a long time, he stood staring
down at the body. He felt no emotion, neither anger
nor remorse. He was, instead, in a state of quandary.
He thought it possible that the man was a robber. One
of a murderous breed who would bushwhack any
stranger unfortunate enough to happen along. Yet he
was no great believer in coincidence. And being
jumped by two unknown men within the space of a
week qualified on all counts. Which led him to the
worst of all conclusions.

He'd been set up—and ambushed.

The thought jolted him into bleak awareness.
Still, however deeply felt, it was tempered by uncertainty. Aside from the lawyer William Dexter, no one
knew his actual destination. Nat Boswell, who was
familiar with undercover work, might very well have
seen through his disguise as a reporter. All the more

so in light of the detailed questions he'd asked about Hole-in-the-Wall. But that presupposed a motive on the part of one or both of the men. Try as he might, he simply couldn't think of a reason why either Dexter or Boswell would have him ambushed. One thing, nonetheless, was absolutely clear. The ambush today, added to the gunfight in Cheyenne, still beggared coincidence. There was a smell about it of something planned. Or worse, something arranged.

He decided to sleep light, and watch his backtrail.

Starbuck rode into Houk's ranch late the following day. The washed blue of the plains sky grew smoky along about dusk, and lamps were already lighted in the main house. He'd timed his arrival perfectly, for there was an unwritten law on cattle spreads. A stranger was always asked to spend the night.

Ed Houk was a bony man, with shrunken skin and knobby joints. His features were seared by years of wind and sun, and his eyes were lusterless as stones. Somewhere in his early thirties, he looked older, and gave the impression of a man burned out by hard times and hard work. His outfit consisted of three hired hands and a herd of some five hundred longhorns. Whether he was a widower or simply unmarried was unclear. He volunteered little information about himself.

By the same token, he exhibited no curiosity about Starbuck. He accepted the name he was given— Arapahoe Smith—and asked no questions of a personal nature. After supper in the cook shack, he invited Starbuck up to the main house for a drink. The accommodations were sparse, and the whiskey he served was genuine popskull. Seated in cowhide chairs they sipped quietly, their talk general. Starbuck rolled himself a smoke and Houk methodically filled his pipe. After tamping down the tobacco, he struck a match and sucked the pipe to life. Then he leaned back in his chair and studied Starbuck with a look of deliberation.

"You're about to burst your britches, so go ahead and ask."

Starbuck gave him an odd smile. "Ask what?"

"About Hole-in-the-Wall."

"What gave you that idea?"

Houk took the pipe from his mouth. "There's men on the scout driftin' through here all the time."

"Who said I'm on the scout?"

"Nobody," Houk said solemnly. "Course, it don't make no nevermind to me one way or the other. I tend to my own knittin'."

Starbuck paused, looked him straight in the eye. "Suppose I was on the run?"

"Then you've got questions," Houk replied. "Everybody does, the first time they come to Hole-in-the-Wall. I just try to steer 'em in the right direction."

"Why so hospitable?"

Houk briefly explained. A code prevailed between himself and the men who haunted Hole-in-the-Wall. He watched the front door, and never gave the time of day to anyone with the look of a lawman. In return, the outlaws allowed him to live in peace and never raided his stock. The arrangement worked to the benefit of everyone involved.

"You must have a trusting nature." Starbuck casually flicked an ash off his cigarette. "How do you know I'm not a lawman?"

"Well—" Houk hesitated, took a couple of puffs

on his pipe. "First off, I ain't that bad a judge of character. You got the look about you, and I ought to know it by now. Then, there's your horse."

"What about him?"

"Boys on the dodge don't ride nothin' but the best. I never seen one yet that was a cheapskate when it come to horses. So I pegged you the minute I saw that bay gelding."

"By jingo!" Starbuck grinned, flashing his dead tooth. "Guess you got my number."

"I generally size a feller up pretty quick."

"No argument there!" Starbuck frowned, suddenly thoughtful. "A minute ago you said something about a front door?"

"Yeah?"

"I always heard there was only one door into Hole-in-the-Wall."

Houk chuckled, puffing a cloud of smoke. "You're talking about Buffalo Creek Canyon?" When Starbuck nodded, he went on. "That's whiffledust the boys spread around for lawmen. Works like a charm, too! Everybody in the whole goldang country thinks it's gospel truth."

"You mean there's more than one entrance?"

"Four altogether." Houk ticked them off on his fingers. "There's Buffalo Creek. Then there's an old Sioux trail over the Big Horns. Then there's Hole-in-the-Wall and Little Hole-in-the-Wall."

"Jeezus!" Starbuck was genuinely astounded. "I thought Buffalo Creek—the canyon—was Hole-in-the-Wall."

"Everybody does." Houk chortled slyly. "That's 'cause outsiders think the Big Horns are the 'Wall.' Ain't so, and never was."

"I don't follow you."

"Lemme draw you a map. Otherwise, I'm liable to confuse you more'n you already are."

Houk got a stub pencil and a scrap piece of paper. He began sketching with quick, bold strokes. As the map took shape, it revealed there was more to Hole-in-the-Wall than commonly thought. The hidden valley was some thirty miles in length, north to south, and roughly two miles in width. On the west, it was bounded by the Big Horns. On the east, it was bounded by towering sandstone cliffs, labeled the Red Wall. Some thirty-five miles in length, the Red Wall merged with the Big Horns in the north and the foothills in the south. The true Hole-in-the-Wall was a gap through which the Middle Fork of the Powder River flowed westward into the valley. The Little Hole-in-the-Wall was simply an ancient game trail leading eastward over the sandstone cliffs. The old Sioux trail, westward through the mountains, was nearly impassable. Buffalo Creek Canyon, the southern entrance to the valley, was by far the easiest approach. Houk penciled a number of Xs where the mouth of the canyon opened onto the valley.

"These here"—he tapped the Xs—"are the boys' cabins. Course, them are the ones that headquarter here regular. There's lots more that comes and goes as the mood suits 'em. They generally pitch camp somewheres, or hole up in a cave. All sorts of caves over here on the slope of the Big Horns."

Starbuck pondered the map a moment. "What's on the other side of the Red Wall?"

"Powder River country," Houk commented. "Whole slew of big cattle outfits over that way."

"Have they got an 'arrangement' with the boys?"

"Nope!" Houk laughed and slapped his knee. "They're fair game, all year round!"

"So they don't know about all these ways in and out of the valley?"

"Besides me, there's only one other outfit that knows."

"Oh?" Starbuck inquired evenly. "Who's that?"

"Now I'm gonna throw you for a real loop!"

Houk pointed with his pencil. He traced the path of Buffalo Creek, which flowed the length of the valley. His pencil stopped where the creek intersected the Middle Fork of the Powder. He made an X southwest of the juncture.

"That there's the Bar C spread."

"A ranch!" Starbuck stared at him, dumbfounded. "Are you saying there's an outfit in the valley itself?"

"Shore am!" Houk cackled. "Started up last summer, and they've turned it into a real nice operation. Foreman's a prince of a feller—name's Hank Devoe."

"I take it they *do* have an arrangement with the boys?"

"Live and let live," Houk said philosophically. "When you stop and think about it, the Bar C's way ahead of the game. Ain't *nobody* gonna come into that valley and try rustlin' their beeves!"

"Or yours either," Starbuck said, stringing him along. "Not while you're the boys' watchdog on the front door."

"I reckon one good turn deserves another."

Starbuck took him a step further. "Now that you mention it—you said you'd steer me in the right direction."

"Try my best," Houk said affably. "What've you got in mind?"

"You know a fellow by the name of Mike Cassidy?"

Houk slowly knocked the dottle from his pipe. "What if I do?"

"He's a friend of a friend," Starbuck lied heartily. "I was told to look him up when I got here."

"Who by . ... just exactly?"

"Somebody he'd know"—Starbuck paused for emphasis—"down at Robbers Roost."

"Tell you what—" Houk stopped, head cocked to one side. "Have a talk with Hank Devoe. If Cassidy's in the valley, Hank'll know where he's at."

Starbuck agreed, and let it drop there. With no great effort, he turned the conversation back to the valley. One question led to another, and before long he and the rancher were hunched over the map. The outcome was all he'd hoped for, and more.

Ed Houk told him all there was to know about Hole-in-the-Wall.

Chapter Seven

Oncoming summer touched the high country. At midday the canyon walls shimmered and the sun at its zenith seemed fixed forever in a cloudless sky. No wind stirred and the only sound was the rushing murmur of Buffalo Creek.

Starbuck halted the gelding in a patch of shade. He looped the reins around the saddlehorn and took the makings from his pocket. He creased a rolling paper, spilled tobacco from the sack, and slowly built himself a smoke. Striking a match on his thumbnail, he lit the cigarette and inhaled deeply. His gaze scanned the rocky gorge, which was narrow and winding, hemmed in by steep walls on either side. He understood now why lawmen never ventured into Hole-in-the-Wall. The canyon approach was some ten miles long, and every switchback along the snaky creek was a natural ambush site. A man soon began waiting for the crack of a rifle shot.

Some hours earlier, Starbuck had ridden out from Houk's ranch. The cattleman sent him off full of flapjacks and good cheer, with the map tucked in his shirt pocket. A few miles northeast the rangeland petered out into a succession of hogback ridges. The terrain rose sharply thereafter, the Big Horns majestic in the early-morning sunlight. Then, suddenly, Buffalo Creek

made an abrupt bend into the canyon. The plains wind
dropped off into an eerie stillness; there was a sense
of being entombed within the foreboding gorge. Nothing moved, and the gelding's hoofbeats echoed off
the canyon walls with a ghostly clatter. Around every
turn it was as though something waited, and the long
ride had a telling effect. On edge and on guard, a
man's nerves were soon strung wire-tight.

Gathering the reins, Starbuck nudged the bay in
the ribs and rode on. He deliberately turned his mind
from the canyon to the gossipy revelations of Ed
Houk. Last night, with a load of rotgut under his belt,
the rancher had grown talkative. Hole-in-the-Wall, according to Hank, was home to cattle rustlers and horse
thieves, as well as a collection of robbers and stone-
cold killers. At any given time, their number varied,
for their activities took them far and wide. Still, even
a conservative estimate ranged upward of fifty or
more. Under one name or another, the majority were
fugitives from justice, with a price on their heads.
And most were determined never to be taken alive.

Contrary to popular opinion, the outlaws were not
organized. Some operated in small gangs, or teamed
up for a particular job. But for the most part, Hole-
in-the-Wall was populated by men with a philosophy
all their own. Far too independent to conform—
especially to the outside world's laws and strictures—
they saw no reason to impose codes on themselves
within the mountain stronghold. No man was his
brother's keeper, and their general attitude was a
rough form of individualism that pivoted around devil
take the hindmost. By choice, their lives were beset
with danger, and the eternal threat of a hangman's
noose. Yet, while they lived, they enjoyed a form of

freedom as addictive as opium. All they needed to earn a livelihood was a fast horse and a little savvy about cows. Or a quick gun and no great conscience.

Understandably enough, Houk in no way considered himself slightly windward of the law. He saw himself and the owners of the Bar C spread as neutrals in somebody else's war. Their cattle outfits were on the fringe of civilization, and the law of might makes right prevailed. Forced to fend for themselves, they had formed an attitude toward the outlaws that was part trade-off and part accommodation. No one asked questions—or condemned the inhabitants of Hole-in-the-Wall—and no harm resulted. Whether they approved of the outlaws was beside the point, germane to nothing in the isolation of the High Plains. With no personal reason to be against the lawless element, they simply took a stand of live and let live. The badmen came and went as they pleased, and the ranchers studiously minded their own business. The trade-off was a mix of pragmatism and common sense. No one lost and everyone profited—each in his own way.

Shortly after the noon hour, Starbuck emerged from the canyon. Before him lay the valley of Hole-in-the-Wall. Some thirty miles long and two miles in breadth, the valley was split by a latticework of streams that fed into the Middle Fork of the Powder River. The streams were bordered by trees, and the valley floor resembled an emerald sea of graze. Cradled beneath high northern peaks, it was sheltered from blustery winds, and the forested mountainsides provided abundant game even in the coldest months. There was water, plenty of wood, and ample forage

for livestock. To a cattleman—or an outlaw—it
lacked for nothing.

The Red Wall, directly across the valley, rose in
a sheer thousand-foot palisade of rock. The wind-
swept battlement stretched north and south as far as
the eye could see, one great mass of vermilion-hued
sandstone. To the west, the slope of the Big Horns
climbed steadily skyward. Farther north, the mountains converged with the Red Wall, and ultimately
vanished in cloud-covered pinnacles. The green of the
valley stood out in sharp contrast between the sandstone wall and the blue-hazed mountains. There was
a smell of crystal-clear air and sweet grass. And an
almost oppressive sense of serenity.

The outlaw cabins were located where Buffalo
Creek entered the valley and made a leisurely bend
to the north. Spread out along the slope of the mountains, the cabins were constructed of logs and appeared large enough for no more than two or three
men. Starbuck counted eight buildings altogether,
each with its own log corral. There were no men in
sight, and he assumed the noonday heat had driven
them indoors. The corrals, however, gave testament
to a comment made by Ed Houk last night. Outlaws
valued their horses above all other possessions; a reliable mount often spelled the difference between life
and death. Whether bought or stolen, the animals
were selected with meticulous care. Speed and stamina were the qualities sought, and men who rode the
owlhoot considered top-notch horseflesh an investment in their trade. The horses in the corrals merely
underscored the point. There wasn't a crowbait in the
lot.

Starbuck held the bay to a walk. His inspection

of the cabins was casual, and he swung wide of the slope. Across the valley he spotted Little Hole-in-the-Wall, the old game trail, leading over the escarpment to Powder River country. From what Houk had told him, rustlers occasionally used the trail to spirit stolen livestock over the wall and into the valley. The primary entrance from the east, however, was some miles farther north. There, within the gap carved out by the Middle Fork of the Powder, was the true Hole-in-the-Wall. Horses and cattle were routinely driven through the gap from ranches in eastern Wyoming.

Once in the valley, there was little problem in hiding stolen livestock. The mountain slopes to the west were laced with hidden gullies and box canyons which made perfect holding pens. The outlaws also constructed cleverly concealed pole corrals in stands of trees along the streams. Farther up the slope, where timber was more abundant, dead trees were used to build an enclosure that resembled a blowdown. In each instance, the corrals were camouflaged and designed to fit in with the natural surroundings. The purpose, so far as Starbuck could determine, was to protect the livestock from fellow thieves. No one attempted to recover stolen stock from Hole-in-the-Wall.

Nor were the outlaws in imminent danger. The valley afforded them several natural hideouts, all of which were virtually invisible to an outsider. On the slope to the west, canyons and gullies concealed men with even greater ease than rustled livestock. Along the base of the Red Wall there were numerous caverns, with subterranean passages leading from one to the other. Anyone familiar with the layout could hide for days, perhaps months, with no fear of discovery.

Yet that, too, was a matter of small likelihood. No
one was foolhardy enough to chase outlaws into the
valley. Hole-in-the-Wall was a world unto itself, at
once mysterious and deadly. And forever inviolate.

Ed Houk had revealed all these secrets and more
last night. Starbuck was nonetheless leery; his cynicism had never betrayed him before, and a grain of
salt seemed prudent where the rancher was concerned.
For all his garrulous good humor, Houk hadn't been
totally forthcoming. The odds dictated that he knew
exactly where to locate Mike Cassidy. But he'd
evaded the question by steering Starbuck to the Bar
C foreman, Hank Devoe. All that led to a reasonable
assumption, and reinforced the need for caution.
Houk was playing for time, and fully intended to warn
Mike Cassidy. Before nightfall, the outlaw would
have gotten the message. A stranger was inquiring
about him—by name.

Starbuck considered it a matter of spilt milk. He'd
asked the question—taken a calculated risk—and
there was nothing to be gained in regrets. For now,
however, he'd lost the element of surprise. His next
step would be determined largely by what he learned
from Hank Devoe. He steeled himself to give a mem-
orable performance for the Bar C foreman. He would
underplay the role, thereby lending Arapahoe Smith
a certain larger-than-life deadliness. The character of
a mankiller was, after all, one he understood completely. With only minor variations, the part was very
much made to order.

He would play himself.

The Bar C headquarters was impressive. Substantial
log buildings within the compound included a main

house, a large bunkhouse with attached cook shack, and several smaller outbuildings. Some distance beyond the bunkhouse was a log corral.

The compound was situated on a stretch of grassland ten miles north of the outlaw cabins. Easily identified, the spot was located where Buffalo Creek emptied into the Middle Fork of the Powder. Across the creek was another landmark—Steamboat Rock—a massive chunk of sandstone shaped along the lines of a paddle-wheeler. A mile or so due north of the compound, the river made a sharp turn eastward through the Red Wall. This narrow gap, formed by erosion along the riverbed, was the true Hole-in-the-Wall. The valley itself extended northward for another twelve miles beyond the compound. There the Red Wall joined the Big Horn Range.

Starbuck rode into the compound late that afternoon. By the size of the operation, he judged the Bar C would have a crew of no fewer than ten cowhands. The owners were a couple of wealthy cattlemen who seldom came anywhere near the ranch. He'd been told by Ed Houk that they lived in Cheyenne, and gave their foreman a free hand in running the outfit. If true, that made Hank Devoe a man of some stature in the valley. Operating a spread in the middle of Hole-in-the-Wall—while maintaining a neutral position toward the outlaws—would require the tact of a diplomat on foreign ground. And above all else, it would demand a tightlipped attitude toward outsiders.

Several things indicated that Devoe was no slouch at walking on thin ice. When the outlaws went east of the Red Wall, into Powder River country, their raids were generally conducted at night. Allowing time for trailing the cows westward, that meant they would pass through Hole-in-the-Wall and enter the valley somewhere after sunrise. Which, in turn, meant the stolen livestock would be driven past the Bar C headquarters in broad daylight. It followed, then, that Devoe would have firsthand knowledge of the brands on the rustled cows. From there, it required no mental genius to deduce which ranches had been raided. He would, moreover, know the names of the outlaws who had pulled the job. All in all, it was dangerous information, especially if Devoe leaked it to the wrong people. Apparently he wore blinders and possessed the ability to button his lip. Otherwise, he would have long since taken a one-way trip to the boneyard.

Starbuck dismounted outside the main house. A moment later an ox of a man stepped through the door and walked forward. He was a big, rawboned fellow, standing well over six feet, with not an ounce of suet on his frame. His jaw was stuffed with a quid of tobacco, and his eyes were impersonal. His gaze swept Starbuck's grizzled appearance, lingering an instant on the conchas belt and the crossdraw holster. Then he stopped, and nodded.

"Howdy."

"Hullo yourself." Starbuck's tone was low, slightly abrasive. "I'm looking for Hank Devoe."

"You've found him." Devoe stuck out his hand. "I don't believe I caught your name."

"Arapahoe Smith." Starbuck shook once, a hard up-and-down pump. "I was told you're the man to see at Hole-in-the-Wall."

"Who told you that?"

"Ed Houk."

"You a friend of Ed's?"

"Nope," Starbuck said bluntly. "Never set eyes on him before yesterday."

"Why'd he send you to me?"

"Mostly because he's a piss-willie."

Devoe hesitated, clearly surprised. "Ed wouldn't take kindly to anybody talkin' like that."

"I don't give a good goddamn whether he would or not."

"You might if it got back to him."

"Nothing I wouldn't say to his face."

"Suppose I told you Ed's a friend of mine?"

"That's your problem."

"And if I took exception to you callin' him names?"

"Then you've bought yourself a bigger problem."

Starbuck's manner was cold, and deadly. He'd learned early in life that confidence counted far more than the odds. A man assured of himself bred that same conviction in other men, and as a result, forever held the edge. His performance was calculated to create an impression, one that left no room for doubt. Arapahoe Smith was a man with an explosive temper and a short fuse. A killer.

Devoe's appraisal of him was deliberate. After a time, the foreman turned his head and spat a brownish squirt of tobacco juice. He watched as it hit the ground and kicked up a puff of dust. Then he looked around.

"What makes you think Ed's a piss-willie?"

"I asked him a simple question," Starbuck said flatly. "He gave me a song and dance, and passed it along to you. I got the impression he don't hardly take a leak without asking permission."

"All depends on the question." Devoe paused,

shifted the quid to the other side of his mouth. "Around here, there's some questions better left un-answered."

"I'm not one for loose talk, myself. All I want's a civil answer and no ring-around-the-rosy."

"Awright, go ahead and ask your question."

"Whereabouts would I find Mike Cassidy?"

Devoe hawked as though he'd swallowed a bone. "Judas Priest! It's no wonder Ed gave you the fast shuffle."

Starbuck's eyes took on a peculiar glitter. "I rode five hundred miles to hear the answer. So do yourself a favor, and don't hand me another dummy routine."

"Mr. Smith," Devoe said hesitantly, "if I was to talk out of school about Mike, I wouldn't last long anyway. To get answers, you got to give a few. Otherwise my lips are sewed shut."

"What'd you have in mind?"

"For openers—" Devoe stopped, met his gaze. "Who are you and where're you from?"

"I already told you." Starbuck looked annoyed. "The name's Arapahoe Smith."

"So you did," Devoe agreed. "But you left out the where from."

"Robbers Roost."

"Are you wanted?"

"I sure as hell didn't ride all the way up here for the scenery."

"What's the charge?"

"Murder." Starbuck grinned crookedly. "A fellow asked me one too many questions, and I put a leak in his ticker."

Devoe eyed him in silence a moment. "You a friend of Mike's?"

"A secondhand friend," Starbuck noted dryly. "Somebody down at Robbers Roost gave me his name."

"Why so?"

"I had to light out pretty sudden, and Hole-in-the-Wall seemed the natural place to come. He told me Cassidy was a square shooter."

"That's it?" Devoe persisted. "You're lookin' for a place to lay low—nothin' more?"

"Nothin' more?" Starbuck rocked his head from side to side. "I don't get your drift."

"Lemme say it another way," Devoe rumbled. "If you're a lawman—or you've got some personal score to settle with Mike—then I'd advise you to make dust and not look back. It's the only way you'll ever leave here alive."

"I'm no lawdog!" Starbuck bristled. "And I never even met Cassidy. So how the Christ could it be anything personal?"

"All I'm tryin' to do is warn you."

"Don't do me any favors." There was a hard edge to Starbuck's voice. "You've had your answers and now I'll have mine. Whereabouts do I find Cassidy?"

Devoe looked down and studied the ground. "I hope you're who you say you are, Mr. Arapahoe Smith. If you're not, then take my word for it—we're both dead men!"

Starbuck laughed. "I aim to live awhile yet."

"I'm mighty relieved to hear it."

"And I'm still waiting for directions."

Devoe considered a moment, then gave him a slow nod. "I take it you come in by way of Buffalo Creek Canyon?"

"You take it right."

"Head back that direction," Devoe said, motioning down the valley. "You recollect them cabins, on the west side of the creek?"

"I got pretty good eyesight."

"Try the third cabin headed south. Last time I heard, that's where Mike called home."

"He bunk alone?" Starbuck asked. "Or does he have a pardner?"

"Search me." Devoe shrugged noncommittally. "I stick to this end of the valley."

Starbuck walked to his horse. He stepped into the saddle, then his gaze settled on Devoe. His mouth quirked and he bobbed his head.

"I always remember a favor, Mr. Devoe."

"That's a comforting thought, Mr. Smith."

Starbuck chuckled and rode off down the valley.

Chapter Eight

A sky of purest indigo was flecked through with stars. On the creek bank, Starbuck stood lost beneath the shadow of the trees. His eyes searched the patchwork sky, as though some magical truth were to be found there. He found instead the tangled skein of his own thoughts.

By any assessment, the situation was a mess. Starbuck prided himself on being a realist, and there was no avoiding the fact that he'd worked himself into a corner. He was in the wrong place at the wrong time, and everyone in Hole-in-the-Wall knew he was there. Worse, he was trapped in a quagmire of his own integrity. He thought it a pretty pickle for a man in the detective business.

One source of concern was Hank Devoe. Starbuck was under no illusions about the Bar C foreman. Hardly a fool, Devoe would hedge his bet. He was concerned for his own life, and with good reason. He'd broken faith with Mike Cassidy, and the consequences were not difficult to imagine. Within Hole-in-the-Wall, such a breach would be considered the cardinal sin; and the penalty was death. His fear of the hardcase named Arapahoe Smith was a momentary thing, quickly come and gone. His fear of retribution from the outlaw quarter was deeply entrenched,

an overriding imperative. By now, he would have
done the sensible thing and warned Cassidy. An old
and widely practiced diplomatic ploy, it was known
as covering your ass. And diplomacy was Hank Devoe's game.

Upon riding away from the ranch, Starbuck's bravado had abruptly vanished. He had bullied Devoe
into talking, and thereby furthered completion of his
assignment. At the same time, he had compounded an
already dicey situation. He now knew where to find
Cassidy; but Ed Houk's warning would have alerted
the outlaw. So he was expected, and his cover story
would never withstand close questioning by Cassidy.
To approach the cabin in daylight—without the element of surprise—was no longer an option. He'd lost
the edge.

A mile or so from the ranch, Starbuck had forded
Buffalo Creek. Thereafter he stuck to the treeline as
he made his way down the valley. The sun was dip-
ping westward toward the mountains when he halted
opposite the outlaw cabins. He left the bay to graze,
tied by a slack length of rope to a tree. Then, moving
through the wooded grove, he found a vantage point
where he could smoke and think without being seen.
His guess was that Hank Devoe had wasted no time
in getting a message to Cassidy. On top of the warning from Houk, that would make the outlaw doubly
vigilant. All of which made a sorry state of affairs
even sorrier.

Starbuck's original plan was a washout. As he'd
done on past cases, he had thought to infiltrate a gang
of outlaws by passing himself off as a man on the
dodge. Once his credentials were established, he
would have bided his time and awaited an opportune

moment. On one pretext or another he would have then picked a fight with Cassidy and killed him. An unknown who called himself Arapahoe Smith would have been credited with the killing, and no one the wiser. At that point he would have gotten on his horse and vanished without a trace. Assignment completed.

None of that had happened for the simplest of reasons. His plan, from the very outset, was based on a false premise. There was no gang at Hole-in-the-Wall. There was, instead, a loose confederation of outlaws. Which left him with nothing to infiltrate, no way to worm his way into a collection of loners. Forced to ask too many questions too fast, he'd alarmed Ed Houk and inadvertently alerted Cassidy. The upshot was not unlike entering the valley at the head of a brass band. The thump of a bass drum and the clash of cymbals would hardly have attracted more attention. So now he had no choice but to improvise as he went along. There was no alternative plan, and no way to resurrect the original scheme. He was playing it fast and loose—one step at a time.

The immediate problem was Mike Cassidy. Not how to kill him, but rather how to kill him in an acceptable manner. Starbuck was no assassin. He believed certain men deserved to die, and he felt no twinge of conscience about hurrying them along to the grave. Yet he operated by a code that allowed him to live with himself in the aftermath. He never back-shot a man, and in all the years he'd worked his trade, he had never bushwhacked anyone. His gun was for hire, but his soul wasn't for sale. He took a wanted man from the front or not at all.

Expediency was nonetheless central to his code. A manhunter was no paladin of social conduct, and

killing men was by no means a game. Only one rule
existed: survive the encounter and live to fight another
day. Starbuck gave the other man a chance—a very
slim chance—but he gave no man the edge. His cus-
tomary practice was to get the drop on an outlaw and
order him to surrender. Barring that, he openly challenged a wanted man and shot him down on the spot.
He killed quickly and cleanly, and without remorse.

Tonight, he would kill again in a similar fashion.
His position in the trees afforded him an unobstructed
view across the valley. From dusk until dark, he had
watched Cassidy's cabin like a hawk zeroed on a
barnyard hen. The distance was not quite a mile, and
he'd had no trouble spotting the lone figure of a man.
At sundown, a couple of horses in the corral had been
grained and watered, and afterward the man had split
some firewood. With darkness, a lamp was lighted in
the cabin and a tendril of smoke drifted upward from
the chimney. None of the other outlaws came near the
cabin, and the sign seemed plain enough to read. Cassidy was a loner.

Starbuck saw it as an exercise in stealth. His approach to the cabin would be made quietly, without
spooking the horses. Once there, he would make positive identification through the cabin window. He'd
memorized Cassidy's description from his rogues'
gallery, and there would be no mistake on that score.
Then, with his gun drawn, he would kick in the door.
The outcome was a foregone conclusion. Cassidy's
instinctive reaction would be to fight, make a try for
his gun. He would die trying.

Under cover of darkness, Starbuck would then
make his way back to the creek. It was a tossup
whether the shooting would draw the other outlaws

from their cabins. They might come to investigate, or they might consider it none of their affair. Either way, it made little difference in the overall scheme of things. By that time, Starbuck planned to be well on his way downstream. He would lead the bay a mile or so into the canyon before he mounted. Then he would ride through the night and on into the next day. Arapahoe Smith would be roundly cursed at Hole-in-the-Wall. And seen no more.

Which was a fitting end to an assignment properly executed.

Satisfied it would work, Starbuck walked back through the woods. He made supper on creek water and jerky from his saddlebags. He suppressed the temptation for a cigarette, unwilling to risk the operation on the flare of a match. Later, when the job was done, would be time enough. He watered the bay at the creek, and afterward snubbed him tight to a tree. Then he turned and moved swiftly into the pale starlight.

He drifted across the valley quiet as woodsmoke.

Starbuck crept along an arroyo that snaked westward behind the cabin. Some thirty yards away, he halted and slowly surveyed the corral. He was alert to any sound, any telltale indication the horses had winded him or sensed his presence. The animals stood hipshot in the silty starlight. He quit the shadows and scrambled out of the defile.

Skirting the corral, he catfooted across the open ground. At the rear of the cabin, he stopped and let his heartbeat slow. Then, icy calm restored, he peered cautiously around the corner. A cider glow filtered through the window, casting puddled light on the earth. A few steps farther on was the door. He heard nothing, and he quickly scanned other cabins in the near distance. There was no one in sight.

Stepping around the corner, he flattened himself against the wall and inched toward the spill of light. He removed his hat and eased to a halt beside the window. Then, with the utmost care, he edged one eye around the casement. He burned every detail of the room into his mind.

The cabin was crude as a wolf's den. A rough-hewn table, with a couple of homemade chairs, occupied the center of the room. Skillets and cast-iron pots were scattered randomly beside an open fireplace. In the corner was a washstand, and directly above it were shelves stacked with tinned goods. Along the far wall, wedged into a corner, was a double bunk. On the upper bunk was a bare mattress; the lower bunk was covered with rumpled blankets and a single pillow. The wall nearby was draped with clothes hung on pegs; saddles and a motley collection of gear were piled on the floor. The right front wall, immediately beside the entrance, was not visible. The window angle created a blind spot from the door to the far corner. A lamp on the table bathed the whole room in flickering shadows.

There was a man seated at the table. He held a deck of cards and spread out before him was a hand of solitaire. He was swarthy, with splayed features and dark hair and a drooping mustache. Heavily muscled, with a thick neck and powerful shoulders, he had the look of a bruiser. His eyes appeared yellow, almost amber, in the lamplight. A jagged scar traced the line of his jawbone.

The man and the rogues' gallery description were

a perfect match. His name was Mike Cassidy.

Starbuck jammed on his hat and pulled the Colt. Stooping low, he ducked under the window and moved to the door. He drew a deep breath and gently thumbed back the hammer on the sixgun. Then he aimed a savage kick at the latch. The door burst open and slammed inward with a splintering groan. He charged through and halted just inside the room. His arm leveled, the Colt steady as a rock.

"You're under arrest, Cassidy!"

Cassidy took the news with unshaken aplomb. He riffled three cards off the top of the deck and laid a red nine on a black ten. Then he looked up and smiled.

"Evenin'," he said almost idly. "Been expectin' you."

"You heard me!" Starbuck pressed him. "You're wanted in Utah—on a hanging charge!"

"Hanging!" Cassidy repeated, amused. "Damned if that don't beat all."

"You got a choice," Starbuck said tightly. "Come along peaceable or I'll shoot you where you sit!"

"Wanna bet?"

A doubt suddenly struck Starbuck deep in the pit of his stomach. Something was wrong here, all ass-backwards to what he'd expected. He felt a strong misgiving about killing the man in coldblood. Yet Cassidy seemed to be inviting death.

"One last warning!" he said harshly. "On your feet or you're a dead man!"

Cassidy gave him a strange grin. "Take a look behind you, Mr. Smith. You're liable to change your mind."

"Forget the tricks and do like I say!"

"It's no trick." Cassidy glanced past him, and nodded. "Tell the man, Butch."

"Drop it! Pronto!"

Starbuck went stock-still. The voice was very close, and he realized someone had been hidden behind the door. Understanding flooded over him as though his ears had come unplugged. He's been suckered into a trap!

"I ain't gonna tell you again, mister!"

The voice was sharp, commanding. With great care, Starbuck lowered the hammer on his sixgun and dropped it. Cassidy threw back his head and roared with laughter. Then he kicked his chair aside and moved around the table.

"You got balls," he said, halting a pace away. "Yessir, you shorely do! I about halfway thought you wouldn't show."

"Guess you got the word," Starbuck said, not asking a question. "Houk and Devoe make pretty fair messenger boys."

"Yeah, they do," Cassidy admitted readily. "Course, I wouldn't've been caught with my drawers down no-how. I knowed you was comin' long before you got here."

"You—!"

"Shut your trap!" Cassidy's mood suddenly turned sullen. "You just speak when you're spoke to! Savvy?"

"Whatever you say."

"Awright, let's start with something simple. Like, for instance . . . what's your name?"

"Arapahoe Smith."

"Don't be a wiseass," Cassidy growled. "Your real name?"

"Arapahoe Smith."

"You're not listenin'!" Cassidy jabbed a finger into his chest. "We'll try another one. Who d'you work for?"

"The law," Starbuck lied with a straight face. "I'm a U.S. deputy marshal."

"Horseshit!" Cassidy exploded. "Who hired you? Who sent you here?"

"The U.S. marshal, Utah Territory."

Cassidy's face mottled with anger. His gaze shifted to whoever stood beside the door. Starbuck saw the look, caught an undercurrent of something unspoken, and suddenly understood. He braced himself too late.

A pistol barrel cracked him across the skull. His eyes spun out of focus and pinwheels of light flashed through his head. Then Cassidy stepped forward and buried a gnarled fist in his stomach. His mouth popped open in a roaring whoosh of breath and he folded at the waist. Cassidy punched him in the jaw and he went down as though he'd been poleaxed. The whole right side of his head turned numb, and the brassy taste of blood filled his mouth. He gasped for air, his lungs on fire.

Cassidy dropped to one knee, grabbed a handful of hair. "Gimme the straight dope or you're gonna get more of the same! Who hired you?"

"Nobody."

Lifting his head, Cassidy drove a hard chopping right into his mouth. "What's your name?"

"Arapahoe—"

A paralyzing blow split his eyebrow. "Who sent you here?"

"I told—"

"You ain't told me nothin'!" Cassidy shouted. "Now smarten up and let's hear it!"

Starbuck shook his head like a man who had walked into cobwebs. His vision was muzzy and showery spots leaped before his eyes. Blood oozed down over his cheekbone and an ugly cut split his upper lip. His mouth moved, the words fragmented.

"Go . . . to . . . hell . . ."

Wordlessly, with a sort of methodical stoicism, Cassidy resumed the beating. The blows were measured and brutal, delivered with cold ferocity, like a butcher working over a side of beef. When he finished, Starbuck's face was a bloody mask, no longer a handsome sight. Cassidy still gripped a handful of hair, and he wrenched Starbuck's head back with a vicious twist. Then he leaned forward, eyeball to eyeball.

"One last time"—his mouth zigzagged in a cruel grimace—"who hired you?"

There was a moment of leaden silence. Starbuck's eyes were glazed, and he retched, spitting blood. He swallowed and gagged, and coughed a wad of bright reddish phlegm. At last he groaned, slowly regained his senses, and tried to focus through swollen eyelids. A crazed smile touched his lips and froth bubbled at the corner of his mouth.

"Kiss my ass."

Cassidy stared at him with stunned disbelief. Then his eyes flashed and his expression turned murderous. He pulled a Colt forty-four from the holster on his hip and eared the hammer to full-cock. Then he pressed the snout of the pistol against Starbuck's temple. His finger tightened on the trigger.

"Talk!" His voice was wild, homicidal. "Talk or I'll blow your head off."

Chapter Nine

A sinister stillness settled over the cabin. For a time neither of the men moved, and between them there was a sense of suppressed violence. Cassidy's eyes were hard and feral, and he stared down the gun barrel with a look of cold menace. At last, with a savage oath, he dropped Starbuck on the floor.

"Stupid sonovabitch!"

Staring down a moment, he suddenly turned and walked away. He lowered the hammer on his pistol and shoved it into the holster. His face was ocherous and he moved to the washstand, where he snatched a whiskey bottle from the overhead shelves. He pulled the cork and took a long swig, shuddering as the liquor hit bottom. Then he stalked to the table and lowered himself heavily into a chair. His expression was black and angry bafflement.

Starbuck felt dazed, punchy. His head buzzed and the room seemed to swirl in a dizzying motion. He ached all over, as though he'd been run through an ore crusher and torn apart. He levered himself up on one elbow and blinked several times, struggling to clear his head. From some distant corner of his mind, a thought surfaced and swam forward through a murky haze. He groped with it a moment, muddled and confused; then there was a slow dawning. Still, his mind was dull and sluggish, and he couldn't quite comprehend what seemed a vital enigma. He wondered why Cassidy hadn't killed him.

A hand scooped his sixgun off the floor. He glanced up and saw a young boy, somewhere in his middle teens. The youngster was of medium height and slim build, with a blunt pug nose and a square jaw. His hair was like a shock of wheat, and an unruly cowlick spilled down over his forehead. He wore rough work clothes and mule-eared boots, and a long-barreled Colt Peacemaker was strapped on his hip. Yet there was laughter in his eyes and a clownish smile, something of the prankster. He looked at once full-grown and still very much a kid.

The youngster stuffed the sixgun in the waistband of his trousers and backed away. He kept one eye on Starbuck, but his attention was clearly directed to Cassidy. He moved to the table and straddled a chair. His face clouded with a thoughtful frown, almost like a child toying with some new and inexplicable riddle. He sat watching the older man for a time. Then he hunched forward, elbows locked over the top of the chair. His voice was husky, surprisingly deep.

"Mike?"

"What?"

"You gonna bite my head off if I ask you something?"

"How'll I know till you ask?"

"Well . . ." A beat of hesitation, then he rushed on. "What stopped you? Holy moly, I figured you was gonna kill him deader'n a doornail!"

"I come goddam close!" Cassidy's eyes blazed. "I never wanted to kill nobody so bad in my whole life!"

"Then why'd you let him off?"

"Aww hell, Butch!" Cassidy grunted sharply. "I couldn't kill him! Don't you see that would've spoilt any chance I got?"

"Any chance for what?"

"Lookee here," Cassidy explained with weary patience. "Somebody hired him, didn't they? Somebody paid him blood money and sent him here to stop my clock. Am I right or not?"

"Yeah," Butch said eagerly. "And—?"

"So he's a hired gun, plain and simple!"

"All the more reason to kill him."

"No, you dope!" Cassidy took a slug from the whiskey bottle, wiped his mouth. "How'll I know who hired him lessen he talks?"

"Oooo!" Butch's mouth ovaled in wonder. "Dead men tell no tales—right?"

"On the button," Cassidy acknowledged. "Wasn't for that, I would've shot him the minute he come through the door."

"Only one trouble, Mike."

"What's that?"

"How you gonna make him talk?"

"What d'you mean?"

"Well, look at him!" Butch jerked a thumb over his shoulder. "Cripes sake! What more could you do?"

"Bastard's tough, awright." Cassidy laughed without humor. "I've whipped lots of men, but I never saw one take that kind of punishment. Did you hear him? Told me to kiss his ass!"

"Guess you gotta admire his sand."

"Either that or he's dumber'n a dog turd."

"Whichever, it's six of one and half a dozen of another."

"How so?"

"You still gotta figure a way to make him talk."

"Ain't it a fact?" Cassidy spat on his large-knuckled hands and rubbed them together. "Maybe I'll try a little Injun torture. That'd cure his lockjaw—real quick!"

"Wooiee!" Butch grinned, his teeth flashing like rows of dice. "You never told me you knowed anything about Injun torture!"

"A trick or two." Cassidy gave him a catlike smile. "Come to think of it, I reckon it'd be plumb fittin'."

"I don't get you."

"Arapahoe Smith!" Cassidy jeered. "Anybody that takes a dog-eater's name ought to be treated like one!"

"Now that you mention it," Butch wondered aloud, "what made you think that wasn't his real name?"

"Simple!" Cassidy snorted. "A hired gun wouldn't use his own handle at Hole-in-the-Wall."

"Why not?"

"'Cause it'd be like signin' his own death warrant. Oncet word got around, he wouldn't live ten minutes! Somebody would kill him figgerin' he was out to kill them."

"Maybe." Butch puzzled on it a moment. "Or maybe he's what he says he is . . . a lawman."

"Possible," Cassidy conceded grudgingly. "I'd tend to doubt it, though."

"Well, he sure as the devil had his facts straight. All that stuff about Utah and you being wanted on a hanging charge. How do you explain that?"

"I dunno." Cassidy looked bemused. "Tell you the truth, the whole goddamn thing don't make no rhyme nor reason."

"Say he was a marshal." Butch leaned forward, earnest. "Seems to me that'd spell it out in spades. It's only natural the law would come after you sooner or later."

"Nope, it won't wash!" Cassidy announced hotly. "There ain't a lawdog alive that'd poke his nose into Hole-in-the-Wall. We got 'em buffaloed—the whole kit-'n'-caboodle—and that's gospel fact!"

"Yeah, but you said it yourself. Nobody ever took that kind of beating and kept his mouth wired shut. Maybe he's one lawman who don't scare so easy."

"He's a hired gun!" Cassidy spat angrily. "Don't make no nevermind what he says. He come here to kill me—and that's that!"

Butch's eyes skittered away, then he cleared his throat. "So what do we do now?"

"I ain't sure," Cassidy noted bitterly. "His kind are a dime a dozen, cheaper'n dirt! There'll be another one after him and then another one and another one. Once it starts, it don't end."

"What don't end?"

"Somebody wants me dead!" Cassidy's face congealed into a scowl. "I gotta learn that somebody's name and personally arrange his funeral. Otherwise, he'll keep on sendin' hired guns till one of 'em gets the job done."

"No doubt about it," Butch agreed. "Somebody aims to put you six feet under."

"Only one salvation to the whole thing. Some-

body else *don't* want me dead. Except for him, I'd be
pushin' up daisies right now!"

"Wonder who he is?"

"Wisht to hell I knew." Cassidy paused, mulling
it over. "Anybody that sends you a warnin', the least
he could do is leave his name."

"Queer the way that come about. You'd think
somebody—Davis or one of the girls—would remember who dropped the word."

"Ain't it the goddamn truth!" Cassidy rasped.
"Beats me how he waltzed in there and spoke his
piece, and not one solitary soul recollects nothin'
about him. I mean, it ain't every day some jasper
leaves word one of your friends is about to get his
ticket punched." He shook his head, eyes rimmed
with disgust. "I can't even figger why he left a warnin'! Who the hell do I know that'd go out of his way
to save my bacon?"

"Vicey versy too," Butch added quickly. "Who
does he know that wants your bacon smoked?"

"If we knew that," Cassidy grumbled, "we
wouldn't be sittin' here scratchin' our heads. We'd
have the name of whoever it was that sent some butthole up here to shoot me!"

"You called it right, Cassidy—a butthole!"

Cassidy and Butch jumped. Starbuck was
propped up on his elbow, watching them. He'd listened, slowly recovering his senses, throughout the
entire conversation. He was battered but alert, and
now he eased himself into a sitting position. He fixed
Cassidy with a questioning look.

"All right if I get on my feet?"

"I think I like you better on the floor."

"Don't blame you." Starbuck gave him a ghastly

smile. "Only I don't talk so good on my backsides."

"Talk?" Cassidy regarded him with wary hostility. "What do you wanna talk about, just exactly?"

"The man who hired me."

A fleeting look of puzzlement crossed Cassidy's face; then his expression became flat and guarded. "Why the sudden change of heart?"

"I got an earful of what you were saying."

"Yeah?" Cassidy eyed him suspiciously. "So?"

"A little bird tells me we've been played for saps."

"You'll have to spell it out plainer'n that."

"We were set up!" Starbuck said fiercely. "Everything that happened here tonight was rigged to get us both killed!"

Cassidy and Butch exchanged a baffled look. Then the outlaw's gaze swung back to Starbuck. His face was pinched in an oxlike frown.

"You're gonna be in a helluva fix if you ain't able to make that stick."

"Won't hurt you to listen."

"Why not, Mike?" Butch interjected. "He might just know something we don't!"

"Well . . ." Cassidy hesitated, then nodded to Starbuck. "None of your monkeyshines! You try anything funny and I'll put your lights out."

"I've got nothing up my sleeve."

"Slow and easy does it," Cassidy said, motioning. "Butch, let him have your chair. You come on around here with me."

Butch obediently rose and circled the table. He stopped beside Cassidy, his hand resting on the butt of his pistol. Then, watchful and alert, they waited.

Starbuck took a tight grip on himself. He climbed

unsteadily to his feet and stood for a moment, rocked by a wave of dizziness. He was aware Cassidy might yet kill him. Still, there was strong indication that someone was manipulating them like puppets on a string. He'd decided to level with the outlaw, and take his chances. The time for guile and subterfuge was past.

Some moments elapsed before his head cleared. Finally, he walked to the chair and sat down. He pulled a handkerchief from his hip pocket and gingerly dabbed the cuts on his lip and brow. His left eye was swollen almost completely shut, and he thought it entirely likely his nose was broken. The handkerchief stemmed the flow of blood, and at last he realized he could stall no longer. It was time now to talk for his life.

"You weren't far off," he said, staring across the table at Cassidy. "The name's Luke Starbuck. I'm a detective, working out of Denver."

"I've heard the name." Cassidy fixed him with an evil look. "You've got yourself quite a reputation as a man-killer."

"No argument there," Starbuck said slowly. "No apology, either. It's part of the detective business."

"And you were sent here to kill me—weren't you?"

"Yeah, I was," Starbuck nodded soberly. "The price was ten thousand dollars and no questions asked."

"Ten—" Cassidy glowered at him with pop-eyed amazement. "Christ on a crutch! Somebody wanted me dead real bad."

"Unless I'm wrong, the whole scheme was cooked up to get me. You were just a bonus prize."

"Scheme?" Cassidy repeated blankly. "What d'you mean by that?"

Starbuck briefly explained. He related the gist of his meeting with the lawyer William Dexter. He next detailed the reason behind the assignment—robbery of the Butte mining company—and the client's name, Ira Lloyd. Then he recounted the gunfight in Cheyenne and the ambush on the trail to Hole-in-the-Wall. He saw now that neither of those incidents was happenstance. He'd been waylaid both times, and tonight was merely a last-ditch effort in an elaborate assassination plot. Somebody had sandbagged the odds to make triple certain he would wind up dead. And that somebody's name was Ira Lloyd.

"In other words," Starbuck concluded, "he figured if his own boys missed, then you'd get me. That's why you were warned I was on my way to Hole-in-the-Wall. He wanted you primed and ready to shoot the minute a stranger asked your name."

"Maybe." Cassidy examined the notion. "Leastways it'd explain why I got the warnin' so roundabout."

"I heard Butch mention Davis and the girls. Who's Davis?"

"Al Davis," Butch said with a wide, peg-toothed grin. "He owns the saloon and cathouse down at Cheever's Flats."

"What's Cheever's Flats?"

"A tradin' post," Butch replied. "North of Ed Houk's place, about a day's ride."

"Exactly what kind of warning was it?"

"Cut and dried," Cassidy informed him. "The fella said a hired gun was gonna settle my hash."

"No explanation?"

"None a-tall."

"Well, the reason's pretty clear now."

"Yeah?" Cassidy said shortly. "Like what?"

"Vengeance." Starbuck rocked his hand, fingers splayed. "Or maybe double vengeance. Lloyd probably figured we'd kill each other."

"Don't make no sense!" Cassidy gave him a baleful look. "I never been to Butte and I never pulled no payroll job. And I damn sure don't know nobody named Ira Lloyd!"

"All the same," Starbuck insisted, "there has to be a link, something that connects us together. Lloyd didn't just pull our names out of a hat."

"What link?" Cassidy crowed. "You and me ain't exactly got a lot in common!"

"Maybe." Starbuck rubbed his chin, thoughtful. "Maybe not."

"No maybe about it! You're upwind of the law and I'm downwind. Where's the connection?"

"Well, in a manner of speaking, we both wallow at the same mud hole."

"You just lost me."

"Look at it this way," Starbuck suggested. "It's possible we know some of the same people. Don't forget, I spend a lot of time with men in your . . . line of work."

"Then how come we never crossed paths before?"

"I didn't say that," Starbuck corrected him. "I'm talking about an indirect link. Somebody we both had dealings with at one time or another."

"Hmmm." Cassidy considered a moment. "You mean somebody I might've rode with?"

"That wouldn't be a bad place to start."

"Won't take long, either," Cassidy observed. "Not countin' Butch, I've only had two partners in my whole life. One was Latigo Spence. We worked together close to four years down in Utah. The other was Dutch Henry Horn. We used to steal horses and pull a few holdups, mostly in Texas."

A strange light came into Starbuck's eyes. "When was that?"

Cassidy's brow seamed in concentration. "Near as I recollect, we busted up the summer of '75. We had a fallin' out—bastard wouldn't divvy the split proper—and I winged him."

"You shot him?"

"Damn right!" Cassidy trumpeted. "He pulled a gun on me!"

"What happened then?"

"Nothin' much." Cassidy shrugged, remembering. "I went on to Utah and started workin' out of Robbers Roost." He paused, suddenly aware of Starbuck's expression. "Why all the questions about Horn?"

"Because he's our link."

"How so?"

"I killed Dutch Henry the summer of '76."

Starbuck quickly related the story. On his first job as a range detective, he'd been hired to track down a gang of horse thieves. Some months later, at a desolate spot in No-Man's-Land, the gang had been wiped out by a posse of ranchers and cowhands. The leader escaped, however, and Starbuck had trailed him to Colorado. There, in the town of Pueblo, the chase had finally ended. Starbuck killed Dutch Henry in a gunfight.

For a long while no one spoke. Cassidy stared down at the table, and Starbuck gazed off into space with the look of a man who had stumbled upon an unexpected revelation. Then, with a coarse grunt, Cassidy shook his head.

"So we both knew Dutch Henry? What's that got to do with anything?"

"It's a link." Starbuck regarded him with a level gaze. "Unless I miss my guess, it's the only link."

Their eyes locked, and after a moment Cassidy slowly nodded. "You figgerin' what I think you're figgerin'?"

Starbuck cracked a smile. "I wouldn't be surprised."

"You're gonna pay this Ira Lloyd a visit?"

"I'd say it's time . . . way past time."

Chapter Ten

A dingy haze lighted the sky at false dawn.

Cassidy and Starbuck stepped from the cabin and stood talking quietly. Between them was the unspoken respect of one hard man for another. There was nothing akin to friendship, and under different circumstances each would have killed the other without a moment's hesitation. Only a common danger united them, and it was more a mutual pact than a bond. Today they were allies.

Starbuck's features were puffy and discolored. Several hours' sleep had restored his vitality, but the shellacking he'd taken was certain to leave scars. He looked vaguely as if he'd had his face shoved into a meat-grinder. His nose was now crooked at a slight angle and his left eye was a kaleidoscope of black and blue. His eyebrow was caked with dried blood, as was the scabbed-over cut on his bottom lip. For all that, he nonetheless thought himself the luckiest of men. He was still alive.

Last night his position had been touch and go for a long while. Even though Cassidy bought his story, the undercurrent of hostility hadn't entirely disappeared. He sensed his life was forfeit at any moment; Cassidy's normal reaction would have been to kill him and personally settle the score with Ira Lloyd.

Neither of them was comfortable with the thought of another man doing their killing. Yet he'd argued far into the night that he was the natural choice for the job. Cassidy was known—and wanted—fair game outside Hole-in-the-Wall. Starbuck, on the other hand, was at liberty to move about at will. He was, moreover, the man with the larger grievance. The whole scheme had been rigged with his death in mind. That gave him first rights—prior claim.

With some reluctance, Cassidy had finally agreed. He was by no means content with the arrangement; but he felt Starbuck's argument had merit. Fair was fair, and the one with the bigger bone to pick was the one who deserved a crack at the job. Then, too, he was something of a realist himself, and willing to give credit where credit was due. Starbuck was the more experienced mankiller, and experience counted. All the signs thus far underscored what seemed an indisputable point. Killing Ira Lloyd would be no simple chore.

The bargain struck, they'd left it there. Starbuck's sixgun was returned, and he'd been offered a bunk for the night. Butch was sent to fetch his horse from the creek, and Cassidy went back to his bottle. Before drifting off to sleep, Starbuck had decided the new alliance would stand only so much strain. He intended to start the hunt at Cheever's Flats, and it was a point he'd neglected to mention. He had no idea whether Cassidy would object, but he wanted no more words, no further argument. He wanted to be gone from Hole-in-the-Wall. And the sooner the better.

Standing now with Cassidy, his attention was drawn to the corral. Butch had the bay gelding saddled, and was leading him through the gate. Starbuck was intrigued, his curiosity aroused. The youngster was happy-go-lucky, with a sunny disposition and no evidence of a mean streak. He was the exact opposite of Cassidy, and seemed an unlikely outlaw, aspiring or otherwise. For partners, the man and the kid were an odd match, hardly birds of a feather. It was something to ponder.

Butch walked the gelding to the front of the cabin. He stopped and handed the reins to Starbuck. Then he grinned with brash impudence.

"You stick around"—he ducked his head at the bay—"and somebody's liable to steal him out from under you."

Starbuck smiled. "That somebody's name wouldn't be . . ." His voice trailed off, and he cocked his head to one side. "I guess I never thought to ask. What is your name, anyway?"

"Cassidy!" Butch swelled with pride. "Same as Mike's!"

"You two related?"

"Naw!" Butch's grin widened. "Lots of folks think that 'cause of us being partners. We're not kin, though. I just took Mike's name when we teamed up."

"How'd you get together?"

"Blind luck," Butch confessed. "I got in a little scrape and lit out for Robbers Roost. Mike took me in and taught me the business. Owe it all to him!"

"Quit braggin'," Cassidy ribbed him. "You ain't no great shakes as a horse thief . . . not yet."

"Says you!" Butch laughed. "I got the natural touch—born to it!"

"What you got," Cassidy said with grumpy good humor, "is a gift for gab." He paused, glanced at Starbuck. "Never knowed a squirt to toot his own horn so much."

"From what I hear," Starbuck said wryly, "he's got a good teacher. Your wanted dodger's still plastered all over Utah."

"Now that you mention it"—Cassidy squinted at him—"that brings us around to some unfinished business."

"What's that?"

"You being a lawman." Cassidy looked uncomfortable. "Or leastways a detective."

A vein pulsed in Starbuck's forehead. "So?"

"Well, first off, lemme say I ain't too proud of the way I roughed you up last night. Except for Butch crackin' you on the head, you'd've probably dished out as good as you got."

Starbuck brushed away the apology. "I reckon you had cause. In your position, I would have done the same—or worse."

"I come close to that, too."

"So I remember."

Cassidy paused, regarding him with a dour look. "I let you off the hook, and I'd like a favor in return."

"Unfinished business means you're calling the marker?"

"Guess it does," Cassidy said, deadly earnest. "I want your word you'll keep what you learned about Hole-in-the-Wall to yourself."

Starbuck stared at him a long time, finally drew a deep breath. "You ask a lot."

"No more'n I gave," Cassidy said grimly. "Would've been lots easier to send you up the flume and end it permanent."

A moment passed, then Starbuck shrugged. "All right, you've got my word."

"That's good enough for me."

"How'd you know I would go along?"

"I didn't." Cassidy's eyes burned with intensity. " 'Course, without your word, you wouldn't never have made it through the canyon." He gestured toward the other cabins. "Some of the boys would've dry-gulched you."

Starbuck nodded, digesting the thought. "What's to stop them from doing it anyhow?"

"A handshake." Cassidy extended his hand. "That's the signal we've come to an understandin'."

Starbuck pumped his arm vigorously. "Let's make sure they get the message."

"Don't trouble yourself." A slow smile spread over Cassidy's face. "You're in the clear . . . now."

"We're square, then." Starbuck forcefully stressed the point. "The marker's paid in full."

Cassidy made a small nod of acknowledgment. "You don't owe me nothin'."

"I'll remember that," Starbuck said quietly, "if we ever meet again."

"Hope we don't!" Cassidy suddenly chuckled. "Got an idea it'd wind up a double funeral!"

"No argument there, Mike."

Starbuck waved to Butch and swung aboard the gelding. He rode toward the creek, aware he was being closely scrutinized by men in the other cabins. The first rays of sunrise broke over the sandstone ramparts as he turned into the canyon. He gigged the bay and left Hole-in-the-Wall behind him.

All the way through the canyon Starbuck examined various possibilities. He mentally rehashed what he'd uncovered and played the devil's advocate with himself. He arrived at only one conclusion.

For a detective, he was the prize bonehead of all time. He'd outsmarted himself, and he had underestimated everyone involved in the case. Worse, he had violated the supreme rule by which a manhunter lived. He'd let them do it to him—not the other way around.

There was no denying the facts. It all fit together like a template, events dovetailed one to the other with unquestionable timing. Despite himself, he had to admit he'd been gaffed by William Dexter. He had swallowed the lawyer's story—bait and all—leaping at the challenge of infiltrating Hole-in-the-Wall. Then, with his judgment already clouded, he had ignored one coincidence after another. He was cocky and overconfident, and only from the vantage point of hindsight had he paused to evaluate the situation. That lapse had almost gotten him killed.

Now, with a grudging sense of realization, he knew he couldn't afford another mistake. He had no idea why Ira Lloyd wanted him dead. He hadn't the faintest clue to the mine owner's connection with Dutch Henry Horn. A connection out of the past, moldering with age and the unmistakable smell of revenge. Yet one thing was very certain. Ira Lloyd was slippery and shrewd, and possessed an absolute genius for treachery. Not a man to be taken lightly, or allowed an even break. The game was dirty pool, no rules and winner take all. The loser got buried.

Late that morning, Starbuck emerged from the canyon onto the plains. His thoughts were hardened around indrawn resolve. He was determined to regain the edge, and force the fight on ground of his own choosing. Then he would kill the man who had tried to kill him.

He rode north into the Big Horn Basin.

Cheever's Flats was a crude collection of three buildings. A trading post, owned by John Cheever, stocked supplies for ranchers and outlaws and those traveling the old Bridger Trail. Next door was a blacksmith shop, and across the way was what people charitably termed a road ranch.

A combination saloon and whorehouse, the establishment was operated by Al Davis. His customers were only slightly rougher than his girls, and he considered himself a High Plains entrepreneur. He sold snakehead whiskey and rented his soiled doves by the trick or by the hour.

The last streamers of light dipped below the horizon as Starbuck rode into Cheever's Flats. Then the sky turned dusky mauve and the buildings suddenly lay cloaked in shadow. He angled across to the road ranch and stepped from the saddle. Tying the bay to a hitch rack, he walked directly to the door and banged it open. He entered with a bluff air of assurance.

The interior was dimly lighted and silent as a tomb. A pair of harridans, both of them ugly as sin, had a table staked out at the rear of the room. Neither of the girls appeared anxious for business, and they scarcely glanced at him as he stepped inside the door. On the opposite wall was a plank bar, and a lone

customer stood bellied up to the counter. The barkeep
was heavyset, with a ginger-colored walrus mustache
and a mail-order toupee. He looked like an overstuffed Kewpie doll with tusks.

Starbuck crossed to the bar. He picked a spot at
the far end of the counter, away from the solitary
drinker. The barkeep ambled over, and he nodded.
"Whiskey."

"Dollar a shot, friend."

"I didn't ask the price," Starbuck said curtly.
"Just bring me a bottle and a glass."

"Suit yourself."

"I generally do."

While he waited, Starbuck rolled a smoke. He
struck a match on the counter and lit up, inhaling a
long drag. The barkeep returned with a bottle and
glass, and poured. He blew smoke in the fat man's
face.

"You Al Davis?"

"I was the last time I checked."

"Keep it short and simple," Starbuck ordered. "I
ain't here to be entertained."

"No offense." Davis' voice was phlegmy, with
the hoarse rasp of a boozer. "What can I do for you?"

"Mike Cassidy sent me." Starbuck blew a perfect
smoke ring toward the ceiling. Then, waiting for it to
widen, he puffed a smaller one straight through the
center. "You're gonna gimme some information Mike
wants. He said to tell you he'd count it a personal
favor."

Davis gave him a blank stare. "What sort of information?"

"A week or so back," Starbuck said stolidly,

"somebody wandered in here and left a warnin' for Mike. You recall that, don't you?"

"I—" Davis' face went pale, and he couldn't seem to keep his hands still. "Why do you ask?"

"You told Mike you couldn't remember the jasper or what he looked like."

"No, I didn't either," Davis protested. "I told Mike I never knew who said it."

"Then that makes you an even bigger liar."

"Wait a minute!" Davis said indignantly. "You got no right to come in here and start calling me names!"

Starbuck's smile seemed frozen. "I'll call you dog and you'll wag your tail! 'Cause if you don't, I'll kick your lardass right up between your shoulders. You begin to get the picture?"

Davis' eyes went round as saucers. "I think I got it."

"You're smarter'n you look." Starbuck studied his downcast face a moment. "Now, we'll make this quick and painless. I want a description of whoever it was that left the warnin'."

"Description?"

"You ain't deaf, are you?"

"No." Davis averted his eyes, darted a quick glance along the bar. "I don't know as I could do that."

Starbuck got the uncanny impression he was being told something without words. He leaned into the counter, motioned Davis closer. "You afraid to talk?"

"Yessir, I am," Davis said in a hoarse whisper. "Mortally afraid."

"Why so?"

"That's him!" Davis hissed. "The one at the end of the bar!"

"You're sure?" Starbuck demanded. "No mistake?"

"None," Davis muttered softly. "He come in not ten minutes ago. Asked me if I'd had any news from Hole-in-the-Wall."

"How come you suddenly remembered him?"

"Just did," Davis said weakly. "When he asked me that, I placed his face from last time."

"If you're lyin'," Starbuck growled, "I'm gonna turn your blubber into worm meat."

"Honest to Christ, I'm telling you! It's him!"

Starbuck was still leaning on the bar. He casually dropped his hand below the counter and eased it inside his vest. His fingers closed around the butt of the Colt and he slipped it from the crossdraw holster. Then he turned his head just far enough to rivet the man with a look.

"Mister, I'd like a word with you."

The man was unremarkable in appearance. He wore soiled range clothes and a battered slouch hat. He was of average height, trimly built, with the kind of face lost in a crowd. The only thing noteworthy was the pistol positioned close to hand. It looked well oiled, and much used. He straightened slightly, then turned. His gaze settled on Starbuck.

"You talking to me?"

"Nobody else," Starbuck said with a wintry smile. "I understand you've been askin' questions about Hole-in-the-Wall?"

"What's that to you?"

"All depends."

"On what?"

"On who you know at Hole-in-the-Wall."

"Try me and see."

"How about Mike Cassidy?"

"Never heard of him."

"You're plumb certain?"

"Positive."

"Then how come you're back here checkin' on things?"

"What things?"

"The warnin' you left Cassidy . . . about me?"

"Hold off a—"

The gun appeared in the man's hand and he fired a hurried snap shot. The slug plowed a furrow in the counter at Starbuck's elbow. He shifted, swinging the Colt from beneath his vest, and touched off the trigger. The pistol roared, spat a sheet of flame.

A surprised look came over the man's face. He dropped the gun and raised both arms, like a preacher warding off evil spirits. Then a splotch of red widened across his chest and his legs went rubbery. He sat down heavily on the floor.

Starbuck approached and knelt beside him. "You're dead, so it don't matter now. Tell me about Ira Lloyd."

"Who's he?"

"The man who hired you to kill me."

"That's a . . . laugh."

"Quit stalling!" Starbuck commanded. "You don't owe Lloyd nothing. Spill it while you got time!"

"Nothing . . . to . . . say."

"C'mon, talk! What've you got to lose?"

"Starbuck"—the man smiled and a trickle of blood leaked out of his mouth—"you fool."

His grin became a wet chuckle, then a strangled

cough. Suddenly he choked and vomited a great gout of blood down across his shirtfront. His eyeballs rolled back in his head and he dropped dead.

Starbuck passed a hand over the man's eyes. Then he rose to his feet and stood staring down at the body. He heard again those last words and any lingering doubt was dispelled. Proof positive lay dead at his feet. The bastard had called him by name! And hammered him to the cross with one last breath.

He was indeed a fool!

Chapter Eleven

The sun was a fiery ball lodged in the sky. Across the plains, a shimmering haze like spun glass bathed the land in a glow of illusion. Far in the distance, waves of heat pulsed and vibrated, distilling small mirages under glaring shafts of light. A faraway knoll sometimes seemed touchable and the plains went on forever.

Starbuck was roughly a hundred fifty miles northwest of Hole-in-the-Wall. He'd followed the old Bridger Trail for three days, with the Big Horn Range to the east and the Absaroka Mountains to the west. Early that morning, north of Stinking Water River, he'd crossed the line into Montana. Now, with the sun fading westward, he intersected the Bozeman Trail. A tributary of the Yellowstone flowed through the juncture, providing fresh water and plentiful graze for the gelding. He decided to pitch camp for the night.

A stand of trees along the stream afforded shelter and a ready supply of deadwood. He unsaddled, then hobbled the bay and turned him loose on a grassy stretch near the shoreline. He dumped his gear on the ground and left the rifle propped against a tree. After collecting an armload of wood, he built a small fire. Nights were brisk, the temperature plummeting when the sun went down and a cheery blaze was one of the few comforts on the trail. He loaded a galvanized coffeepot and put it to boil on a couple of rocks beside the flames. Supper would consist of hardtack and a rabbit he'd shot late that afternoon. His treat would be a tin of peaches he'd been hoarding.

With the campsite in order, he spread his bedroll beneath the trees. He built himself a smoke and lit it with a stick from the fire. He was reminded of the joke Indians told among themselves. A white man kindled a roaring blaze and backed off from it, whereas a red man built a small fire and hovered near its warmth. The thought did little to improve his humor, and nothing at all to dispel his guarded mood. He stretched out on the bedroll and lay back with his head pillowed on the saddle. He stared at the muslin blue of the sky and wondered where it would all end.

The killing at Cheever's Flats was still very much on his mind. Several things were immediately apparent. The dead man, despite his denial, was yet another of Ira Lloyd's stooges. He'd returned to Cheever's Flats for the express purpose of verifying whether Starbuck had been killed at Hole-in-the-Wall. In the event that gambit had failed, he was doubtless under orders to pick up Starbuck's trail and arrange an ambush. The most troublesome aspect, however, was confirmation of something Starbuck had until then merely suspected. The dead man—along with the two bushwhackers killed previously—had known him on sight. Clearly, his attempts to disguise his identity hadn't worked.

All of which added a new dimension to Ira Lloyd. The mine owner had orchestrated a far-flung assassination plot. He had retained William Dexter, whose

role in the affair was still somewhat murky. Then he'd
hired at least three veteran gunhands and set them to
tracking Starbuck across the vastness of the High
Plains. Obviously a stickler for detail, he had let nothing escape his attention. He had acquired Starbuck's
photo—probably from one of several articles in the
Police Gazette—and each of the hired killers had
quite plainly committed it to memory. There was an
overall coordination to the plot that smacked of someone with a keen mind; not unlike a wily chess player,
Lloyd had made his moves with a certain analytical
perception of men and events. Then, too, the magni-
tude of the operation indicated a large outlay of funds.
No cheapskate, Lloyd was clearly willing to spend
whatever it took to get the job done. He was determined and relentless, a man of craft and spidery patience. He wouldn't quit until Starbuck was dead.

A similar thought was uppermost in Starbuck's
mind. He possessed his own brand of bulldog tenac-
ity, and the word "quitter" was not part of his lexicon.
Yet he was still operating somewhat in the dark. His
gut feeling told him that Lloyd somehow anticipated
his every move. There seemed to be a contingency
plan every step along the way, and no end to the
number of assassins who dogged his trail. At Cheever's Flats, he'd taken precautions to insure he wasn't
followed. After searching the dead man, he had gone
directly from the saloon to the trading post. There, he
replenished his victuals and indulged himself with the
purchase of a coffeepot. Then he rode south, toward
Hole-in-the-Wall. Only after full dark had he reversed
course and turned north. So he was relatively certain
no one shadowed his backtrail.

What lay ahead was an altogether different story.

He planned to follow the Bozeman Trail, which paralleled the Yellowstone in a westerly direction. Another couple of days would put him at Fort Ellis, and some miles past there he would swing northwest, toward the Missouri River. Four days from now, barring the unforeseen, he would arrive in Butte. Thus far, however, his hindsight had been considerably keener than his foresight. The trail ahead was rough country, desolate and virtually devoid of habitation. Ambush sites were around every crook and turn; the terrain was made to order for bushwhackers. For all he knew, another of Lloyd's assassins awaited him even now. Based on events to date, he could only surmise that Lloyd would anticipate him once more. Whether the next attempt would be made on the trail—or in Butte itself—was anybody's guess. Yet he needed no crystal ball for a look into the future. A pattern had been established, and patterns were seldom broken. There would be another attempt on his life.

The coffeepot suddenly rattled. He stubbed out his cigarette on the ground and climbed to his feet. With his jacknife, he cut green branches and fashioned a spit. Then he dressed out the rabbit and put it to cook over the fire. Afterward he walked to the stream to clean his knife. He hunkered down and then stopped, grunting softly to himself. He stared at the blood on his hands.

And thought of Ira Lloyd.

Butte was situated directly on a mountain. The town sprawled over and around the mountain, which was shaped like a woman's breast and filled with the world's richest lode of copper. Unlike other mining camps, there was a sense of permanence to the community. Butte was the prized play-toy of millionaires.

Starbuck rode into town around midday. He left the gelding at a livery stable, and spent the next couple of hours drifting from saloon to saloon. His grubby appearance made him one of the crowd, for the miners were rough-garbed and covered with powdery grime. He casually engaged men in conversation, and kept them talking with an occasional question. He was a good listener—a master of subtle interrogation—and a few rounds of drinks bought him all the inside information. He discovered Butte was on the brink of open warfare.

The story told by the miners typified what was happening all across the West. In the 1870s, when gold was the lodestone in Butte, a man worked his claim by hand. Within a few years, however, the gold diggings petered out. At that point, large corporations bought up the claims and began exploitation of minerals locked deep within the bowels of the mountain. By the end of the decade, copper was king, and the town was controlled by bankers and financiers. Absentee owners, generally a consortium of wealthy businessmen, pulled the strings from New York and San Francisco. Their singular interest was profit—at any cost.

Technology was the key to the financiers' takeover. A new invention—dynamite—was used to blast through the rock and excavate tunnels. Underground drilling, formerly done by hand, was now accomplished with power drills, operating on compressed air. Working in tandem, dynamite and power drills made it possible to burrow far beneath the earth's surface. Some operations were thousands of feet below ground and extended for miles through a labyrinth of tunnels.

As the mines probed ever deeper into the mountainside, the danger to workers multiplied at an alarming rate. Safety measures were virtually nonexistent, and accidents became commonplace. Men were killed and maimed by cave-ins, sometimes drowned when subterranean springs flooded the tunnels, and frequently incinerated when fire swept through the timbered mine shafts. Adding fuel to the workers' discontent was a miserly pay scale of thirty cents an hour. The inevitable result was revolt and violence.

Only two years ago, the battle between management and miners had flared into open hostility at Leadville, Colorado. Workers went on strike—demanding four dollars for an eight-hour shift—and the mines closed. Owners and miners armed themselves, and Leadville teetered on the edge of anarchy. The state militia was activated and the miners were ultimately forced back to work. Yet the battle cry had been sounded all across the West.

Embittered workers rallied to the exhortations of radical union organizers. With armed men on both sides, a strike more often than not developed into a bloody confrontation. Murder, complete with bombings and midnight assassinations, was the rule. Still, the owners controlled the courts and the law, and as a last resort, the militia. Strikes were generally broken by the might of force, and the miners seldom realized any lasting benefit. The struggle, nonetheless, continued unabated. A climate of revolution spread like wildfire throughout western mining camps.

Even now a strike was brewing in Butte. Starbuck learned that labor leaders were organizing the miners along military lines. Weapons were being distributed, and rifle squads were openly training in the surrounding hills. The plan was to call a general strike, and challenge the owners with their own tactics. The hired guns of management—known as goon squads—and the militia would be met by organized resistance. The battle lines were drawn and an explosion was imminent. Butte was where the union leaders would take their stand.

Starbuck discovered the impending strike directly affected his own plans. The Grubstake Mining Company—owned by Ira Lloyd—had suspended operations. The mine had been closed almost a month past, with no prior warning of a shutdown. Several miners attributed the closing to the threat of a strike. Grubstake management apparently preferred to sit out the battle and wait until the dust settled. As for Ira Lloyd himself, the name was unknown in Butte's saloons. George Horwell, the general manager, had operated the mine for the last three years. The day after the shutdown he had simply vanished from town. No one could hazard a guess as to where he'd gone.

Late that afternoon, Starbuck went to have a look for himself. The Grubstake was located on the west side of the mountain, near the bottom of the slope. Everything he'd heard was substantiated by what he found. The windows and door of the office were boarded up, and the mine shaft was sealed off by heavy timbers. There was no watchman, and no evidence anyone had been near the place in several weeks. For all practical purposes, the mine appeared abandoned.

Unless William Dexter was a fool, he'd known the Grubstake was closed when he offered Starbuck

the assignment. Then, too, it seemed curiously strange
that Ira Lloyd was a cipher to everyone in Butte. On
top of that, there was the additional mystery of
George Horwell, the Grubstake manager. Why he'd
disappeared and where he'd gone were equal parts of
the overall riddle. The upshot of all these imponderables was a cul-de-sac. A dead end that seemingly
stopped at Butte.

Starbuck took a room in one of the local hotels.
His investigation was stymied and he was momentarily at a loss. A bath and a decent meal and a good
night's sleep seemed very much in order. He would
think on it overnight and then decide his next move.

For the next move might very well be the last.

Starbuck rolled out of bed and padded barefoot to the
washstand. He poured water from a pitcher into a
cracked basin and briskly scrubbed his face. After
rinsing his mouth, he smoothed his hair back and
caught his reflection in the mirror. The vestiges of
Hole-in-the-Wall marked his features.

The bridge of his nose was slightly off center and
an angry scar still puckered one eyebrow. The puffi-
ness was gone from his lip, but a hairline crease was
visible. He looked vaguely like a pugilist who had
stepped into the prize ring once too often. He wondered how Lola would react when she got a glimpse
of the rearrangement. Then he laughed at himself for
wondering at all.

After supper last night, he'd gone on a quick
shopping spree. A men's emporium was able to outfit
him in a suit and accessories that were reasonably
passable. He had swapped the Stetson for a derby,
and chucked the range garb, including the vest and

the conchas belt, into a trash bin. His last purchase was a straight razor and a soap mug. Then he'd walked down to the livery stable and sold the bay. He got a good price, but it made the chore no easier. The horse had served him well.

Pouring fresh water, he lathered his face and shaved with dull concentration. His thoughts this morning were not on the bay, and only fleetingly on Lola Montana. He was, instead, mentally preparing himself to assume a new guise. He finished shaving and toweled his face dry. Then he dressed, remembering to remove the fake dead tooth, and walked out the door. He left nothing of Arapahoe Smith behind.

By eight o'clock, he'd had breakfast and inquired directions to the sheriff's office. A cheap cigar was wedged in the corner of his mouth, and the derby was cocked at a rakish angle. He thought it added just the right touch to his cover story. Hurrying along the street, he worked himself into the proper mood of outrage. He stormed into the sheriff's office with a look of bellicose indignation.

Hiram Urschel was less lawman than politician. He was bald and potbellied, and wore thick, wire-rimmed glasses. He was also the tool of the mine owners, and currently sitting on a powder keg called Butte. He looked nervous as a whore in church.

"Earl Suggs," Starbuck announced, shaking his hand. "Western District Manager for the Olympic Mining Equipment Company."

"Yessir," Urschel replied without much interest. "What can I do for you, Mr. Suggs?"

"I have just now," Starbuck remarked stiffly, "come from the Grubstake mine. Or perhaps I should say—what's left of the mine!"

"You have some connection with the Grubstake?"

"I do indeed!" Starbuck thundered. "To the tune of a hundred thousand dollars."

"A hundred—"

"Precisely!" Starbuck assumed a wrathful stance. "An Olympic smelter—Model ZB10—ordered by Grubstake and due to arrive here tomorrow morning!"

"Oh!" Urschel nodded sagely. "Grubstake ordered the smelter and promised payment on delivery. That the idea?"

"Scoundrels!" Starbuck stumped to the window and back again, puffing clouds of smoke. "Sheriff, I desperately need your assistance! Otherwise I am in dire jeopardy of losing my job. Where might I find the Grubstake's owner, Mr. Ira Lloyd?"

"Don't know any Lloyd," Urschel advised him. "The owner of record is a man named William Dexter. He's headquartered in Denver."

"I—" Starbuck was genuinely astounded. "How did you come by that information?"

Urschel nervously drummed his fingers on the desktop. "Guess there's no harm in telling you that. I was asked to contact all the mine owners and coordinate things when this strike blows. I wrote Dexter about six weeks ago." He paused, wiped his nose. "The only reply I got was the one you've seen for yourself. He closed down the mine."

"And you've never heard of Ira Lloyd?"

"Not till you mentioned the name."

"Have you ever met Dexter?"

"No, I haven't," Urschel admitted. "Course, that's neither here nor there. Most of the mines are owned by syndicates or fronts—"

"Fronts?"

"Dummy corporations," Urschel explained. "So it's not surprising we never see the individuals themselves."

"Sheriff, just between us . . ." Starbuck winked and munched his cigar. "Would you say Dexter is a front man?"

Urschel gave him a hard, wise look. "That'd be my educated guess."

"Do you recall when he bought the Grubstake?"

"Well, as I recollect, it was about three years ago. Sometime the spring or early summer of '79."

"Uh-huh!" Starbuck deliberated a moment. "What about the manager, George Horwell? Any idea where I might locate him?"

"Wouldn't have the least notion."

"Out of curiosity"—Starbuck made an offhand gesture with his cigar—"what does he look like . . . his general appearance?"

"Let's see," Urschel said in a mild, abstracted way. "Early thirties, brown hair, medium height, slim build; pretty average. Why do you ask?"

"No reason."

Starbuck thought the reason was best kept to himself. He now knew what had happened to the Grubstake manager. George Horwell had died on a barroom floor at Cheever's Flats. Which partially explained his disappearance from Butte, and raised yet another intriguing question.

Was Horwell otherwise known as Ira Lloyd? Or, carrying it a step further . . . *was there an Ira Lloyd?*

Chapter Twelve

Starbuck pulled into Union Station three mornings later. From Butte he had traveled to Salt Lake City, and there he'd caught the overnight train to Denver. He looked worn and hollow-eyed from the long trip, and his mood was one of quiet steel fury. He planned to brace William Dexter.

All the way from Butte he'd brooded on his next step. There were no easy answers, only hard questions. The man he'd killed at Cheever's Flats was undoubtedly George Horwell, the Grubstake manager. Whether or not Horwell and Ira Lloyd were one and the same was less certain. Try as he might, he had thought of no way to establish a connection. Nor was there any practical way to determine Horwell's link to Dutch Henry Horn. As for the knottier question—did Ira Lloyd actually exist?—he was in a complete quandary. Key pieces to a very convoluted puzzle were still missing.

Yet certain factors were beyond question. By whatever name, someone had organized an elaborate assassination plot. There was a direct link between that someone and a ghost from his past, Dutch Henry Horn. Which meant there had been a concerted effort to keep tabs on him over the last seven years. His reputation as a detective was known, and someone

had skillfully employed it as a device to lure him into
a trap. Further, though the reason was unclear, there
was obviously some reluctance to assassinate him in
Denver. Otherwise there was no need to rig such a
complex scheme, one that enticed him out of the city.
He could easily have been killed on homeground.

So all roads led back to Denver. The case had
begun with William Dexter, and he was clearly the
key to the missing pieces. There was, moreover, the
very real possibility that he alone had orchestrated
the assassination plot. If true, that would explain his
ownership of the Grubstake mine and unravel, at last,
the mystery of Ira Lloyd. For if William Dexter had
invented Ira Lloyd, the case was closed. With the exception of one final question.

What was his link to Dutch Henry Horn?

Starbuck was determined to have an answer. He'd
been shot at and beaten to a pulp, and conned so
thoroughly he felt like the greenest of rubes. He was
in no mood for polite conversation or civilized tactics.
His plan was simple and direct, versed in terms even
a hotshot Denver lawyer would understand. He intended to put a gun to Dexter's head.

From the train depot, Starbuck took a hansom cab
uptown. He got off at the corner of Eighteenth and
Larimer, and walked directly to the Barclay Building.
An elevator deposited him on the fifth floor, and he
proceeded along the hallway to a suite of offices. Entering the waiting room, he found a male secretary
seated behind a desk. The man was slightly built,
somewhat bookish in appearance. He glanced up from
a stack of paperwork, nodded pleasantly.

"Good morning."

Starbuck halted before the desk. "Tell Dexter I

want to see him. The name's Luke Starbuck."

The man's smile faltered. "Apparently you haven't heard, Mr. Starbuck."

"Heard what?"

"About Mr. Dexter," the man stammered. "He— he's dead."

"Dead!" Starbuck stopped, as though he'd walked into a wall. His mouth hardened, and when he spoke the words were clipped, brittle. "How'd it happen?"

"He was shot . . . murdered."

"By who?"

"No one knows." The man swallowed, eyes grim. "He worked late one night, and the next morning—it was awful—I found him myself."

Starbuck's tone was inquisitorial. "Any signs of a struggle?"

"No, sir."

"Was he robbed?"

"Oh, no!" the man blurted. "There was considerable cash in his wallet and he was wearing a very valuable timepiece. His person was . . . undisturbed."

"Anything missing from the office files—records or correspondence?"

"Nothing insofar as we've been able to determine. The police were here and went through everything very thoroughly. His safe was open—that's where he kept confidential records—and they even inspected that. Everything appeared in order."

"When was he killed?"

"Yesterday," the man said miserably. "Or to be more precise, night before last. I found him yesterday morning."

Starbuck's expression was wooden. Yet any

doubt was blown from his mind like jackstraws in a wind. *Ira Lloyd did exist!*

The timing told the tale. The lawyer had been murdered one day before Starbuck returned to Denver. As for a motive, it was patently clear he'd been silenced. Forced to talk, he could have revealed the whereabouts of Ira Lloyd. Or more important—since the name was probably phony—the true identity of Ira Lloyd. The sequence of events was not difficult to piece together.

Some ten days ago, Starbuck had killed Horwell. Then he'd appeared in Butte and begun asking questions. Somehow word had reached Lloyd, and he had correctly anticipated Starbuck's next move. With Butte a washout, Starbuck would return to Denver and put the screws on Dexter. Having failed to kill Starbuck—and unwilling to risk exposure—Lloyd had taken the only remaining countermove. He'd killed Dexter.

Starbuck pondered it at length. His eyes narrowed in concentration and he mentally shifted the pieces on the chess board once more. Then he nodded to himself, satisfied with the result. Finally, his gaze shifted to the man behind the desk.

"What's your name?"

"Frank Huggins."

"Do you know me, Mr. Huggins?"

"Yessir," Huggins murmured. "That is to say, I know who are you are, Mr. Starbuck."

"Suppose I took you into my confidence?" Starbuck arched one eyebrow in question. "Would I be safe in assuming you'd keep it to yourself?"

"Oh, yessir!" Huggins said with a catch in his voice. "I would never betray a confidence!"

"I'd want your word," Starbuck warned him. "And I can't abide a man who breaks his word."

Huggins bobbed his head. "You have my solemn oath, Mr. Starbuck."

"Good enough." Starbuck paused, let him hang a moment. "I was working on a case for Mr. Dexter. Unless I'm wrong, the subject of that investigation is the man who killed him."

"You really mean it?"

"I'd bet on it," Starbuck said with conviction. "But I'll need your help to prove it."

"Anything!" Huggins offered. "Anything at all!"

"I need a look at Mr. Dexter's confidential files— the ones in the safe."

"Oh, my!" Huggins said doubtfully. "The police wouldn't like that, Mr. Starbuck. Chief Kelsey himself ordered me not to touch anything until they've finished their investigation."

"Who's to know?" Starbuck smiled. "I won't tell him if you don't."

"Well—"

"You want to help catch the killer, don't you?"

"Yes, of course!"

"Then here's your chance," Starbuck urged. "I'll be in and out before you know it."

"I . . ." Huggins hesitated, then suddenly squared himself up. "I'll do it! I owe that much to Mr. Dexter."

"That's the ticket!"

Starbuck quickly crossed the room. He entered Dexter's private office and stopped just inside the door. The office was richly appointed, with a carved walnut desk, several wingback chairs, and plush carpeting. Someone had carefully washed the desktop, but the outline of bloodstains was still visible. A cursory inspection indicated the lawyer had been shot while seated in the judge's chair behind the desk. From the pattern of the bloodstains, he had then slumped forward on the desk, apparently shot in the head. All signs pointed to a swift and efficient job. An execution, and not the work of a stranger.

After a look around, Starbuck began with the desk. He spent the next half hour rummaging through Dexter's personal effects. He was searching for anything that might provide a lead to either Ira Lloyd or the Grubstake Mining Company. Curiously, there was no correspondence from George Horwell, the mine manager. Odder still, there was no file pertaining to the mine itself. It was as though all traces of the Grubstake had been expunged from Dexter's records.

The squat wall safe was a trove of information. The contents revealed that Dexter's business interests had been varied and immensely profitable. A large bookkeeping ledger was particularly enlightening. There, page by page, was a detailed record of the lawyer's financial dealings. His association with men of power and wealth ranged from Denver to San Francisco, with notable emphasis on mining investments. The pages were in chronological order, providing a calendar with dates and company names and dollar figures. Between April, 1879, and May, 1879, Starbuck made a startling discovery. A page had been neatly razored from the ledger.

The missing page was proof in itself. He recalled an item gleaned from his conversation with the sheriff in Butte. Three years ago—which translated to the spring of 1879—William Dexter had purchased the Grubstake mine. The time frame fit perfectly, and the missing page, by its very absence, was strong testimony. All transactions relating to the Grubstake had been removed from the ledger. Which meant Dexter was, in the end, a mere front man.

The motive behind the killing was now corroborated. No record existed connecting Dexter to Ira Lloyd. Nor was there any fear of the lawyer's talking.

A dead man was indeed a silent partner.

Starbuck paused at the corner of Fourteenth and Larimer. He lit a cigarette and stood looking at the police station. He was thinking without any charity of Chief Elwood Kelsey. Their dislike was mutual and of long duration. Yet he saw no alternative to requesting the chief's cooperation. He desperately needed a lead.

A dull and grinding weariness had fallen over him on his walk from the Barclay Building. Any trace of Ira Lloyd had ended at the lawyer's office. There was no next step, for the missing page from the ledger had effectively erased the trail. His investigation was blunted, and with nowhere left to turn, his only option was the police. He would attempt, however briefly, to resurrect William Dexter. A voice from the grave might yet be made to speak.

Inside the police station, Starbuck was left to cool his heels for nearly an hour. He understood the slight was intentional, a low form of insult meant to embarrass him. Denver's chief of police was contemptuous of private detectives in general, and he reserved a particularly virulent animosity for Starbuck. Based in part on envy, his attitude blackened in direct proportion to Starbuck's reputation. A quote in a newspaper interview had revealed the sum and substance

of his spite. He had publicly labeled the manhunter a
licensed killer.

Smoking quietly, Starbuck waited on a bench in
the hall. He'd learned long ago that the man who lost
his temper generally lost the fight. The winner, inevitably, was the man who provoked his opponent
into some heedless act. He took a tight grip on himself, and ruthlessly suppressed his anger. He couldn't
afford to lose today.

At length, a uniformed officer ushered him into
the chief's office. Elwood Kelsey was a beefy man,
with the bulbous nose of a heavy drinker and the girth
of one who indulged himself in the good life. His eyes
were small and mean, and he looked marvelously like
a bright pig. He let Starbuck stand, hat in hand.

"You wanted to see me?"

"I'm working on a case." Starbuck regarded him
with great calmness. "I'd like your assistance."

"God's blood!" Kelsey declared hotly. "Aren't
you the bold one! Do you really believe I'd give you
the time of day?"

"You will when you hear my client's name."

"And who might that be?"

"William Dexter."

Kelsey was visibly startled. "Why would Dexter
hire a—someone like you?"

"He retained me to find a man," Starbuck lied
easily. "I have reason to believe that same man killed
him."

"What's the man's name?"

Starbuck was alert to any reaction. "Ira Lloyd."

"Never heard of him." Kelsey's eyebrows drew
together in a frown. "Who is he?"

"A stock promoter," Starbuck said guilelessly.

"Works out of Butte . . . mostly mining stocks."

"What was his business with Dexter?"

"Let's trade." Starbuck met his gaze with an amused look. "You tell me your secrets and I'll tell you mine."

"Why should I help the likes of you?"

"You've got no choice," Starbuck bluffed. "I know something you don't . . . and it might solve the case."

"Bastard!" Kelsey's lips were tight and bloodless. "Go ahead, then! Ask your questions and be damned!"

"What physical evidence did you turn up at Dexter's office?"

"None," Kelsey answered with defensive gruffness. "Whoever murdered him left the place clean as a hound's tooth."

"How about the coroner's report?"

"One shot," Kelsey said in a resigned voice. "Powder burns on the right temple and no exit wound."

"No exit wound," Starbuck repeated slowly. "What caliber gun?"

"A thirty-two," Kelsey replied. "All the same, the autopsy showed death was instantaneous."

"So he knew the killer." Starbuck was thoughtful a moment, then went on. "Any eyewitnesses? Someone who saw the man entering or leaving the building?"

"Not so far."

"Was the door to Dexter's office forced?"

"No." Kelsey's tone was emphatic. "Either it wasn't locked, or he admitted the killer without incident."

"Anything else?" Starbuck insisted. "Anything unusual or out of place . . . maybe something you confiscated as evidence?"

"Nothing." Kelsey halted, glaring at him. "Now it's your turn! What was Dexter's interest in this fellow Lloyd?"

Starbuck embroidered on his original fairy tale. "Lloyd swindled one of his clients. Don't ask which one, because Dexter never told me."

"Where's Lloyd now?"

"I lost his trail in Butte."

"Butte?" Kelsey gave him a dirty look. "Are you saying you can't place Lloyd in Denver at the time of the murder?"

"I can't place him at all." Starbuck stitched a smile across his face. "I've never laid eyes on the man."

"You tricked me!"

"No, Chief," Starbuck said without irony. "You tricked yourself."

"I'll get you!" Kelsey's fist crashed into the desktop. "By the sweet Jesus, I'll run you out of Denver!"

Starbuck stared him straight in the eye, challenging him. "You haven't got the balls for it—or the clout."

Kelsey reddened with apoplectic rage. Starbuck flipped him a salute and walked to the door. Outside, however, the smile slipped and he admitted to himself it was a hollow victory. While he had won the game of wits, nothing of any value had been uncovered. He'd hopscotched his way back to square one.

Late that afternoon Starbuck entered the First National Bank. An hour earlier he had called a political marker with Lou Blomger, the underworld czar of Denver. In his pocket was a court order, duly executed by a circuit judge. He thought it a shot in the dark, but nonetheless worth a try. He'd exhausted his options.

Andrew Reed, the bank president, was portly and urbane, with foxy eyes and bone-china teeth. He was a high priest of Denver society, and a man of such vanity that he knelt only before mirrors. He looked up as Starbuck pushed through the swinging door of the balustrade and approached his desk. His greeting was civil but cool.

"Good afternoon, Mr. Starbuck."

"Afternoon." Starbuck handed him the court order. "As you'll see, that authorizes me to inspect the bank records of William Dexter."

"Highly irregular!" Reed squinted owlishly, rapidly scanning the paper. "May I inquire your purpose?"

"Confidential," Starbuck said vaguely. "But just between us, there's some hitch in getting Dexter's will probated."

"Indeed?" Reed spread his hands in a bland gesture. "I presume you are representing the widow?"

Starbuck shrugged off the question. "Hope there won't be any problem having a look at the records."

"Perish the thought!" Reed smiled dutifully. "The First National always honors a lawful request."

"Judge Peters told me you were a man of high principle."

"We all serve the public, Mr. Starbuck. Indeed we do!"

Reed summoned the head teller and issued instructions. Starbuck was then led along a corridor and

into a back room filled with filing cabinets. He asked
to see William Dexter's records for the last three
years. A clerk went through the files, and returned
with three enormous ledgers. Seated at a table, Starbuck began with the ledger marked 1879. He soon
struck paydirt.

Beginning the summer of 1879, a draft from the
Grubstake Mining Company had been deposited to
William Dexter's business account on the first of each
month. Leafing through the ledgers, Starbuck discovered the practice had continued month by month,
without interruption. The amounts were sizable and
grew progressively larger, indicating the mine had
prospered. Then, only a month ago, the deposits had
abruptly ceased. The date coincided with the closing
of the mine.

There were hundreds of entries in the ledgers,
covering Dexter's transactions in myriad business
ventures. The sheer volume of it left Starbuck bleary-
eyed, and his concentration on the mine almost cost
him a vital clue. Then, so suddenly it took his breath
away, he tumbled to a pattern. On the first of each
month the Grubstake Mining draft had been credited
to the account. On the fifth of each month a draft had
been drawn and debited against the account. The
practice had been regularly followed, month after
month, and the tipoff was a simple matter of calculation. The debits—to the penny—were ten percent
less than the amount of the Grubstake deposits.

The conclusion was inescapable. William Dexter,
functioning as a front man, had taken ten percent off
the top for overseeing the Grubstake operation. Those
monthly drafts for the balance were clearly earmarked
for the lawyer's silent partner. The entries in the ledg-

ers showed the drafts were always made to the order
of the same firm, in the same location. The Black
Hills Land Company. Deadwood, Dakota Territory.

Starbuck knew where to look for Ira Lloyd.

Chapter Thirteen

They were naked. The night was warm and modesty unnecessary. Stretched out on the bed, a tangle of arms and legs, their breath grew shorter. He kissed the nape of her neck, and they silently caressed and fondled. He cupped one of her breasts and the nipple swelled erect. She moaned, exhaled a hoarse, whimpering cry. Then his hand slowly slid down her stomach and went lower still until she shuddered convulsively.

"Oh Luke," she gasped in his ear. "Oooo—"

A knock sounded at the door. Starbuck raised himself up on one elbow, his head turned toward the sitting room. She pulled him back down in a fierce embrace. Her voice was furry and passionate.

"Forget it!" she whispered urgently. "They'll go away!"

The knock turned to a hammered pounding. Starbuck kissed the tip of her nose and gently disengaged himself from her arms. He rolled out of bed and moved to the wardrobe.

"Jeezus Christ!" Lola cursed furiously. "What a sense of timing!"

"Won't take long," Starbuck grumbled. "I'll send the bastard packing!"

"Watch yourself, lover!" Lola cautioned, sud-

denly wary. "One beating gives a man's face character. No need to overdo a good thing!"

"You've got my vote on that."

Starbuck hastily slipped into shirt and pants. He
took the Colt from beneath his pillow and walked to
the bedroom door. The pounding grew louder as he
padded barefoot across the sitting room. He hurried
the last few steps through the foyer.

"Hold your horses!" he yelled. "I hear you!"

The Colt at waist level, he cautiously flattened
himself against the wall. Then he cracked open the
door and took a quick peek. A look of astounded disbelief swept his features.

"Butch!"

"Howdy, Arapahoe!" Butch grinned. "Bet you
wasn't expectin' me."

"I sure as the devil wasn't!" Starbuck opened the
door wider. "How the hell'd you find me, anyway?"

"Asked around." Butch sauntered into the foyer.
"Finally got a line on you from a barkeep in some
dive."

"Where'd you come from?"

"Cheyenne," Butch replied absently. "I left my
horse there and caught a train. Got in a couple of
hours ago."

"Well—" Starbuck closed the door, still bemused. "C'mon in and tell me about it. What's up?"

Butch stopped just inside the entranceway. He
stood for a moment eyeballing the sitting room, and
his grin dissolved into a look of wonder. He tilted his
hat back on his head, whistled softly.

"Holy cow!" he muttered. "You got yourself
some digs!"

"Nothing much." Starbuck motioned him to a

chair. "Take a load off your feet and give me the lowdown."

"Don't mind if I do." Butch dropped into an easy chair, and suddenly noticed his bare feet. "Sorry I woke you up, Luke. What I got to say wouldn't keep till morning."

Starbuck flicked a glance toward the bedroom door, then shrugged. He saw the bulge of a sixgun beneath the youngster's jacket, carried on the off side and jammed into the waistband. The pistol was no surprise, but the kid materializing out of the night was like a dash of ice water. He laid his Colt on the coffee table and took a seat on the sofa.

"What's so important you'd risk coming to Denver?"

"Aww, I'm safe enough," Butch said confidently. "No dodgers out on a little fish like me. Course, the same don't hold true for Mike! That's why he asked me to come in his place."

"Mike sent you?" Starbuck asked, confounded. "All the way from Hole-in-the-Wall?"

"Well, don't you see, he wasn't sure whether you'd settled matters up in Butte. How'd things work out?"

"I was a day late and a dollar short. No sign of our friend."

"Then my trip wasn't wasted! Mike figured we'd be better off safe than sorry."

"You still haven't told me why?"

"Got a message for you," Butch replied. "Mike says—"

Lola appeared in the bedroom door. Her hair hung loose and she was wrapped in a filmy peignoir. The sheer fabric accentuated her full breasts and the curve of her hips. She glided into the room and struck a provocative pose beside the sofa.

"Who's your friend, lover?"

Starbuck was amused by her dramatic entrance, and her choice of costume. His arm moved in an idle gesture. "Lola Montana, meet Butch Cassidy."

"Hello, Butch," Lola purred. "Any friend of Luke's is a friend of mine."

Butch swept off his hat and bounded to his feet. His mouth sagged open and he ogled her with a look of slack-jawed amazement. He seemed to have lost his voice.

"What's the matter, honey?" Lola flashed a theatrical smile. "Cat got your tongue?"

"No, ma'am!" Butch sputtered. "Pleased to make your acquaintance."

"*Ma'am?*" Lola uttered a low, throaty laugh. "God, I must be losing my touch!"

"No, ma'am!" Butch twisted his hat into knots. "I mean—no offense, ma'am—you ain't lost nothin'!"

"That's sweet! I think I'm going to like you, Butch."

Lola fluttered her lashes and sized him up with a quick once-over. Her immediate impression was of a young ruffian fresh off a cattle drive. He smelled of horses and leather, and distant familiarity with a bathtub. Yet, beneath the dithering and callow manner, there was the sense of a kid aged beyond his years. She wondered what business he had with a manhunter.

"Lookee here now, Luke!" Butch blushed beet red, took a step toward the door. "I'm sorry as all get-out! Wouldn't've busted in here if I knowed you had . . . company."

"Simmer down," Starbuck said genially. "You're not interrupting anything that won't keep."

"Why, of course not!" Lola trilled. "We were just sitting around chewing the fat!"

Starbuck caught the mockery in her eyes, and chuckled softly. "Lola's a good sport, Butch. She knows it's business before pleasure with me."

"You're sure?" Butch glanced from one to the other. "I ain't all that wet behind the ears. You just say the word and I'll get lost!"

"Stick around," Lola said with a sigh of resignation. "I'll just make myself scarce and let you boys get on with your talk. I don't mind."

Starbuck made a spur-of-the-moment decision. In all the time he'd known her, Lola had never once pried into his business affairs. She respected his privacy with grace and with no hint of resentment. Yet, at times, he sensed she was hurt by his cynical distrust, which until now had included her. The thought suddenly occurred that she deserved better. He decided to give it a try.

"You stick around, too." He patted the sofa. "Have a seat, and let's hear what Butch has to say. He's come a long way to say it."

Lola felt her heart skip a beat. She realized their relationship—at that very instant—had undergone a change. Tonight, for the first time, he was extending his trust. She knew she'd passed a critical test, and sensed they were now something more than lovers. She promised herself he would never regret the decision.

When she was seated, Starbuck turned his attention to Butch. "You said you've got a message?"

"Yeah, I do." Butch resumed his chair. "Mike wasn't sure whether it meant anything, but he sent me along all the same. He figured you ought to judge for yourself."

"Go on."

"Well, he got to doing some powerful thinking after you left Hole-in-the-Wall. He wouldn't admit it, but the two of you being set up by this Ira Lloyd must've thrown him for a loop. Anyway, he remembered something he'd all but forgot."

"About Dutch Henry Horn?"

"For a fact," Butch said, suddenly solemn. "Dutch Henry was a widower."

"I'll be damned!" Starbuck was momentarily nonplussed. "I never heard anything about Dutch Henry being married."

"Nobody else, either," Butch noted. "Mike said she was some sort of big, dark secret. When him and Dutch Henry rode together, none of the rest of the gang knowed about her. Only reason he told Mike was because they were partners."

"Where did she live?"

"Outside Fort Worth a ways. Dutch Henry had a farm he used for a cover."

"Did Mike ever meet her?"

"Nope." Butch shook his head. "He never had no reason to go there, and he wasn't invited."

"When was she supposed to have died?"

"Near as Mike recollects, it was about a year before him and Dutch Henry parted company. So that would've made it sometime late summer of '74."

"If Mike never saw her or the farm"—Starbuck

fixed him with a stern look—"then how come he's so sure she actually died?"

"He asked himself the same question," Butch admitted. "There for a while he even toyed with the notion that Ira Lloyd might turn out to be Horn's wife. If she hadn't died, it could've been her tryin' to kill you both with one stone."

"What changed his mind?"

"Like I said," Butch reminded him, "Mike give it a lot of thought. He remembered Dutch Henry was busted up something terrible when it happened. So, all things considered, he figures it was on the up and up."

"But he still doesn't know—not for certain."

"No," Butch conceded. "Not for certain."

Starbuck nodded and was silent, thoughtful. When he looked up, there was a strange expression in his eyes. "Something else occurs to me."

"What's that?"

"As I recall, Dutch Henry was in his late thirties when I killed him."

Lola started with an involuntary gasp. It was the first and only time he'd ever referred to the darker side of his work. Starbuck and Butch glanced at her, and she smiled sheepishly. Then Butch picked up the thread of the conversation.

"I got an idea you're onto the same thing Mike was thinkin'."

"It makes sense," Starbuck said quite seriously. "A man that old—and married—it's just natural he'd have some kids. Add seven years and they'd be grown by now."

"Grown and chock-full of hate for the man that killed their daddy."

"Don't forget Mike," Starbuck amended. "He winged Dutch Henry in a shootout. That would explain why somebody put us at each other's throats."

"Them was Mike's words exactly."

"I'd say it's the best bet yet."

"Only one trouble," Butch said glumly. "We don't know where to lay our hands on Ira Lloyd. We don't even know if he's a him or a her!"

"Things turned around today," Starbuck informed him. "I got my first solid lead since this whole mess started. It's a pip, too!"

Butch's eyes lit up like soapy agates. "You know who Lloyd is?"

"No, not just exactly," Starbuck remarked. "But I've got a damn good idea where to find him."

"Where?"

"Deadwood."

"Dakota Territory?"

"Let me catch you up on what's happened."

Starbuck briefly recounted everything that had occurred since he'd departed Hole-in-the-Wall. He told of the shooting at Cheever's Flats, and how he'd eventually identified the dead man as George Horwell. Then he detailed his investigation of the Grubstake mine and his conversation with the sheriff in Butte. All of which, he noted wryly, had led him step by step into a dead end. From there, he outlined the return to Denver and the salient factors in William Dexter's murder. He went on to relate what he'd learned from Dexter's secretary and Chief Kelsey. Finally, he explained the discovery he'd made while sifting through the bank records. Though it was a paper trail, the ledgers had left him convinced on one point. Ira Lloyd was somehow connected with the Black Hills Land Company.

"So Deadwood's the place to look," he concluded. "Our man's headquartered there—whatever name he goes by."

"I dunno," Butch said skeptically. "Them ledgers don't exactly *prove* it's Lloyd. Sounds like Dexter had so many irons in the fire it'd be hard to tell one way or the other."

"There's more to it than that." Starbuck paused, and the timbre of his voice changed. "Late yesterday I went back and had another talk with Dexter's secretary. He let slip a real curious item."

"What d'you mean?"

"Dexter only left Denver twice a year on business."

"Where'd he go?"

"That's the curious part." Starbuck pondered a moment, and then, almost as though he were thinking out loud, he went on. "Dexter never told anyone where he was headed. According to his secretary, it was all hush-hush and top-drawer secret."

"So you drew another blank?"

"No," Starbuck elaborated. "I went to the train station and questioned the ticket agents. Things got curiouser and curiouser once I jiggled their memory."

"You did it!" Butch whooped wildly. "You found out where Dexter went on those trips!"

"Yankton." Starbuck's pale eyes glittered, and a wide grin spread across his face. "Dakota Territory."

"Yankton?" Butch appeared bewildered. "I thought you said Lloyd's headquarters was in Deadwood."

"Yankton's the territorial capital. The train line

from the east ends there, and Cheyenne's the closest railhead to the west. The last leg of the trip to Deadwood—whatever direction you're coming from—has to be made by stagecoach."

"Are you saying Dexter went on by stage to Deadwood?"

"Maybe," Starbuck mused. "On the other hand, Deadwood's a little rough for a city slicker like Dexter. I'm willing to bet him and Lloyd got their heads together in Yankton. It figures he'd deliver a report on the Grubstake operation at least twice a year."

"Why, sure!" Butch said, suddenly grasping it. "If he was headed for Deadwood, why go the long way around through Yankton?"

"Exactly," Starbuck affirmed. "The shorter way would've been Cheyenne, and on from there by stage. He'd have saved a couple of days in both directions."

"By golly, that pretty well nails it down!"

"One other thing." Starbuck's expression turned sober, somehow pensive. "Dexter was killed with a thirty-two. That's a gentleman's gun and I've got a strong suspicion Lloyd did the job himself."

"You mean he was here in Denver?"

"I doubt he would've trusted the job to a hired hand. Not to mention the files on the Grubstake and the missing page out of Dexter's ledger. He had to get it right the first time—no mistakes."

"Well, a thirty-two might be a gentleman's gun, but he sure don't act like one. Not the way he kills people."

Starbuck's jawline tightened. "His killing days are about to stop."

Butch gave him a quick, intent look. "You're headed for Deadwood, aren't you?"

"I was." Starbuck pulled at his ear, reflective. "Figured to leave tomorrow morning. But I think I just changed my mind."

"Why so?"

"A day more or less won't matter. We might do well to check out a few headstones—down in Pueblo."

"What's in Pueblo?"

"That's where I killed Dutch Henry."

The shadow of a question clouded Butch's eyes. "Am I going deaf, or did you say 'we'?"

"Why not?" Starbuck commented. "That way there's no loose ends. You'll be able to give Mike the whole story."

"Suits me," Butch said with an impish grin. "I don't get much chance to work the right side of the law."

"Tell you what." Starbuck hesitated, considering. "Go downstairs and see the desk clerk. Have him fix you up with a room, and tell him I said to put it on my bill."

"Say, thanks a lot, Luke!"

"I'll roust you out about sunup."

"Sunup!" Butch rolled his eyes. "Why so early?"

"The train for Pueblo leaves at seven."

"You know, I got an idea rustlin' cows beats the whey outta this detective business."

Starbuck laughed and showed him to the door. Walking back to the sitting room, he stopped and stood for a moment, lost in concentration. Lola bounced off the sofa and moved to join him. Her eyes suddenly shone and she mimicked his dour expression. She slipped inside his arms.

"No more detective business tonight!"

"Yeah?"

"Yeah!" she said with a bawdy wink. "We've got some business ourselves. Unfinished business!"

"Well—" Starbuck playfully swatted her rump. "Never leave a job half done. That's my motto!"

Lola purred and led him toward the bedroom. Her look was one of smoky sensuality, and she shed the peignoir as they went through the door. Her bare white bottom blink-blinked like a beacon in the night.

Starbuck went willingly.

Chapter Fourteen

His gaze was drawn to the outhouse. The door was shut and the latch bar firmly in place. But the latch-string stopped swaying even as he watched. Someone was in the outhouse.

Starbuck suddenly whirled, leveling the Colt, and drilled a hole through the outhouse door. Thumbing the hammer back, he drew a steady bead on the door, then called out in a hard voice.

"Dutch Henry, you got a choice. Come out with your hands up, or I'll turn that privy into a sieve."

"Hold off, Starbuck! I'm comin' out, you win!"

The latch bar lifted and the door cracked open. Horn stood in a spill of sunlight, his arms raised above the doorsill. He blinked, watching Starbuck with a sardonic expression.

"You're a regular bulldog once you get started, aren't you?"

"Toss your gun out of there, Dutch! Slow and easy, nothin' fancy."

"I laid it on the seat before I opened the door."

"Then lower your hands—one at a time!—and you'd better come up empty."

"Hell, I know when I'm licked." Horn lowered his left hand, palm upraised. "See, no tricks and no—"

His right arm dropped in a flash of metal. Starbuck triggered three quick shots. The slugs stitched a neat row straight up Horn's shirtfront, bright red dots from belly to brisket. Knocked off his feet by the impact, Horn crashed into the back wall of the privy, then sat down on the one-holer. A pistol fell from his hand, and his head tilted at an angle across one shoulder. His eyes were opaque and lusterless, staring at nothing.

Starbuck walked forward and halted at the door. He lowered the hammer on his Colt, gazing down on the dead man. A smile tugged at the corner of his mouth, and he slowly shook his head.

"You should've known better, Dutch. You sure should've."

The memory echoed distantly, as though carried to him through the corridors of time. He stared out the window, watching as the train pulled into Pueblo. He saw the town had changed little in seven years, and wondered if anyone still remembered Dutch Henry Horn.

Or the young range detective who had killed him.

The train ground to a halt outside the depot. Starbuck and Butch were the first passengers off the lead coach. They stepped onto the platform and hurried toward the end of the stationhouse. The night train for Denver departed at six, and Starbuck planned to be aboard. He thought an afternoon would suffice for what he had in mind.

Walking uptown, Starbuck experienced a strong sense of *déjà vu*. The sleepy main street was much as he recalled it, and Pueblo itself had grown hardly at all in the intervening years. The hotel still occupied one corner of the main intersection, and catty-corner across from it was the bank. The afternoon was blistering hot, and it required no effort of will to transport himself backward in time. He saw it all as though it had happened yesterday.

The summer of 1876 he had tracked Dutch Henry Horn to Pueblo. There the trail vanished, but he had reason to believe Horn was hiding out in the surrounding countryside. He took a room at the hotel, confident the outlaw would show up in town. His wait lasted nearly a month; his days were spent on the hotel veranda, where he kept a lookout on the intersection. Finally, when he'd all but lost hope, his patience paid off. Dutch Henry, accompanied by two men, rode past the hotel. Suspecting nothing, they dismounted outside the bank.

Starbuck hurried to a nearby hardware store and bought a shotgun. Then, as the men exited the bank, he challenged them in the street. He killed Horn's companions in the ensuing shootout, but the outlaw ducked around the corner and fled on foot. The chase ended across town, behind an adobe cantina. There he cornered Horn in an outhouse, and killed his third man in less than ten minutes. He was duly arrested, and only then did he discover that Horn was known locally as Frank Miller. Operating under an alias, the outlaw had purchased a ranch outside town and established himself as a cattleman. He was widely respected, and the citizens of Pueblo cared little that his true occupation was as the ringleader of a gang of horse thieves. Starbuck had escaped town one jump ahead of a lynch mob.

Today, walking along the street, Starbuck recalled the incident as the turning point in his life. The

assignment had been his first job as a range detective.
From there, with his reputation made, he'd gone on
to other cases and wider renown. That long-ago afternoon had truly been a milestone, and he saw it now
with a note of irony. The death of Dutch Henry Horn
had put him in the detective business to stay.

In a sense, he owed Dutch Henry a debt of grat-
itude. Or perhaps it was owed to Dutch Henry's ghost,
and the time of reckoning had at last come around.
Someone seemed determined to collect on the debt,
and collect in kind. An eye for an eye and a pound
of flesh, the account settled in blood. Vengeance was
the purest of all motives, and by far the most sinister.
Starbuck had known men to wait longer than seven
years, and their revenge was no less sweet for the
wait. He wondered again what Ira Lloyd was to Dutch
Henry Horn.

At the courthouse, Starbuck went directly to the
county clerk's office. His request to inspect certain
backdated records was met with studied reluctance.
The clerk finally acceded, and with Butch in tow, he
was led to a storage room. The shelves were stacked
with musty ledgers dating back to Civil War times.
Left alone, he and Butch dug around until they located the tax rolls for 1876. Under the name Frank
Miller, they found no indication of family or survi-
vors. Their next try was the probate files, and all their
suspicions were at last confirmed. Frank Miller had
an heir—a son.

The records established that one James Miller had
inherited the entire estate. As the sole heir, his legacy
consisted of the Diamond X Ranch and several thousand head of cattle, certain parcels of town real estate,
and some $40,000 on deposit at the bank. For tax

purposes, the estate had been assessed at $212,000 and so entered on the county rolls.

A further search of probate-court records provided corroboration of James Miller's parentage. In his last will and testament, Dutch Henry Horn had used the alias Frank Miller. Following his death, and the subsequent publicity, his true identity had become public knowledge. The court ruled that the father's sins in no way jeopardized the son's right of inheritance. Dutch Henry Horn's estate was legally unencumbered, and judged to be wholly apart from his criminal activities. James Miller, twenty-one at the time, was awarded uncontested title to all lands and property.

His true name, duly noted in the court record, was James T. Horn.

Starbuck's immediate concern centered on James Horn's present whereabouts. It was entirely possible he still owned the Diamond X Ranch. In that event, he might be easier located than originally thought. Still, whether in Deadwood or Pueblo, one thing was abundantly clear.

Ira Lloyd was James Miller, otherwise known as James Horn.

After weighing the situation, Starbuck decided to play it close to the vest. He needed information about James Horn; assuming the man was to be found at the ranch, there was every likelihood it would bloodshed. Yet he had no wish to risk another lynch mob in Pueblo. Wary of alerting the county clerk, who looked to be a gadfly, he made no further inquiry. He determined, instead, to try another tack.

Outside the clerk's office, Starbuck huddled briefly with Butch. He intended to pay a call on the sheriff, and he thought the conversation would best be conducted in privacy. There was, moreover, some slim chance the youngster might be recognized, and he saw no reason to tempt fate. He sent Butch to wait for him on the courthouse steps. Then he walked down the hall to a door marked SHERIFF, PUEBLO COUNTY. He entered without knocking.

The man seated at the desk was lean and muscular, with weather-beaten features and a soup-strainer mustache. His gestures were restrained, his manner brisk and businesslike. He greeted Starbuck in a deep baritone voice.

"Help you?"

"Hope so." Starbuck smiled affably and stuck out his hand. "I'm Luke Starbuck."

"Ernie Tucker." The lawman's handshake was firm and his appraisal swift. "You the detective fellow, works out of Denver?"

"You got me dead to rights, Sheriff."

"Thought so," Tucker said evenly. "I was a deputy when you caused that little rhubarb a few years back."

Starbuck stared at him. "In that case, you'll recall I was only doing my job."

"Never said you wasn't." Tucker smiled, waved him to a chair. "I always figured it was good riddance to bad rubbish. Course, some folks around here don't agree."

"Yeah," Starbuck said, seating himself. "They're probably the same ones who wanted to stretch my neck."

"Say, that's right!" Tucker boomed. "Ol' Walt Johnson saved you from a lynching bee!"

"Johnson still the town marshal?"

"No more." Tucker's smile faded. "He got turned out to pasture the year after you killed Frank Miller."

"Too bad," Starbuck said tonelessly. "He was a good lawman."

"Like I said, some folks have got long memories."

"So I've learned . . . the hard way."

Tucker ruffled his brow, watchful. "What brings you to Pueblo?"

"Frank Miller." Starbuck's expression was stoic. "Or as he was better known—Dutch Henry Horn."

"That's water under the bridge, isn't it?"

"Yeah, it was," Starbuck agreed. "Till somebody started trying to kill me."

"I don't follow you."

"There's been three attempts on my life in the last month. I have reason to believe the man behind it is Dutch Henry's son—James Horn."

"Not very likely," Tucker observed. "Nobody's seen hide nor hair of him since he sold out."

"Sold out?" Starbuck's gaze narrowed. "Are you talking about the ranch?"

"Everything," Tucker said, gesturing out the window. "Town property and the ranch, the whole ball of wax. He showed up a week or so after his daddy was buried. Quick as the deeds were transferred, he put everything on the auction block. Walked away with a potful of money—a big potful!"

"How long was he here?"

"A month, maybe a little more."

"That's fast work, considering he was barely grown."

"Well, there weren't any flies on him! No, sir, he

was smart as a whip. Got top dollar for the whole shebang!"

"Where'd he come from?"

"Back east somewhere," Tucker said, with mild wonder. "Turned out Miller—Horn—had sent him off to college. Hell, you could've knocked half the town over with a feather! Nobody even knew Horn had a son."

"What was he like?"

"Quiet, but not snooty or nothing. Course, you could tell he was educated! The minute he opened his mouth there wasn't no doubt on that score."

"Did he look anything like Dutch Henry?"

"Did he ever!" Tucker laughed. "It was down-right spooky! Tall and thick through the shoulders, that same tight-lipped look around the mouth. Had his daddy's eyes too—chalk blue. Queerest eyes I ever saw on a man."

"When he left here," Starbuck inquired easily, "where'd he go?"

"Nobody knows." Tucker shrugged. "The day he sold the last piece of property, he went down to the bank and got himself a draft for the whole bundle. Then he climbed on the train and took off without a by-your-leave. Nobody knew he was gone till he'd already done it!"

"Any word of him since?"

"Not a peep," Tucker said, shaking his head. "I always figured he went back east. That's what I would've done in his place."

"Why?"

"Well—" Tucker spread his hands. "What with his daddy being a horse thief and all, that would've been the natural thing to do. A young fellow wouldn't want a thing like that hanging over his head."

"How'd he feel about the way Dutch Henry died?"

Tucker leaned back in his chair, hands steepled, tapped his forefingers together. "What you're really asking is how he felt about you killing Dutch Henry?"

"That's close to the mark."

"I never heard him say," Tucker ventured. "I'll tell you one thing, though. I don't think he harbored a grudge and I don't think he'd come looking for you. He just didn't seem like the type."

"Well, Sheriff," Starbuck said, rising to his feet, "somebody's looking for me and he's working at it full time."

Tucker eyed him with a shrewd look. "You aim to kill him, don't you?"

"I don't aim to let him kill me."

"For my money, you're barking up the wrong tree."

"I guess we'll just have to wait and see."

Starbuck nodded and walked to the door. He stepped into the hall and proceeded toward the front of the courthouse. His eyes were grim, fixed straight ahead. He thought it time to put Pueblo behind him.

He'd found his ghost.

The night was pitch dark. Cinders and sparks from the engine whistled past the coach like tiny meteors. The car lights were turned low and nearly all the passengers were asleep. A rhythmic clackety-clack of wheels on steel rails punctuated the stillness.

Starbuck was staring out the window. His expression was abstracted and faraway. He'd been sitting quietly for a long while, lost in inner deliberation.

The puzzle, fitted together piece by piece, was now almost whole. In his mind's eye, he saw a vivid mosaic of where he'd been and where he was headed. Only one small part still remained out of focus and somewhat incomplete. Yet he wasn't worried, for the answer awaited him in Deadwood and he knew who to ask. A man there was in his debt.

"Penny for your thoughts."

His preoccupation was broken by Butch's voice. He turned and found the youngster watching him with a sober gaze. He lifted his shoulders in a shrug, smiled.

"Save your penny and take a guess."

"Deadwood?"

"Yeah, that and young Mr. Horn."

"You reckon you'll be able to find him? He's a regular wizard at coverin' his tracks."

Starbuck's eyes took on a distant, prophetic look. "I'll find him."

"Wonder what he's like?"

"Why do you ask?"

"Oh, I guess I've been doing a little woolgatherin' myself. Hard to figure a man like Horn."

"How so?"

"Well, I'll tell you one thing!" Butch cocked his head in a funny smile. "If I had me a college education and all that money, I sure wouldn't be running around killin' people. Nosireebob!"

"What would you be doing instead?"

"For openers, I would've kept the Diamond X."

"Dutch Henry's ranch?" Starbuck was surprised. "Operating a cattle spread's no picnic. It's a hard life."

"You're telling me!" Butch laughed. "I was

raised up on a farm, and when I got big enough, I hired on as a cowhand. Hard work and me ain't exactly strangers!"

"Where was this?"

Butch gave him a quick, guarded glance. "Utah."

"You got folks there?"

"Maybe."

"Forget I asked," Starbuck said amiably. "I wasn't trying to poke around in your personal business."

"Well—" Butch squirmed uncomfortably in his seat. "I don't suppose it'd hurt nothin'. Anybody Mike trusts is okay in my book."

"Wouldn't go any further," Starbuck promised him. "I was just interested, that's all. A man don't meet many rustlers your age."

Butch's story was a familiar one on the frontier. His parents, Max and Ann Parker, homesteaded a quarter section in southern Utah. Devout Mormons, they sowed their fields and prayed to a benevolent God for a rich harvest. All they reaped was misfortune; three straight years of drought left the crops withered and the land parched. The Parkers lost their homestead, and turned to other work to keep food on the table. Max hired out as a teamster, hauling timber, and Ann found employment at a dairy. Times were rough and the Parkers struggled to eke out an existence.

Their eldest son, Robert LeRoy Parker, was one of six children. Only fourteen at the time, the boy went to work on a neighboring ranch to supplement the family income. He was inexperienced, somewhat impressionable, and he quickly fell in with a drifter named Mike Cassidy. Posing as a saddle tramp,

Cassidy was actually engaged in stealing cattle and trailing them to ready markets in the Colorado mining camps. To young Roy, the rustler offered a life of excitement and an escape from drudgery. The law soon tumbled to their scheme, and they took off for Robbers Roost. There, fully committed to riding the owlhoot, the youngster adopted his mentor's name. He assumed the alias Butch Cassidy.

"You already know the rest," Butch concluded with an offhand gesture. "We got run out of Utah and ended up at Hole-in-the-Wall."

Starbuck studied him a moment. "Suppose you got the chance to make a clean break? Would you take it?"

"Probably not." Butch caught his eye for an instant, looked quickly away. "Mike always says, the trouble with life, it's so goddang daily. I guess that holds for me too. The straight and narrow just don't suit my style."

"How do you know?" Starbuck asked. "You've never really given it a try."

"I tried it long enough to get burnt out on psalm singin' and an empty belly."

"Well, I'm no soul-saver," Starbuck said, grinning. "But if you ever change your mind, look me up. I might be able to steer you into something that wouldn't be so 'goddang daily'."

"I'm obliged, Luke." Butch kept his gaze averted, slightly shamefaced. "I'll likely stick to rustlin', though. The way I got it figured, it beats workin' for wages."

"Suit yourself." Starbuck let it drop there. "You want to stay over in Denver awhile?"

"Naw!" Butch said cheerfully. "Mike's like an

old hen. I'd better get on back before he comes lookin' for me."

"There's a morning train to Cheyenne."

"Guess I'll catch it," Butch said without hesitation. "That'll put me on the trail to Hole-in-the-Wall by tomorrow night."

Starbuck nodded and resumed staring out the window. He pondered the future of a likable kid turned outlaw. Sooner or later, a hangman's noose or a stiff prison sentence was in the cards. Or perhaps a quicker death, at the hands of a manhunter. The thought struck a nerve, and he silently wished the youngster Godspeed. Hole-in-the-Wall was, in the end, the only choice.

He hoped they would never meet again.

Chapter Fifteen

The stage slid to a dust-smothered halt. There were nine passengers crammed inside and six more clung to the top of the coach. The driver set the foot brake with a hard kick and looped the reins around the lever. Then he leaned over the side and let loose a raspy shout.

"All out for Deadwood!"

Starbuck was the first passenger to alight from the coach. His hair was dyed raven black and a spit-curl mustache was glued to his upper lip with spirit gum. A black eyepatch, which was held in place by a narrow headband, covered his left eye. The patch broke the line of his features and further distracted attention from his general appearance. The getup he wore was an advertisement of sorts, almost a uniform. He was attired in a black frock coat and somber vest, topped off by a low-crowned hat. A diamond stickpin gleamed from his four-in-hand tie and a larger stone sparkled on his pinky finger. He looked every inch the professional gambler.

Dusting himself off, Starbuck moved to the rear of the coach. There he waited while the luggage was unloaded from the storage boot. He took a thin black cheroot from inside his coat and snipped the end with one clean bite. Then he fished out a match and lit the cigar. Puffing smoke, he hooked his thumbs in his vest and scanned the street. All around him was a tableau of bedlam in motion.

Deadwood was surrounded by the pine-forested mountains of the Black Hills. The town proper twisted through a narrow gulch, and wooden stairways intersected terraced side streets up and down the slopes. Wagons drawn by oxen clogged the main street, and bullwhackers scorched the air with curses and the sharp pop of their whips. The boardwalks were thronged with men, and the riotous atmosphere of a gold camp pervaded the town. There was a sense of carnival madness to the milling crowds and the deafening hubbub.

Some six years past, the gold rush had transformed a wooded gulch into a boomtown. Yet, like most mining camps, Deadwood still wasn't much to look at. It was simply bigger and brassier, with a population of thirty thousand, and more arriving every day. The upper end of Main Street was packed with stores and rat-infested cafés, three banks and some thirty hotels, and one public bathhouse. The lower end of town—known locally as the Bad Lands—was a beehive of saloons, gaming dives, and cheap brothels. Sanitation was virtually unknown, and ditches carved out of the rocky terrain served as sewers. The stench of refuse and unwashed men was overpowering.

Starbuck hefted his valise and walked downstreet. He thought it unlikely anyone expected him in town. The link to Deadwood, established by the bank records in Denver, was his card in the hole. James Horn had no way of knowing he'd stumbled upon the connection and at last put the pieces together. Still, he had gone to extreme measures to insure he wasn't followed. After a day's layover in Denver, spent collecting the paraphernalia for his disguise, he had secretly made his way to Cheyenne. There he'd boarded a stagecoach for the three-hundred-mile run to Dakota Territory. The trip had consumed three days and two nights, with stops in several lesser mining camps in the western reaches of the Black Hills. Today, lost in the crowds, he seemed just another gambler touring the circuit. His cover name was Ace Pardee.

At the corner of Main and Lee, he spotted the Custer Hotel. Aptly named, it honored the man responsible for Deadwood's very existence. General George Armstrong Custer, in 1874, had commanded an expedition into the Black Hills. Apart from a thousand soldiers, he was accompanied by a geologist and two reporters. The discovery of gold was duly publicized in newspapers throughout the nation. Hundreds of prospectors, in direct violation of the Laramie Treaty of 1868, immediately invaded the holy ground of the Sioux. Within a year, the hundreds turned to thousands, and the Black Hills gold rush was on. By early 1877, with the army unable to stem the flood, the government legislated yet another treaty into extinction. The Sioux's sacred Paha Sapa—the Black Hills—were opened to settlement. And Deadwood roared to life.

Starbuck was an iconoclast where government was concerned. He considered bureaucrats the blight of mankind, and lumped all politicians into two categories, the corrupt and the stupid. The army was viewed with a somewhat more charitable outlook. Yet he made an exception in the case of George Armstrong Custer. Long ago, he'd tagged the flamboyant general as an exhibitionist, with delusions of grandeur.

The Black Hills expedition was symptomatic of Custer's thirst for recognition and fame. Only two years later that same thirst led to the Battle of the Little Big Horn. By all accounts, Custer had his eye on the presidency and needed a splashy victory to garner the nomination. The 7th Cavalry had been sacrificed not to quell the Sioux, but for the greater glory of the one called Yellowhair. In Starbuck's opinion, that made Custer something worse than a meddling bureaucrat or a corrupt politician. He was a fool.

On general principles, Starbuck checked into another hotel. He paid in advance and was shown to a cubbyhole on the second floor. The furnishings consisted of a swaybacked bed, one wooden chair, and a washstand. A chipped and fading johnny-pot occupied one corner of the room. He dumped his valise on the bed and stripped to the waist. Then, gingerly avoiding his dyed hair, he took a quick bird bath. After a shave, he toweled dry and slipped into a clean shirt. Somewhat refreshed, he put on the gambler's outfit and went downstairs. The desk clerk obligingly pointed him toward the Bad Lands.

A couple of blocks down the street, Starbuck happened upon another landmark. The No. 10 Saloon, located on the edge of the Bad Lands district, was famed as Wild Bill Hickok's last watering hole. There, on a warm August day in 1876, a deadbeat named Jack McCall had shot Hickok in the back of the head. The assassin was ultimately hanged, and his victim was laid to rest in Deadwood's budding cemetery. The funeral marked the birth of a legend.

Like many westeners, Starbuck had a jaundiced view of the man a journalist had once dubbed Prince of the Pistoleers. Hickok had reputedly killed several dozen men in gunfights, and touted himself as the most deadly shootist on the frontier. It was commonly believed he could drill the cork into a bottle without touching glass, and further, that he could handle two guns simultaneously, blazing away from the hips and never missing the target. He was credited as well with having brought law and order to at least two Kansas cowtowns, Hays City and Abilene. The truth was somewhat more mundane.

Starbuck, through friends in the law community, had gradually put together a factual account. The Prince of Pistoleers was a showboat and braggart, who followed the axiom of shoot first and ask questions later. He was known to have killed six men, four of whom had been gunned down in coldblood. The only man he'd ever killed in the line of duty—in a face-to-face shootout—was a drunken gambler in Abilene. Thereafter, he had toured the East as an actor, capitalizing on his notoriety. As a peace officer, he was a joke, and as a gunman, he was little more than a common killer. Among those who knew him best, he was renowned as a man who never gave the other fellow a ghost of a chance. He always rigged the game.

A pragmatist himself, Starbuck took few chances. Yet he was contemptuous of any man who killed in coldblood. Showboats like Hickok, who pandered to the press, were almost beneath contempt. Throughout his lifetime, Wild Bill had courted dime novelists and eastern journalists who dealt in sensationalism. The result was an entire mythology based on invention, distortion, and outright lies. Hardly a noble servant of the law, Hickok was a spinner of windy tales, all of them about himself. The eastern reading public was

ravenous for western heroes, particularly those who
were painted larger than life and possessed all the
sterling attributes. Hickok simply gave them what
they wanted to hear.

Walking along the street, Starbuck was struck by
a curious juxtaposition in time. General George
Armstrong Custer had gone under at the Little Big
Horn in June, 1876. Not quite two months later Wild
Bill Hickok had been murdered in the No. 10 Saloon.
Never had any two men deserved less to be enshrined
in the mythology of a nation. Yet, in an orgy of print,
both of them had been immortalized in newspapers
as well as books and periodicals. The general public
accepted what it read as truth carved in stone. So it
was that Custer and Hickok had achieved in death
what they had vainly pursued in life—the glory of
everlasting fame.

Sadder still were the unsung paladins of the frontier. The men who deserved public acclaim, men who
actually were legend in their own time. Yet, because
they shunned the limelight and sought no personal
glory, their names were virtually unknown outside the
western territories. Starbuck felt himself privileged to
have met a few of them personally. Foremost in his
mind were three peace officers of unquestionable
courage: Tom Smith, Heck Thomas, and Dallas Stou-
denmire. He was on his way now to meet yet another
such lawman. A grizzled veteran by the name of Seth
Bullock.

Starbuck made a leisurely tour of the Bad Lands.
To all appearances, he was a gambler out surveying
the prospects. Deadwood, the richest of all gold
camps, was a magnet for the sporting crowd. The
stakes were high, the play was fast, and suckers were

soon parted from their money. The vice district was contained within a few square blocks, and there the action was nonstop, night and day. Whores, whiskey, and games of chance were the principal attractions. A man out to see the elephant saw it all in Deadwood.

While he walked, Starbuck searched his memory for everything he knew about Seth Bullock. Their acquaintance stemmed from his correspondence with peace officers throughout the West. He'd first written Bullock last year, selecting him for the best of all reasons. No better contact existed in Dakota Territory.

Seth Bullock was universally feared and respected by the outlaw element. He had served as a sheriff in Montana before joining the rush to Deadwood in '76. Upon arrival, he'd opened a hardware store, prospering as the boom got under way. Yet he was bothered by the lawlessness and violence of a raw mining camp. In league with other responsible citizens, he had organized a Board of Commissioners to police the town. Their first act was an ordinance restricting the vice district to lower Main Street. Their second act was the appointment of Bullock as sheriff, and with it a mandate to enforce the law. Within a year, he'd driven the outlaws out of Deadwood and convinced the sporting crowd to toe the line. In 1878, the territorial attorney general had secured his appointment to the post of U.S. deputy marshal. He was the law in Deadwood.

Over the years, Bullock had become a man of influence and prominence in Dakota Territory. After one term as sheriff, he'd devoted himself to various business enterprises. In addition to the hardware store, he invested in several mining ventures and established a cattle ranch on the Belle Fourche River. Yet, despite his wealth, he had retained his commission as a U.S. deputy marshal. He was one of that rare breed of men who served the law out of personal commitment and a sense of duty. He still risked his life chasing stage-coach robbers and murderers, and he'd acquired a fearsome reputation with a gun. He was the man to be reckoned with in the Black Hills.

Starbuck wanted advice and information. He nonetheless thought it wiser to approach Bullock in secret. Their association, should it become public knowledge, might very well affect the plan he'd mapped out. Accordingly, he went to the end of the Bad Lands district, then crossed to the opposite side of the street. He casually strolled back uptown, pausing now and then to check out a gambling dive. At the corner of Main and Wall, he stepped into the hardware store. A couple of clerks were busy waiting on customers, and paid him no notice. He browsed his way toward the rear of the store, moving slowly toward a door marked private. He knocked once and entered unannounced.

The man seated behind the desk was tall and lithely built. He had piercing gray eyes, a droopy mustache, and wild bushy eyebrows. His nose was hawklike, almost hooked, and his jawline slanted to a prominent chin. He held a pistol trained on Starbuck's belly button.

"You oughtn't to pop in on a man without an invite."

Starbuck stood rock-still. "You must be Seth Bullock."

"Who might you be?"

"Luke Starbuck."

"That a fact?" Bullock eyed his funereal attire.

"If you're Starbuck, how come you're tricked out like a tinhorn?"

"I'm working undercover," Starbuck told him. "I trailed a murderer here and thought you might be able to give me an assist."

"If you're who you say you are"—Bullock gave him a dark look—"what was the last thing I wrote you about?"

Starbuck smiled. "Your last letter was in reply to my inquiry about a bank robber, Jack O'Hara. You said he hadn't been reported in Dakota Territory."

"Well, I'll be damned!" Bullock holstered his pistol and rose with an outstretched hand. "It's a pleasure, Luke. I've been wanting to meet you for a long spell now."

"Same here." Starbuck accepted his handshake. "I would've telegraphed ahead, but it's too risky. The bird I'm after probably has ears all over town."

"Who'd he murder?"

"A lawyer in Denver."

"What's his name?"

"James Horn," Starbuck said slowly. "Alias Ira Lloyd."

"Never heard of either one."

"That figures," Starbuck remarked. "He's one cagey son-of-a-bitch."

"Sounds the least bit personal." Bullock motioned, then resumed his seat. "Grab yourself a chair and lay it out for me."

Starbuck sat down and took a moment to light a cheroot. Then he told Bullock the entire story. He skipped certain details about Hole-in-the-Wall, honoring his word to Mike Cassidy. Yet the salient points were covered in sum and substance. The link to the

Black Hills Land Company was underscored as the most vital lead in the case. He concluded with a physical description of James Horn.

"I put his age at twenty-seven," he noted. "Any of that ring a bell?"

Bullock's voice was troubled. "Skyrockets would be more like it."

"You know him?"

"Oh, hell, yes!" Bullock paused, jawline set in a scowl. "He goes by the name of John Eastlake."

"How long has he lived in Deadwood?"

"Since day one!" Bullock said with a grim smile. "He showed up the fall of '76 and started throwing money around like it was going out of style. Bought himself a whole batch of claims, and then he organized the land company. Today, he owns about half the real estate down in the sporting district, and he's the second or third biggest mine owner in town. So he's nobody to mess with unless you've got the goods."

"What's that supposed to mean?"

"Pretty obvious," Bullock speculated. "He tried to kill you and now you're set on returning the favor."

"So?"

"How'd you figure to do it?"

"Call him out," Starbuck said coldly. "Pick the time and show my hand—force him to fight?"

"Won't work!" Bullock waved the idea aside. "He knows you'd kill him. So why should he fight?"

"He'll fight before he'd let me expose him as a murderer!"

"What evidence you got that it was him who killed the lawyer?"

Starbuck looked surprised, then suddenly irritated. "None."

"You can't even prove for a fact that Eastlake is Horn—can you?"

"No." Starbuck's features were immobile. "Even if I could, it wouldn't change things. There's nobody left to testify against him . . . they're all dead."

"So that's that!" Bullock dusted his hands. "You call him out and he'll just laugh in your face. Then he waits till things cool down and hires himself another backshooter to get you. His kind don't never do their own dirty work! You ought to know that, Luke."

"Yeah, you're right." Starbuck gave him a bitter grin. "I guess I lost sight of that . . . took it too personal."

"Who wouldn't!" Bullock pursed his lips and nodded solemnly. "Course, there's more than one way to skin a cat."

Starbuck studied him a moment, eyes dark and vengeful. "I'm open to ideas."

"One thing I didn't mention." Bullock leaned forward, very earnest now. "Eastlake's a big muckamuck hereabouts in politics. There's talk that he's the bagman for Deadwood. I can't prove it, but the word's around if you listen close. He collects graft from the sporting crowd and funnels it to the governor."

"Why would the governor take graft?"

Bullock laughed without mirth. "Guess you never heard of Nehemiah Ordway. He's crooked as a barrel of snakes, always was! Some folks got fed up with it and organized a reform party. So now he's in a do-or-die fight to save his hide."

"Where does Horn come into it?"

"He don't want Deadwood reformed! That'd

undercut his political base, not to mention all the property he owns in the vice district. So him and the governor are thick as spit!"

"What's all that got to do with me?"

"You want Eastlake—Horn—don't you?"

"I'm still listening."

Bullock was suddenly very quiet, eyes boring into him. "I can't nail them, but you could. You're a pro at working undercover, and that's the only thing that'll turn the trick. You help me and we'll send 'em to prison till their teeth rot out!"

"I don't want Horn in prison." Starbuck's voice was edged. "I want him dead."

"Half a loaf's better than none," Bullock said shrewdly. "I know Dakota Territory from A to Zizzard, and I could steer you to all the skeletons. Course, along the way, you might get a crack at Eastlake. He'd likely fight if you threatened to bust his bubble here in Deadwood—destroy what he's built."

There was a prolonged silence. Starbuck rubbed his jawline and gazed off into space. He seemed to fall asleep with his eyes open, lost in some deep rumination. Presently he blinked, took a couple of quick puffs on his cheroot, and swung back to Bullock.

"You want the governor real bad, don't you?"

"Luke, just the thought of it makes my mouth water!"

"All right," Starbuck said with a clenched smile. "You got yourself a partner."

"All the way down the line . . . root hog or die?"

"All the way till the day we bury James Horn."

Chapter Sixteen

"Fifty simoleons!"

"Bump you a hundred."

"I fold."

"Too rich for my blood."

"I'm right behind you."

"Call the raise!"

Starbuck turned his hole card. "Three ladies."

"Bite my butt!" The miner who had called the raise tossed in three tens. "Pardee, it's a gawddamn good thing yore on the level. That kinda luck just ain't natural!"

"Luck's got nothing to do with it."

"Not that old chestnut!" the miner grumbled testily. "Poker ain't a game of chance, it's all skill—right?"

"Nope." Starbuck smiled, raking in the pot. "The secret's simpler than that . . . I pray a lot."

The other players whooped and jeered, and the miner mumbled something inaudible under his breath. Starbuck's mood was jovial and unruffled, the mark of a professional plying his trade. A gambling man always humored the losers and left them in a congenial frame of mind. He chuckled lightly at his own joke and began stacking the money on an already sizable pile of winnings. The next dealer gathered the cards and started shuffling.

The game was one of many under way in the Gem Theater. A combination saloon, gaming den, and brothel, the Gem was the most infamous dive in the Bad Lands. The owner, a loudmouthed slick named Al Swearingen, was something of an institution in Deadwood. His faro layouts and roulette tables were honest, and he served unwatered whiskey. Yet his square-deal policy stopped when it came to the bordello upstairs. He lured innocent girls out from the East, promising them stage jobs, and then converted them into dollar-a-trick whores. Everyone in town thought it all balanced out in the end. Honest games were preferable to cathouse morality.

Starbuck had made the Gem his unofficial headquarters. Over the past two weeks, he'd established himself as a gambler of some skill. He won consistently, working most of the dives in the Bad Lands, and he had made no enemies in the process. At the same time, he'd been at some pains to ingratiate himself with the sporting crowd. He was a free spender, quick to laugh, and always ready with a bawdy story. The man he'd cultivated more than any other was Al Swearingen. After hours, they frequently shared a bottle, and Swearingen had yet to realize he was being pumped for information. He considered Ace Pardee a prince of a fellow, one of the fraternity. And Starbuck slowly learned what made the wheels go round in Deadwood.

The dossier he'd put together on John Eastlake was now complete. The composite drawn was that of an ambitious man, who was at once munificent with his friends and ruthless with anyone who opposed his will. Yet he was noted as a man of character, scrupulous in all his business dealings, and a civic booster without rival. On the surface, he was dedicated to the greater good of the community and the advancement of his own burgeoning empire. Beneath the surface, however, there was a darker undercurrent. Unveiled there was the man inside—James Horn.

An astute entrepreneur, Horn exhibited foresight and a flair for organization. His intellect was demonstrated in the manner in which he'd structured his business empire. All his holdings were sheltered under the umbrella of the Black Hills Land Company, with a manager responsible for each division. He leased out his mining properties, thereby avoiding capital expenditure, and took a hefty cut of the profits in lieu of a fee, The proceeds were then plowed back into added mining ventures and the acquisition of real estate. The constant reinvestment and expansion had made him the most influential businessman in Deadwood. He owned pieces of two banks, a couple of hotels, and mining properties throughout every camp in the Black Hills. His real-estate holdings in the vice district were a veritable money tree. There, following the same formula employed in the mining division, he acted as a partner rather than a landlord. His cut was twenty percent straight off the top.

Payoffs for political graft were uncovered with remarkable ease. Operating openly, with uncanny sleight of hand, Horn simply integrated the payoffs into his vice-district revenues. The dives quartered in buildings he owned were visited once a week by a collector and two bruisers riding shotgun. The initial tipoff came from Al Swearingen, who tended to consume a good deal of his own liquor. Over a bottle one night—with Starbuck all ears—he bemoaned the payoffs, which, added to the twenty percent rental fee, were driving him to the poorhouse. Starbuck confirmed the lead by tailing the collector and his goons; their route covered the whole of the Bad Lands, every whorehouse, dance hall, and busthead saloon. Without exception, everyone shelled out, and Horn was clearly unworried by loose talk or legal repercussions. The reason was patently obvious.

Horn controlled the political apparatus of Lawrence County. His power base was Deadwood, the county seat, and the courthouse was his fiefdom. He operated behind the scenes, a shadowy kingfish who handpicked all candidates for office. Those he selected represented themselves as champions of the working man, decrying the excesses of wealthy mine owners and the business community. As a result, the coalition he'd put together was made up of beguiled miners and the sporting crowd, who voted a straight ticket every time out. Opposition had gradually withered, until now there was only token resistance when elections rolled around. From a practical standpoint, it had ceased to be a contest in Lawrence County. He owned the ballot box.

On a higher plane, Seth Bullock had enlightened Starbuck regarding territorial politics. Dakota was a stewpot of corruption and graft. Elected officials operated on the theory of enrichment through legislation, passing laws that lined their own pockets or generated kickbacks from vested interests. Legislators went to Yankton, the territorial capital, imbued not with honesty but with schemes for personal benefit. One newspaper editor, in a scathing editorial, indicted the lot: "We will match Dakota against all the world in ancient or modern times to produce as many official thieves and purchasable legislators."

The division of spoils was never better illustrated than in the frauds involving Indian reservations. Syndicates composed of merchants and legislators seized on the opportunity for economic exploitation. The Sioux were shortchanged on rations and forced to endure privations that bordered on genocide. The profits were astronomical, and the practice was widely condoned. A few Indians more or less rated small attention.

A greater concern in the political arena was the struggle over statehood. One faction believed Dakota should remain a ward of the federal government. A coalition of vested interests, such as the railroads, and Washington politicos, who controlled the purse strings, had joined with the governor to maintain territorial status. The opposition, intent on self-rule, believed Dakota should sever the cord and petition for statehood. Under the banner of the Dakota Citizens' League, its membership was a strange amalgamation of farmers, prohibitionists, and civic reformers. The battle was joined in the byways and corridors of the territorial capital.

Governor Nehemiah Ordway stood to lose the most if Dakota was granted statehood. Appointed to office two years ago, he had undertaken a Byzantine plan to create a vast political machine. Only after the fact, when it was much too late, did the opposition realize the full extent of his scheme. By controlling federal patronage, Ordway had established alliances with powerful leaders throughout Dakota. Not the least of those aligned with the governor was John Eastlake.

Statehood, in Eastlake's view, was bad for Deadwood and Lawrence County. Territorial status was a
looser form of government, with less control exerted
from Yankton. The county political apparatus, not to
mention patronage jobs and public funds, was more
easily managed when left in the hands of a few men.
Then, too, the Dakota Citizens' League was the kiss
of death for the wide-open mining camps of the Black
Hills. Once reformers got control of Yankton, the
whorehouses, saloons, and gaming dens would
quickly become a thing of the past. In the end it
boiled down to self-interest, and what was bad for
Deadwood was equally bad for John Eastlake. He'd
thrown his support to Governor Ordway.

Nor were the motives of Seth Bullock derived
wholly from altruism. Starbuck had learned that the
lawman was seeking revenge of a different sort. In
the county elections of 1877, Bullock had been turned
out of office as sheriff. His opponent had been backed
by Horn, who at the time was making his first bid to
assume the reins of power. In concert with Yankton
politicians, Horn had engineered a stunning victory.
Bullock, despite his reputation as a town tamer, went
down to defeat. A proud man, he was also one who
never forgave an affront. He considered Horn an en-
emy, and he was out to settle an old score. By top-
pling the governor, he would bring the political
structure of Lawrence County tumbling into ruin. And
leave Horn—John Eastlake—standing amidst the rub-
ble.

Only one thing in the investigation had given
Starbuck pause. By listening more than he talked,
he'd uncovered a curious revelation. Some years ago
Horn had married a refined eastern lady, who di-

vorced him not six months after the wedding. There was speculation among the sporting crowd that she couldn't take the rough life of a mining camp. Yet there were other rumors afloat in the gossipy world of the Bad Lands. Horn reportedly had some kinky sex habits, involving leather straps and the infliction of pain. Among the whores of the vice district he was known as the Marquis de Eastlake. Starbuck was amused but hardly surprised. It was a window into Horn's character.

In subsequent days, it became apparent to Starbuck that he'd done all the spadework possible in Deadwood. There was nothing of any substance left to learn about Horn and the local political ring. Nor was anything unearthed to date particularly incriminating in itself. He had devoted considerable thought to the problem, and he always returned to the graft payoffs. It seemed unlikely Horn would entrust the transfer of the money to anyone else; the fewer witnesses the better when illegal funds were passing hands. Then, too, Bullock had told him that Horn made periodic trips to Yankton, generally once a month. So he saw only one recourse, the logical next step. He must somehow tie Horn and the graft payoffs to Governor Nehemiah Ordway.

The plan he evolved was larded with risk. Horn most certainly had his photograph, and might very well see through his disguise. Over the past two weeks, all quite unobtrusively, he had observed Horn from a distance. On one occasion he had loitered across from the land company, and on another he had discreetly tailed Horn through the business district. Yet he'd cautiously avoided any face-to-face meeting. As a result, his disguise had never been tested. That worried him more than he cared to admit.

While it was extreme, there seemed no alternative to shadowing Horn on his next trip to Yankton. Only in that manner could he establish a direct link to the governor. The stage ride to the territorial capital took several days, and he would be caged with Horn inside the coach the entire time. The chance of being recognized was not to be discounted; even a slip of the tongue could destroy his cover. Still, however calculated the risk, the option was to sit on his thumb and do nothing. He was determined to see the case through, and he at last made the decision to go for broke. Ace Pardee would accompany Horn to Yankton.

There were two stages a day to the capital. One departed early in the morning and the other at noon. The date of Horn's next trip, and which stage he would board, were known only to Horn himself. So Starbuck hedged his bet by arising every morning at the crack of dawn. He would then stroll casually past the stage line shortly before departure time. The ploy was repeated again at noon, always with a quick visual check of the passengers. Finally, on the morning of the fourth day, he got a break. As he stepped out of the hotel, he spotted Horn walking along the street, suitcase in hand. He hurried back to his room, collected his valise, and settled accounts with the desk clerk. Then he made a beeline for the stage office.

Purchasing a ticket was the first test. Horn was waiting outside with several other passengers, standing somewhat apart. He glanced in Starbuck's direction, then his eyes moved on. Encouraged, Starbuck went inside and paid the fare to Yankton. When he emerged, the passengers were already in the process of boarding. He hoisted himself into the coach and took the only vacant seat, directly across from Horn. A few moments later the luggage was loaded and the driver popped his whip over the rumps of the six-horse hitch. The stage began the long climb out of Deadwood gulch.

The morning passed uneventfully. The passengers were for the most part drummers and businessmen. Some caught a catnap while others talked quietly as the coach jounced and swayed through the mountains. If Horn knew any of them, it was not apparent by his actions. He made no attempt to join in the conversation, and none of the men addressed him directly. He sat wrapped in silence, withdrawn into the privacy of his own thoughts. His visage was meditative.

Starbuck felt as though he were in the presence of a dead man. What seemed a lifetime ago—after he'd infiltrated the gang of horse thieves—he had once spoken briefly with Dutch Henry Horn. The recollection was vivid, and today it was as if he found himself seated across from a specter. Horn was the very image of his father, both in looks and in manner. There was something impenetrable about him, an aura of personal insensitivity. His composure was monumental, and he seemed not just aloof but genuinely comfortable with his own company. Only his eyes moved, alert and penetrating, the color of carpenter's chalk. He stared out at the countryside, his mouth a tight gashlike line. He looked every bit as dangerous as his father.

On the outskirts of Rapid City, the stage stopped for a late noon meal. While a fresh team was being hitched, the passengers trooped inside the relay station. The meal consisted of fried fat pork, beans and biscuits, and muddy coffee. Starbuck avoided Horn, taking a place at the opposite end of the table. After the meal, however, there was no way to keep his distance. Courtesy of the road dictated that each passenger resume his original seat. When the stage pulled out, they were once more across from each other. He slowly became aware that Horn was covertly watching him.

A mile or so out of town, Horn suddenly faced him directly. The full impact of his strange, dispassionate gaze was unsettling. His features were expressionless.

"Have we met?" he asked. "You look familiar."

"Don't think so." Starbuck went into his tinhorn routine. "Course, we could've bumped into one another at the Gem. I hang out there pretty regular."

"Then you must know Al Swearingen?"

"Why, sure thing!" Starbuck said with dazzling good humor. "Al's the salt of the earth, none better! He a friend of yours too, Mr.—?"

"Eastlake." Horn smiled without warmth. "Swearingen's a business acquaintance, not a friend. I take it you're a gambler?"

"Bet your boots!" Starbuck hooked his thumbs in his vest, grinned broadly. "Ace Pardee's the name and poker's my game. Open for business six days a week and all day on Sunday!"

Horn regarded him with an odd, steadfast look. "Are you new to Deadwood, Mr. Pardee?"

Starbuck sensed it was no idle question. For all the dyed hair and eyepatch, Horn clearly detected some similarity to his photo. He nerved himself to give a sterling performance.

"Got in a couple of weeks ago," he said affably. "By way of Frisco and points west."

"What brings you to Dakota Territory?"

"The root of all evil!" Starbuck boomed out jovially. "Heard there was gold in them thar hills! And I'll tell you true, Mr. Eastlake"—he lowered his one eyelid in a sly wink—"it surely weren't no rumor!"

"I thought a gambler never quit a winner."

"Don't believe I exactly follow you?"

"If Deadwood's so lucrative," Horn inquired in a reasonable tone, "why travel all the way to Yankton?"

Starbuck laughed a wild braying laugh. "You're not a politician, are you, Mr. Eastlake?"

"No," Horn said shortly. "Why do you ask?"

"I heard there's a freeze-out game in Yankton. Some of them crooked legislators and fat-cat railroad boys are gonna shoot for the moon! Figured I'd go have a look-see."

"You don't say?"

"Well, I don't say it too loud!" Starbuck uttered a roguish chuckle. "I wouldn't want to warn 'em Ace Pardee's on his way!"

Horn abruptly lost interest. "I wish you luck, Mr. Pardee."

"Say, looky here now!"

Starbuck produced a deck of cards from his inside coat pocket. He deftly shuffled on his knees and gave the deck a smooth one-handed cut. The other passengers were spellbound by his dexterity, and sat watching him with the expression normally reserved for sword swallowers. He riffled the cards with a flourish and gave them a come-on grin.

"Why wait till Yankton!" he said with a gleam in his eye. "Anybody play the game of poker?"

A couple of the drummers and one of the businessmen allowed themselves to be talked into a game. With a valise balanced on their knees, they hunched forward and a hand of stud was quickly dealt. Horn looked on with icy detachment for a moment, then went back to staring out the window. Starbuck suppressed a laugh and turned his attention to the cards.

He knew he'd passed the test.

Chapter Seventeen

John Eastlake spent two days in Yankton. He registered at the Dakota Hotel and went about his business in an open manner. No effort was made to conceal either his movements or the purpose of his trip.

Upon arrival, Starbuck checked into a seedy hotel across town. A nearby pawnshop, which sold used clothing, provided him with an outfit for yet another disguise. He chose a suit one size too large, a pair of worn brogans, and a battered slouch hat. The eyepatch and spit-curl mustache were retired to his valise, and replaced with a scraggly black beard. Though fake, the beard was a theatrical prop, crafted of real hair and genuine in appearance. To complete the masquerade, he adopted a shuffling gait and the stooped posture of a man aged by hard times. He looked very much the ragtag tramp.

Posing as a panhandler, Starbuck was all but invisible in the hustle and bustle of downtown Yankton. He shadowed Horn day and night, easily melding into the background. As John Eastlake, the Deadwood kingfish, Horn was warmly received by the political oligarchy. On the first day, he met with a succession of legislators from around the territory. Early the second morning he went to the capitol and met privately with Governor Nehemiah Ordway. There was no attempt at secrecy, and to all indications his meeting with the governor was by appointment. His business accomplished, he then returned to the hotel and checked out. He boarded the afternoon stage for Deadwood.

Starbuck was left in a maze of doubt. His surveillance had uncovered nothing incriminating and no hint of corruption. Nor was any damaging inference to be drawn from the meetings. Businessmen and lobbyists were constantly seeking favors from both the governor and members of the legislature. John Eastlake was simply one of a very large crowd.

Further obscured was the matter of graft. There was every reason to believe that Horn, in his meeting with the governor, had passed along the payoffs from Deadwood's sporting district. Yet there was no proof—nor any glimmer of an eyewitness—that money had actually exchanged hands. In short, there was no evidence of illegality and no way to substantiate the existence of corrupt practices. The surveillance, start to finish, was a washout.

Following Horn's departure, Starbuck was somewhat at a loss. He returned to his hotel room and flopped down on the bed. Hands locked behind his head, he stared at the ceiling in a brooding funk. His investigation had run up against a stone wall, and he saw no way to surmount the problem. Horn was on cordial terms with the governor and a gaggle of legislators, and clearly no stranger to the corridors of the capitol. Still, for all his high-placed connections, there was no crime involved. The business of Dakota Territory, as everyone readily admitted, was politics. Horn appeared as legitimate as the next man.

Starbuck nonetheless saw it through a prism of his own attitude. In his experience, those who tended the vineyards of government were by nature the worst of all bloodsuckers. He marked again that venal men in a political marketplace were corrupted by a system that thrived on skullduggery. Some men were corrupted by ambition and a thirst for power, and others were merely creatures of their own avarice. Almost all of them, however, were some strain of parasite. The few who weren't inevitably suffered a fate similar to that of the original reformer. The mob spiked them to a cross.

All of which served to infuriate Starbuck even further. There seemed little likelihood he would preside over the crucifixion of James Horn. Without hard evidence, his investigation was scotched and his odyssey of nearly two months was at a standstill. He had the sensation of a man sinking ever deeper into quicksand. He was going nowhere but down.

By late afternoon, he'd muddled the impasse from every angle. No workable plan presented itself, and a sort of sluggish pessimism crept over him. Then, ever so slowly, the germ of an idea took shape. The thought occurred that Horn would never entrust his well-being into the hands of other men. Nor would he hazard his fate to the vicissitudes of the political arena. Power brokers were forever jockeying for position, and today's alliances were as ephemeral as a zephyr. When crooks parted ways, only a fine line separated the oxes from the foxes. Someone was always thrown to the mob, a sacrificial offering. And James Horn was not a man to get caught with his pants down.

One thought led to another in rapid sequence.

Any equation involving Horn and political survival translated into only one possible answer: blackmail. The man had the character of an assassin and all the social virtues of a scorpion. In the event of political upheaval, he would emerge the high priest, the one who performed the sacrifice. To guarantee that outcome, it followed he would have some form of leverage, an insurance policy. Whatever the nature of that insurance, several things were beyond speculation. It would be in writing, documentation of some sort that would provide evidence of graft and corruption. Moreover, it would indict a wide spectrum of politicians, most especially the governor of Dakota Territory. A man with all that need never fear exposure, for the mere threat of blackmail would insure his own impunity. James Horn was just such a man.

The premise seemed to Starbuck almost a lead-pipe cinch. He sat bolt upright in bed, concentrating hard. The only questions that remained were where, and how, he might lay his hands on Horn's insurance policy. He thought he knew where to look.

Hurrying out of the hotel, he walked directly to the train depot. He scribbled a short message to Verna Phelps, and passed it through the window to the station telegrapher. The wire was cryptic, worded in a code known only to himself and Verna. When deciphered, it read simply:

CONTACT TYRONE QUINN. HIRE HIM FOR A BLIND JOB AND PUT HIM ON THE FIRST TRAIN TO YANKTON.
                           STARBUCK

The telegrapher evidenced no great curiosity. He was accustomed to secret messages in the convoluted world of Dakota politics, and toted up the charge without a word. Starbuck waited while he hunched over his key and tapped out the wire. A schedule posted on the wall provided information on routes and arrival times. By way of Denver, there was only one connection to Yankton. Tyronne Quinn would arrive day after tomorrow.

Outside, Starbuck lit a cigar and strolled back uptown. He was confident Verna would handle the chore with dispatch and efficiency. He was equally certain Tyrone Quinn would accept the job without hesitation. He made a practice of obligating members of the Denver underworld, and only last year he'd saved Quinn from a long term in prison. The man was incorrigible, a professional thief and master safecracker. But when the marker was called, a professional always paid his debts. Quinn would be on the train.

Looking ahead, Starbuck formulated a loose plan. Time and distance were the critical factors, and he proceeded on the assumption Quinn would arrive in Yankton as scheduled. In that event, they would then board the stage for Deadwood the following morning. To all appearances, they would be fellow gamblers, traveling to the mecca of the Black Hills. By the end of the week they would pull into Deadwood, and the weekend seemed the perfect time for the job. Horn's land-company office would be closed on Sunday, so that made Sunday night the target date. Some inner hunch told him the office safe, rather than Horn's home, was the place to look. As to the safe itself, he foresaw no problems. Quinn would open it like a tin of sardines.

Which made Monday the day of reckoning. Between now and then, assuming the safe divulged.

Horn's secrets, he would decide on the next step. He
figured there were a couple of options, one of them
involving Seth Bullock.

The other was strictly lone hand . . . all the way.

It was late evening. Gold Street was empty, gripped
in a weblike darkness. A pale sickle moon dimly
lighted the sky, and streetlamps flickered at the corner
of Main. The sound of a raucous Sunday-night crowd
carried distinctly from the Bad Lands.

Starbuck kept watch on the distant intersection.
Tyrone Quinn took a locksmith's pick from his vest
pocket and inserted its slim, flat tip into the door lock.
Gingerly, working by feel, he probed and tested;
within seconds there was a soft *click*. He replaced the
pick in his pocket and turned the doorknob. Without
a word, they stepped inside the Black Hills Land
Company. Quinn swiftly closed and locked the door.

A moment passed while Starbuck studied the layout of the outer office. Then he led the way to a door
on the far side of the room. There seemed little question it was the entrance to Horn's inner sanctum; a
double set of locks had been installed in the door.
Quinn went to work with his flat-nosed pick and the
door quickly swung open.

The office was furnished with good taste. A large
desk dominated the room, and grouped before it were
three wingback chairs. Along the near wall was a
leather sofa and the floor was carpeted. Yet, for all
the expensive furnishings, security was quite plainly
the overriding consideration. There were no windows,
and the double-locked door was the only entrance. On
the far wall stood a massive steel safe.

Closing the door, Quinn moved directly to the

safe. A candle and a round metal disk appeared from his inside jacket pocket. While Starbuck watched, he struck a match and lit the candle. The snuffed match was returned to his pocket; he dripped hot wax on the metal disk and sealed the butt of the candle firmly in place. Expertly, he examined the safe, all the time muttering to himself. At last, he set the candle on the floor and knelt down. He glued one ear to the safe door and briskly rubbed his hands together. Then he began rotating the combination knob.

Tyrone Quinn possessed a magic touch. Somewhat esthetic in appearance, he was short and wiry, with the watery eyes of a sparrow. His hands were delicate, the fingers smooth and tapered. He oiled them daily with glycerine and before a job he lightly sandpapered the finger pads to create a sensitive feel no less acute than antennae. Tonight, his fingers were alive, the nerve endings like exquisite sensors. It took only seven minutes until the last tumbler rolled into position.

Quinn smiled, and rose to his feet. "Any idea when your man was born?"

"No," Starbuck said shortly. "What the hell's that got to do with anything?"

"A matter of curiosity," Quinn replied in a reedy voice. "The combination is left 5—right 12—left 55. If he's twenty-seven, then that's when he was born. Lots of people use their birthdate as a combination . . . it helps 'em to remember."

"Let's get on with it."

Quinn shrugged and turned the handle on the safe. Then he opened the double doors and stepped aside. Candlelight revealed several rows of shelves at the top and a large storage area at the bottom. Star-

buck moved to the safe and began his search with the
topmost shelf. The material he found was largely confidential files and accounting ledgers relating to the
land company. On the last shelf were stacks of cash
totaling something less than two thousand dollars.
Hidden behind the money was a Colt double-action
revolver. He turned his attention to the bottom storage
area.

Outdated ledgers and files stuffed with old correspondence occupied most of the space. After paw-
ing through it item by item, he suddenly stopped and
leaned forward. He reached deep into the safe and
pulled from the rear a wide leather satchel. Opening
the clasp, he took out a small ledger and flipped
through the pages. Listed there, with a page for every
dive in the Bad Lands, were entries representing the
graft collections. One column of figures noted the
amount collected; a second column, calculated to
the penny, represented seventy-five percent of the total. Neatly lettered above the second column was the
name ORDWAY, and the conclusion was obvious.
The governor got the lion's share for his political war
chest. The balance, a full twenty-five percent, was
skimmed off the top by James Horn. Quite probably,
it went to fund his county organization.

Starbuck dug farther into the satchel. Whatever
he expected, he was amazed by what he found. Horn
had gathered incontestable documentation on the governor's corrupt practices. An affidavit by the publisher
of the Deadwood *Sentinel* indicated Ordway had organized a wide-ranging conspiracy among the territory's newspapers. Government printing contracts,
which represented a substantial volume of business,
had been awarded to a select group of publishers. In

return, the newspapers supported Ordway and voiced his political sentiments in all press coverage. The effect was a propaganda machine of staggering proportions.

Other documents revealed that patronage had been used in a criminal manner. Ordway, as territorial governor, was empowered to appoint county commissioners throughout Dakota. An affidavit from a Lawrence County commissioner indicated Ordway had transformed patronage into a scheme to line his own pockets. The appointments were conducted somewhat like an auction, with the office going to the highest bidder. The commissioners, moreover, served at the governor's pleasure. He could remove them from office as quickly as he had appointed them. The result was a stranglehold on the men who dispensed government funds at the county level. Ordway owned every commissioner throughout the whole Dakota Territory.

Starbuck was grimly amused by his discovery. The contents of the satchel were indeed an insurance policy. Horn, with one stroke, could send the governor and a phalanx of county commissioners to federal prison. The conspiracy with newspaper publishers, while not so serious, was also an indictable offense. Whether or not the affidavits had been obtained by coercion was a moot point. In a court of law they would prove irrefutable, and reduce the political structure of Dakota to a shambles. Despite himself, Starbuck felt a grudging sense of admiration. Horn was a crafty infighter, and he played for keeps.

Hefting the satchel, Starbuck turned toward the door. Quinn closed the safe and spun the combination knob. The candle was extinguished and returned to

the safe-cracker's pocket. On the way out, both the
door to Horn's office and the street door were once
more locked. There was no sign of their entry and
nothing was disturbed. The job had consumed not
quite an hour.

Starbuck was silent as they walked toward the
corner. Then, nearing the intersection, he glanced
sideways at Quinn. His eyes were stony.

"I want you on the morning stage to Cheyenne.
Take the train from there to Denver."

Quinn bobbed his head. "Whatever you say,
Luke."

"One last thing," Starbuck said flatly. "You never
heard of Deadwood or the Black Hills Land Company, Savvy?"

"Never fear!" Quinn laughed nervously. "Mum's
the word!"

"I'll hold you to it," Starbuck warned him. "Don't
let me hear any rumors floating around the Tenderloin
when I get home."

Quinn understood perfectly. Only the bare details
of the job had been revealed to him, and he had no
idea whose safe he'd just cracked. Nor was he interested in pursuing the matter further. He owed a debt
and he'd paid off, and that was that. Silence was part
of the bargain, not so much professional courtesy as
common good sense. For he also understood his life
was forfeit if he developed a loose lip. Starbuck tolerated no man who broke an agreement, and there was
no court of appeal. The verdict stood.

At the corner, they stopped in a pool of light from
the streetlamp. Starbuck was once again in the guise
of Ace Pardee. The black eyepatch and the mustache
intrigued Quinn, but he wisely suppressed his curi-

osity. He'd asked no questions over the past several days and he asked none now. All he knew about Starbuck's work was what he read in the papers, and that was all he wanted to know. A mankiller who operated undercover was best left to his own secrets.

"I'm obliged, Tyrone." Starbuck extended his hand. "You haven't lost your touch."

"It's a gift," Quinn said modestly, pumping his arm. "I play tumblers the way some people play a piano. We all have our calling."

"Maybe so." Starbuck let go his hand. "Just make sure you hear the call for the Cheyenne stage."

"Why, I wouldn't miss it for the world! No, indeed, I surely wouldn't!"

Quinn waved and walked off in the direction of the hotel. Starbuck watched him a moment, then turned downstreet. From the Bad Lands, he heard laughter and shouts, and the discordant blare of a brass band. Sunday night was always a big night in the sporting district, and he saw throngs of miners on the boardwalk outside the dives. Uptown was deserted, and a look around revealed he had the street to himself. His pace quickened.

A block farther on he approached Seth Bullock's hardware store. At the corner, he paused and slowly inspected the street in both directions. There was no one in sight, but he took a moment longer to scan the darkened doorways of shops and businesses. Then, satisfied he wasn't being followed, he turned onto Wall Street. The lamplight faded and he moved through the night to the rear of the building.

He ducked into the alleyway behind Bullock's store.

Chapter Eighteen

Early the next morning Starbuck left his hotel and walked toward Gold Street. His mood was somber, and he scarcely noticed passersby as he reflected on the problem at hand. He was absorbed with thoughts of mortality.

Outside the land company he paused and squared his shoulders. Then he opened the door and entered with a determined stride. He halted in the outer office, assessing the situation at a glance. Several clerks were seated at their desks, and three partitioned cubicles were ranged along the front wall. The men inside the cubbyholes were quickly identified as the managers of Horn's various enterprises. He grinned broadly and nodded to the nearest clerk.

"I'd like to see Mr. Eastlake."

"Oh?" The clerk gave his tinhorn attire and the eyepatch a swift once-over. "Is he expecting you, Mr.—?"

"Ace Pardee," Starbuck replied jovially. "Your boss told me to drop around anytime."

"Well, in that case, I'll just inform—"

"No need for ceremony! I'll announce myself."

Starbuck laughed with hearty good cheer. Before the clerk could move, he quickly crossed the room to the unmarked door. Throwing it open, he plastered a wide smile on his face and stepped into Horn's office.

"Hullo there, Mr. Eastlake!"

Horn jumped, shoving away from his desk. He rose partway out of his chair, then resumed his seat as Starbuck closed the door. His features took on a guarded look.

"How was Yankton, Mr. Pardee?"

"Broke the game!" Starbuck said ebulliently. "Walked away with all the marbles and then some!"

"Congratulations." Horn's face was blank, his eyes opaque. "What can I do for you?"

"Thought we might talk a little business."

Horn stared at him. "Business?"

"Political business." Starbuck lowered himself into one of the wing chairs, pulled out a cheroot. "Turns out we've got some mutual acquaintances."

"I see." Horn regarded him thoughtfully. "Are you referring to the poker game in Yankton . . . the legislators you trimmed?"

"Nope." Starbuck lit up and puffed a cottony wad of smoke. "I was thinking of Nehemiah Ordway."

"Ordway?" Horn stiffened, fully alert. "What interest do you have in the governor?"

"Well, for openers"—Starbuck studied the tip of his cigar—"you and him swill at the same trough."

Horn sat perfectly still. "I suggest you explain yourself, Mr. Pardee."

"All in good time." Starbuck casually flicked an ash onto the carpet. "I learned something else while I was in Yankton."

"I warn you, Mr. Pardee!" Horn's features set in a grim scowl. "I don't like being toyed with."

"Why, perish the thought!" Starbuck said smoothly.

"I just figured you'd want to know everything I know."

"Very well." Horn folded his hands, eased back in his chair. "I'm listening."

"The Dakota Hotel," Starbuck observed. "The one you stayed at in Yankton? I bribed the night clerk."

"I fail to see your point."

"Oh, it's a doozy! He let me have a gander at the hotel register. A few months ago—early May, to be exact—you and William Dexter were there at the same time."

"Dexter?" Horn seemed turned to stone. "I'm not familiar with the name."

Starbuck laughed in his face, "Suppose I jiggle your memory! There are bank records in Denver that tie you to Dexter. Once a month, he transferred funds from the Grubstake mine to the Black Hills Land Company. Get the picture now?"

"Go on."

"You killed Dexter, and you cleaned out his office files. But you overlooked the bank, and that's where I made the connection. Dexter was your number-one errand boy."

Horn's mouth clamped in a bloodless line. "Who are you?"

"Starbuck." A slow, dark smile creased Starbuck's features. "Luke Starbuck."

"I—" Horn paused, jolted into sudden awareness. "I thought it was you, that day on the stage. You're to be commended, Mr. Starbuck. You fooled me completely."

"That makes us even," Starbuck said with a note

of irony. "You had me fooled from the day Dexter hired me."

"Hired you?" Horn said a bit too quickly. "I know nothing of any such arrangement."

"Come off it!" Starbuck brushed aside the objection. "You did your damnedest to get me killed. I can quote it to you chapter and verse! Mike Cassidy and Hole-in-the-Wall, the smoke screen in Butte. You name it and I've got the goods."

"Indeed?" Horn tensed, his expression watchful. "Why would I want to have you killed?"

"You're James Horn," Starbuck said with a clenched smile. "Your father was Dutch Henry Horn. Want me to go on?"

"I'm impressed, Mr. Starbuck. Your reputation as a detective apparently has some basis in fact."

"What's a fact," Starbuck said firmly, "is that I've got you by the short hairs."

"I think not," Horn countered. "There's nothing to connect me to Dexter's death, and no proof I attempted to have you killed. In case you've forgotten, you shot all the witnesses, Mr. Starbuck."

"You're a little slow," Starbuck pointed out. "I'm talking about politics, not murder."

"Oh, yes!" Horn gave him a quizzical look. "You did mention the governor, didn't you?"

"The governor and graft payoffs, and a wholesale market in patronage."

"Would you care to be more specific?"

"Ordway has seven newspapers—including the Deadwood *Sentinel*—locked into a conspiracy. They all dance to his tune."

"I doubt it seriously."

"He also controls every county commissioner in

the territory. And they all paid through the nose before he'd confirm their appointment."

"Unfounded rumors!" Horn advised loftily. "No one would believe a word of it!"

"Yeah, they will," Starbuck said with conviction. "I sort of accidentally-on-purpose stumbled across the proof."

"How interesting," Horn replied with cold hauteur. "Exactly what does that have to do with me, Mr. Starbuck?"

"I mentioned graft payoffs a minute ago."

"And?"

"You're the bagman for Deadwood."

"Absurd!" Horn announced. "A total fabrication!"

"Wanna bet?" Starbuck's eyes hooded. "I cracked your safe last night."

Horn's face went chalky. "You're lying!"

"Wrong again," Starbuck said woodenly. "I got the affidavits and the ledger that shows the split between you and Ordway on the graft. It's all I need to send you up for ten, maybe twenty years."

"I still say you're bluffing!"

"One way to find out." Starbuck motioned toward the safe. "The combination is left 5—right 12—left 55."

There was a moment of stunned silence. Then Horn rose from his chair and crossed the room. He approached the safe in the manner of a condemned man mounting the gallows. Dropping to one knee, he quickly spun the combination knob and heaved open the doors. A brief search of the storage compartment convinced him the affidavits and the ledger were missing. All the color drained from his face and his

eyes dulled, appeared to turn inward. His head felt
queer, almost as though his eardrums were blocked,
and his brow glistened with beads of sweat. Finally,
with his back still to Starbuck, he bowed his head and
placed one hand on the lower shelf. His voice was
shaky.

"Why haven't you gone to Bullock? You have
the proof."

"I was tempted to do that very thing. Then, on
second thought, I figured the marshal could wait."

"Don't mock me!" Horn said sharply. "Why are
you here?"

"Guess."

"You intend to kill me, don't you?"

"Yeah, I do," Starbuck said simply. "I reckon I
wouldn't sleep nights . . . even with you in prison."

"You fool!" Horn said with raw hatred. "It won't
end here. Kill me and you're a dead man for certain!"

"I'll chance it."

Horn could scarcely mistake the finality of the
statement. The death knell had sounded, and he was
a doomed man. It flashed through his mind that he
had nothing to lose. He could submit and die on his
knees. Or he could try and yet live.

His hand brushed past the stacks of money and
clutched the hidden revolver. He twisted around, still
on one knee. He awkwardly banged his arm on the
door of the safe, almost lost his balance. Then a look
of stark terror suddenly crossed his features. He froze.

Starbuck was on his feet, waiting. The Colt six-
sixgun was extended at arm's length, and there was a
metallic whir as he thumbed the hammer. An instant
of tomblike stillness slipped past while they stared at
each other. Then he smiled and fired.

The slug drilled through Horn's forehead. The top of his skull exploded, blown off in a misty spray of brains and gore. He toppled over, driven backward by the impact, and fell wedged inside the safe. One leg kicked, his bootheel drumming the floor in afterdeath. His eyes rolled upward, then a wheezing rattle escaped his throat and he lay still.

Starbuck felt nothing. The man had tried repeatedly to kill him, and would have tried again. Whatever else he was, the son of Dutch Henry Horn was no quitter. One day, somewhere down the line, there would have been a time of retribution. So, in the end, it was kill or get killed. Which made it the simplest of all choices.

Only one emotion touched Starbuck. He was glad James Horn was dead. And somehow relieved, almost sanguine. It had been a long hunt.

Nor was he yet out of the woods. He moved to the door and flung it open. The men in the outer office were on their feet, their faces taut with apprehension. He leveled the sixgun and they hastily cleared a path. No one spoke as he crossed the room; his eyes and the Colt swept constantly from side to side. Once past the row of desks, he turned and kept them covered as he backed to the door. He stepped outside and holstered his pistol. Then he hurried toward the corner.

On Main Street, Starbuck turned downtown. He strode rapidly in the direction of Bullock's store, located on the next corner. The business district was already bustling with activity, and throngs of people jammed the boardwalk. Weaving in and out, he snaked through the crowd, ignoring the stares of passersby. When he was halfway down the block, a sudden shout behind him brought everything on the street to a standstill. He glanced over his shoulder and saw one of the land-company clerks standing at the corner. The shout became a shrill scream, wild and frenzied.

"Stop that man! He murdered Mr. Eastlake!"

Starbuck broke into a headlong sprint. Deadwood was infamous for vigilante justice, and the man known as John Eastlake was the town's leading citizen. In the hands of a mob, he knew he would be lynched without trial or hearing. He bulled past a hard-faced miner who attempted to block his path. Then he jerked the sixgun and wiggled the barrel with a menacing gesture. The crowd split apart, some hugging the walls of buildings and others scattering into the street. He took the last few steps and darted into the hardware store. He kept the Colt trained on the door.

Seth Bullock rushed forward from his office. Outside, a clot of townspeople quickly gathered on the boardwalk, and more came running. Word spread along the street like wildfire, and there was a buzz of excitement mingled with dark mutterings. Bullock halted beside him, one eye on the crowd. His face was etched with bewilderment.

"What the hell's all that about?"

"I braced Horn," Starbuck said stolidly. "He went for a gun and I killed him."

"Holy Jesus!" Bullock cursed. "Get on back to my office and lock the door."

"I'd sooner take my chances here."

"Don't argue! I want you out of sight—now!"

Starbuck hesitated, then slowly backed toward the rear of the store. Bullock grabbed a shotgun off a nearby rack and emptied a box of shells on the counter. He swiftly loaded both barrels and snapped the breech closed. Then he walked to the door and stopped, the scattergun centered on the mob. His voice was harsh, commanding.

"Clear out! The man's my prisoner and I've got a load of buckshot for anybody that disagrees. Go on, gawddamnit—get moving!"

The shotgun was steady, and the barrels looked big as mine shafts. The crowd stared back at him a moment; then those in the front rank turned away. The movement broke the spell and the mob dispersed to the opposite side of the street. Bullock slammed the door and locked it. His eyes were grim as he walked toward the office.

While Bullock listened, Starbuck briefly recounted the events of the past two days. He outlined how the safe had been cracked and explained in some detail the ledger dealing with graft collections. For reasons of his own, he omitted any mention of the affidavits linking Governor Ordway to political corruption. He concluded with a straightforward account of Horn's death.

"Thought so," Bullock said when he finished. "You went there plannin' to kill him, didn't you?"

"What's the difference?" Starbuck replied. "He's dead and that ends it. All I want now is a ticket out of Deadwood."

"How d'you figure to do that? The sheriff and the whole courthouse crowd were Horn's stooges. You'll be charged with murder sure as thunder!"

"I've got something to trade."

"Yeah?" Bullock eyed him narrowly. "What's that?"

"The ledger," Starbuck said with a tired smile. "It indicts the courthouse crowd the same as it did Horn.

What's in there could send every last one of them to
prison. I'll swap it for a ticket on the Cheyenne
stage."

"God a'mighty!" Bullock glowered at him in
tongue-tied rage. "That'd let Ordway off the hook
too! We wouldn't have a case against nobody!"

"No way around it, Seth." Starbuck gave him a
downcast look. "It's that or they'll have me decorat-
ing a tree by sundown."

"You rigged it!" Bullock said with sudden understanding. "You rigged it so you could kill Horn
and walk away clean! All the time you wasn't
thinkin' about nobody but yourself!"

"You believe what you want to believe. It doesn't
change a thing."

"Where's the ledger?"

"Hidden," Starbuck said evasively. "I'll tell you
where after the coroner's inquest."

"What inquest?"

"That's the rest of the deal." A wintry smile
lighted Starbuck's eyes. "I want the whole story on
the record. Horn's real identity, and how he tried to
have me assassinated. And I want a coroner's jury to
clear me of killing him—all neat and official and in
writing!"

"You really think a bunch of politicians are gonna
buy that? Hell, they'll probably figure you're tryin'
to set 'em up for a double-cross!"

"No inquest, no ledger," Starbuck said equably.
"I don't see they've got any choice."

Bullock chewed at his mustache before answering. "Why should I go out of my way to make your
deal? You've done spoilt my game all to hell and
gone!"

"Trust me, Seth." Starbuck stared straight into his gaze. "You won't regret it."

Silence thickened between them. Finally, with a great shrug of resignation, Bullock cleared his throat. "Guess I couldn't rightly let 'em stretch your neck. I'll go see what we can work out."

After the lawman was gone, Starbuck locked the door and fired up a cheroot. He took a chair, puffing smoke, and propped his boots on the desk. He looked pleased as a tomcat spitting feathers.

The stagecoach stood outside the Deadwood station. To the east, the sun crested the mountains like a fiery globe. Several passengers were milling about, awaiting the call to board. Their destination was Cheyenne.

Starbuck and Bullock were off to one side, talking quietly. The coroner's inquest, held yesterday afternoon, had created a sensation. Starbuck's testimony regarding John Eastlake's true identity had turned the town topsy-turvy. The assassination plot, corroborated by Bullock, had put the final onus on the dead man. The verdict was justifiable homicide, and the news had been flashed to papers all across the territory. The courthouse crowd, having fulfilled their end of the bargain, had spent an uneasy night. One piece of business still remained.

Squinting into the sun, Starbuck lowered his voice. "You know that loading dock out behind your store?"

"In the alley?" Bullock cocked his head. "What about it?"

"Dig down a foot or so over at the left side. You'll find a leather satchel buried there. The ledger's inside."

"Well, I'll be damned!"

"You'll find something else, too." A slow smile tugged at the corner of Starbuck's mouth. "There's a couple of affidavits that ought to put Ordway on the rockpile till he's an old man."

Bullock looked astounded. "Affidavits about what?"

"When you've read them, you'll understand. I'd suggest you go have a talk with the attorney general. Once he's empaneled a grand jury and issued subpoenas, the lid will blow sky high. There'll be all kinds of newspaper publishers and county commissioners ready to turn songbird."

"Newspaper—"

"Not so loud!" Starbuck cut him short. "Just read the affidavits. You'll hang Ordway, and along with him your own courthouse crowd. There's plenty of rope for everybody."

Bullock considered briefly, then nodded. "How come you didn't tell me all this yesterday?"

Starbuck wagged his head. "The game's not over till the last hand is dealt. I always like to have an ace up my sleeve."

"Judas Priest!" Bullock laughed and smote him across the back. "You're one of a kind, Luke! Goddamn me if you're not!"

The driver let loose a leather-lunged shout. While the other passengers climbed aboard, the two men vigorously shook hands. There was a sense of celebration in their parting, and no maudlin words. Starbuck simply waved and stepped into the coach. Then he settled back in his seat with an inward sigh of relief.

He wasn't sorry to put Deadwood behind him.

Chapter Nineteen

Verna Phelps thought the article in poor taste. She adjusted her pince-nez and spread the Denver *Post* on her desk. A grisly account of the Deadwood killing was featured on the front page. Written with a certain ghoulish detail, the article pandered to the reading public's morbid sense of curiosity. She considered it a low form of yellow journalism.

Over the past week Starbuck had become a coast-to-coast news item. The story was first picked up by the *Police Gazette*, and quickly spread to papers all across the country. With bold headlines and purple prose, the tale of a detective who had killed both father and son was played as high drama. The seven-year lapse between killings, combined with the assassination plot, gave it an added degree of sensationalism. The furor in the nation's press served to enhance Starbuck's reputation, and his notoriety. He remained the most celebrated manhunter in the West.

The door opened and Verna glanced up from the paper. A fashionably dressed woman stepped into the office. She wore a tailored waistcoat, with an accordion-pleated skirt and a stylish hat decorated with an ostrich feather. She was slender, somewhere in her late forties, but well preserved and still very

attractive. Verna folded the paper and nodded pleasantly.

"Good afternoon. May I help you?"

"Yes, please." The woman's voice was surprisingly genteel. "I wish to see Mr. Starbuck."

"Do you have an appointment?"

"I—" The woman smiled uncertainly. "I apologize, but I wasn't aware an appointment was necessary."

"May I inquire the nature of your visit?"

"A personal matter . . . confidential."

"I'm sorry," Verna said briskly. "Mr. Starbuck
does not handle domestic cases. I suggest you try another agency."

"Oh, no!" The woman's lip trembled. "I assure
you it has nothing to do with domestic difficulties. I
wish to retain Mr. Starbuck on a business matter!"

"Perhaps you could provide me with the particulars?"

The woman averted her eyes. "I can only say it's
a matter of the gravest importance. Anything else will
have to be said to Mr. Starbuck personally."

"I see." Verna frowned, still not convinced. "May
I ask your name?"

"Mrs. Roger Latham."

"Are you a resident of Denver, Mrs. Latham?"

"Yes, of course."

"Your current address?"

"Why do—" Mrs. Latham stopped, nervously
clutching her purse. "It's 1038 Welton."

"Capitol Hill?"

Mrs. Latham inclined her head. "Quite near the
governor's mansion."

"Please wait here."

Verna rose and moved to the door of Starbuck's office. She rapped lightly and entered, closing the door behind her. Several moments passed, the low murmur of voices audible from within the other room. Then the door opened and Verna reappeared.

"Won't you come in, Mrs. Latham." She motioned, stepping aside. "Mr. Starbuck will see you."

"Oh, thank you!"

The woman glided across the room and went past her. Starbuck was seated, his desk littered with an accumulation of correspondence. He stood, nodding to Verna, who quietly closed the door. Then he indicated a chair.

"Please be seated, Mrs. Latham."

"You're most kind, Mr. Starbuck. I do apologize for interrupting your busy schedule."

"No need." Starbuck waited until she took a chair before he sat down. "I was just clearing my desk. Nothing that won't wait."

Mrs. Latham looked at him fully for the first time. Her gaze was oddly clinical, almost an inspection. She smiled and shifted her purse to her lap.

"I must say you're not what I expected, Mr. Starbuck."

"Beg your pardon?"

"Well—" Her hand fluttered like a wounded bird. "A man in your profession conjures a certain image. I thought you would . . ."

Her voice trailed off, and Starbuck made an idle gesture. "No horns and no cloven hooves, Mrs. Latham. I do the Devil's work, but it ends there."

"Is that how you see it—the Devil's work?"

"A figure of speech," Starbuck said easily. "How

can I help you? I understand you're here on a matter
of some importance."

"Yes, I am." A pulse throbbed in her neck. "I
wish to retain your services."

"To what purpose?"

"A man stole something from me. Something
very dear and very precious."

"You want me to run him down, reclaim your
property?"

"No." Her mouth narrowed and her eyes took on
the dull gleam of an icon. "I want him killed."

A sudden foreboding swept over Starbuck. He
found himself unaccountably disquieted, every sense
alert. He could see anger, resentment, and a trace of
fear in her eyes. There was a strangeness about her—
some haunting familiarity—and unbidden a tantaliz-
ing thought popped into his mind. He wondered on it
a moment, almost let it slip away. Then he listened
and heard again the last words of James Horn.

Kill me and you're a dead man for certain.

The woman across the desk watched him with
utter directness. She was marvelously in control of
herself, and yet there was something attenuated in her
manner. She sat rigid, and a pinpoint of anguish
lighted her gaze. He warned himself to proceed cautiously.

"How'd you happen to pick me?"

"You have no peer, Mr. Starbuck." She un-
snapped the clasp on her purse, and took out a worn
news clipping. "I realized that when I read of your
last case."

Starbuck accepted the clipping. He scanned it
quickly and saw that it dealt with the Deadwood killing. There was no byline and the dateline simply read

Dakota Territory. Yet the typeface was distinctive, unlike any he'd ever seen before. He casually placed the clipping on the desk.

"Offhand, I'd say that came from an eastern newspaper."

"Yes." Her voice dropped. "The New York *Morning Telegraph.*"

"So you're not from Denver?"

"No."

"And you're not Mrs. Roger Latham?"

"No."

"Who are you, then?"

"Haven't you guessed?" She pulled a small pocket revolver from her purse. "I credited you with somewhat keener deductive powers, Mr. Starbuck."

"I'm generally quicker," Starbuck said lamely. "Course, the story I got was that you'd died some years back. I reckon Dutch Henry had his reasons for lying."

"Henry was a vain fool," she replied. "His pride wouldn't allow him to admit I divorced him."

"Or that you'd remarried?"

"Bravo!" she said without irony. "How clever of you, Mr. Starbuck."

"Only makes sense," Starbuck said, playing for time. "James was attending some eastern college when he got word his daddy had been killed. He came west to collect his inheritance and he never went back. The way that tallies out, he was trying to put something—or someone—behind him. I'd judge it wasn't you."

"No." Her expression was wistful, somehow vulnerable. "James loathed his stepfather almost as much as he loved Henry. The inheritance provided him with the wherewithal to start a new life . . . to escape."

"You must've missed him all those years?"

"Terribly," she admitted. "James and I were always very close. He wrote, of course, and whenever he came east on business, we always managed a visit. But it was never the same after Henry's death."

"I'm almost sorry I had to put Dutch Henry away."

"Regrets hardly seem in character for you, Mr. Starbuck."

"Not that, exactly." Starbuck feigned a hangdog look. "If I hadn't killed Dutch Henry, then you wouldn't have lost your son. See what I mean?"

"I bear you no grudge for Henry's death. He was scarcely a loss to mankind."

"The boy was, though," Starbuck added quickly. "Except for his daddy's influence, he would've turned out all right. Seemed like Dutch Henry had a hold on him—even from the grave."

"Are you trying to play on a mother's sympathy?"

"No, ma'am!" Starbuck protested. "I'm just saying life's not fair. Your son deserved better, a whole lot better!"

"Tell me, Mr. Starbuck"—her tone was raw with bitterness—"were those your thoughts the day you killed him?"

Starbuck slowly shook his head. "At the time, he was doing his level best to kill me."

"I read the newspaper articles."

"Then you know what I testified to at the coronor's inquest. He was mad for revenge, and he'd tried to have me assassinated several times. He wouldn't have stopped until I was dead."

"Do you honestly believe that matters?"

"I think it would if you gave it some thought."

"You killed my son!" She drew a deep, unsteady breath, and her voice rose quickly. "I gave that a great deal of thought, Mr. Starbuck! All the way from New York I thought of nothing else!"

"Ask yourself a question," Starbuck said gently. "What would you gain by killing me?"

"Please, Mr. Starbuck!" Her words were hard, contemptuous. "Don't beg pity! I have none left— none!"

"I'm not begging." Starbuck regarded her without guile. "I'm talking reason, common horse sense."

"Are you indeed?" she said stiffly, her lips white. "Very well, allow me to indulge you. What earthly reason would stop me from killing the man who killed my son?"

"You have too much to lose."

"Lose!" Her laugh was laced with scorn. "I have nothing left to lose. I've already lost it all—everything that matters!"

"A good look in a mirror might convince you otherwise."

"A mirror?"

"A look at yourself," Starbuck explained. "You're a cultured woman. You started out on a hard-scrabble farm—with an outlaw for a husband—and you've made yourself over into a lady. A real, honest-to-god lady! You shouldn't throw that away."

"Now you're attempting to play on my vanity!"

"Am I?" Starbuck asked softly. "You've got position and wealth, and a husband who thinks the world of you. I'd call that a plain fact, not vanity."

"How—" She seemed to falter, then rushed on.
"How do you know those things?"

"A blind man could see it," Starbuck remarked.
"The way you dress, the refined way you speak, all
that says a lot about your husband. You must've told
him about Dutch Henry—lies wouldn't have held up
all these years—and he still married you, didn't he?"

She studied him a moment. "You should have
been a lawyer, Mr. Starbuck. You plead a case very
eloquently."

"It's your case, not mine. You shoot me and
you're the big loser."

"I rather doubt that."

"Do you?" Starbuck said with genuine concern.
"No matter how much you grieve your son, that'll
pass. Some things you live with all your life. Killing
a man in coldblood tops the list."

"The way you killed James?"

Starbuck sensed he'd lost. Her expression became
immobile and her eyes glittered with hatred, naked
and revealed. There was no remorse, no pity, in her
look. A tightening around the mouth told him she was
about to pull the trigger.

The door burst open. She was momentarily distracted, and in that split instant, Starbuck flung himself headlong to the floor. Then she fired; the slug
drilled through the backrest of his chair and thunked
into the wall. Her features twisted in a crazed look
and she swiftly rose to her feet. She leaned across the
desk.

"No!" Verna cried from the doorway. *"Don't!"*

She ignored the command. Bracing herself
against the desk, she thrust out her arm and pointed
the revolver at Starbuck. Her hand shook violently as

her finger curled tighter around the trigger. Verna took dead aim with a double-barrel derringer and shot her in the leg. Her mouth froze in a silent oval, then the revolver barked and a bullet whizzed past Starbuck's head. She stared at him a moment, and suddenly the light went out in her eyes. Her legs collapsed and the gun dropped from her hand. She slowly folded to the floor.

Starbuck stood and moved around the desk. He looked first at the woman, then his gaze shuttled to the doorway. Verna appeared steady, not in the least shocked by what she'd done. He shook his head in open wonder.

"Where'd you get the derringer?"

"Out of my pocketbook."

"I never figured you to carry a gun."

Verna sniffed. "You never bothered to ask. As it happens, I am an expert markswoman."

"Lucky for me you are," Starbuck said gratefully. "How'd you know she wasn't on the level?"

"The address," Verna observed. "She told me she lived at 1038 Welton. I checked it in the city street directory. Welton ends at the 800 block."

"Loose ends," Starbuck said absently, staring at the woman. "Guess you'd better run fetch a doctor. No sense letting her bleed to death."

"Oh?" Verna looked surprised. "I do believe there's hope for you yet!"

"How so?"

"Perhaps you're not the cynic you think."

"Whatever I am"—Starbuck's mouth lifted in an ashen grin—"you're a sweetheart. I wouldn't trade you for all the tea in China!"

Verna flushed and tittered a giddy laugh. She

turned quickly away, pausing only long enough to
drop the derringer on her desk. Then she hurried out
the door.

Still chuckling to himself, Starbuck knelt beside
the fallen woman. He took her wrist between thumb
and forefinger; her pulse was strong and her color
appeared good. On the verge of rising, his attention
was drawn to her purse. He opened it and pawed
through the contents. A brief search turned up a
silver-filigreed calling-card case. He recognized it as
the type commonly carried by society ladies and
wealthy matrons. He extracted an embossed card and
read it with mild shock.

Her name was Mrs. Cornelius Vanderbilt II.

A gentle breeze drifted through the window. The bedroom was dark, lighted only by the dim glow of a
lamp from the sitting room. Lola lay quietly in the
crook of his arm, her head pillowed on his shoulder.
She was satiated, drifting on the tranquil flame of
their lovemaking. Yet she was wide awake, and
thoughtful.

Earlier, he'd told her about the shooting. Verna's
part was related in some detail, and she had emerged
the heroine of the piece. All else, including his conversation with Horn's mother, had been somewhat
fuzzy in the telling. Oddly, he'd skipped over several
salient points, leapfrogging from the shooting to the
bare bones of the aftermath. The woman had been
taken to the hospital, and a full recovery was expected. The particulars, all the savory little tidbits, had
been bypassed. He'd simply stopped there, and said
no more.

At the time, Lola had curbed her curiosity. But

now, with her imagination running wild, she could restrain herself no longer. She snuggled closer, her breath warm and velvety against his ear.

"Lover?"

"Hmmm?"

"What will happen to her . . . Horn's mother?"

"Nothing."

"Nothing!" Lola pushed up on one elbow. "Aren't you going to press charges?"

"Nope."

"Why not?" Lola demanded. "She tried to kill you!"

"Happens all the time."

"Very funny! What happens when she tries again? You know she'll try!"

"I got a hunch that says she won't."

"Ooo God! It's like pulling teeth! What kind of hunch?"

"Well—" Starbuck nibbled her nipple, grinned. "I reckon she's got it out of her system now. We had a long talk at the hospital, and I'm satisfied bygones are bygones. She agreed to leave town the minute the doctors give her the okay."

"Where will she go?"

"Beats me."

"What name does she go by?"

"Mizz Horn," Starbuck said dreamily. "What else?"

"Some detective!" Lola lifted an eyebrow, studied him with mock seriousness. "What you need is a keeper. Or better yet—a bodyguard!"

"No," Starbuck said, nuzzling her breast. "All I need's a body!"

"Any old body?" Lola inquired with a naughty
wink. "Or somebody special?"

"What do you think?"

Lola's laugh was a delicious sound. "I think I'm
all the body you can handle, Mr. Starbuck!"

"Do you, now?"

"You don't believe me?"

"Let's just say I'm willing to be convinced."

"How long do I have?"

"All the time it takes."

"Braggart!" Lola darted his ear with her tongue.
"You won't last that long!"

"Try me and see."

The moon went down over Denver before they
were finished. She fell away limp and exhausted, but
secretly pleased with herself. However far he roamed,
even when he strayed, she knew he would never forget tonight. She'd spoiled him for other women, and
the memory would linger. A bright ember, quickly
fanned to flame, and always there. His bed was hers.

Starbuck slept the sleep of the weary warrior. He
dreamed not of ghosts but of people. He held her
close and thought no more of death.

Epilogue

Telluride, Colorado
June 24, 1889

"How many were in the gang?"

"Seven or eight." The express messenger sounded doubtful. "I didn't exactly have time to count noses."

Starbuck nodded. "Your report to the main office said the holdup took place outside Placerville?"

"You familiar with the valley?"

"Not all that much."

"Well, there's a bridge that crosses the San Miguel. I'd put it maybe five miles this side of Placerville. That's where they hit us."

"How'd they stop the train?"

"It was in my report," the messenger said testily. "They dropped a rock slide across the tracks."

"Just checking," Starbuck replied casually. "How about a description? Anything special you remember?"

"I damn sure remember the one that gave the orders! He kept a gun in my ear the whole god-blessed time!"

"What'd he look like?"

"Your size, maybe a little taller. Had black hair

and a mustache, and chewed tobacco. Sonovabitch
spit like a grasshopper!"

"Hear any names?"

"Not that I recollect."

The train whistle tooted three sharp blasts. Starbuck hastily concluded the interrogation. He had all
the information he needed, and he saw no reason to
delay departure. After shaking hands, the messenger
hoisted himself into the express car. The engine chuf-
fed a cloud of steam and the driving wheels spun,
slowly took purchase on the tracks. A few moments
later the train pulled away from the platform.

Starbuck turned and walked past the stationhouse.
On his way uptown, he mentally reviewed all he'd
learned. The description fitted a known train robber,
Charlie Stroud. Operating out of Robbers Roost,
Stroud led a gang whose numbers varied according to
the job. His territory extended south into New Mexico
and Arizona, and he had pulled a string of holdups
over the last year. He was elusive and a good tacti-
cian; running him to ground would be no easy task.
Robbers Roost was as inhospitable as ever, still a hazardous undertaking for any lawman. Which made it
even more so for a detective.

By now the trail was cold. The train had been
robbed almost a week ago, and the gang had made
off with some thirty thousand dollars in loot. Hired
to run them down, Starbuck had arrived in Telluride
only last night. The town was located in southern Colorado, on the western slope of the Rockies. Overlooking the San Miguel Valley, it was one of the
newer mining camps, with a railroad spur and a thriving business community. To the northwest, some two
hundred miles distant, lay Robbers Roost.

Starbuck judged it to be a four- or five-day ride. Adding another week or so to make contact with the outlaws, that would allow time for him to sprout a scruffy beard. From his valise, which he'd left in the hotel, he would select whatever else was needed to complete his disguise. All that remained was to buy a horse and pick up a used saddle. He turned onto Main Street and went looking for a stable. A block ahead he spotted Searle's Livery.

As he approached the stable, he saw three men push through the bat-wing doors of a nearby saloon. They stopped, huddling on the boardwalk in conversation. He automatically checked out the two men facing him, but neither of them was familiar. The third man, whose back was to him, appeared to be doing most of the talking. He dismissed them from mind and angled off toward the livery. Then the third man turned sideways, gesturing obliquely across the street. His features were distinct in the bright morning sun.

Thunderstruck, Starbuck halted dead in his tracks. Almost seven years had passed since they'd last met. The lithe frame was taller now, heavier and padded with muscle. The face was older, somewhere in the early twenties, visibly toughened by time. Yet there was no mistaking the broad brow and the square jaw, and the quick youthful look of a jester. The man doing the talking was Butch Cassidy.

Abruptly, the conversation ended. Butch dismissed the other men with a gesture, and they hurried down the boardwalk. Starbuck got himself untracked, walking toward them at a leisurely pace. He passed them as they turned into the dim interior of the stable. Proceeding upstreet, he stepped onto the boardwalk and strolled toward the saloon. Butch was still turned away, lost in thought. Starbuck followed the direction of his gaze and grunted softly to himself. Across the street, catty-corner to the saloon, was the San Miguel Valley Bank.

"Hello, Butch." He stopped a pace away. "How's tricks?"

Butch jumped, then whirled around. His jaw dropped open and his features corkscrewed in a look of doglike amazement. His eyes were veined with disbelief.

"I'll be go to hell!" he croaked. "Luke Starbuck!"

"In the flesh."

"Where'd you come from?"

"The depot." Starbuck jerked a thumb over his shoulder. "Passed your friends, and saw you standing here big as life."

"Couple of my drinkin' buddies," Butch said with an uneasy smile. "What brings you to Telluride?"

"Train robbers," Starbuck remarked. "Somebody pulled a holdup down around Placerville last week."

"No kiddin'?" Butch inquired innocently. "You still in the detective business, are you?"

"Only trade I know," Starbuck commented. "How about you? You're a long way from Hole-in-the-Wall."

"Yeah, I called it quits up there almost four years back."

"Where do you call home these days?"

"I drift around . . . nowhere special."

Starbuck's look betrayed nothing. "Whatever happened to Mike Cassidy?"

"You won't believe it!" Butch laughed, and for a moment there was a vestige of the clownish youngster in his features. "That old scutter done up and quit the owlhoot! Last I heard, he'd settled down somewheres south of the border. Got himself a señorita and a whole passel of kids!"

"Good for him," Starbuck said warmly. "How long ago was it he quit?"

"Summer of '85." Butch's expression turned sober. "That's when I packed it in at Hole-in-the-Wall. Wouldn't never've been the same, not without Mike."

"So you've been drifting around ever since?"

"More or less."

Starbuck sensed a sudden tension. Butch's gaze went past him, and he turned his head slightly. Out of the corner of his eye, he saw the other two men cross the street, leading three saddled horses. They glanced toward the saloon, and Butch nodded with an almost imperceptible movement. Then they continued on to the hitch rack outside the bank. After the horses were tied, one of the men stooped down and pretended to check the cinch on his mount. The other man took up a post near the bank entrance.

"Mike had the right idea," Starbuck said evenly. "You ought to try it yourself."

"Well, like I told you once, life's too goddang daily. A fellow stands still and before you know it, he takes root."

"Is that why you aim to rob the bank?"

Butch gave him a lightning frown. "Stay out of it, Luke! It's none of your concern!"

"Wish it weren't," Starbuck said in a low voice. "But here in Colorado, I'm sworn to uphold the law. I'd have to stop you."

"You'll die tryin'!" Butch ducked his chin toward the bank. "Those boys are meaner'n bitch wolves.

You stick your nose where it don't belong and they'll kill you dead!"

"I'd still be obliged to try."

"Christ on a crutch!" Butch grimaced, darted a quick look around. "Awright, lemme level with you, Luke. We've got the town marshal in our hip pocket! Bought him for a share of the pie and a promise he'd make himself scarce while we pulled the job. Now, you just stop and think about it! If the local lawdog don't care—why the hell should you?"

Starbuck regarded him with a cool look of appraisal. "Even if it's true, it doesn't change things. I'm here and I'd be bound to stop you."

"Goddamnit, you owe me!" Butch muttered fiercely. "I could've shot you that time at Hole-in-the-Wall! I had you dead to rights and all I did was crack your skull. You know you owe me, Luke!"

Starbuck looked him straight in the eye. "You're sure you want to call the marker that way?"

"You damn betcha I'm sure!"

"Then you've got yourself a deal, Butch."

"Well, now, I always knew you was a man that paid your debts!"

"One last condition," Starbuck said tightly. "You kill anyone and I'll drop you the minute you walk out of that bank."

"Fair enough!" Butch crowed. "I ain't never killed nobody in my life. I don't aim to start now!"

"We're even, then." Starbuck's voice was edged. "Next time all bets are off."

"What makes you think there'll be a next time?"

"Sooner or later somebody will want your ticket punched."

"And they'll call on you to do the job . . . that it?"

Starbuck's mouth set in a hard line. "Let's just say I'm the chief ticket-puncher hereabouts."

Butch began a question, then appeared to change his mind. He shrugged and turned away, mumbling as he walked off. "See you, Luke."

"Hope you don't and wish you're right."

There was no reply. Butch crossed the street without looking back. He nodded to the man at the hitch rack, whose assignment was to guard the horses and warn passersby away. Then he mounted the boardwalk and joined the man at the door. Together, they entered the bank. A moment later the door closed and the blind was drawn.

Starbuck moved back into the shade. He leaned against the wall of the saloon and took his time lighting a cigarette. Over the years, he'd wondered about Butch, recalling their train ride from Pueblo. The youngster had turned him down then—refusing a chance to go straight—and things clearly hadn't changed. The only difference was that Butch had now raised his sights. He had himself a gang and he felt cocky enough to tackle a bank. Still, for all his bravado, it was apparently his first try at the big time. Starbuck had heard nothing of him on the grapevine, and there were no wanted posters bearing his name. For seven years, he'd been a cipher among western outlaws. Today, all that went by the boards.

Old memories flooded back in a rush. Starbuck tried to remember the last time he'd thought of Hole-in-the-Wall and Deadwood. And James Horn. As near as he could recall, it was sometime the spring of '84. He'd received a letter from Seth Bullock, advising him a grand jury had finally returned an indictment against Governor Nehemiah Ordway. That it had

taken Bullock two years to secure an indictment
merely underscored Ordway's political power in Dakota Territory. The outcome of the trial, held that
summer, bordered on travesty. Ordway's lawyer entered a motion to quash the indictment; the brief con-
tended that a territorial governor, appointed by the
president, was not subject to the jurisdiction of a territorial court. The judge granted the motion, and all
charges were dismissed. No effort was made to secure
an indictment by a federal grand jury.

Starbuck was scarcely surprised by subsequent
events. Less than two weeks after the trial, President
Chester Arthur removed Ordway from office. While
hardly a whitewash, the president's action nonetheless
ended any hope of criminal prosecution. Ordway,
with no fear for the future, devoted himself to a business empire founded on the graft and bribes he'd accepted while governor. Nor was he tarred and
feathered in the political arena; his reputation was still
intact, and his influence on the Potomac suffered none
at all. The Northern Pacific Railroad hired him as a
lobbyist, and a good part of his time thereafter was
spent in Washington. He emerged a man of wealth
and prominence, and in the process he disproved the
old axiom about crime. He'd made it pay.

Once more, Starbuck's cynicism regarding politicians had withstood the test. There was no justice
for those who held membership in the Order of
Strange Bedfellows. His investigation, all the evidence of graft and corruption, had proved little more
than an exercise in futility. His time in Deadwood had
produced only one tangible result. He'd killed a man
who deserved to die. In retrospect, he saw that summary justice was the only lasting justice. He thought

it a sad commentary on life, and yet it was enough for him. He still lived, and James Horn was dead.

His reverie into the past abruptly ended. The bank door opened and Butch stepped outside. He was trailed by his cohort, who carried a gunnysack stuffed with cash. Their guns were drawn and they walked directly to the hitch rack. Along the street, several townspeople gawked a moment in disbelief, then quickly scattered for cover. Butch and the other men stepped into the saddle and reined their horses away from the bank. No cry of alarm was raised and no one attempted to stop them. All of Telluride seemed to hold its breath.

Starbuck moved from the shade into the sunlight. He took a final drag on his cigarette and ground it underfoot as the robbers neared the corner. Butch glanced in his direction, and for an instant their eyes locked. An unspoken message passed between them, and in that fragmented moment the youngster's face looked somehow like a sad clown. Then he laughed and gigged his horse.

With Butch in the lead, the robbers rounded the corner. They spurred their mounts into a gallop and rode north out of town. Yipping and howling, they aimed their sixguns skyward and blasted off several rounds. The getaway was loud and noisy, somehow amateurish, and almost comic to watch. They were like exuberant schoolboys, filled with their own devilment, tossing lighted strings of firecrackers into the air. Their horses abreast, they pounded out of Telluride in a cloud of dust. A short stretch down the road they vanished from sight.

Starbuck took the pragmatic view. The kid had called the marker and their account was now settled.

Yet he saw today as a beginning, not an end.

Butch Cassidy was wild as the wind, bound and determined to live unfettered by rules. The Telluride bank robbery truly branded him an outlaw, and he possessed all the attributes of the breed. One day his picture would appear on wanted posters and a price would be put on his head. Then an angry banker or a railroad baron would issue a summary death warrant. From that moment onward, the youngster would be living on borrowed time.

Starbuck turned and walked toward the livery stable. He had a train robber to catch, and the first order of business was to get himself aboard a horse. Still, for all that, there was no escaping his own vision of the future. When the time finally rolled around, he somehow knew he was the one who would be summoned. It was in the cards, ordained by the caprice that governed such things. He would be assigned the job of killing Butch Cassidy.

He promised himself to do it swiftly.

America's Authentic Voice of the Western Frontier

Matt Braun
Bestselling author of *Bloody Hand*

HICKOK & CODY

In the wind-swept campsite of the Fifth Cavalry Regiment, along Red Willow Creek, Russia's Grand Duke Alexis has arrived to experience the thrill of the buffalo hunt. His guides are: Wild Bill Hickok and Buffalo Bill Cody—two heroic dead-shots with a natural flair for showmanship, a hunger for adventure, and the fervent desire to keep the myths of the Old West alive. But what approached from the East was a journey that crossed the line into dangerous territory. It would offer Alexis a front row seat to history, and would set Hickok and Cody on a path to glory.

"Braun tackles the big men, the complex personalities of those brave few who were pivotal figures in the settling of an untamed frontier."
—Jory Sherman, author of *Grass Kingdom*

"Matt Braun has a genius for taking real characters out of the Old West and giving them flesh-and-blood immediacy."
—Dee Brown, author of *Bury My Heart at Wounded Knee*

GOOD PLAN GONE BAD . . .

A shot sounded from within the bank and one of the tellers stumbled through the door. He lost his footing and fell face first onto the sidewalk. On his heels, the three inside men burst out the door and ran for their horses. Frank was in the lead, followed by Jesse, and last in line was Bob Younger. Bunched together, they dodged and weaved, snapping off wild shots as they headed for the hitch rack. The marshal and Elias Stacey opened up on them in a rolling barrage. The bank window shattered and bullets pocked the wall of the building all around them. Younger's horse reared backward and toppled dead as he grabbed for the reins. Beside him, still in the middle, Jesse bent low under the hitch rack.

Starbuck, tracking them in his sights, had not yet fired. From the moment they darted out of the bank, he'd waited for a clear shot. His concentration was on Jesse, but the other men were in the way, spoiling his aim. Then, as Younger's horse fell dead, he saw an opening. He touched off the trigger as Jesse rose from beneath the hitch rack . . .

PRAISE FOR SPUR AWARD–WINNING AUTHOR MATT BRAUN

"Matt Braun is head and shoulders above all the rest who would attempt to bring the gunmen of the Old West to life."
—Terry C. Johnston, author of the Plainsmen series

"Matt Braun has a genius for taking real characters out of the Old West and giving them flesh-and-blood immediacy."
—Dee Brown, author of *Bury My Heart at Wounded Knee*

OTHER TITLES BY MATT BRAUN

TOMBSTONE
THE SPOILERS

EL PASO
THE WILD ONES

KINCH RILEY
INDIAN TERRITORY

HANGMAN'S CREEK
JURY OF SIX

DODGE CITY
DAKOTA
A DISTANT LAND
WINDWARD WEST
CROSSFIRE
THE HIGHBINDERS
THE WARLORDS
THE SPOILERS
HICKOK AND CODY
THE OVERLORDS
TOMBSTONE
RIO GRANDE
THE BRANNOCKS
THE GAMBLERS
RIO HONDO
THE SAVAGE LAND
NOBLE OUTLAW
CIMARRON JORDAN
LORDS OF THE LAND
ONE LAST TOWN
TEXAS EMPIRE
JURY OF SIX

AVAILABLE FROM ST. MARTIN'S PAPERBACKS

MANHUNTER

MATT BRAUN

St. Martin's Paperbacks

This novel is a work of historical fiction. Names, characters, places and incidents relating to non-historical figures are either the product of the author's imagination or are used fictitiously, and any resemblance of such non-historical figures, places or incidents to actual persons, living or dead, events or locales is entirely coincidental.

MANHUNTER / DEADWOOD

Manhunter copyright © 1981 by Matthew Braun.
Deadwood copyright © 1981 by Matthew Braun. Published by arrangement with Pocket Books.

Cover photo © Creatas/Inmagine.

ISBN: 0-312-94604-X
EAN: 978-0-312-94604-3

Printed in the United States of America

Manhunter Sphere Books Ltd edition / 1982
St. Martin's Paperbacks edition / March 2003

Deadwood Pocket Books edition / December 1981
St. Martin's Paperbacks edition / August 2003

St. Martin's Paperbacks are published by St. Martin's Press, 175 Fifth Avenue, New York, NY 10010.

10 9 8 7 6 5 4 3 2 1

To Bess and Paul
whose belief and support
are beyond measure

Author's Note

The Old West produced a unique collection of rogues and rascals.

Outlaws and grifters, gunfighters and gamblers, they formed a roll call unsurpassed for shady exploits. Certain of these men were supreme egotists, actively courting fame and glory. They manipulated the media of the day, and the media, with a public clamouring for larger-than-life heroes, was delighted to oblige. Dime novelists, abetted by newspapers and periodicals, transformed these rogues and rascals into the stuff of legend. Later, with a remarkable disdain for the facts, movies and television added their own brand of hype to an already false mythology. The end result was a pantheon of stalwart gunmen and chivalrous desperadoes.

For the most part, it was folklore founded on invention and lies. And it was sold to America by hucksters with an uncanny knack for distorting the truth.

Jesse James was one of the myths fobbed off on a gullible public. Far from the Robin Hood of legend, he was a paranoid outcast who robbed banks and trains rather than work for a living. He was also a master of propaganda. Throughout his career as an outlaw, he wrote articulate and persuasive letters to the editors of several midwestern newspapers. The letters were duly reprinted, and accounted, in large measure, for the belief that he "robbed the rich and gave to the poor." In reality, he was something less than charitable; there is no documented instance of his assisting the needy or championing the cause of oppressed people. He was, moreover, a sadistic killer without mercy or remorse. Still Jesse James captured the public's imagination, and he did it with a certain flair. He was his own best press agent.

Yet every myth has some foundation in fact. The Old West produced many mankillers who were both honourable and courageous. For the most part, however, they shunned the limelight. Because they weren't seeking fame or immortality, they made poor source material for dime novelists and hack journalists. The upshot was that their attributes were grafted onto the rogues and rascals. America, as a result, ended up revering men who deserved no place in our folklore. The truly legendary characters of the era became little more than footnotes in the pages of history.

Luke Starbuck was one such man. His character is a composite of several Old West detectives, who were the most feared mankillers of the day. They worked undercover—generally in disguise—and thus their exploits are not widely known. In *The Manhunter* Starbuck accepts an assignment that pits him against Jesse James. Though the events depicted are historically accurate, certain liberties have been taken regarding time and place. Yet the characters are real, and the revelations unearthed by Starbuck are fact, not fiction. His investigation at last brings to light the truth about Jesse James. A hundred years overdue, it is nonetheless a story that needs telling.

The Manhunter also reveals Starbuck's role in the

death of Jesse James. A compelling tale, it was until now shrouded in mystery. Luke Starbuck told no one of the part he played. For he was a man of many parts and many faces. None of them his own.

CHAPTER 1

The men rode into town from the north. Their horses were held to a walk and they kept to the middle of the street. Unhurried, with three riders out front and two more trailing behind, they proceeded towards the centre of town. No one spoke.

The community, like many midwestern farm towns, was bisected by a main thoroughfare. The business district, small but prosperous, consisted of four stores, a saloon and a blacksmith shop, and one bank. There were few people about and little activity in the downtown area. A typical Monday morning, it was the slowest time of the week. Which, in part, accounted for the five riders. Their business was better conducted in confidence and without crowds.

The men were unremarkable in appearance. Neatly dressed, they wore drab woolen suits and slouch hats. Three were clean-shaven and the other two sported well-trimmed beards. All of them were above average height, but only one, somewhat large and burly, was noticeable for his size. Their mounts were an altogether different matter. At first glance, the animals appeared to be common saddle stock. On closer examination, however, a uniform sleekness and conformation became apparent. The horses were built for endurance and stamina, staying power over long distances.

In the centre of town, the riders wheeled to the left and halted before the bank. There was a military precision to their movements, smooth and coordinated, somehow practiced. The two bearded men stepped down and handed their reins to the third man in the front rank. Without hesitation, the two riders in the rear positioned their mounts to cover the street in both directions. A moment passed while one of the bearded men took a long look around. His bearing was that of a field commander and he subjected the whole of the business district to a slow, careful scrutiny. Then, followed by his companion, he turned and entered the bank.

Inside the door, he stopped and quickly scanned the room. The cashier's window and the vault were to the rear. He noted that the vault door was closed and, to all appearances, locked. To his immediate left, seated behind a desk, the bank president was engaged in conversation with three middle-aged men. By their dress and manner of speech, they were gentlemen landowners and therefore no threat. He pulled a .45 Smith & Wesson revolver from a shoulder holster inside his suit jacket.

"Get your hands up! Keep 'em up and you won't get hurt!"

There was an instant of leaden silence. The cashier froze, watching him intently. At the desk, the president stared at him with disbelief, and the three customers swiveled around in unison. Suddenly, eyes wide with terror, one of them panicked and bolted from his chair.

"Robbers! The bank's being robbed!"

A gun exploded and the man staggered, clutching at his arm. His face went ashen, then he passed out, collapsing at the knees, and dropped to the floor. One eye on the cashier, the gang leader glanced over his shoulder. His companion, standing just inside the doorway, held a pistol trained on the men at the desk. A wisp of smoke curled upward from the barrel.

"Goddamnit!" he said gruffly. "Did you have to shoot him?"

"Seemed like the thing to do. Leastways it made him close his trap."

"Maybe so," the gang leader snapped. "But that gunshot will draw a crowd just sure as hell."

"I don't recollect that ever stopped you before."

"All right, forget it! Keep them birds covered while I tend to business."

With that, he walked to the rear of the bank and stopped before the cashier's window. He casually rested the butt of the Smith & Wesson on the counter, and nodded to the cashier.

"What's your name?"

"Martin," the cashier muttered. "Robert Martin."

"Well, Mr. Martin, how would you like to make it home to supper tonight?"

"I'd like that."

"Then get busy and open that vault. No fool tricks or I'll blow your head off. Hop to it!"

Martin eyed him steadily a moment, then turned towards the vault. A roar of gunfire, several shots in rapid succession, suddenly sounded from outside. The gang leader looked around and saw his companion peering out the door.

"What's all that about?"

"Nothin' serious. Some of the locals got nosy and the boys warned them to stay off the street."

"Keep a sharp lookout."

Turning back, he started and let loose a harsh grunt. Robert Martin had the cash drawer open and was clawing frantically at a revolver hidden beneath a stack of bills. The gang leader pulled the trigger and his Smith & Wesson spat a sheet of flame. The slug punched through Martin's forehead and tore out the back of his skull. A halo of bone and brain matter misted the air around his head, and he stood there a moment, dead on his feet. Then he folded at the waist and slumped to the floor.

"Dumb bastard!" the gang leader cursed savagely. "Told you I'd blow your head off!"

Leaning across the counter, he began scooping bills out of the cash drawer and stuffing them into his pockets. Once the drawer was empty, he wheeled about and marched towards the front of the bank. He signalled the bearded man at the door.

"Let's go! We're all done here."

"What about the vault?"

"No time! Another couple of minutes and the whole town'll be up in arms."

"The boys won't like it. They rode a long ways for a payday."

"Tough titty!" he barked. "You should've thought of that before you got an itchy trigger finger. C'mon, let's clear out!"

The din of gunfire swelled as they moved through the door. Still mounted, the gang members outside were winging random shots through store windows along the street. The merchants and townspeople had taken cover, and as yet there was no return fire. Crossing the broadwalk, the bearded men hastily swung into their saddles. Then, with everyone mounted, the robbers reined about and rode north out of town.

A short distance upstreet the gang leader abruptly brought his horse to a halt. Where the business district ended, the residential area began, and both sides of the street were lined with modest homes. Outside one house, a teenage boy stood at the edge of the yard. His eyes were filled with a mix of fear and youthful curiosity. He watched with wonder as the rest of the robbers skidded to a stop and turned their mounts. The gang leader calmly drew his pistol and extended it to arm's length. He stared down the sights at the boy.

"Come out to get an eyeful, did you?"

The youngster swallowed, licked his lips. "I didn't mean no harm, mister."

"Your mama should've taught you better manners."

Thumbing the hammer on his pistol, the gang leader sighted quickly and fired. A brilliant red splotch appeared on the pocket of the boy's shirt. He reeled backward, then suddenly went limp and fell spread-eagled in the yard. As he hit the ground, the other bearded robber kneed his horse forward, blocking the gang leader.

"Why'd you do that? Why'd you kill him?"

"I felt like it."

"For God's sake, he's just a kid!"

"So what."

"*So what!* You took your spite out on a kid. That's what!"

"Watch your mouth."

"The hell I will!"

The burly rider reined his horse closer. "What's the matter, Frank?"

"Ask Jesse."

"I'm askin' you."

"We didn't finish the job! Jesse said there wasn't time to clean out the vault, and now he's mad at himself."

"Wasn't time?" The large man scowled, turned his gaze on the gang leader. "Then how come you had time to stop and kill that kid?"

"Don't push me, Cole."

"And don't you try throwin' your weight around! We didn't ride to hell and gone just to come away with chicken feed."

"I told you to lay off! I won't tell you again."

"Well, I'll damn sure tell you something! Me and the boys are gonna go back and empty that vault. You can come or stay as you please."

"I'm warning you—!"

"Jesse, one of these days you're gonna warn me once too often."

A shot cracked and they instinctively ducked as a slug whizzed past their heads. Looking around, they saw a man standing in the middle of the street downtown. He had a rifle thrown to his shoulder, and as he fired the second time other men rushed to join him. The gang leader booted his horse and rapped out a sharp command.

"Too late now! Let's ride!"

A barrage from downtown settled the matter. With lead whistling around their ears, the robbers bent low and kicked their mounts into a headlong gallop. Moments later they cleared the edge of town and thundered north along a rutted wagon road.

Their leader, well, out in front, never once looked back.

CHAPTER 2

Starbuck wiped his razor dry and walked from the bathroom. He selected a fresh linen shirt from the bureau, then took a conservative brown suit from the wardrobe. After knotting his tie, he slipped into a suit jacket and checked himself in the mirror. No dandy, he was nonetheless particular about his appearance.

Turning from the mirror, he moved to the bed and took a .45 Colt from beneath the pillow. He shoved the gun into a crossdraw holster worn on his left side, positioned directly above the pants pocket. The holster was hand sewn and wet-moulded to the Colt, crafted in such a manner that his belt snugged it flat against his body. The natural drape of his jacket concealed the entire rig and eliminated any telltale bulge. Only those who knew him well were aware that he went armed at all times.

Fully dressed, he walked towards the door leading to the sitting room. His suite in the Brown Palace Hotel was comfortable, though modest in size, and handsomely appointed. Off and on, after establishing headquarters in Denver, he had debated buying a house. His detective business kept him on the move—often for months at a stretch—and the cost of maintaining a suite on a per-

manent basis sometimes seemed exorbitant. Yet a house
would have tied him down, and he wasn't a man who
formed attachments easily. Besides, the hotel provided
room service and laundry, not to mention a certain freedom of movement. All things considered, he was satisfied with the arrangement. It somehow suited his style.

Entering the sitting room, he nodded to the girl and
took a seat beside her on the sofa. A singer, her stage
name was Lola Montana, and she was the star attraction
at the Alcazar Variety Theater. She was also his current
bed partner, and for the past few weeks she had slept
over almost every night. Still, in his view, she was a
pleasant arrangement, with no strings attached.

A room-service cart was positioned beside the sofa.
Earlier, they had shared a breakfast of ham and eggs,
topped off with sourdough biscuits and wild honey.
Now, luxuriating over a cup of coffee, Lola sat with her
legs tucked under the folds of a filmy peignoir. The swell
of her breasts was visible through the sheer fabric and
she noted his appreciative glance. She vamped him with
an engaging smile.

"You look real spiffy this morning, lover."

"I sort of like your getup, too. Hides just enough to
give a fellow ideas."

"Ooo?" She slowly batted her eyelashes. "I thought
by now you knew all my secrets."

"Let's just say you showed me a few surprises last
night."

She laughed a low, throaty laugh. "The way I remember it, you rang the bell a couple of times yourself."

"Worked out even, then, didn't it?"

"How so?"

" 'Cause you rung the ding-dong clean out of mine."

His bantering tone delighted her. Normally reserved,
he was a man of caustic wit but little natural humour.

Like everyone else in Denver, she knew he was a man-hunter—by some accounts, a mankiller—and a detective of formidable reputation. Danger intrigued her, and from the outset she'd been captivated by the fact that he looked the part as well. Corded and lean, with wide shoulders and a muscular build, he stood six feet tall. His eyes were pale blue, framed by a square jaw and light chestnut hair, and he gave the uncanny impression of seeing straight through another person. She thought his look not so much cold as simply devoid of emotion. The quiet, impersonal look of a man who would kill quickly, and without regret.

Today, however, his manner seemed light, almost chipper. She took that as a good sign, and wondered if he'd decided to unbend a little, let her have a glimpse of the man beneath the hard exterior. She felt no real conviction that it was true, and yet . . . a girl could always wish.

"Why not take the day off?" She stretched like a cat, and gave him a beguiling grin. "We could just loaf around, and who knows—maybe I'd show you some more surprises."

"Don't tempt me," Starbuck said genially. "The day's already half gone, and I've got some errands that won't wait."

"You know what they say, all work and no play."

"That's a laugh! You've kept me so busy, I haven't hardly had time to tend to business."

"Detective business?" she inquired innocently. "Or monkey business?"

Starbuck cocked one ribald eye at her. "I'll give you three guesses, and the first two don't count."

"Mr. Mysterious himself!" She mocked him with a minxlike look. "Got a hot case cooking, honeybun? C'mon, you can tell Lola."

"Strictly back burner," Starbuck said vaguely. "Nothing worth the telling."

She laughed spontaneously, in sheer delight. "You're one of a kind. Luke! I've just been told to butt out and damned if you didn't make me like it. That's real talent!"

"Ask me no questions and I'll tell you no lies."

Starbuck understood it was a game, lighthearted and meant in jest. Unlike many women he'd known, she wanted nothing of him. A good time and a few laughs— along with their romps in bed—were all she sought from the liaison. She possessed a kind of bursting vitality, and she seemed to have discovered the instant recipe for fun. Then, too, there were her physical attributes, which amounted to an altogether stunning package. She was smallish and compact, with coltish grace and a dazzling figure. Her features were mobile and animated, with a wide, sensual mouth, and her hair hung long and golden. She was impudent and puckish, with a sort of mischievous verve, and the tricks she brought to his bed never failed to amaze him. All in all, she was his kind of woman, sportive and undemanding, with no claims on tomorrow or the future. He thought it might last awhile.

"All right, lover," she said cheerfully. "Off to the races! Get your business done and we'll save our playtime for tonight."

"That sounds like a proposition."

"There's one way to find out."

"Then I reckon I'd better drop around to the theatre tonight."

"You miss my show and you'll never find out! How's that for a proposition?"

"Best offer I've had today."

She leaned forward and brushed his lips with a kiss. "See you there?"

"Count on it."

Starbuck rose and walked to the foyer. He took a wide-brimmed Stetson from the closet, jammed it on his head, and then shrugged into his overcoat. When he stepped into the hall, Lola poured herself another cup of coffee and lounged back on the sofa. A slow kittenish smile touched the corners of her mouth.

Outside the hotel Starbuck turned onto Larimer Street. It was a bitter cold day, with savage winds howling down from the northwest. A metallic sky rolled overhead and snow flurries peppered his face. As he passed the police station, he pulled up the collar of his coat and stuck his hands in his pockets. With the wind pushing him along, he rounded the corner and headed directly across town.

Several minutes later he crossed Blake Street. His destination was a small shop wedged between a pool hall and a hardware store. On the window was a neatly lettered sign, chipped and fading with age.

DANIEL CAMERON
GUNSMITH
PISTOLS—RIFLES—SHOTGUNS

An overhead bell jing-a-linged as Starbuck hurried through the door. The walls along both sides of the shop were lined with racks of long guns, and towards the rear a glass showcase was filled with pistols. Beyond the showcase, a grey-haired man turned from a workbench at the sound of the bell. Starbuck brushed snow off his coat and moved down the aisle.

"Afternoon, Daniel."

"Well, Luke!" Cameron warmly shook his hand. "I was beginning to think you'd forgotten our project."

"No," Starbuck said equably. "Too many irons in the fire, that's all."

"So I've heard." Cameron let a sly smile cross his face. "Apparently Lola Montana is a full-time . . . avocation."

Starbuck grinned. "If that means she keeps me busy, you're right. Course, I wouldn't exactly call it a chore."

"No need to explain." Cameron lifted his hands in an exaggerated gesture. "A man needs diversion! Enjoy it while you're young."

"I'm doing my damnedest," Starbuck said with heavy good humour. "How're things with you? Any luck?"

"Luke, I think I'm onto something. Not precisely what we're after, but close. Very close."

"Tell me about it."

"I'll do better than that. Come along and judge for yourself."

A master gunsmith, Cameron possessed an innovative mind and an unquenchable thirst to explore. Always receptive to a challenge, he had agreed to tackle a problem posed by Starbuck. The bullets commonly available were efficient killers but poor manstoppers. An outlaw, though mortally wounded in a gunfight, would often live long enough to empty his pistol. What Starbuck wanted was a bullet that would stop the other man instantly, neutralise him on the spot and take him out of the fight. For the past several weeks, engrossed in the project, Cameron had experimented with radical new bullet designs. Today, he proudly demonstrated the end result.

In the back room of the shop, Cameron lined up three Colt .45 shells on a table. The first was a factory loading, with the standard round pug-nosed bullet. The next shell, loaded with Cameron's new design, had a slug with shoulders which gradually tapered to a flat nose. The last shell was unlike anything Starbuck had ever seen. In

effect, Cameron had turned his new slug upside down
and loaded it backwards. The nose of the slug was now
inside the casing, and the base, which was blunt and
truncated, was now seated in the forward position. After
a brief explanation, Cameron loaded the shells into a
Colt sixgun.

Along the rear wall were arranged three bales of wet
newspaper that had been tightly bound with rope. The
distance was less than five yards, and each of the bales
was marked with a bold X in the centre. Cameron aimed
and fired, shifting from one bale to another, splitting the
X with each shot. Then he walked forward, followed by
Starbuck, and cut the bales open with a jackknife. The
experiment spoke for itself.

The standard pug-nosed bullet had penetrated three-
quarters of the way through the first bale. The bullet was
virtually unmarred and still retained its original shape.
The flat-nose slug, which was slightly deformed, had
penetrated more than halfway through the second bale.
Within the third bale, the reverse-loaded slug had penetrated scarcely one-third of the way through the wet
newspaper. Yet the truncated base, upon impact with the
bale, had been deformed beyond recognition. The entire
slug had expanded, squashed front to rear, and emerged
a mushroom-shaped hunk of lead.

"Quite an improvement," Cameron said, holding the
slug between his fingertips. "The factory load expended
all its energy drilling through the bale. Even my new
design did much the same thing. But the reverse load!
As you can see, the mushroom effect caused the bullet
to impart its energy quickly and with massive shock."

Starbuck was impressed. "Would it work the same
way on a man?"

"Much better," Cameron assured him. "The shock effect on human tissue would be far greater than it is on wet newsprint."

"Would it stop him cold?" Starbuck persisted. "Dead in his tracks?"

"Good question." Cameron's expression was abstracted. "I suppose we won't know that until you shoot someone, will we?"

"What about accuracy?"

"Now there we have a slight hitch. At long range, it's not as accurate as a factory load. On the other hand, most of your work is fairly close up. What would you estimate . . . five yards, ten at the outside?"

"I reckon it'd average that or less."

"Then you have no problem." Cameron tossed him the slug. "Go try it on someone, Luke! I'm willing to bet it's a manstopper."

Starbuck left the shop with a box of the new shells in his overcoat pocket. His faith in Daniel Cameron, however, rode in the crossdraw holster on his belt. The Colt was now loaded with blunt-nosed slugs.

Starbuck's next stop was his office. Located around the corner from the Windsor Hotel, the office was a second-floor cubbyhole, with no sign on the door and spartan as a monk's cell. Essentially it was a clearinghouse, with a secretary to handle correspondence and light bookkeeping chores. All else, especially matters of a confidential nature, Starbuck committed to memory.

His secretary, Verna Phelps, greeted him with prune-faced civility. Her desk and chair, along with a battered file cabinet, were the only furnishings in the room. Her cool manner stemmed from the fact that she hadn't seen Starbuck in almost two weeks. Though Denver was a cosmopolitan city—with a population approaching 100,000—one of the holdovers from its frontier days was an active and highly efficient gossip mill. Almost from the start, she had known the unsavory details of Starbuck's latest dalliance. And in her most charitable moments she considered Lola Montana nothing short of a wanton hussy.

With no great urgency, Starbuck sifted through a stack of mail now several days old. One by one he dropped letters from various railroads, stagecoach lines, and mining companies on the desk. A man of means—with investments in commercial real estate and a portfolio of major stocks—he had no compelling financial need to work. Then, too, his reputation allowed him to accept only those assignments that piqued his interest.

Several of his previous cases were celebrated for the notoriety of the outlaws involved. He had been instrumental in ridding New Mexico of Billy the Kid and largely through his efforts Wyatt Earp had been run out of Arizona. Apart from his eminence as a detective, he was also noted as a mankiller. By rough calculation—since he never discussed the topic—journalists estimated he had killed at least eighteen men. As a result, his fame had spread across the West, and he could now pick and choose from among the jobs offered. Yet fame, with the attendant publicity and newspaper photos, had destroyed the anonymity he'd once enjoyed. These days, he operated undercover, and always in disguise.

One letter caught his interest. Postmarked St. Louis, it was signed by the president of the International Bankers Association. Short and somewhat cryptic in tone, it requested his presence in St. Louis at the earliest possible date. He studied the letter a moment, then stuck it into his pocket. Looking up, he indicated the stack of mail he'd dropped on the desk.

"Write those outfits and tell them I'm unavailable till further notice."

A spinster, Verna Phelps had plain dumpling features and her hair was pulled severely away from her face into a tight chignon. She heartily applauded Starbuck's work as a detective, and took a certain grim satisfaction in the number of outlaws he'd killed. Yet she disapproved of his personal life, and viewed his conduct with women as reprehensible. Now, with a dour nod, she shuffled the letters into a neat pile.

"Are you accepting the St. Louis offer?"

"Maybe," Starbuck said noncommittally. "All depends on what they've got in mind."

"How long will you be gone?"

Starbuck shrugged. "Look for me when you see me."

"Very well." Her voice was tinged with reproach. "And the hotel suite? Shall I look after it as usual, or will your lady friend be staying on while you're gone?"

"Never give up, do you, Verna?" Starbuck smiled, and shook his head. "Follow the usual routine. Have the suite spruced up and tell the desk to send any messages over to you."

"Just as you wish, Mr. Starbuck."

"Hold down the fort." Starbuck waved, turning towards the door. "I'll be in touch."

Verna Phelps gave a rabbity sniff and watched him out the door. She marvelled at his devilish ways and his taste for cheap, tawdry women. Then, blushing beet red, she was jolted by a sudden thought.

She wondered how it might have been . . . if she were younger.

Starbuck arrived at the Alcazar Variety Theater late that evening. The owner greeted him warmly, and escorted him to his usual table down front. A complimentary bottle of champagne materialised, and he settled back to enjoy the show.

Several men, seated at nearby tables, exchanged friendly nods. But no one attempted to approach Starbuck, or engage him in conversation. A private man, he tolerated few questions. Nor would he indulge drunks or the idly curious. He was known on sight, and what he did for a living was no secret. Still, though he was widely admired, he never spoke of his business to anyone. That too was known, and while some people considered it eccentric, his wishes were respected. The sporting crowd of Denver had long ago learned to take him on his own terms. Or not at all. Which suited him all the way around. He was alone even in the largest crowd.

Tonight, a solitary figure lost in his own thoughts, his mind centred wholly on the moment. Tomorrow he would entrain for St. Louis, and whatever happened would happen, all in good time. Before tomorrow, there was one last night with Lola, and not an hour to be wasted. His anticipation was heightened all the more as the curtain rose and the orchestra struck up a catchy tune. Lola went prancing across the stage, her legs flashing and her breasts jiggling over the top of a peekaboo gown. The audience roared and she gave them a dazzling smile. Then her husky alto voice belted out across the hall.

> *"Oh, don't you remember sweet Betsy from Pike,*
> *Crossed the great mountains with her lover Ike,*
> *With two yoke of oxen, a large yellow dog,*
> *A tall shanghai rooster and one spotted hog!"*

CHAPTER 3

St. Louis itself was worth the trip.

Starbuck arrived on a blustery January evening. From Union Station, he took a hansom cab to one of the fashionable hotels on Olive Street. There he registered under an assumed name and gave San Antonio as his hometown. To all appearances, he was a well-to-do Texan visiting the big city on business.

A precautionary measure, the deception had by now become second nature. Only a couple of months past, the *Police Gazette* had done an article that labelled Starbuck the foremost mankiller of the day. He had no idea whether his notoriety extended as far eastward as Missouri. Yet he was a man who played the odds, and assumed nothing. Outside Denver, he always travelled under an alias.

After supper in the hotel dining room, he went for a stroll. St. Louis, with a population exceeding the half-million mark, was the largest city he'd ever visited. The downtown district was a hub of culture and commerce. Theatres and swank hotels, office buildings and banks and business establishments occupied several square blocks between Market Street and Delmar Boulevard. A sprawling industrial section, which had gravitated early to the riverfront, lay stretched along the levee. Steamboats were rapidly losing ground to railroads, and the city had developed into a manufacturing centre for clothing, shoes, and various kinds of machinery. Still, for all its advancement, St. Louis remained a major market for hides and wool, horses and mules, and a wide assortment of farm produce. However cosmopolitan, it had not yet fully made the transition from its frontier origins.

On the waterfront, Starbuck stood for a long while staring out across the Mississippi. The Eads Bridge, completed only eight years before, spanned the great river like a steel monolith. Far in the distance, he saw the lights of towns ranged along the Illinois shoreline. Not easily impressed, he was nonetheless taken with the sight. He had travelled the West from the Gulf of Mexico to the Pacific Coast, but he'd never had occasion to look upon the Mississippi. The breadth of the river, with girded steel linking one bank to the other, seemed to him a marvel almost beyond comprehension. He thought back to his days on the Rio Grande, and slowly shook his head. Age and experience, he told himself, altered a man's perception of things.

A nomadic westerner, Starbuck had grown to manhood in Texas. The Civil War, which had left him without family or roots, taught him that killing was a matter of expediency. Thereafter, he accepted abuse from no man, and quickly accommodated those who overstepped themselves. For a time he drifted from ranch to ranch, a saddletramp beckoned onward by wanderlust. Then, all within a period of a few years, he went from trailhand to ranch foreman to range detective. Quite by coincidence, one job leading to another, he discovered his niche in life.

Once his reputation as a manhunter spread, Starbuck

branched out from chasing horse thieves and common
rustlers. Offers from stagelines and railroads afforded
greater challenge, and there he came into his own as a
detective. Despite his renown, however, he was never
really satisfied with yesterday's accomplishments. He
enjoyed what he did for a livelihood, and he took pride
in his work. Yet something of the old wanderlust still
remained. He forever sought greater challenges, and he
was cursed with an itch to move on to the next case. A
blooded hunter, his quarry was man. And only when the
chase was joined was he truly content.

Now, his gaze fixed on the Mississippi, he wondered
what tomorrow would bring. His wire had confirmed the
time and place for the meeting. Otis Tilford, president
of the International Bankers Association, was expecting
him first thing in the morning. An assessment would be
made, and assuming he passed muster, an assignment
would be offered. The only imponderable was whether
or not he would accept. He was looking for tomorrows,
not yesterdays, and nothing else would turn the trick.
Nothing and no-damn-body.

He turned from the wharves and walked towards his
hotel.

The Merchants & Farmers Bank Building stood on the
corner of Fourth and Delmar. Starbuck entered the lobby
shortly before nine o'clock and took an elevator to the
third floor. At the end of the hall, he spotted a door with
frosted glass and gilt lettering. He moved directly along
the corridor, observant and suddenly alert. The lettering
on the door was sparkling fresh.

Inside the waiting room he closed the door and doffed
his hat. A mousy-looking woman, with grey hair and
granny glasses, sat behind a reception desk. She looked
him over, stern as a drill sergeant, and nodded.

"May I help you?"

"I'm Luke Starbuck. I have an appointment with Mr. Tilford."

"Yes, of course." She rose, bustling around the desk. "Please have a seat, Mr. Starbuck. I'll inform Mr. Tilford you're here."

Starbuck watched as she hurried down a hallway. Then, still standing, he slowly inspected the waiting room. All the furniture, including the receptionist's desk and a couple of wingbacked chairs, looked as though it had been delivered only that morning. A door on the opposite side of the room was open, and through it he saw several clerks in what appeared to be a general office. Their desks and a row of file cabinets along the far wall also looked fresh off a showroom floor. Whatever he'd expected, something about the layout put him on guard. He made mental note to do lots of listening, play it close to the vest. And volunteer nothing.

The receptionist reappeared, motioning him forward. "Will you come this way? Mr. Tilford can see you now."

"Much obliged," Starbuck said pleasantly. "I was just admiring your offices. Got a real handsome setup."

"Thank you."

"Been here long?"

"I beg your pardon?"

"Well, everything looks so new and all. I thought maybe you'd just opened for business?"

"No." She did not elaborate. "This way, Mr. Starbuck."

Starbuck followed her down the hall. She ushered him into a spacious office and stepped aside. The room was panelled in dark wood, with ornately carved furniture and a plush carpet underfoot. A coal-burning fireplace glowed cherry red, and directly opposite was an imposing walnut desk. Behind it, seated in a tall judge's chair, was a man who looked like a frog perched on a toad-stool. He was completely bald, with a wattled neck and beady eyes, and his oval face was peppered with liver spots. When he rose, extending his hand, his posture was shrunken and stooped. Yet, oddly enough, his voice was firm and lordly.

"Welcome to St. Louis, Mr. Starbuck."

"Pleasure's all mine, Mr. Tilford."

"Please be seated." Tilford let go his hand, and dropped into the judge's chair. "I trust your trip was without incident."

"More or less." Starbuck took an armchair before the desk. "One train ride's pretty much like another."

"No doubt." Tilford appeared to lose interest in the subject. "I appreciate your quick response to our request."

"When a man says 'urgent,' I take him at his word."

"Commendable," Tilford said, no irony in his tone. "All the more so since your services are much in demand these days."

"Don't believe everything you read in the *Police Gazette*."

Tilford's laugh was as false as an old maid's giggle. "On the contrary, Mr. Starbuck! I found the article most informative. Few men have your zeal."

"Oh?" Starbuck asked casually. "How so?"

"Once you accept a case, you display a remarkable tendency to see it through to a conclusion. Would you consider that a fair statement?"

"I generally finish what I start."

"Precisely." Tilford gave him an evaluating glance. "And more often than not you finish it permanently. Correct?"

Starbuck regarded him thoughtfully, "Why do I get

the feeling you know the answer before you ask the question?"

"I too am a man of zeal," Tilford replied loftily. "I had you checked out thoroughly before sending that wire."

"Sounds reasonable." Starbuck smiled humourlessly. "Hope you got your money's worth."

"The queries were of a personal nature. A man in my position develops certain alliances, and we often exchange information. All on a confidential basis, of course."

"Anyone I know?"

"What's in a name?" Tilford spread his hands in a bland gesture. "Suffice it to say you come highly recommended by the Central Pacific and Wells Fargo."

"I reckon they had no room for complaint."

"Indeed!" Tilford wagged his head. "You are too modest by far, Mr. Starbuck. I am reliably informed that you have no equal when it comes to meting out justice to outlaws."

"There's all kinds of justice."

"True." Tilford pursed his lips and nodded solemnly. "But only one kind of any lasting value. Wouldn't you agree, Mr. Starbuck?"

Starbuck took out the makings and rolled himself a smoke. He struck a match, all the while watching Tilford, and lit the cigarette. Then, inhaling deeply, he settled back in his chair.

"Suppose we get down to cases?"

"By all means." Tilford leaned forward, stared earnestly at him. "I presume you are familiar with the James-Younger gang?"

Starbuck looked at him without expression. "Jesse James?"

Tilford made a small nod of acknowledgement. "Over

the last seventeen years James and his gang have robbed dozens of banks and trains—"

"So I've heard."

"—and killed at least a score of innocent people."

"I wouldn't argue the figure."

"And yet," Tilford said in an aggrieved tone, "they are free to come and go as they please throughout Missouri."

"I understood," Starbuck observed neutrally, "that the Pinkertons had been brought in on the case."

"Quite true." Tilford's eyelids drooped scornfully. "Some eight years ago the Pinkerton Agency was retained for the express purpose of putting a halt to these depredations."

"That long?" Starbuck blew a plume of smoke into the air. "Guess they've had a run of bad luck."

"You're too charitable," Tilford said, not without bitterness. "To put it bluntly, Allan Pinkerton has accomplished nothing—absolutely nothing!—and he has been paid very handsomely for doing it."

"Nobody's perfect," Starbuck commented dryly. "Maybe it's time for the worm to turn."

"I seriously doubt it." Tilford shook his head in exasperation. "A coalition of banks and railroads still has Pinkerton under retainer. In my view, however, it's a waste of money. Given another eight years, he would be no closer than he is today."

"Sounds like you hold the Pinkertons in pretty low opinion."

"Unless I'm mistaken"—Tilford watched him carefully—"that is an opinion we share, Mr. Starbuck."

Starbuck flipped a hand back and forth. "Let's just say I think they're a little bit overrated."

"How would you like an opportunity to prove your point?"

"Try me and see."

"Very well." Tilford's voice dropped. "We wish to retain your services, Mr. Starbuck. Within reasonable limits, you can name your own price."

"Exactly what services did you have in mind?"

Tilford's face took on a sudden hard cast. "We want Jesse James killed."

Starbuck's gaze was direct now, his ice-blue eyes alert. "Who is 'we?' "

"Why, the International Bankers Association. I thought you understood—"

"Try another tune." Starbuck fixed him with that same disquieting stare. "The lettering on your door looks like the paint's hardly had time to dry. Every stick of furniture in your office is brand new, and unless I miss my guess, so's your association." He paused, his eyes cold and questioning. "I'll ask you again, and this time I want some straight talk. Who is 'we?' "

A shadow of irritation crossed Tilford's features. "You are a very discerning man, Mr. Starbuck. I commend you on your powers of observation. However, I am not in the habit of being interrogated. Nor do I appreciate your rather cavalier manner."

"That's your problem," Starbuck said woodenly. "Either I get an explanation or we don't do business. Take your pick."

Tilford reflected a moment. "Very well," he answered at length. "A number of bankers around the Midwest deplore Pinkerton's lack of results. We have severed our ties with the railroad and banking coalition, and formed our own organisation. Our purpose is legitimate and quite straightforward. We intend to eradicate Jesse James and those of a similar persuasion."

"How do you fit into the picture?"

"I am president and chief stockholder of the Merchants & Farmers Bank. In short, I own the bank downstairs and the building in which we are seated."

Starbuck played a hunch. "From what I've heard, James normally concentrates on small-town banks. So that lets you out, unless you've got some personal score to settle. Suppose you tell me about it?"

"Are you a mind reader as well as a detective, Mr. Starbuck?"

"Tricks of the trade," Starbuck said flatly. "I'm waiting for an answer."

Tilford regarded him somberly. "Last July the evening train out of Kansas City was robbed. The conductor and a passenger by the name of McMillan were murdered in cold blood. Jesse James, and his brother Frank, were positively identified as the killers. Frank McMillan was my son-in-law."

"Tough break." Starbuck stubbed out his cigarette in an ashtray. "Any special reason you took it so personal?"

"I sent Frank to Kansas City on business. He was an officer of this bank, the husband of my only daughter, and the father of my grandchildren. As should be obvious, I feel responsible for his death."

"In other words," Starbuck ventured, "you want an eye for an eye. You formed the association—and gave it a high-sounding name—in order to put a legitimate front on personal vengeance."

"Not altogether," Tilford countered. "By ridding society of Jesse James, I am also performing a public service. I see those as compatible goals—a worthy endeavour!"

"Why kill him?" Starbuck inquired. "Why not bring him to trial and let him hang? That way the state executes him . . . instead of you."

"He must be killed!" Tilford's voice was heated and vindictive. "No jury in this state would convict Jesse

James. Nor would any court dare impose the death penalty."

"What makes you so sure?"

Tilford rose and moved to the wall directly behind him. With some effort, he lifted a large leather satchel off the floor and dropped it on his desk. Then, his expression grim, he resumed his chair.

"Inside that satchel you will find the Pinkerton file—eight years of investigation and surveillance—on the James-Younger gang. I obtained a duplicate of the file in the hope it would speed your own investigation. Aside from that, it will also convince you that Jesse James can never be convicted in the state of Missouri."

"Out of curiosity"—Starbuck gave him a quizzical look—"how did you come by it?"

"A friend," Tilford explained. "One who owns a railroad and contributes large sums to the settlement of Allan Pinkerton's fee."

Starbuck studied the satchel, thoughtful. For most of his professional career he had lived in the shadow of the world's most famous detective agency. The idea of going head to head with the Pinkertons—and beating them—was a challenge he found too tempting to resist. At last, with an overdrawn gesture, he looked up at Tilford.

"I don't work cheap."

"Ten thousand now," Tilford said gravely, "and ten thousand more when the job is completed. With one added proviso."

"Which is?"

"You are to kill Frank James as well."

"Want your pound of flesh, don't you?"

"I want them dead, Mr. Starbuck! Dead and buried—and forgotten."

"Hell, why not?" Starbuck shrugged. "I reckon one deserves it as much as the other."

"Then we have an agreement?"

"You ante up and we're in business. Two for the price of one, delivery guaranteed."

"Where will you start?"

Starbuck smiled cryptically. "Where Pinkerton should have started."

"Oh?" Tilford appeared bemused. "Where might that be?"

"Let's just say it won't be out in the open."

CHAPTER 4

The Pinkerton file was compelling stuff. Starbuck found himself fascinated almost from the first field report, which was dated January 23, 1874. He also found confirmation of what he'd suspected all along.

Jesse James was no garden-variety outlaw.

For three days and nights, Starbuck holed up in his hotel room. The file, he determined early on, could not be let out of his sight. One look by a snooper would jeopardise the need for secrecy, and pose the even greater threat of a leak to the press. Accordingly, he refused to allow the maids inside, and he himself never set foot outside. All his meals were ordered from room service, and on the first night he sent a bellman to fetch a quart of whiskey. Like a monk sequestered in a cell, he was alone with himself. And the file.

His first chore was to devise some system of organisation. The file was voluminous, and from the outset it was apparent that Allan Pinkerton had a fondness for long, rambling memos. The agency's founder exhorted everyone in his employ—from division chiefs to field operatives—with page after page of detailed instructions regarding the investigation. The flow of paperwork was compounded by the sheer number of personnel involved in the case. Apart from Pinkerton's two sons, who were responsible for field operations, there were a dozen or more investigators active at all times. The avalanche of reports and memos, generated from different parts of the country, was stupefying to contemplate. A method was needed to separate the chaff from the wheat.

Starbuck broke the material down into categories. Allan Pinkerton's directives, which contained little of value, were consigned to an ever-growing pile. Speculative reports were next in line, and armchair analyses by division chiefs formed still another stack. On-the-scene reports, written by field operatives, were divided into those dealing with conjecture and those that dealt in hard intelligence. The latter category, scarcely to Starbuck's surprise, made up the smallest pile. Nevertheless, taken as a whole, the file provided an absorbing overview. Chronicled there was the violent history of the James-Younger gang.

Like many men brutalised by the Civil War, Jesse and Frank James found it difficult to adjust to peacetime. During the hostilities they had ridden with Quantrill's guerrillas, and those savage years had instilled in them a taste for action. Bored and restless, they avoided the family farm and made no effort to earn an honest livelihood. Quickly enough, they developed a reputation as the chief troublemakers of Clay County.

To make matters worse, the Federal occupation forces sought retribution against their defeated enemies. Yet the James brothers were in no greater danger of reprisals than the balance of Quantrill's ex-guerrillas. The vast majority of former Confederates settled down and went to work, determined to put the war behind them. Other men, however, felt society had turned on them, and that a life of robbery and murder was justified. Such was the backdrop against which Jesse and Frank James took the outlaw trail.

At the time, Jesse James was eighteen years of age. Still, for all his youth, he was a blooded veteran and an experienced leader of men. Headstrong, with magnetic force of character, he dominated Frank, who was three years his senior. The Younger brothers, who were boyhood friends and former comrades under Quantrill, were recruited into the gang. Cole Younger, the eldest of the four brothers, was the same age as Frank James. Yet, like Frank, he submitted to the will of a fiery young hothead. By late winter of 1865, the gang was formed, all of them ex-guerrillas and stone-cold killers. Their leader was Jesse James.

Only ten months after the Civil War ended, the long string of depredations committed by the James-Younger gang began. On the morning of February 3, 1866, they rode into Liberty, Missouri, and robbed the Clay County Savings Association of $70,000. It was the first daylight bank robbery in American history, and created a furor in the nation's press. It also served as the template by which the gang would operate over the years ahead. In the course of the holdup, the bank teller and an innocent bystander were callously murdered. The only shots fired were those fired by the gang, and they escaped unharmed. The scene would be repeated time and time again.

For the next eight years the gang roamed the Midwest, robbing trains and looting banks. Their raids were conducted with military precision, and ranged over an area encompassing Missouri, Kansas, Arkansas, Kentucky, and Iowa. The dead littering their backtrail grew in number with each holdup, yet pursuit was rare. Even though the law knew their names, no concerted effort was made to track them to their homeground in Mis-

souri. Like will-o'-the-wisps they appeared from nowhere—hitting fast and hard—then vanished without a
trace. And the bloodletting went on unabated.

Early in 1874 the Pinkerton agency entered the case.
Their failure was monumental, and resulted in an immediate loss of prestige. One of their agents, operating
undercover, was captured in Clay County. With his
hands tied behind his back, he was executed personally
by Jesse James. As an added humiliation—and a warning to all lawmen—his body was left to be savaged by
wild hogs. The incident kindled in Allan Pinkerton an
unyielding hatred for the outlaws. His memos thereafter
took on the fervour and tone of a holy war.

A few months later Pinkerton suffered yet another
loss of face. On a brisk March day, two operatives, accompanied by a deputy sheriff, were surprised by Jim
and John Younger. The encounter occurred on a back-
country road, and in the ensuing shootout both Youngers
were wounded. One of the detectives and the deputy
sheriff were killed on the spot. The second Pinkerton
escaped during the confusion, and thus lived to tell the
tale. While John Younger ultimately died of his wounds,
the message quickly made the rounds among peace officers. Any outsider who ventured into Clay County—
whether Pinkerton or lawman—would be made to pay
the price. And then left to the wild hogs.

In the end a combination of partisan politics and the
terror inspired by the gang defeated the Pinkertons. If a
group of former Quantrill raiders held up a bank or
robbed a train, the common wisdom was that no great
harm had been done. Bankers and railroad barons, who
were considered thieves themselves, could easily afford
the loss.

Friends and relatives, moreover, were always willing
to hide the outlaws. Of no less significance, they also

provided the gang with an efficient and highly reliable intelligence network. No stranger entered the backwoods of Clay County without arousing comment, and word swiftly found its way to those who supported the robbers. Those who were unsympathetic simply tended their own business and made every effort to remain neutral. Forced to choose, few would have taken sides with Yankee detectives in any event. A veil of silence hung like a wintry cloud over all of Clay County.

After losing two operatives, Allan Pinkerton waited almost a year before he again challenged the James boys on homeground. On the night of January 25, 1875, a squad of Pinkerton agents surrounded the home at the family farm. Jesse and Frank, with several members of the gang, had ridden away only hours before. Inside the house were Jesse's mother, his stepfather, Dr. Reuben Samuel, and his young half brother, Archie Samuel. A servant, awakened when the operatives pried open a window shutter, sounded the alarm.

The Pinkertons, determined to capture or kill the James boys, immediately tossed a large iron bomb through the window. While the family stumbled about in the dark, the bomb exploded. A piece of shrapnel struck Jesse's mother and tore off her right arm below the elbow. Across the room, young Archie was hit in the chest by another jagged shard and died instantly. Only the quick thinking of Dr. Samuel, who hastily applied a tourniquet to his wife's arm, saved her from bleeding to death.

With the house ablaze, and no sign of the James boys, the detectives panicked and fled. Later the Pinkerton agency denied that the object hurled through the window was a bomb. By then, however, the damage was done. Censure from the community and several prominent politicians forced Allan Pinkerton to withdraw his operatives from Clay County. Thereafter the Pinkertons were vilified as assassins and child killers. And the legend of Jesse James took on a whole new dimension.

Oddly enough, that aspect of the case stirred Starbuck's admiration. The Pinkerton file documented beyond question that Jesse James was a social misfit with a deep-rooted persecution complex. Nor was there any doubt that he was a mad-dog killer—lacking mercy or remorse—who dispatched his victims with cold ferocity. Yet he was also a master of propaganda. With cunning and calculation, he had captured the public's imagination and transformed himself into a heroic figure. In a very real sense, he was his own best press agent, and one with a certain flair for words. However grudgingly, Starbuck had to admit he'd done a slam-bang job of whitewashing himself and his murderous deeds.

Throughout the years, James had written articulate and persuasive letters to the editors of influential midwestern newspapers. The letters were duly reprinted, and accounted, in large measure, for the myth that "he robbed the rich and gave to the poor." Comparisons were drawn between Jesse James and Robin Hood, the legendary outlaw of Sherwood Forest. Not entirely in jest, newspaper editorials made reference to "Jesse and his merry band of robbers."

Apocryphal tales were widely circulated with regard to his charitable nature and his compassion for the poor. One story, typical of many, credited Jesse with donating a bag of gold to help establish a school for Negro children in Missouri. The gold, naturally, was reported to have been liberated from the coffers of a money-grabbing banker. In time, with such tales multiplying, Jesse became known as a champion of the oppressed and downtrodden. To backwoods Missourians and gullible Easterners alike he came to represent a larger-than-life figure. A Robin Hood reborn—who wore a sixgun and puckishly thumbed his nose at the law.

In Starbuck's view, the fault could be traced directly to the Pinkertons. Had they done their job, Jesse James would have been tried and hanged, and long forgotten. Instead they had botched the assignment from beginning to end. By hounding James for eight years they had turned themselves into the villains of the piece and transformed him into the underdog. Their abortive raid on the family farm had merely capped an already miserable performance. A child's death, and the horror of an innocent woman losing her arm, had been perceived by the public as unconscionable. That one act had stamped the Pinkertons as skulking cowards, somehow more outside the law than the man they hunted. And Jesse James, mindful of public reaction, had quickly seized on the opportunity. Without the Pinkertons, he would have been just another outlaw, foxier than most but nothing to rate front-page headlines. With the Pinkertons, he had become a mythical creature and a national sensation. A legend.

On the evening of the third day Starbuck finally put the file aside. His eyes were bloodshot from reading and his head felt like an oversoaked sponge. He poured himself a stiff shot of whiskey and slugged it back in a single motion. Then he stretched out on the bed, hands locked behind his head, and stared at the ceiling. Slowly, with infinite care, he examined what he'd gleaned from the file.

Several things were apparent now. Foremost among them was the fact that Otis Tilford had given him the straight goods. Nowhere in Missouri could Jesse James be tried in a court of law and found guilty. Even in the event he were captured, there was little likelihood of securing an indictment. The time for that was long past, and would never again return. Underdogs who became living legends were immune to the laws that governed lesser men. So the alternative was obvious, and precisely as Tilford had stated. Jesse James had to be killed.

Insofar as the job itself was concerned, Starbuck realised he faced a formidable task. All the obstacles that had defeated the Pinkertons would likewise hinder his own investigation. The people of Clay County were clannish, openly suspicious of any stranger, and would doubtless prove none too talkative. To compound the problem, they were rightfully fearful of the James-Younger gang, and aware of the consequences to anyone who spoke out of school. The reasonable conclusion, then, was that he would make little headway in Clay County itself. Without solid information—a lead of some sort—it would be a waste of time and effort. Not to mention the great probability he'd wind up bush-whacked on a back-country road some dark night.

Still, based on what he'd read in the file, there was a definite pattern to the gang's activities. After pulling a job every six months or so, they always vanished without a trace. Generally a month or longer would pass before they were again reported in Clay County. Which meant they went to ground and laid low following a holdup. The Pinkertons, even with their bureaucratic mentality, had tumbled to the pattern.

Yet, at the same time, the Pinkertons had overlooked what seemed a salient point. A passing comment in one of the reports noted that Cole Younger had sired a daughter by Belle Starr. Almost as an afterthought, the report indicated that Belle Starr was now living in Indian Territory. No other connection had been made regarding the gang, particularly with respect to Jesse James. Nor had it occurred to the Pinkertons to check it out further. Either Indian Territory wasn't their cup of tea, or else they considered the item a worthless bit of trivia. Whichever, it seemed to Starbuck an oversight.

There was a link, however tenuous, between Cole Younger and his former lady love. Coupled with the fact that the gang vanished after every job, it made for interesting speculation. Moreover, from the standpoint of a robber, it was a link that made eminent good sense. A hideout in Indian Territory would be damn hard to beat. Not only was it a sanctuary for outlaws, but the nearest law was the U.S. marshal's office at Fort Smith. No better place existed for a man to lose himself until the dust settled. And taken to its logical conclusion, the thought was equally true for an entire gang. Perhaps more so.

Starbuck had no idea whether Cole Younger and Belle Starr were still on speaking terms. That Jesse James and the gang used her place as a hideout was an even greater question mark. Yet the link existed, and thus far it was his only lead. A place to start.

CHAPTER 5

Starbuck stepped off the train at a whistle-stop in Indian Territory. A way station for travellers and freight, the depot was located on the west bank of the Arkansas River. On the opposite shore stood Fort Smith.

Hefting his warbag, Starbuck walked towards the ferry landing. No stranger to Indian Territory, he was reminded of an assignment that now seemed a lifetime ago. Some seven years past, on his first job as a range detective, he had trailed a band of horse thieves through the Nations. The homeland of the five Civilised Tribes— Cherokee, Chickasaw, Choctaw, Creek, and Seminole— it was so named because they had chosen to follow the white man's path. Bounded by Texas, Kansas and Arkansas, the Nations were still a long way from civilised.

No less ironic, in Starbuck's view, was the name of the railroad line. The Little Rock & Fort Smith Railroad extended to the depot on the western shoreline, and the river roughly paralleled the boundary separating Arkansas and Indian Territory. But there was no bridge spanning the river, and thus the railroad stopped short of its namesake. Ferryboats were the sole means of conveying freight and passengers from the depot to Fort Smith. As a practical matter, the railroad terminus was on Indian land, and separated from the white man's world by far more than a river. From the depot westward there was a sense of having taken a step backward in time.

Now, standing on the foredeck of the ferry, Starbuck stared across the river at Fort Smith. Originally an army post, the town was situated on a sandstone bluff overlooking the juncture of the Arkansas and Poteau rivers. With time, it had become a centre of commerce and trade, serving much of Western Arkansas and a good part of Indian Territory. Warehouses crowded the waterfront, and in the distance the town itself looked to be a prosperous frontier community. The largest settlement bordering the Nations, it boasted four newspapers, one bank, and thirty saloons which enjoyed a captive trade from transients bound for the great Southwest. By federal law, the sale of firewater was banned throughout Indian Territory.

When the ferry docked, Starbuck inquired directions to the U.S. marshal's office. From the wharf, he followed Garrison Avenue, the main street that ran through the centre of town. On the far side of the business district, he approached the garrison of the old army post. Abandoned some years before by the military, the compound was now headquarters for the Federal District Court of Western Arkansas. And the indisputable domain of Judge Isaac Charles Parker—the Hanging Judge.

Starbuck, like most Westerners, thought Judge Parker had been slandered by the Eastern press. His jurisdiction covered Western Arkansas and all of Indian Territory, a wilderness area which encompassed some 74,000 square miles. To enforce his orders, he was assigned two hundred U.S. deputy marshals, and the almost impossible task of policing a land virtually devoid of law. Four months after taking office, he had sentenced six convicted murderers to be hanged simultaneously.

The thud of the gallows trap that day called the attention of all America to Judge Parker. Newspapermen poured into Fort Smith, and a crowd of more than 5,000 gathered to witness the executions. The press immediately tagged him the Hanging Judge, and decried the brutality of his methods. In the furor, the purpose of his object lesson was completely lost. Yet the reason he'd hung six men that day—and went on to hang eighteen more in the next six years—lay just across the river.

Gangs, of white outlaws made forays into Kansas, Missouri and Texas, and then retreated into Indian Territory. There they found perhaps the oddest sanctuary in the history of crime. Though each tribe had its own sovereign government, with courts and Light Horse Police, their authority extended only to Indian citizens. White men were untouchable, exempt from all prosecution except that of a federal court. Yet there were no extradition laws governing the Nations; federal marshals had to pursue and capture the wanted men; and in time the country became infested with hundreds of fugitives from justice. Curiously enough, the problem was compounded by the Indians themselves.

The red man had little use for the white man's laws, and the marshals were looked upon as intruders in the Nations. All too often the Indians connived with the outlaws, offering them asylum; and the chore of ferreting out entire gangs became a murderous task. It was no job for the faint of heart, as evidenced by the toll in lawmen. Over the past six years nearly thirty federal marshals had been gunned down in Indian Territory.

The old military garrison was a grim setting for the grim work carried out by Judge Parker and his staff. A bleak two-storey building housed the courtroom and offices for the federal prosecutors. As many as ten cases a day were tried, and few men were acquitted. The majority were given stiff sentences—all the law would allow—and quickly transported to federal prisons. Convicted murderers were allowed one last visit with immediate family. Then they were hung.

Another stone building, formerly the post commissary, was situated across the old parade ground. A low one-storey affair, it was headquarters for the U.S. marshal and his complement of deputies. In the centre of the compound, within clear view of both buildings, stood the gallows. Constructed of heavy timbers, it had four trapdoors, each three feet wide and twenty feet long. If occasion demanded, there was adequate space for twelve men to stand side by side and plunge to oblivion on the instant. The structure was roofed and walled, so that executions could be performed even in bad weather. Judge Parker, among other things, believed that justice should be swift—and timely.

Crossing the compound, Starbuck observed activity near the gallows. A crowd, growing larger by the minute, was gathering outside a roped-off area which formed a horseshoe around three sides of the structure. The onlookers were composed of townspeople and farmers, their wives and children, and a collection of travellers distinguishable by their dress. A holiday atmosphere seemed to prevail, and an excited murmur swept over them as a bearded man slowly mounted the stairs. Hushed, the spectators watched as he walked to the centre trap and began testing the knotted hemp nooses. All business, he went about his work with an air of professional detachment.

Starbuck figured it was his lucky day. From the looks of things, he would get to see the Western District Court in action. With one last glance, he went up the steps to the old commissary building. Inside, directly off the hallway, he entered what appeared to be the main office. A man was seated at a battered rolltop desk, hunched forward over a litter of paperwork. He looked up without expression, and waited.

"Afternoon," Starbuck said amiably. "I'd like to see the U.S. marshal."

"You've found him," the man replied, rising from his chair. "I'm Jim Fagan."

Starbuck accepted his handshake. "Luke Starbuck."

Fagan was bearish in appearance, with square features and a shaggy mane of hair. Yet there was a rocklike simplicity in his manner, open and unassuming. He let go Starbuck's hand, cocked his head to one side.

"Starbuck." he repeated aloud. "Why, hell, yes! You're the detective fellow, aren't you? The one that got his picture in the *Police Gazette*."

"Wish to Christ I hadn't," Starbuck admitted unhappily. "In my line of work, it don't pay to have your face plastered all over the country."

"Take a load off your feet." Fagan gestured to a chair beside the desk. "Not often we get a look at a real-live detective."

Starbuck seated himself. "Don't believe everything you read. Lots of that stuff was hogwash, pure and simple."

"Now you're gonna spoil my day! Near as I recollect, that article said you had a hand in puttin' the skids to Wyatt Earp and Billy the Kid. You mean to tell me it's not so?"

"No," Starbuck conceded. "I'm just saying reporters invent about half of what they write. Never known one yet that stuck to the straight facts."

"Guess you got a point." Fagan leaned back in his chair, suddenly earnest. "Well, now, what brings you to Fort Smith? Hot on a case, are you?"

"After a fashion," Starbuck commented. "Wondered what you could tell me about Belle Starr."

"What's to tell?" Fagan said with mild contempt. "Her and Sam Starr—that's her husband—rustle livestock and pull penny-ante holdups. Strictly small-time."

"What kind of holdups?"

"Nuisance stuff," Fagan observed. "Trading posts, backwoods stores . . . every now and then they smuggle a load of whiskey into the Nations. Between them, they haven't got brains enough to take on a bank or train."

"Why haven't you arrested them?"

"We've got our hands full with the *real* hardcases. Course, that don't mean their number won't show. One of these days we'll get 'em for horse stealing or some such—only a matter of time."

"So there's nothing hanging over their heads right now?"

"Nothing particular." Fagan's gaze sharpened. "What's your interest in Miz Belle? She's a slut, common as dirt. Otherwise she wouldn't have married herself off to a reformed dog-eater."

"Her husband's an Indian?"

Fagan nodded. "Full-blooded Cherokee."

"I understand they've got a place over in the Nations."

"On the Canadian River," Fagan affirmed. "Way the hell back in the middle of nowhere. Not marked on any map, but it's called Younger's Bend."

Starbuck looked startled. "Younger's Bend?"

"Well, so the story goes, Belle had herself a kid by Cole Younger. That was some years ago, but apparently she's not one to forget an old sweetheart."

"You're saying she named her place after Cole Younger?"

Fagan slowly shook his head. "I can see how you

made your mark as a detective. You've got a knack for askin' all the questions—without answering any yourself."

"No offence," Starbuck said, smiling faintly. "Old habits are hard to break."

"Suppose we try," Fagan said in a firm voice. "You dodged it a minute ago, so I'll ask again. What's your interest in Belle Starr?"

Starbuck gave him a thoughtful stare. "Anything I say would have to be off the record."

Fagan unpinned his badge and tossed it on the desk. "Shoot."

"I'm after Jesse and Frank James. I've got reason to believe they're using Belle Starr's place as a hideout."

"The hell you say!" Fagan looked at him with some surprise. "Where'd you get a notion like that?"

"A word here, a word there," Starbuck said evasively. "Nothing solid, but a man plays his best hunch."

"One way to find out," Fagan informed him. "I've got a chief deputy that sort of oversees the Cherokee Nation. Want me to call him in?"

"Will he keep his lip buttoned?"

"I'll guarantee it." Fagan threw back his head and roared. "Heck Thomas! Get your dusty butt in here—now!"

A moment passed, then the sound of footsteps drifted in from the hallway. The man who appeared through the door was tall and rangy, with close-cropped hair and a wide handlebar moustache. His eyes were grey and impersonal, and his features were set in the stern expression befitting a church deacon. Starbuck marked him as a mankiller, which immediately put them on common ground.

After a round of introductions, Fagan briefly explained the situation. Heck Thomas listened impassively, arms folded across his chest, saying nothing. At last, when his boss concluded, his gaze shifted to Starbuck.

"Belle and Sam aren't too high on our list, you understand?"

"So Marshal Fagan told me."

"Anything I pass along would be mostly hearsay and rumour."

"No harm in listening."

"Well—" Thomas paused, lifted his shoulders in a shrug. "Every now and then I get word that a bunch of strangers have been seen at Belle's place. Just that—a bunch of strangers—no names, no descriptions."

"You never had reason to check it out?"

"Nope," Thomas said simply. "Belle's probably screwed half the male population of Indian Territory. So it don't spark much curiosity when we hear there's strange men hangin' around her place."

"These strangers," Starbuck inquired, "were they white men?"

"I don't remember anybody sayin' one way or the other."

"How often have you heard they were there?"

"Oh, once or twice a year. Course, keep in mind, I never heard it was the same men every time. Like I said, no names, no descriptions . . . nothin'."

Starbuck thought it was far from nothing. The appearance of strangers at Belle Starr's place—once or twice a year—dovetailed very neatly with the disappearance of the James gang following their periodic holdups. The information was promising, and substantiated what until now had been a shot in the dark. His instinct told him he was on the right track.

For the next few minutes, he questioned Thomas at length about Belle Starr. The lawman required little prompting, and gave him an earful regarding the lady

bandit's tawdry personal life. Then, moving to a large
wall map, Thomas traced the route to Younger's Bend.
He allowed it was an easy two days' ride, but cautioned
Starbuck to keep his eyes open. The Nations was no
place for a man to get careless. And that applied most
especially, he added, to a lawman.

Starbuck inquired the best place to buy a horse, and
Fagan directed him to a stable on the south side of town.
After a few parting remarks, he shook the marshal's
hand and thanked him for his assistance. Thomas, waiting near the door, motioned him into the hallway and
walked him outside.

On the steps they halted and looked towards the gallows. The death warrant had been read and a minister
was intoning a final prayer. Four condemned men stood
positioned on the centre trap, their hands tied behind
their backs and black hoods fitted over their heads. The
bearded man Starbuck had seen earlier moved down the
line, snugging each noose tight, careful to centre the knot
below the left ear. Then he turned and walked directly
to a wooden lever behind the prisoners. The crowd, mor-
bidly curious, edged closer to the scaffold.

"Who's the hangman?"

"Name's George Maledon," Thomas said stolidly.
"Takes pride in his work. Likes to brag he's never let a
man strangle to death. Always breaks a fellow's neck
first crack out of the box."

"How many men has he hung?"

"That bunch'll make twenty-eight."

A loud *whump* suddenly sounded from the gallows.
The four men dropped through the trapdoor and hit the
end of the ropes with an abrupt jolt. Their necks snapped
in unison, and their heads, crooked at a grotesque angle,
flopped over their right shoulders. The spectators, staring
bug-eyed at the scaffold, seemed to hold their breath.

Hanging limp, the dead men swayed gently, the scratchy creak of taut rope somehow deafening in the stillness. One eye on his watch, the executioner finally nodded to the prison physician. Working quickly, the doctor moved from body to body, testing for a heartbeat with his stethoscope. A moment later he pronounced the four men officially dead.

Starbuck grunted softly to himself. "Damn shame Judge Parker's not running the whole country."

"How so?"

"Well, from what I've seen, there're more men that deserve hanging than gets hung. Jesse James and his crowd would be prime examples."

"Ain't it a fact!" Thomas paused, then laughed. "Sure you don't want a job? We could use a man with your style over in the Nations."

"Thanks all the same." Starbuck turned, his hand outstretched. "I'll stick to Judge Colt. Never have to worry about the verdict that way."

"Hallelujah!" Thomas grinned and pumped his arm with vigour. "Good huntin' to you, Luke."

Starbuck nodded and walked off in the direction of the street. Heck Thomas watched him a moment, wondering on the outcome with Belle Starr and her Cherokee lapdog. Then, as the spectators began dispersing, his attention was drawn to the gallows. The hanged men, one by one, were being unstrung. Somehow, though Thomas wasn't all that superstitious, it seemed prophetic. A favourable sign.

Starbuck ought to have himself a whale of a time at Younger's Bend.

CHAPTER 6

By late afternoon of the following day Starbuck was some fifty miles west of Fort Smith. The horse he'd bought was a roan gelding with an easy gait and an even disposition. Along with a secondhand saddle and worn range clothes from his warbag, he looked every inch the fiddle-footed cowhand. Which was precisely the role he'd chosen to play at Younger's Bend.

Early on in his career Starbuck had discovered something in himself that went hand in hand with the detective business. He possessed a streak of the actor, and seemed to have a natural flair for disguise. Every assignment differed, and the range of roles he'd played would have challenged a veteran thespian. Over the past few years he had posed as a saddletramp and stockbuyer, con man and grifter, tinhorn gambler and sleazy whoremonger. Experience had taught him that outward appearance fooled most folks most of the time. The balance of the deception required the proper lingo and a working knowledge of the character he portrayed. For that, he had developed the habit of studying other people's quirks of speech and their mannerisms. Operating undercover, his very survival rested on the skill of his

performance. So it was he'd honed the trick of trans-
forming himself, both outwardly and inwardly, into
someone else. Once he assumed a disguise, he simply
ceased to be Luke Starbuck.

For Younger's Bend, he already had a pip of a cover
story in mind. All day, riding west from Fort Smith, he'd
added a touch here and a touch there. Based on past
assignments—the trial and error of mastering his craft—
he knew that a credible cover story must always strike
a delicate balance. A general rule was the simpler the
better, with a guileless, straightforward approach. Yet an
element of the outlandish—even something bizarre—
added icing to the cake. A happy-go-lucky character
who was half fool and half daredevil was the most con-
vincing character of all. Somehow people never suspected a jester whose sights were set on the brass ring.
A combination of down-at-the-heels cowhand turned
bank robber seemed to Starbuck a real lulu for the task
ahead. He thought it would play well at Younger's Bend.

Shortly before sundown Starbuck approached the
juncture of the Arkansas and Canadian rivers. Farther
west lay the Creek Nation and some distance south lay
the Chocktaw Nation. Younger's Bend, which was on
the fringe of the Cherokee Nation, was ideally situated
to the boundary lines of all three tribes. By rough calculation, he estimated Belle Starr's place was some forty
miles upstream along the Canadian. The general direction was southwest, and with no great effort he would
arrive there around suppertime tomorrow evening. That
fitted perfectly with his plan, for it was essential that he
be invited to stop over at least one night. With no reason
to travel farther, he decided to pitch camp on the banks
of the Arkansas.

A stand of trees was selected for a campsite. There,
with deadwood close to hand, a fire would be no prob-

lem. Along with a Winchester carbine he'd bought in
Fort Smith, Starbuck dropped his saddlebags and blanket
roll at the base of a tree. After being unsaddled, the roan
was hobbled and turned loose to graze on a grassy
stretch near the riverbank. A fire was kindled, and as
dusk fell a cheery blaze lighted the grove.

All in keeping with his role, Starbuck was travelling
without camp gear or victuals. He dined on a cold supper
of hardtack, store-bought beef jerky, and river water. An
hour or so after dark, he picketed the roan between a
couple of trees at the edge of the grove. Afterwards, with
an eye to comfort, he spread his blankets near the fire
and covered them with a rain slicker. By then a damp
chill had settled over the land, and he decided to call it
a night. With his saddle for a pillow, he crawled between
the blankets and turned up the collar of his mackinaw.
Overhead the indigo sky was clear and flecked through
with a zillion stars.

Unable to sleep, he soon tired of counting stars. His
thoughts drifted to Younger's Bend, and the reception
he might reasonably expect. Then, item by item, he began a mental review of all he'd learned about Belle Starr.
With everything contained in the Pinkerton file, added
to the rundown by Heck Thomas, it made a hefty package. None of it was good—a sorry account of an even
sorrier woman—but revealing all the same. And damned
spicy in spots.

Myra Belle Shirley was born in Jasper County, Missouri. Her father, who owned a blacksmith shop and livery stable, was widely respected and prominent in
politics. At the proper age, like all proper young ladies,
Myra Belle was enrolled in the Carthage Female Academy. There she was taught grammar and deportment,
and learned to play a passable tune on the piano. But
she was something of a tomboy, and more interested in

horses and guns than ladylike refinement. By the time abolitionist Kansas and pro-slavery Missouri went to war, she was an accomplished horsewoman and no slouch with a pistol.

The border states were savaged during the Civil War, at the mercy of guerrilla bands on both sides. Only fifteen when Quantrill pillaged and burned Lawrence, Kansas, Myra Belle was impressed by the way he had raised a band of volunteers and turned them into a small army of bloodthirsty raiders. Among them was her idol and secret lover, Cole Younger.

In 1863, Myra Belle's older brother was killed when federal troops razed Carthage. Wild with grief, she fled home and rode off to join Cole and the guerrillas. For the balance of the war, crazed with revenge, she served as an informant and spy for Quantrill. Then, with the South's surrender, Cole and the James boys took off on their own. She had no choice but to return to her family.

The summer of 1865 Myra Belle's father pulled up roots and moved the family to Texas. Outside Dallas, he bought a farm and dabbled in horse trading. Once more enrolled in school, Myra Belle seemed to have settled down and lost her taste for excitement. Then, early in 1866, Cole Younger rode into the farm with his three brothers and the James boys. Fresh from their first bank robbery, they were flush with money and lavished extravagant gifts on the family. A month or so later, when the gang rode back to Missouri, Cole left an even more lasting memento of the visit. Myra Belle, now a ripe eighteen, was pregnant.

When the child was born out of wedlock, the scandal rocked the farm community. Branded a hussy, Myra Belle left her daughter with her parents and fled to Dallas. There, working as a dance-hall girl, she dropped Myra from her name and became known simply as Belle.

There, too, she met and married a young horse thief named Jim Reed. Several years were spent on the run, flitting about from Texas to California, with the law always one step behind. At last, with no place to turn, Reed sought refuge in Indian Territory. Belle shortly joined him, and her career as a lady bandit began in earnest.

The Reeds were given sanctuary by Tom Starr, a full-blood Cherokee. Starr and his eight sons were considered the principal hell-raisers of the Cherokee Nation. Their land was located on a remote stretch of the Canadian River, and considered unsafe for travel by anyone not directly related to the Starr clan. Nonetheless, those who rode the owlhoot were welcome, and even white outlaws found haven there. Belle, the only white woman present, was accorded royal treatment by the Starrs. Then, in the summer of 1874, she abruptly became a widow. Jim Reed, trapped following a stagecoach robbery in Texas, was slain by lawmen.

Never daunted, Belle soon shed her widow's weeds and married Sam Starr. The fact that Sam was a full-blood gave Belle no pause whatever. By the marriage, she gained dower rights to her husband's share in the communal lands of the Cherokee Nation. For the first time in her life she was a woman of property; being white, she was also queen bee of the ruffians who found refuge with the Starr clan. Together she and Sam formed a gang comprising renegade Indians and former cowboys. All were misfits, none of them too bright, and Belle easily dominated the entire crew, her husband included. She promptly dubbed their base of operations Younger's Bend.

The eldest of Old Tom Starr's sons, Sam had a parcel of land located farther downstream on the Canadian. From here, the gang rustled livestock, robbed backwoods stores, and occasionally ran illegal whiskey across the border. Belle was the planner—the brains—and shrewdly brought the men together only when a job was imminent. Afterwards, the gang members scattered to Tulsa and other railroad towns to squander their loot. Meanwhile, back at Younger's Bend, Belle and Sam were virtually immune to arrest. Their home was surrounded by wilderness and mountains, and the only known approach was along a canyon trail rising steeply from the river. So inaccessible was the stronghold that lawmen—both Light Horse Police and federal marshals—gave it a wide berth. After ten years in Indian Territory, Belle was riding high and in no great danger of a fall. She was living the life Myra Belle Shirley had sought since girlhood. And she gloried in the notoriety accorded the Nation's one and only lady bandit, Belle Starr.

To Starbuck, it was a challenge with an unusual twist. Yet tonight, warmed by the embers of the fire, he concluded the lady bandit was vulnerable on several counts. Aside from the vanity normal to any woman, there was the added vanity of a woman who had made her mark in a man's world. A woman who ruled her own robbers' roost and considered herself the femme fatale of the James-Younger gang. Such a woman, unless he missed his guess, was likely to have chapped lips from kissing cold mirrors. And a man who played on her vanity might very easily induce her to brag a little. Or maybe a lot, particularly where it concerned an old beau and lingering sentiment. A sentiment expressed in the name itself—Younger's Bend.

Worming deeper into his blankets, Starbuck turned his backside to the fire. He closed his eyes and drifted towards sleep, thinking of tomorrow. And the lady who was no lady.

* * *

In the lowering dusk Starbuck emerged from the canyon trail. Before him, surrounded by dense woods, lay a stretch of level ground. Not fifty yards away, a log house stood like a sentinel where the trail ended. One window was lighted by a lamp.

A flock of crows cawed and took wing as he rode forward. From the house a pack of dogs joined the chorus, and he smiled to himself. On horseback or on foot, there was little chance anyone would approach Younger's Bend unannounced. He noted as well that trees had been felled in a wide swath from the clearing around the house to the mouth of the canyon. The purpose—an unobstructed field of fire—was obvious. He felt a bit like a duck in a shooting gallery.

The door of the house opened and a woman stepped onto the porch. Her features were indistinct, but the lines of her figure and the flow of her dress were silhouetted against lamplight from inside. She hushed the dogs with a sharp command, and stood waiting with her hands on her hips. Starbuck reined to halt in the yard, mindful he wasn't to dismount unless invited. He smiled politely and touched the brim of his hat.

"Evenin', ma'am."

"Evening."

"You'd likely to be Miz Starr."

"Who's asking?"

"Clyde Belden."

"I don't recall we've met, Mr. Belden."

"No, ma'am," Starbuck said briskly. "I was steered to you by a mutual friend."

"Would this friend have a name?"

"Sure does," Starbuck said with the slow whang of a born Missourian. "None other than Jim Younger his-self."

There was the merest beat of hesitation. "Come on

inside, Mr. Belden. Just be careful to keep your hands in plain sight."

"Anything you say, Miz Starr."

Starbuck stepped down out of the saddle and left the gelding ground-reined. From the corner of the house, a man materialised out of the shadows. He moved forward, holding a double-barrel shotgun at hip level. In the spill of light from the window, Starbuck immediately pegged him as Sam Starr. He was lithely built, with bark-dark skin, muddy eyes, and sleek, glistening hair. His pinched face had an oxlike expression, and he silently followed along as Starbuck crossed the porch and entered the house. Lagging back, he stopped halfway through the door, the shotgun still levelled.

When Belle Starr turned, Starbuck got the shock of his life. Based on her long string of lovers, he'd expected at the very least a passably attractive woman. Instead, she was horsefaced, with a lantern jaw and bloodless lips and beady close-set eyes. Her figure was somehow mannish, with wide hips and shoulders, and almost no breasts beneath her drab woolen dress. While his expression betrayed nothing, Starbuck thought she looked like a cross between ugly and uglier. He'd seen worse, but only in a circus tent show.

Inspecting him, Belle's eyes were guarded. He figured the chances of being recognised were slight. It was unlikely the *Police Gazette* had any wide readership in the Nations; only through a fluke would she have seen the issue bearing his photo. Then, too, his face was now covered with bearded stubble, which tended to alter his appearance. At length, watching him closely, she put him to the test.

"What makes you think I know Jim Younger?"

"He told me so!" Starbuck beamed. "Course, I haven't seen him in a spell, but that don't make no nevermind. The day I headed west he told me all about you and Younger's Bend."

"Then you're from Missouri?"

"Born and bred," Starbuck said with cheery vigour. "All us Beldens come from over around Sedalia way."

Belle gave him a veiled but searching look. "I suppose you rode with Jim during the war?"

"No such luck! I got called up and served with the regulars. Jim and me didn't make acquaintance till after the shootin' stopped."

"You mean you rode with him afterwards?"

"Naw," Starbuck said sheepishly. "Jim and me was just drinkin' pals. He used to talk to me about it some, but I didn't have the sand for it in them days."

"So how did he come to mention me?"

"Well, like I said, I decided to cut loose and head west. Wanted to be a cowboy, and I shore got my wish! Been up the trail from Texas ever' year since the summer of '78."

"You left out the part about Jim."

"Ain't that just like me!" Starbuck rolled his eyes with a foolish smile. "I get started talkin'—well, anyway, Jim told me if I ever got in a tight fix to look you up. So here I am!"

Belle studied him in silence a moment. "What sort of fix?"

"Robbed me a bank!" Starbuck lied heartily. "Walked in all by my lonesome and cleaned 'em out!"

"Where?"

"Vernon," Starbuck informed her. "That's a little burg on the Texas side of the Red River. Figgered it was a good place to get my feet wet."

"Wait a minute." Belle blinked and looked at him. "Are you saying that was your first job?"

"Shore was." Starbuck gave her a lopsided grin.

"Pulled it off slicker'n a whistle, too. Got pretty near two thousand in cold cash!"

"Why now?" Belle appeared bemused. "After all this time what changed your mind?"

"Got tired of workin' for thirty a month and found. Thought it over and decided ol' Jim was right. There's easier ways to make a livin', lots easier."

"So what brings you here?"

"By jingo!" Starbuck boomed out jovially. "Where's a better place to lose yourself? The way Jim talked, you're the soul of Christian charity. I just figgered I'd hightail it into the Nations and make your acquaintance. Better late than never!"

Belle seemed to thaw a little. "Clyde, I'd say you've got more sand than you gave yourself credit for."

"Why, thank you, ma'am." Starbuck swept his hat off. "Comin' from you, I take that as a puredee compliment."

"Do you now?" Belle sounded flattered. "What makes you say that?"

"Why, you're famous, Miz Belle! Ole Jimbo thinks the sun rises and sets right where you stand. And it ain't just him either! I've heard Jesse and Cole brag on you till they plumb run out of wind. That's gospel fact!"

"Ooo, go on!" Belle cracked a smile. "I don't believe a word of it!"

"Miz Belle, I do admire a modest lady. You make me proud to say I'm an ol' Missouri boy. Yessir, you shorely do!"

From the doorway Sam Starr cleared his throat. Belle glanced in his direction and he jerked his head outside. Then he backed away and turned out of the lamplight spilling through the door. Belle frowned, clearly displeased by her husband's presumptuous manner. After a moment, her gaze shifted to Starbuck and she smiled.

"Have a seat." She waved him to a crude dining table. "I'll be with you in a minute."

"Thank you kindly." Starbuck took a chair and tossed his hat on the table. "Don't rush on my account, Miz Belle. I got time to spare."

Belle merely nodded and walked swiftly from the room. Outside, she wheeled right and strode to the end of the porch. Sam was stationed where he could watch the door, the shotgun cradled over one arm. His view through the window was partially obstructed by the angle, but he could see the edge of the dining table and Starbuck's hat. Belle stopped, fixing him with an annoyed squint. Her voice was harsh, cutting.

"What the fuck's your problem?"

"Not me," Sam grunted coarsely. "That feller in there's the problem."

"If you've got something to say, why don't you just spit it out?"

"You ain't gonna like it."

"Try me and see."

"We got to kill him, Belle. Kill him now!"

CHAPTER 7

Starbuck sat stock-still. He listened as Belle's footsteps rapidly crossed the porch, then there was silence. His smile vanished and his eyes flicked around the room.

The interior of the house was smaller than it appeared from outside. Stoutly built, with chinked log walls, it consisted of a central living area and a separate bedroom. The battered table and chairs stood before an open fireplace with a mud chimney. A commode with a faded mirror occupied the wall beside the bedroom door. An ancient brass bed, visible through the door, gleamed in the flames from the fireplace. To the rear of the main room was a wood cooking stove and rough-hewn shelves packed with canned goods. A jumble of odds and ends was piled in the far corner.

On the whole, it was sparse on comfort and smelled like a wolf den. Yet Starbuck wasn't concerned with tidiness or the accommodations. He was looking for a backdoor—all too aware his Colt was no match for a shotgun at close quarters, and suddenly uncomfortable that the only exit was the door through which he had entered. His attention turned to the powwow under way on the front porch. There was no question he was the

topic of conversation, but considerable doubt existed as
to the verdict. He subscribed to the theory of "shoot first
and talk about it later," and a vantage point nearer the
door seemed eminently advisable. Then, too, a bit of
eavesdropping might very well improve his odds.

Quietly, Starbuck rose and moved to the fireplace. He
stood with his hands outstretched to the flames, one eye
on the window. No one was watching him—nor was
there any sound from outside—and he concluded they
were still huddled at the end of the porch. Hugging the
wall, he ghosted towards the front of the house. There,
he flattened himself beside the windowsill and pressed
his ear to the logs. The chinking was old and cracked,
seeping air between small gaps, and through it he heard
the drone of voices. A heated argument was under way.

"I don't give a good goddamn what you think!"

"You'd better," Sam grumbled. "I got a nose for those
things."

"Heap big Injun!" Belle mocked him. "You'd starve
to death if somebody hadn't invented tinned goods!"

"You got no call to say that."

"Oh, no? When's the last time you and your mangy
pack of brothers shot a deer—or a rabbit—or even a
squirrel, for Chrissakes? You've got a hunter's nose like
I've got warts on my ass!"

"I'm warnin' you now! You leave my brothers outta
this!"

"Awww, dry up," Belle said in a waspish tone. "The
whole bunch of you couldn't hold a candle to a cigar-
store Indian. Your pa's the only one with any balls—
and it sure as hell didn't get passed along to you!"

"How come you're always throwin' the old man up
in my face?"

"Because nobody ever pulled his tail feathers. Go on,

admit it! You're full-grown and you still wet your pants anytime he looks cross-eyed at you."

"Mebbe you should've married him 'stead of me."

"Maybe!" Belle crowed. "Jesus Christ, no maybe about it! At least he's still got some red-hot Injun blood left in him. Which is more than I can say for you and your butthole brothers."

Sam laughed without mirth. "Won't work, Belle! I ain't gonna get mad."

"Talk sense! What the Sam Hill's that got to do with anything?"

" 'Cause you're tryin' to throw me off the scent and we both know it."

"Here we go again," Belle gibed. "You and your track-'em-through-the-woods nose!"

"I know a lawdog when I smell one."

"Sam, you poor sap! You couldn't smell a fart if somebody caught it in a bottle and let you have the first sniff."

"I am warnin' you, woman. That feller's no bank robber! I'll betcha he don't know Jim Younger nor none of the others either."

"Judas Priest," Belle groaned. "You heard me question him! You were standing there the whole time and I didn't trip him up once. How do you explain that?"

"I didn't say he was dumb," Sam reminded her. "I said he was a lawdog! So it just naturally figgers he'd have all the right answers. Any fool oughta see that."

"Are you calling me a fool, Sam Starr?"

"No, I ain't. I'm only tryin' to talk some sense into your head."

"Well, you can talk till you're blue in the face and it won't change a thing. I told you once and I'm telling you again! I won't let you kill him."

"Too bad your brains ain't where they're supposed to be."

"What the hell does that mean?"

"It means you've got hot drawers, that's what it means."

"You're crazy as a loon!"

"Yeah?" Sam bristled. "You think I don't know the sign when I see it? You got your mind set on him humpin' you, and you ain't gonna listen to reason till he forks you good and proper."

"That's a dirty goddamn lie!"

"Belle, how many men you humped since we got married? Mebbe you lost count, but I haven't. I watched it happen enough times I know what I'm talkin' about. You don't want me to kill him 'cause you got hot drawers. So don't tell me different."

"Well, so what?" Belle lashed out. "I go to bed with any damn body I please. I don't need your permission!"

"Never said otherwise," Sam conceded. "All I'm sayin' is, we'd be better off with him dead. So I'll wait till after you're done and then kill him. How's that?"

"No deal," Belle said sternly. "I will budge a little, though. We'll let him spend the night and then send him on his way. Fair enough?"

"I wish you'd believe me when I tell you he's a lawman. Probably sent personal by the Hangin' Judge hisself."

"You think I don't know a Missouri boy when I see one? He's no more a marshal than you are. Hell's bells, I'm a better judge of character than that!"

"So go on and suit yourself. You always do anyway."

"Sam?"

"Yeah?"

"Don't get any wiseass notions about killing him after he leaves here. You do and I'll wait till you're asleep some night—and then I'll cut your goddamn tally-whacker clean off! You hear me, Sam?"

"I hear you."

Starbuck heard her, too. He was again seated at the dining table when Belle led her husband through the door. Several things were apparent to him from their conversation. Foremost was that he would have only one night to squeeze Belle dry of information. Another factor, which might serve to loosen her tongue, was that she'd bought his story about Jim Younger. Yet, like an alley cat in heat, she had designs on his body, and big plans for the night ahead. One look at her gargoyle face and he began having second thoughts about the detective business. He wasn't sure he could get it up—much less romance her—even in the cause of law and order.

Sam halted near the door and Belle moved directly to the table. Watching her, Starbuck wondered how it would work with a sack over her head. He thought it an idea worth exploring.

"Forgot to introduce you boys," Belle said, gesturing towards the door. "Clyde, want you to meet my husband Sam Starr."

"Howdy, Sam." Starbuck nodded amiably. "Pleasure's all mine."

Sam muttered something unintelligible, and Belle quickly resumed. "How would you like to stay to supper and spend the night?"

"Why, I'd be most obliged, Miz Belle."

"We'd ask you to stay longer, but it wouldn't work out just now. We've got a business deal of our own that won't keep."

"No problem," Starbuck said agreeably. I was just passin' through, anyhow. Only stopped off to pay my respects."

"Too bad in a way." Belle feigned a rueful look. "You

and Sam would probably get a kick out of chewing the fat. But he's got to run over to his pa's place and tend to that business deal. Don't you, Sam?"

"Yeah, sure." Sam gave her a disgruntled scowl, then turned towards the door. "See you in the mornin'."

A few minutes later, Belle watched from the porch while her husband led a horse from the barn and mounted. When the hoofbeats faded into the night, she stepped back inside and closed the door. She smiled like a tigress stalking a goat.

Starbuck, cast in the role of the goat, had a sudden sinking feeling. It looked to be a long night.

Whatever else she was, Belle Starr was no cook. She served Starbuck sowbelly and beans, a pasty hominy gruel, and cornbread baked hard as sandstone. He wolfed it down with gusto—grinning all the while—and topped off the performance with an appreciative belch. The belch was the easiest part, and required no strain. He felt gassy as a bloated hog.

After clearing the table, Belle brought out a couple of tin cups and a quart of rotgut. The whiskey had a bite like molten lead, and tasted as though it had been aged in a turpentine barrel. No sipper, Belle was clearly a lady who enjoyed her liquor. She poured with the regularity of a metronome, and slugged it down without batting an eye. Starbuck, sensing opportunity, matched her shot for shot. She wanted his body and he wanted information, and it all boiled down to who got crocked first. Unless she had a hollow leg, he thought there was a reasonable chance he could outlast her.

In passing, Starbuck noted that he'd been dead on the mark regarding her vanity. She was a woman with a high opinion of herself, and not above putting on airs. Earlier, on the porch with Sam, she had displayed the foul mouth of a veteran muleskinner. Yet with Starbuck, her language bordered on the ladylike, sweeter than sugar and twice as nice. The more she drank, the more he had to admire her style. For a virtuoso of four-letter words, it took considerable restraint to hobble her tongue. He mentally applauded the effort, and bided his time waiting for her to slip back into character. Only then would he make his move.

Along towards midnight, Starbuck's patience was rewarded. The bottle of popskull was approaching empty, and Belle's eyes were fixed in a glassy stare that seemed vaguely out of focus. She wasn't ossified, but her tolerance to snakebite would last well into next week. Starbuck was feeling a little numb himself, warmed by a tingling sensation that extended to his hair roots. Yet he still had his wits about him, and it appeared he'd won the drinking bout. The lady bandit suddenly reverted to her true self. And her choice of words was all the tipoff he needed.

"You know something, Clyde?" Her mouth curled in a coy smile. "For an old Missouri boy, you're a goddamn sweet-looking man."

"Well, Miz Belle"—Starbuck grinned, suppressing his revulsion, and plunged ahead—"you're pretty easy on the eyes yourself."

"Forget that Miz Belle shit. I'm not your mama and you're not wet behind the ears. You follow me?"

Starbuck's grin turned to a suggestive leer. "What'd you have in mind?"

"When I was a girl—" Belle burst out in a bawdy horselaugh. "All the prissy-assed little buttermouths at the Female Academy called it the birds and the bees. Once I took up with boys, I learned it was better known as stink finger and hide the weenie. That answer your question?"

"Sounds the least bit like an invitation."

"I never was one to mince words. A woman's got the same needs as a man."

"Some folks call it horny."

"By God, Clyde, you're a card! Always was partial to a man with a sense of humour."

"What about Sam?" Starbuck jerked his chin at the door. "I'd hate to have him come bustin' in here with that shotgun just when I was all set to flush the birds out of your nest."

"Wooiee!" Belle leaned forward, grabbing his head in both hands, and planted one smack on his lips. "Flush the birds out of my nest! Goddamn, that's rich, Clyde. I do like the sound of it!"

Starbuck felt like he'd been kissed by a dragon. "Not to put a damper on things, but I'd shore like to hear your answer about Sam."

"Who gives a fuck?" Belle gave him a sly and tipsy look. "I sent Sam packing for the night, and that's that! You just rest easy, sport."

Starbuck paused, then smoothly laid the trap. "Well, now, I dunno. Jim told me about you and Cole, but I just naturally figgered—"

"What about Cole?"

"Why, that you was sweet on him. The way Jim talked it went back long before the war."

Belle poured herself a stiff shot and knocked it back. "What else did he tell you?"

"Say, look here—Starbuck broke off with a troubled frown. "I don't want to step on nobody's toes. Maybe I'd best let it drop there."

"No, you don't!" Belle demanded. "You started it, now finish it!"

"Listen, Belle, me and Jim go way back. I shore wouldn't wanna get him in Dutch."

"Oh, for God's sake!" Belle drunkenly waved the objection aside. "I won't hold it against Jim. Now stop dancing around and spill it! What'd he tell you?"

"Nothin' much, really." Starbuck's tone was matter-of-fact. "Only that you let Cole and the boys hide out here after they'd pulled a job. I seem to recollect he mentioned Jesse and Frank, too."

The effects of her last drink suddenly overtook Belle. She squinted owlishly and her speech slurred. "How about Ruston's place?"

Starbuck held his breath. "You mean the other hide-out?"

"Yeah."

"Wait a minute!" Starbuck wrinkled his brow in concentration. "Why, shore, Ruston! Near as I recall, Jim said he'd served with 'im under Quantrill. Now what the blue-billy-hell was his first name? Got it right on the tip of my tongue!"

"Tom," Belle mumbled. "Good ol' Tom Ruston. Wish I had his spread and he had a feather up his ass! We'd both be tickled pink."

Starbuck played along. "Jim said it was some layout."

"One of the biggest." Belle nodded. "And on the Pecos, that's saying a lot! Nothing small-time about Texans."

"You're tellin' me!" Starbuck laughed. "I reckon I've trailed enough cows outta Texas to have a pretty fair idea." He hesitated, choosing his words. "Well, maybe I'll run acrost Jim down there one of these days."

"Not likely." Belle sloshed whiskey into her cup, wholly unaware she had emptied the bottle. "Long as they're safe here, they got no reason to bother Ruston."

Starbuck decided not to press it further. The last piece of the puzzle was now clear, and all that remained was to fit the parts together. With a broad grin, he lifted his

cup in a toast. "Here's to the Youngers! Ol' King Cole
and the best damn brothers any man could ask for."

"I'll drink to that!"

Belle drained her cup in a long swallow and lowered
it to her lap. Whiskey dribbled down her chin and she
burped, clapping her hand to her mouth with a foolish
giggle. She gave Starbuck a dopey smile and reached for
his hand. Then a wave of dizziness rocked her, and her
eyes suddenly glazed. The cup clattered to the floor and
her head thumped forward onto the table.

Starbuck lifted her from her chair and carried her to
the bedroom. She was out cold and lay like a corpse
while he undressed her. Unmoved by her nakedness, he
pulled the covers up to her chin and turned away. At the
door, he glanced back and let go a heavy sigh of relief.

He felt like a condemned man with a last-minute reprieve.

Late the next morning Starbuck led his horse from the
barn and halted before the house. Belle, suffering from
a monumental hangover, stood on the porch. He gave
her a lewd wink and playfully patted her on the thigh.

"You're some woman, Miz Belle Starr. One of a
kind!"

Belle's eyes were bloodshot, vaguely disoriented.
"Clyde, tell me something. How'd things work out last
night?"

"You don't remember?"

"Not just exactly. Did you—uh—flush the birds out
of the nest?"

"Did I ever!" Starbuck whooped. "Scattered 'em all
to hell and gone!"

"Yeah?" Belle seemed bemused. "Well, how was it?"

"Never had none better! You plumb tuckered me out,
and that's the gospel truth."

Belle brightened visibly. "You Missouri boys always was hot-blooded."

"Godalmightybingo! Stink finger and hide the weenie! Wouldn't have missed it for the world, Miz Belle!"

Starbuck tossed her a roguish salute and stepped into the saddle. He turned the gelding out of the yard and gigged him into a prancing trot. At the mouth of the canyon, he twisted around and waved his hat high over-head. Belle, looking fluttery as a schoolgirl, threw him a kiss.

The performance ended as Starbuck rode towards the river. His jaw hardened and his mouth set in a tight line. For the moment, Indian Territory was a washout, and he saw nothing to be gained in scouting the ranch on the Pecos. All of which meant he'd exhausted his options. Jesse James would have to be hunted down on home-ground.

He forded the river and headed north, towards Missouri. And Clay County.

CHAPTER 8

A cold blue dusk settled over the winter landscape.

Lamar Hudspeth waited in the shadows of the barn. With his son at his side, he watched three riders approach along the rutted wagon road. A snowfall, followed by a brief warm spell, had turned the road into a boggy quagmire. The horses slogged through the mud, heads bowed against a brisk wind, snorting frosty clouds of vapour. Their riders reined off the road and proceeded towards the barn at a plodding walk. Hudspeth stepped out of the shadows.

"Cole." He greeted the men by name as they dismounted. "Jim, you're lookin' fit. Evenin', Bob."

"How do, Lamar."

Cole Younger merely bobbed his head. "Jesse here yet?"

"Nope," Hudspeth replied with a shrug. "He'll be along directly though. Probably waitin' till it gets full dark."

"Horseshit!" Cole loosed a satiric laugh. "He's waitin' to see if we get ourselves ambushed. Jesse always was good at lettin' somebody else bird-dog for him."

"You got no call to talk that way, Cole."

"Think not? Then how come we're the first ones here when it's him that called the meetin'? Go on, answer me that!"

"I 'spect he's got his reasons."

"Lamar, there's none your equal when it comes to stickin' by kinfolk. I'll hand you that."

"Speakin' of kin," Hudspeth said, easing into another subject, "I made the rounds today. Stopped by Miz Samuel's place, just to make sure there wasn't no outsiders nosin' about."

"We done the same," Cole remarked, motioning to his brothers. "All of us snuck in to see our women last night. Things appear to be pretty quiet."

"So Miz Samuel said," Hudspeth acknowledged. "She ain't seen hide nor hair of anybody that looks like a Pinkerton."

"Jesse's wife still stayin' with his ma?"

"Well, her being in a family way and all, I 'spect she'll stay there till her time comes."

"Leastways Jesse don't need no bird dog there. One way or another, he manages to sire his own pups."

"Iffen it was me, I wouldn't let Jesse hear you say a thing like that."

"Before the night's over, he's gonna hear lots worse. I got a bellyful, and I aim to speak my piece."

"I reckon you're full-growed." Hudspeth gestured to his son. "The boy'll put your horses in the barn. There's coffee on the stove and angel cake for them that wants it."

"Your woman's braver'n most, Lamar."

"How's that?"

"Bakin' an angel cake for this crew? Damnation, she's liable to get your house struck by lightning!"

Cole laughed and walked off with his brothers. The Hudspeth boy, flushed with shame for his father, led their horses into the barn. For his part, Lamar Hudspeth took no offence at the crude humour. His one concern was that there would be no spillover of animosity tonight. Yet, from all indications, he sensed that it wasn't to be. Cole Younger was plainly looking for an excuse to start trouble.

The Hudspeth farm was located some miles outside the town of Kearney. Hudspeth himself was a law-abiding family man, a deacon in the Baptist church, and modestly active in Clay County politics. He was also a second cousin of Jesse and Frank James. Though he abhorred their methods—for he was a fundamentalist who took the Scriptures literally—he nonetheless believed they were being persecuted by shylock bankers and unscrupulous railroad barons. Like many people, he assisted the James boys and the Youngers at every turn. Since their own homes were unsafe, the gang members found shelter with friends and relatives; constantly on the move, they seldom spent more than a couple of nights in any one spot. The system baffled the law and allowed the robbers to visit their wives and children on a sporadic basis.

After nearly seventeen years, the people of Clay County had grown accustomed to a climate of conspiracy and distrust. Their efforts on behalf of the gang were now commonplace, an everyday part of life. Not unlike measles or whooping cough, it was accepted as the natural order of things.

Lamar Hudspeth, no different from his neighbours, would have scoffed at the notion that he was aiding and abetting outlaws. The James boys were kinsmen, and the Youngers, with the possible exception of Cole, were old and valued friends. Honour dictated that he shield them from harm and forever take their part in the struggle against the Pinkertons. Tonight, as he had on past occasions, he had consented to let them meet in his home. He recognised the danger and gave it no more than passing consideration. They were, after all, family.

A short while after dark Jesse and Frank emerged from the woods north of the house. Hudspeth wasn't surprised, and while he'd denied it earlier, he knew Cole Younger was right all along. Jesse was a cautious man, forever leery of a trap; it was no accident he hadn't arrived on time for the meeting. Instead, waiting in the trees, he had probably watched the house since well before dusk. Hudspeth thought it a sensible precaution, if not altogether admirable. Yet there was no condemnation in the thought. He never judged a kinsman.

Jesse reined to a halt and swung down out of the saddle. He was lean, with stark features and a cleft chin and cold slate-coloured eyes. His beard was neatly trimmed, and he carried himself with the austere, straight-backed posture that bordered on arrogance. He was a man of dour moods and he seldom smiled. His natural expression was rocklike, wholly devoid of sentiment.

By contrast, Frank was courteous and thoughtful, with a warm smile and an affable manner. Quietly studious, he was self-educated and an ardent reader, especially partial to the works of Shakespeare. To the dismay of the other gang members, he liberally quoted the Bard whenever the occasion permitted. Among friends and family, it was an open secret that he supplied the wording for Jesse's articulate letters to the newspaper editors. Except for the dominance of his brother, he might have been a scholar, or a man of the cloth. He was, instead, an outlaw with a price on his head.

After a round of handshakes, Jesse cut his eyes towards the house. "Cole and the boys inside?"

Hudspeth nodded. "Cole's some put out 'cause you

wasn't here first. Hope there won't be any trouble."

"Cole's all wind and no whistle. He just likes to hear himself talk."

"Maybe so," Hudspeth said, without conviction. "He's on a tear tonight, though. Told me he'd had a bellyful and meant to get it out in the open."

"Bellyful of what?"

"Search me," Hudspeth responded. "I just listen, Jesse. I don't meddle."

"One of these days," Jesse said crossly, "I'm gonna fix his little red wagon for good."

"C'mon now, Jess," Frank gently admonished. "Cole doesn't mean any harm. He just flies off the handle every now and then, that's all. Besides, it wouldn't do to forget . . . you need him and the boys."

The men stood for a moment in a cone of silence. Then, to no one in particular, Hudspeth spoke. "Saw your ma today."

"Figured you might." Jesse's expression mellowed slightly. "She all right?"

"Tolerable," Hudspeth allowed. "Got herself a touch of rheumatism, and that's slowed her up some. Course, she ain't one to complain."

"No, it's not her way. How's Zee?"

Hudspeth looked down and studied the ground. "She asked me to pass along a message."

"Yeah?"

"She ain't happy with your ma, Jesse. One woman under another woman's roof puts a strain on everybody concerned. She asked me to tell you she wants a place of her own."

Jesse acted as though he hadn't heard. "Well," he said, after a measurable pause, "I guess we'd best get the meeting started. What with one thing and another, it's liable to take awhile."

Hudspeth pursed his lips, on the verge of saying something more. Then, reluctant to meddle, his gaze shifted to Frank. "Sorry I didn't get by to see Annie. Between chores and all, there just wasn't time enough."

"In our line of work," Frank said with a rueful smile, "wives learn to take catch as catch can. All the same, I'm planning to slip into home tonight when we're done here. I'll tell her you asked after her."

"Let's get on with it." Jesse started off, then turned back. "Lamar, you aim to keep a lookout while we're inside?"

"No need to fret," Hudspeth assured him. "Anybody comes along, I'll send the boy to fetch you lickety-split."

"What about Sarah?"

"She knows to stay in the kitchen. If you'll recollect, she never wanted to hear nothin' about your business anyhow."

With a querulous grunt, Jesse trudged off in the direction of the house. Frank traded glances with Hudspeth, then tagged along on his brother's heels. Upon entering the house, they found the Youngers seated around the parlour. Bob and Jim greeted them civilly enough, but Cole opted for brooding silence. An air of tension seemed to permeate the room.

No one spoke as Jesse hung his coat and hat on a wall peg beside the entrance. Without a word, he crossed the parlour and closed a door leading to the kitchen. Frank, fearing the worst, lowered himself into a rocker and began stuffing his pipe. Then, once more crossing the room, Jesse took a chair directly across from Cole. His eyes were metallic.

"I understand you've got your bowels in an uproar?"

"You understand right."

"Then spit it out, and be damn quick about it!"

Cole reddened, stung by his tone. An oak of a man,

with brutish features and a square jaw, the eldest of the
Younger brothers was ruled by a volatile temper. Yet,
where Jesse was concerned, his outbursts were generally
of short duration. For years he had allowed himself to
be intimidated by the gang leader's autocratic manner.
His deference, though he had never admitted it to anyone, was due in no small part to fear. He knew Jesse
would kill without pretext or provocation, the way a fox
mindlessly slaughters a coop full of chickens. Tonight,
however, he was determined to stand his ground. His
jaw set in a bulldog scowl, and his gaze was steady.

"Me and the boys"—he motioned to his brothers—
"are fed up! We want a bigger say in how this outfit's
run. All the more so since you likely called us together
to plan a job."

Jesse nailed him with a corrosive stare. "Suppose we
leave Bob and Jim out of it. You're the one that's got a
hair across his ass! So let's just keep it between ourselves."

"That ain't so," Cole corrected him. "We talked it out
and we're of a mind. We've got to have more say so in
how things are done."

"Don't make me laugh," Jesse's voice was alive with
contempt. "The three of you together don't have brains
enough to pour piss out of a boot. Without me to do
your thinking for you, you'd starve to death in nothing
flat."

"Bullfeathers!" Cole said defiantly. "We ain't been
doing so hot with you! Our last couple of jobs was
nickel-and-dime stuff. Keep on that way and we'll have
to take up honest work to make a livin'."

"Quit bellyaching! You and the boys have done all
right for yourselves."

"No, we ain't neither! You bollixed our last bank job
and that train holdup last summer was a regular gawd-

damn disaster. All we done was kill a lot of people! And in case it slipped your mind, that ain't exactly the purpose in pullin' a robbery."

An evil light began to dance in Jesse's eyes. He glanced at Bob and Jim, and they seemed to cower before the menace in his gaze. Neither of them spoke, and their hangdog expressions evidenced little support for their brother. At length, Jesse swung back to Cole.

"Sounds like you've got some idea of moving me aside and stepping into my boots."

"Never said that," Cole protested. "All I'm sayin' is that we want a vote in the way things are handled."

"A vote!" Jesse fixed him with a baleful look. "We don't operate by ballot. Only one man around here calls the shots—and that's me!"

"Confound it, Jesse!" Cole said explosively. "That won't cut the ice no more. We're done takin' orders like we was a bunch of ninnies! Either you treat us square or else—"

"Don't threaten me." Jesse's tone was icy. "You do, and I'm liable to forget your name's Younger."

"Whoa back now!" Frank struck into the argument with a gentle rebuke. "You two keep on that way and we'll all wind up losers. Jesse, it wouldn't hurt anything to listen. Why not let Cole have his say?"

"Are you taking sides against me?"

Frank appraised his brother with a shrewd glance. "You ought to know better than to even ask such a thing. I'm just trying to get you to listen, that's all. We have to divvy up the same bone—so where's the harm?"

"Well . . ." Jesse said doubtfully. "I don't mind listening. I just don't want anybody telling me I don't know my business."

"Never said that either," Cole insisted. "But Frank hit the nail on the head. We ain't had a decent payday in a long gawddamn time, and it wouldn't hurt to take a new slant on things."

"A new slant?" Jesse repeated stiffly. "What's that supposed to mean?"

"For one thing," Cole explained, "we've got to give a little more thought to the Pinkertons. The way I see it, they pretty well got us euchred."

"Awww, for God's sake," Jesse said with heavy sarcasm. "You're crazy as a hoot owl! How long's it been since a Pinkerton set foot in Clay County?"

"Fat lotta good that does us! They've figured out we only operate in certain states and they've got everybody nervy as a cat in a roomful of rockers. We haven't hit one bank or one train in the last year that wasn't halfway expectin' to be robbed."

"So what's your idea? Should we start robbing poor boxes, candy stores—what?"

"No," Cole said with an unpleasant grunt. "I think we ought to consider explorin' new territory."

"Don't tell me," Jesse taunted him. "Let me guess. You've got just the place picked out—am I right?"

"Now that you mention it," Cole noted with vinegary satisfaction, "I stumbled across a real humdinger. A friend had some kinfolk move up there, and the way their letters read, the streets are paved with gold."

"Up where?"

"Minnesota," Cole informed him. "Northfield, Minnesota."

"You are nuts!" Jesse snorted. "What the hell's in Minnesota worth robbing?"

"A bank," Cole replied in a sandy voice. "I had my friend write his relatives—all nice and casual—and it turns out Northfield's smack-dab in the centre of things up that way. And there's only *one* bank. A big bank!"

"There's lots of big banks, and lots closer, too. Hell's

fire, Minnesota must be three hundred miles away, maybe more."

"I checked," Cole said without expression. "Northfield's right at four hundred miles from where we're sittin'."

"That corks it!" Jesse said, almost shouting. "Why in Christ's name would we ride four hundred miles to rob a bank?"

"Because it's the last place on earth the Pinkertons would expect us to hit. So far as I'm concerned, that's about the best reason there is. You stop and think on it, and you'll see I'm right."

A thick silence settled over the room. Jesse caught Frank's eye, and they exchanged a long, searching stare. Then, with a sombre look, Frank slowly bobbed his head.

"It makes sense, Jess. I never heard of Northfield, and I doubt that the Pinkertons have either. Matter of fact, it's so far out of our usual territory, they'd probably blame the job on someone else."

Jesse heaved himself to his feet. He began to pace around the parlour, hands stuffed in his pockets. No one spoke, and the tread of his footsteps seemed somehow oppressive in the stillness. After a time, he stopped, his head bowed, studying the floor. At last, as though to underline the question, he raised his head and looked Frank squarely in the eye.

"Are you voting with Cole?"

"Jesse—" Frank paused, weighing his words. "I couldn't vote one way or the other, not till we've got more details. I'm only saying the idea itself sounds good."

"All right," Jesse said in a resigned voice. "Here's the way we'll work it. Since Bob's the best scout we've got, he goes to Northfield to check the layout. I want to know

everything there is to know about the bank and the town.
And most especially, I want you to map out a step-by-
step escape route to Belle Starr's place. You got that
straight, Bob?"

"Sure do, Jesse." Bob grinned, sitting erect in his
chair. "I'll leave first thing in the mornin'."

Jesse considered a moment. "I figure two weeks ought
to do it. That'll push you a little, but not too bad. So
unless I send word to the contrary, we'll all meet back
here two weeks from tonight. Any questions?"

There were no questions. Jesse looked around the
room, and his eyes were suddenly stern, commanding.
"One last thing. Lay low and stay out of trouble. We
don't want to draw attention to ourselves just before we
pull a job." He paused, and added a blunt afterthought.
"Cole, that goes for you more than the others. None of
your monkeyshines down at Ma Ferguson's."

Cole darted a glance at Frank, then shrugged. "No
nookie for two weeks? That's a pretty tall order."

"Tie a string on it and keep it in your pants."

"We ain't all got your willpower, Jesse."

"You've argued with me enough for one night. Just
do like I say."

"Well, I'll give 'er a try. Yessir, I shore will!"

Jesse stared at him a moment. Then, nodding to
Frank, he turned towards the door. With no word of
parting, he shrugged into his coat and stepped into the
night. Frank, trading one last look with Cole, dutifully
tagged along.

The parlour suddenly seemed ominously quiet.

CHAPTER 9

Starbuck rode into Clay County on a bleak February evening. The sky was heavy with clouds and beneath it the frozen trees swayed in a polar wind. His destination was Ma Ferguson's roadhouse.

Upon returning from Indian Territory, he had laid over several days in Kansas City. The delay, though it had grated on him, was unavoidable. He'd needed time to perfect a disguise, and assume yet another identity. There was every reason to believe that the *Police Gazette*—which frequently carried articles about the James-Younger gang—was widely read in Clay County. His photo, which had appeared in the same publication, would have proved a dead giveaway. The upshot, were he to be recognised, was none too pleasant to contemplate. He wisely undertook a transformation in his appearance.

A theatrical supplier was his first stop. Kansas City was a crossroads for show companies, and the supplier stocked all manner of props and costumes. There, Starbuck obtained a bottle of professional hair dye, choosing dark nut-brown as a suitable contrast to his light chestnut mane. The proprietor assured him a dye job would last several weeks, barring a hard rain or any great penchant for hot baths. As an added touch, Starbuck also bought a spit-curled moustache of the same colour. Though fake, the moustache was quality work; even on close examination it looked to be the genuine article. A liberal application of spirit gum guaranteed it would remain glued to his upper lip.

While arranging the disguise, Starbuck had reviewed his mental catalogue on Clay County. From the Pinkerton file, he recalled that the Younger brothers were notorious womanisers. The James boys, for all their quickness with a gun, were faithful husbands and devoted family men. But the Youngers, particularly Cole, were known to frequent a brothel operated by one Ma Ferguson. Located outside the town of Liberty, the bawdy house was situated in the southwestern tip of the county, and apparently catered to the rougher element. Somewhat remote, lying on a back-country road between Kearney and Liberty, it was a place to be avoided by strangers. According to the Pinkerton file, it was considered a certain-death assignment for both law officers and private investigators. No undercover operative had ever attempted to infiltrate Ma Ferguson's cathouse.

Starbuck thought it the most likely place to start. For one thing, he would arouse less suspicion simply because the Pinkertons, for the last eight years, had steered clear of the dive. For another, it would allow him to observe the gang—perhaps strike up an acquaintance—when they were most vulnerable. Men intent on swilling booze and rutting with whores were almost certain to lower their guard. Then, too, the easygoing atmosphere of a brothel fitted nicely with his overall plan. Ma Ferguson's was but an initial step, a matter of establishing himself and gaining the confidence of the girls who worked there. His ultimate goal was to infiltrate the James-Younger gang itself.

Starbuck had devised a cock-and-bull story that was entirely plausible. He would pose as a horse thief—operating out of Dodge City—who was now on the run from Kansas lawmen. Dodge City, billing itself as the Queen of Cowtowns, was also the current horseflesh capital of the West. Along with the longhorn herds driven to railhead, thousands of horses were trailed up each year from Texas. Some were sold there; others were moved north, to distant markets in Montana and Wyoming. Horse thieves, like wolves sniffing fresh scent, had made Dodge City their headquarters. And therein lay his cover story. One thief, forced to take the owlhoot, would draw little in the way of curiosity. It was an occupational hazard, all part of the game. So common, in fact, that wanted posters were no longer circulated on horse thieves.

All that remained was to attract the attention of the Younger brothers. A high roller, throwing his money to the winds, would do for openers. Then, somewhere along the line, he would find a way to impress them, and gain their favour. Only then would they accept him as a thief who aspired to greater things, one who deserved their consideration. And only then, when he'd wormed his way into their ranks, would he get the chance he sought. A shot at Jesse James.

The plan entailed a high degree of risk. One slip—the slightest miscue—and he was a dead man. Yet, at the same time, his charade would represent the safest possible approach. The Youngers would never suspect that a private detective, alone and unaided, would invade their favourite whorehouse. Nor would they guess that his audacity was less invention than necessity. Try as he might, he'd thought of nothing else that would work in Clay County.

Shortly after nightfall, Starbuck rode into the yard of Ma Ferguson's place. The house was a large two-storey structure, brightly lighted and painted a dazzling white. He thought the colour an ironic choice—one seldom associated with ladies of negotiable virtue—and instantly pegged Ma Ferguson for a woman with a sense of humour. Stepping down from the saddle, he loosened the cinch and left the roan tied to a hitch rack out front. Then, dusting himself off, he strode boldly into the house.

The front room, as in most bordellos, was fashioned on the order of a parlour. Sofas and chairs were scattered at random, with a small bar in one corner and an upright piano along the far wall. The hour was still early, and only two customers, townsmen by their dress, were in evidence. The girls, nearly a dozen in number, lounged on the sofas while a black man with pearly teeth pounded out a tune on the piano. Ma Ferguson, a large, heavyset woman in her forties, was seated in an overstuffed armchair. She gave Starbuck's range clothes a slow once-over, then smiled and waved him to the bar.

"First one's on the house, dearie!"

"Thank you, ma'am." Starbuck doffed his Stetson and hooked it on a hatrack. "Don't mind if I do."

Walking forward, he halted at the bar and ordered rye. Before the barkeep finished pouring, a girl appeared at his elbow. Her eyelids were darkened with kohl and her cheeks were bright with rouge. She smiled a bee-stung smile.

"Hello there, handsome."

"Hello yourself." Starbuck gave her a burlesque leer. "Buy you a drink?"

"My mama taught me to never say no."

Starbuck laughed, his face wreathed in high good humour. "I shore hope that don't apply just to drinks."

"Why, honeybunch, you can bet your boots on it!"

The girl was a pocket Venus. She was small and saucy, with a gamine quality that was compellingly attractive. Her delicate features were framed by ash-blonde hair, and her wraparound housecoat fitted snuggly across fruity breasts and tightly rounded buttocks. She fixed him with a smile that would have melted the heart of a drill sergeant.

"Let me guess." Her eyes sparkled with suppressed mirth. "You're a cowboy, aren't you?"

"Close," Starbuck said with a waggish grin. "You might say I'm a horse trader."

"Nooo," she breathed. "Really?"

"Sometimes." Starbuck's grin broadened. "Course, it all depends."

"On what?"

"On whose horses we're tradin'."

She threw back her head and laughed. "Sweetie, I do like a man who likes a joke!"

"Well, little lady, I've got a hunch you're gonna like me lots."

"I'm Alvina." She leaned closer, squashing a breast against his arm. "What's your name . . . horse trader?"

"Floyd Hunnewell." Starbuck cocked one eye askew. "Fresh from Kansas and hot to trot."

"Then you've come to the right place, Floyd."

"Alvina, you shore know how to make a feller feel welcome."

"Honey, you haven't seen nothing yet!"

For the next two nights Starbuck played the braggart. He took a room at the hotel in Liberty; but he saw it only during daylight hours. By dark each evening, he was

Johnny-on-the-spot at Ma Ferguson's bordello. And his nights were spent in Alvina's bed.

Starbuck drank heavily, and flung money around as if he owned a printing press. The effect, considering the mercenary nature of his hostess, was somewhat predictable. Ma Ferguson accorded him the deferential treatment reserved for big spenders, and saw to it that his glass was never empty. She also allowed him to monopolise Alvina. The charge, which included sleeping over, was a mere twenty dollars a night.

Outwardly bluff and hearty, Starbuck acted the part with a certain panache. Sober, he appeared to be a happy-go-lucky drifter, with some mysterious, and inexhaustible, source of funds. With several drinks under his belt, he then turned garrulous, pretending the loose tongue of an amiable drunk. Whores were accustomed to braggarts who seemed possessed of some irresistible urge to toot their horn and confide their innermost secrets. So Alvina found nothing unusual in Floyd Hunnewell's boastful manner, and she dutifully portrayed the spellbound listener. He told her a tale of outlandish proportions.

Improvising as he went along, Starbuck intertwined fact with fabrication. His story, unfolding in bits and pieces, was recounted with an air of drunken self-importance. A Texan born and bred, he'd worked as a cowhand since boyhood. Over the years, he had trailed herds to every cowtown on the Kansas plains. Then, after last summer's drive to Dodge City, he awoke to the fact that he was getting no younger, and no richer. Determined to make something of himself, he looked over the field and decided that horse stealing was an enterprise with real potential. For the past seven months, he had averaged better than fifty head a month, and it was all profit. In total, he had cleared more than ten thousand

and no end in sight. A minor error in judgement had put
the law on his tail, but that was no great calamity. He
could afford to lie low and let the dust settle. Meanwhile,
he was scouting around for a new venture, something
befitting a man of his talents. Horse stealing, he'd decided, was too easy. A fellow who wanted to get ahead
had to raise his sights—aim higher!

Alvina bought the story. It was, after all, no great
shocker. Cowhands turned outlaw were fairly commonplace, and a horse thief in her bed was no cause for
excitement. She'd slept with worse—lots worse—and
never given it a thought. Yet she hadn't slept with anyone lately who was as much fun as Floyd Hunnewell.
For all his crowing and cocksure conceit, he was damned
likable. And to her surprise, he was a regular ball of fire
in bed. The last couple of nights, she'd actually found
herself enjoying it. Which was something to ponder.

To Starbuck, it was all in a day's work. Alvina was
good company—gullible like most whores—and he was
pleased that she'd swallowed his fairy tale so readily.
But that wasn't the reason he had selected her over the
other girls, and stuck with her for two nights running.
Instead, he'd zeroed in on her because she was by far
the prettiest girl in Ma Ferguson's henhouse. Some gut
instinct told him that her pert good looks would make
her the favourite of one or more of the Younger brothers.
By and by, he meant to turn that to advantage.

Late the third evening, Starbuck was seated on one
of the sofas with Alvina. They were talking quietly, sip-
ping whiskey, but his mind was elsewhere. The thought
occurred that he might be in for a long wait. So far there
had been no sign of the Youngers, and he'd heard no
mention of their name. For all he knew, they might have
taken their trade to another whorehouse. Or even worse,
they could be off robbing a bank—and ready to hightail

it for the Nations. By his count, they were already some months overdue at Belle Starr's. Still, there was nothing for it but to curb his impatience and wait it out. Time would tell, and meanwhile Alvina was a pleasant enough diversion. A damn sight more pleasant than that axe-faced bitch he'd wooed at Younger's Bend.

Alvina suddenly stiffened. She caught her breath in a sharp gasp and stared past him towards the door. He turned and saw three men enter the parlour. Though no photographs or drawings existed, the men fitted the general description of the Younger brothers. One of them separated, walking in the direction of the sofa while the other two continued on to the bar. He was powerfully built, with a pockmarked face, coarse sandy hair, and the bulge of a pistol beneath his coat. He halted, nodding to Alvina.

"How's things?"

"Fine." Alvina appeared flustered. "You haven't been around much lately."

"Well, I'm here now. C'mon, we'll have a drink and get ourselves caught up."

"Cousin," Starbuck interrupted politely. "You've done stopped at the wrong pew. The lady's taken for the night."

"Who says?"

"I reckon I do." Starbuck uncoiled slowly and got to his feet. " 'Specially since I paid for the privilege."

"The night's young. You just get in line, and when I'm done, she's all yours."

Starbuck sensed opportunity, and seized it. "Cousin, you must've heard wrong—"

"I've heard all I wanna hear! Close your trap or I'll close it for you."

"Say, looky here." A cocked sixgun emerged like a magician's dove from inside Starbuck's jacket. He scowled, and wagged the tip of the barrel. "I don't much cotton to threats. Suppose you just haul it out of here before I get tempted to make your asshole wink."

"Omigawd!" Alvina jumped to her feet. "Floyd, put it away! Please, honey, I'm asking—"

"Why the hell should I?"

"Because," Alvina whispered, touching his arm. "That's Jim Younger! The big one at the bar is Cole Younger, and the other one is Clell Miller. They'll kill you if you don't back off!"

"Younger?" Starbuck gave her a look of walleyed amazement. "Are you talkin' about *the* Younger brothers?"

"In the flesh," Alvina acknowledged. "Now cool down and play it smart! Like he told you, the night's young."

Starbuck shook his head in mock wonder. Then he lowered the hammer and slowly holstered the Colt. With a lame smile, he glanced at Jim Younger.

"Any friend of Alvina's is a friend of mine."

Younger grunted, and roughly pushed Alvina towards the door. Without a word, she led the way into the hall and they mounted the stairs to the second floor. Starbuck watched after them a moment, trying his damnedest to look unnerved and properly chastised. After a time his gaze shifted to the bar, and he found himself pinned by Cole Younger's stare. He grinned weakly and walked forward, halting a pace away.

"No offence." He stuck out his hand. "Name's Floyd Hunnewell, and I shore don't want no trouble with the Youngers."

Cole ignored the handshake. "You're pretty sudden with a gun."

"Wisht I wasn't sometimes."

Cole regarded him evenly. "You keep pullin' guns on

people and somebody's liable to give you a try."

"Hope there's no hard feelings." Starbuck looked painfully embarrassed. "I'd shore admire to buy you a drink, Mr. Younger."

"I guess not," Cole said bluntly. "We're sort of choosy about who we drink with."

"Well, maybe another time. I wouldn't want you to think I was unsociable, Mr. Younger."

"I'll keep it in mind."

Starbuck turned and walked back to the sofa. He was conscious of Ma Ferguson's beady glare and an almost palpable sense of tension among the girls. With a hang-dog expression, he took out the makings and began rolling a smoke. He made a show of nervously spilling tobacco, and took two tries to light a match. Yet inside he was laughing, positively jubilant.

By sheer outhouse luck, he'd made an impression the Youngers would never forget. The suddenness of his draw—his willingness to resort to gunplay—all that would stick in their minds. Then, too, there was Alvina. Even now, she was probably spilling his story to Jim Younger. And soon enough the word would circulate. Floyd Hunnewell was a wanted man, a horse thief with his eye on bigger things.

All in all, Starbuck thought he'd made a helluva start.

CHAPTER 10

"We've got ourselves a real stem-winder this time!"

"Why's that?"

"Have a look and you'll see."

Bob Younger, recently returned from Minnesota, unfolded a hand-drawn map. The men were gathered around the dining table in the Hudspeth home. Jesse and Frank sat at opposite ends of the table, with Cole on one side and Bob, flanked by Jim, on the other. Bob spread the map in the middle of the table, and everyone leaned forward for a better look. A series of lines, radiating outward like spokes in a wheel, converged on a central spot. He pointed with his finger.

"Here's Northfield. This wavy line's the Cannon River. Whoever named it ought've called it the curlycue. Crookedest sonovabitch you ever saw!"

Jesse glanced up. "What's so important about a river?"

"Oh, nothin' much." Bob smiled lazily. "It just splits Northfield clean down the middle, that's all."

"You're saying the town's divided by the river?"

"See that mark?" Bob indicated two parallel lines. "That's the Northfield Bridge. The river runs roughly

north-south and the bridge crosses it east to west. Sep-
arates the town pretty near half and half."

"So how's the town laid out?"

"Well, it's mostly houses on the west side of the
bridge. Then you cross the bridge headed east and you
come out smack-dab on the town square. That's the main
business centre, with a few stores and some such off on
these side streets. On beyond that, there's more houses."

"Sounds like a fair-sized town."

"You ain't whistlin' Dixie!" Bob's mouth curled. "I
had a few drinks in one of the bars, and got cosy with
some of the locals. They told me the town's pushin' five
thousand and still growin' strong."

No one spoke for several moments. Cole Younger,
already briefed by his brother, sat without expression,
waiting. Frank shot him a sidewise glance, then quickly
looked away. Jesse stared at the map a long while, his
features unreadable. Then, almost to himself, he finally
broke the silence.

"That's considerable bigger than anything we ever
tackled before."

"Bigger haul, too!" Cole said stoutly. "Wait'll Bob
tells you about the bank."

"What about it?"

Bob leaned back, thumbs hooked importantly in his
suspenders. "Them locals I talked to was regular civic
boosters. Told me the bank was just about the biggest
in southern Minnesota. Hell, it's even got a highfalutin
name—the First National Bank!"

"Forget the name." Jesse gave him a sour look.
"How's it fixed for money?"

"Plumb loaded!" Bob let loose a hoot of laughter.
"Them barflies said it's got a vault the size of a barn.
And they wasn't lyin' either! I meandered over and had
a look for m'self."

"You checked out the bank?"

"Figgered I might as well. It was a Saturday, and the town was crawlin' with farmers and their families. I just joined the crowd and waltzed in there nice as you please."

"Tell him about the vault," Cole prompted. "What you saw."

"Well, now!" Bob snapped his suspenders and grinned. "The people was lined up three deep and depositin' money hand over fist. Seems like Saturday is the day all the farmers and folks from neighbourin' towns does their business. You never saw nothin' like it in all your born days!"

"The vault," Jesse reminded him. "Did you get a look or not?"

"I did for certain! The door was standin' wide open, and you could've drove a wagon through the inside with room to spare. Ever' wall was lined with shelves and drawers, and the whole kit 'n' caboodle was stacked knee deep with money. Goddamnedest sight I ever laid eyes on!"

"How much would you estimate?" Jesse eyed him keenly. "Just a rough calculation?"

"Well, don't you see—" Bob spread his hands in an expansive gesture. "Folks come from all over to do their bankin' there 'cause it'd take a cannon to blow the door off that vault. The locals told me nobody'd ever tried a holdup. Not once!"

"Answer the question," Cole said with weary tolerance. "You done told me and Jim. Now tell Jesse. How much?"

Bob swallowed, licked his lips. "I'd judge two hundred thousand. As God's my witness, Jesse—not a penny less!"

Jesse shoved his chair from the table. He rose and

without a word walked to the parlour, where he began pacing back and forth in front of the fireplace. Silence thickened at the table, and the men tracked him to and fro with their eyes. His head was bowed, thinking private thoughts, and a minute or longer passed before he suddenly stopped. Then he turned and moved once more to the table, standing behind his chair. His expression was sombre, and determined.

"I don't like it." He punctuated the statement with a vigorous gesture. "There's got to be a reason that bank's never been robbed. Somebody would've tried—especially with all that money layin' around—unless there was a damn good reason. I say we scotch the idea right here and now."

"No!" Cole's jaw jutted stubbornly. "We've waited a lifetime for this kind of payday. Just because nobody else has busted that bank don't mean it can't be done. And that sure as hell ain't no reason for us not to try!"

Jesse was very quiet, eyes boring into him. "Cole, I've spoke my piece. I say it's a washout, and that's that."

Cole's bushy eyebrows seemed to hood his gaze. "Last time we met, I told you the Youngers wouldn't play tin soldier no more. That goes double after hearin' what Bob saw at Northfield."

"Suppose you spell that out a little plainer?"

"Since you asked—" Cole smiled with veiled mockery. "We're fed up with nickel-and-dime jobs, and we're through playin' it safe. If you haven't got the stomach for Northfield, then we'll handle it our own selves."

A stony look settled on Jesse's face. "You sorry goddamn ingrate! I ought to kill you where you sit."

"Maybe you ought to," Cole challenged him, "but you won't. The way it stands now, you'd have to fight all us Youngers—not just one."

"Don't tempt me! Haulin' your ashes might make it worth it!"

Cole flipped his hand in scorn. "You love yourself too much for that, Jesse. So I don't guess I'm gonna lose any sleep over it."

"By Christ—!"

"Not Christ," Frank interrupted, clearing his throat. "To quote the Bard: 'Hell is empty and all the devils are here.' You two make the line sound prophetic."

Jesse and Cole stared at him blankly. When neither of them responded, he went on. "Why in thunder do you have to fight? We've got enough enemies without turning on one another." He paused, then continued in a temperate voice. "Jess, I'm not taking sides; but you have to face the facts. Unless you bend a little, Cole and the boys will take off on their own. Once it comes to that, we'll likely never get it healed. So maybe you ought to make allowances. We've been together a long time."

Jesse was white around the mouth, his temples knotted. Yet he held his temper, avoiding Frank's steady look, and gave the matter some thought. "All right," he said finally, squaring himself up. "We'll lay out the job and get on with it. But once we're in Northfield—if it don't smell right or anything looks queer, I'll call it off and no questions asked. That's as far as I'm willin' to bend, no farther. So take it or leave it."

The Younger brothers swapped quick glances among themselves. At length, Cole nodded and swivelled his head just far enough to meet Jesse's venomous glare. "I guess we could go along with that. You always said Bob was the best scout in the bunch, and Northfield didn't give him the willies. Don't expect it will you either. Specially when you get a gander at the vault."

"If we get that far," Jesse said, watching him with

undisguised hostility. "Just remember, once we're there, I call the tune as to whether or not we hit the bank. That's the deal."

"You want a blood oath?" Cole cracked a smile. "Or will my word do?"

Jesse let the remark pass. He seated himself, then reached out and pulled the map closer. "Bob, show me the layout. Let's start with the bank."

"Sure thing, Jesse." Bob leaned forward, explaining various marks on the map. "The bank's over here at the east end of the square. Sits right on a corner, where the square leads into Division Street. I figgered the best approach was to come into town from the east—that means we'd be headed west on Division Street—and stop right in front of the bank. That way we can cover the square without exposing ourselves, and we've got nothin' behind us but a few stores. When the job's done, we just turn around and ride out the same way we came in. It's the shortest and safest route, near as I could tell."

"The shortest, maybe." Jesse studied the map with a critical eye. "Not necessarily the safest."

"I don't follow you."

"Your way we've only got one line of retreat. If we were discovered—and these shopkeepers back here on Division Street got up in arms—then we'd be caught between them and the ones on the square. In other words, they'd have us trapped in a bottleneck. I can't say I'd care too much for that idea."

"By gum, you got a point there."

"Where's the town marshal's office?"

"Over here." Bob pointed with a dirty fingernail. "Off the south side of the square, just round the corner."

"Which means he steps out his door and he's roughly kitty-corner to the bank."

"Yeah, I reckon it does."

"What's along the other sides of the square?"

"Oh, just the general run of business and shops. Couple of cafés and that saloon I mentioned. A hotel over on the north side, right about in the middle of the block. Course, down here, on the west side, there's not much of anything. Don't you see, that leads directly to the bridge."

"How wide is the bridge?"

"Well, it'll take two wagons abreast. Looked like they built it specially for the farm trade."

"Across the river"—Jesse directed his attention to the western shoreline—"you show a road headed south. What's down that way?"

"Nothin' much. The road generally follows the river, and a couple of miles south there's a crossroads called Dundas. After that, you hit a long stretch of woods. Then maybe ten miles south there's a fair-sized town called Faribault."

"What's west of those woods?"

"I brought back maps of Minnesota and Iowa. You want me to show you in detail?"

"Later," Jesse said shortly. "For now, just tell me about those woods."

"To the west, there's more of the same. Broken woods, with marshy terrain and lots of small lakes. Due west—maybe thirty miles—there's a town called St. Peter and southwest there's one called Mankato."

Jesse abruptly switched back to the Northfield Bridge. "From here, are there any telegraph lines runnin' south?"

"No, there ain't." Bob pondered a moment. "I guess the towns are too small down that way. Near as I recollect, the poles all took a northerly direction—to Minneapolis."

"Thought so," Jesse said, almost to himself. "Now tell me about the bank. How's it laid out inside?"

Bob took a stub pencil from his coat pocket. Turning the map over, he began sketching a diagram on the opposite side. Watching them, Cole marvelled at Jesse's tactical genius. Always the guerrilla commander, he saw any job along the lines of a military raid. Before an actual date was set for the job, he would have worked out every detail, including their route to Minnesota and the order of retreat once they'd robbed the bank. However grudgingly, Cole had to admit there were none the equal of Jesse James when it came to planning a holdup. The end result would be a textbook study in how to rob a bank and make a clean getaway. All without losing a man or exposing themselves to unnecessary risk.

After studying the floor plan of the bank, Jesse flipped over to the map. He briefly scanned the drawing of Northfield, then nodded to himself in affirmation.

"Here's the way I see it." His finger stabbed out at the map. "That bridge is the key point. Once we occupy it and hold it, we have a clear field of fire that covers the entire square. On top of that, our best line of retreat is south along the road to that stretch of woods. So everything hinges on taking control of the bridge."

"Lemme understand," Cole said, hunching forward for a look at the map. "You're sayin' somebody posted at the bridge could keep the townspeople pinned down while we're in the bank. Is that it?"

"Yeah, that's the first step. Course, we'll also need covering fire when we leave the bank and head back across the square. So like I said—that bridge has got to be held the whole time."

"No question there," Cole agreed. "What about the bank itself?"

"We'll split up into groups." Jesse tapped the map with his finger. "One at the bridge and another outside the bank. Between them, they'll have the square covered in a crossfire from one end to the other. Once they're in place, the third group will enter the bank and pull the job."

"Hold on!" Cole protested. "That'll split us up pretty thin, won't it?"

"Normally it would," Jesse said levelly. "Except I'm figurin' on eight men altogether. Three at the bridge, two outside the bank, and three more inside. With the size of the town, and the way it's laid out, I wouldn't try it with any less."

"So you're talkin' about three more besides ourselves?"

"That's the general idea."

"Well, I don't like it! That means we're gonna have to divvy out eight shares instead of five."

"Either we do it right or we don't do it at all. It'll take eight men to make certain we hold that bridge. And without the bridge—I'm not settin' foot in Northfield!"

"Whereabouts you figure to get 'em? There ain't a helluva lot of men I'd trust to cover my backsides."

"What about Clell Miller?" Bob suggested. "He pulled his weight on that last train job."

"Don't forget Charlie Pitts," Jim added quickly. "He's no slouch either."

"I suppose they'll do," Cole grumbled. "Now try thinkin' of another one that's worth his salt! All the good ones are dead or else they've turned tame as tabby cats."

"Not all," Frank said with a slow grin. "The way Jim tells it, there's a fellow down at Ma Ferguson's who acts more like a bobcat."

"Awww, hell, Frank!" Jim groaned. "I told you that private. Besides, he sucked wind quick enough when push came to shove."

"Only because you had Cole and Clell Miller to back your play."

"Wait a minute," Jesse broke in. "Who're you talkin' about?"

"Some stranger." Jim shrugged it off. "Him and me got into it over a girl, and he pulled a gun. Wasn't all that much to it."

"Tell me anyway," Jesse persisted. "Who is he? What d'you know about him?"

"He's a small-time horse thief. Alvina, that's the girl, told me the law run him out of Kansas. Way he acts, he's had lots of experience runnin'."

"Bullfeathers!" Frank laughed. "You told me he got the drop on you so fast you never knew what happened. Anybody that handy with a gun, maybe we ought to consider him for the third man."

"God a'mighty!" Cole blustered. "You got rocks in your head, Frank. The man's an outsider."

"Cole, answer me this," Jesse said in a cold, dry manner. "What were you doing at Ma Ferguson's in the first place? I thought we agreed you'd stay clear of there."

"No such thing!" Cole muttered. "I told you I'd stay out of trouble—and I did!"

"The hell you did! A man pullin' a gun sounds like the kind of trouble we could do without."

"Jesus Christ! He pulled on Jim, not me!"

Jesse eyed him in disgust. "Maybe Frank's right. We could use some new blood in this outfit. 'Specially a rooster that'd pull on the Youngers."

"Whoa back, Jesse." Frank gave a troubled look. "I was only joking around. Why take it out on Cole?"

"Why not?" Jesse said with heavy sarcasm. "Anybody Cole don't like probably deserves a second look. You go on down to Ma Ferguson's and check out this horse thief. He might be just the man we need."

"You're makin' a mistake," Cole said sullenly. "And

you know goddamn well you're only doing it to spite me."

"C'mon now!" Jesse mocked him. "You mean to say you don't trust Frank's judgement?"

"That ain't what we're talkin' about here."

"What are we talkin' about, then?"

"The same old thing." Cole's jaw muscles worked. "Who beats the drum and who winds up playin' tin soldier."

"Cole, I do believe you got the message."

"You're liable to thump your drum one of these days and nobody'll answer muster."

A ferocious grin lit Jesse's face. "There's lots of tin soldiers, Cole. But I'm the only one that's got a drum . . . and I aim to keep it!"

CHAPTER 11

"You shouldn't be so impatient, lover."

"Hell, I need some action! Fun's fun, but a steady diet of it don't suit my style."

"Thanks a lot!" Alvina crinkled her nose in a pout. "You sure know how to make a girl feel special."

"Holy moly!" Starbuck rolled his eyes upward. "I done spent six nights in a row with you! If that don't make you special, I shore as the devil don't know what would."

"A little sweet talk wouldn't hurt. You were full of it up until tonight."

"Yeah, you're right." Starbuck's tone was grumpy, out of sorts. "It's just that a feller goes stale after a while. Not that you ain't good company! I got no complaints on that score, none a 'tall. But it's like I'm gettin' itchy—and don't know where to scratch."

"Ooo." Alvina clucked sympathetically, kissed him softly on the cheek. "Don't get down in the mouth, sweetie. I told you I'd talk to Jim, and I will. Cross my heart!"

"Probably won't do no good," Starbuck said glumly. "Them Youngers ain't the friendliest bunch I ever run acrost."

"You leave it to me," Alvina assured him brightly.
"Jim Younger thinks more of me than he does his own
wife! One way or another, I'll convince him to at least
talk to you."

"Well, I shore as hell wisht he'd show again! I'm
plumb tuckered out with sittin' on my duff."

Starbuck's gruff manner was no act. Seated beside
Alvina on a sofa, he watched listlessly as the evening
crowd began drifting into Ma Ferguson's. The ivory
tickler was playing a melancholy tune on the piano, and
it somehow suited his mood. For the past three nights—
since the evening he'd braced Jim Younger—he had
planted himself on the sofa and waited. Some inner conviction told him the Youngers would return, and he'd
kept himself steeled to take the next step in his plan. Yet
tonight his conviction was waning rapidly. Unless the
outlaws put in an appearance soon, then it was all wish-
ful thinking. Not a plan but rather a pipe dream. He dully
wondered if he'd sold himself a bill of goods.

"Don't you worry, Floyd." Alvina lowered one eyelid
in a bawdy wink. "Where Jim Younger's concerned, I'm
the hottest stuff in Clay County! He couldn't stay away
if his life depended on it."

"Looks like he's making a pretty good stab at it."

"Oh, pshaw! You know what my mama used to say?"

"What's that?"

"She used to say, 'Worry is the curse of those who
borrow trouble.' "

"I ain't worried," Starbuck grumbled. "It's like I told
you—I'm just tryin' to scratch that itch."

"Well, I can't see why you're so stuck on becoming
a bank robber anyway. The notion probably wouldn't
have occurred to you in a thousand years if you hadn't
bumped into the Youngers the other night."

"Who knows? I was lookin' for a new line of work

and they just happened along at the right time. Nothing ventured, nothing gained."

"From what Jim tells me, they've ventured a lot and gained a little here lately. Talk about a bunch that needs a rabbit's foot!"

"He tells you all his secrets, does he?"

Alvina giggled and batted her eyelashes. "Honey, you just wouldn't believe it! I told you he was sweet on me."

"So their luck's turned sour, then?"

"Let's say they're not exactly rolling in clover."

"Hell, maybe you're right," Starbuck said guilefully. "Maybe robbin' banks ain't what it's cracked up to be."

"Feast or famine, that's the way it looks to me."

"I guess I could always go back to Kansas. Things have likely cooled off by now, and horse stealing ain't all that bad. Least it's regular work."

"Floyd!" Alvina looked wounded. "You said you liked it here!"

"I do," Starbuck said earnestly. "That's why I asked you to put in the word with Younger. But now, you sound like you're tryin' to talk me out of it."

"No, I'm not!" Alvina snuggled closer on the sofa. "You just put Kansas out of your mind. And stop worrying about Jim Younger! I'm one girl that doesn't go back on a promise."

Starbuck felt only a twinge of conscience. He had purposely set out to win her over, and six nights in her bed had proved adequate to the job. He'd treated her with gentleness and affection, and seen to it that their lovemaking was a thing of ardour rather than passionless rutting. All of which was like catnip to a working whore. She'd fallen for him very much in the manner of a schoolgirl surrendering her virginity. And recruiting her to his cause had been accomplished with surpassing ease.

Having failed in his approach to Cole Younger, he'd
thought to hedge his bet with Alvina. Her assistance created a couple of intriguing possibilities. For openers, she
was a veritable fund of information. As she herself had
noted, men often confided more in whores than in their
own wives. Apparently that was the case with Jim
Younger, and whatever tidbits she gleaned would be a
welcome addition to the file. Of greater import, she
claimed some influence over Younger. In the event she
persuaded him to vouch for Floyd Hunnewell, then the
larger part of the problem would be resolved. One rec-
ommendation would lead to another, forming a daisy
chain that would ultimately lead to Jesse James. From
there, it would remain but a matter of time—and opportunity.

Starbuck by no means felt sanguine. Alvina might
prove an asset, and then again her efforts might very
well come to nothing. Yet, from his standpoint, there
was everything to gain, with little or no risk of exposing
his hand. She was an unwitting operative—undercover
in every sense of the word—and more valuable for it.
Should she prove ineffective, then it would have cost
him nothing more than six nights of ardent lovemaking.
And in all truth, the expenditure had required no labour.
He'd thoroughly enjoyed himself.

"See!" Alvina suddenly hissed out of the corner of
her mouth. "I told you he couldn't stay away!"

She popped off the sofa and hurried towards the door.
As Starbuck watched, she greeted Jim Younger with an
exuberant laugh and a teasing peck on the mouth. Behind him, crowding through the doorway, were Cole and
two other men. One of them, not unlike the third pea in
a pod, was clearly Bob Younger. The other newcomer
was slimmer of build, somewhat gangling, with a determined jaw and a neatly trimmed beard. Something about

him bothered Starbuck. A wisp of recognition that was at once familiar and elusive.

The men walked to the bar, with Alvina hanging on Jim Younger's arm. None of them so much as glanced at Starbuck, and he pretended to mind his own business. After a couple of drinks, Jim ordered a bottle from the barkeep; with Alvina in tow, he excused himself and led her towards the hallway. Cole, his voice loud and boisterous, subjected them to a coarse ribbing as they crossed the parlour. Arm in arm, ignoring his jibes, they disappeared up the stairs. Cole laughed uproariously and turned back to his companions. He whacked the bar, ordering a fresh round of drinks.

Several minutes later, the bearded man abruptly shoved away from the bar. He walked directly to the sofa and halted. His eyes were friendly but sharp, very sharp. He nodded to Starbuck.

"Mind if I sit down?"

"Help yourself, cousin. It's a free country."

Starbuck had a feral instinct for the truth. His every sense alerted, and he warned himself to play it loose. For some reason as yet unrevealed, he was about to be put to the test. He knew he dare not fail.

"I'm told," the man said tentatively, "you go by the name of Floyd Hunnewell?"

"You're told right," Starbuck said with a raffish smile. "Appears you've got the advantage on me."

"Most folks call me Frank."

"Well, I'll be jiggered!" Starbuck gave him a look of unalloyed amazement. "I ain't no mental wizard, but my ma didn't raise no dimdots neither. Something tells me you got a brother named Jesse."

Frank gazed at him for a long, speculative moment. "Let's talk about you. I understand you're from Kansas?"

"Now and then," Starbuck said, grinning. "The rest of the time I'm a Texican—and damn proud of it!"

"Strayed a mite far north, haven't you?"

Starbuck regarded him with an expression of amusement. "Women shore do talk, don't they?"

"How so?"

"Why don't we skip the guessin' game? Seems pretty clear Alvina spilled the beans to Jim Younger, and now he's put the bee in your ear. So it boils down to you askin' questions when you already know the answers."

"You're right." Frank smiled genially. "Your ma didn't raise any dimdots."

"Only one thing troubles me." Starbuck leaned back, legs casually stretched out before him. "Why're you askin' me any questions at all?"

"You could be a Pinkerton." Frank let the idea percolate a few moments. "A stranger appears out of nowhere and passes himself off as a horse thief. If you were in my boots—wouldn't that tend to make you leery?"

"*Pinkerton!*" Starbuck said wonderingly. "I been called lots of things in my time, but never nothin' that lowdown. Course, you wasn't exactly accusin' me"—he paused for effect—"or was you?"

Frank smiled in spite of himself. "Fast as you are with a gun, that'd be pushing my luck pretty far, wouldn't it?"

"Shore do regret that." Starbuck chuckled, stealing a glance at the bar. "Guess the Youngers was some put out, huh?"

"No harm done. Jim has a habit of crowding people when he shouldn't. Nobody faults you for pulling a gun . . . so long as you don't do it again."

"In that case—" Starbuck raised an uncertain eyebrow. "How come you and me are sittin' here playing ring-around-the-rosy?"

Frank cocked his head and studied Starbuck thoughtfully. "Jim was naturally curious, especially after you threw down on him so quick. He twisted Alvina's arm and she let it drop that you're on the run. Any truth to it?"

Starbuck wormed around on the sofa and flexed his shoulders. "I'll have to have m'self a talk with Alvina. Her arm twists a little too easy—regular goddamn blabbermouth!"

"She also said you're on the scout for a new line of work."

"So?"

"Wondered why," Frank said almost idly. "You seem to have done fairly well in the horse business."

"Simple enough," Starbuck said lightly. "I don't aim to scratch a poor man's ass all my life. There's ways to make lots more money—and lots faster, too!"

Frank gave him a swift, appraising glance. "Got anything particular in mind?"

"Why?" Starbuck asked, deadpan. "You offerin' me a job?"

"What if I was?"

"I'd still ask why. You don't know me from a hole in the ground, and I ain't exactly in your league. See what I mean?"

"Everybody has to start somewhere."

"That's a fact," Starbuck said slowly. "Howsoever, not everybody starts at the top. Sort of makes me wonder whether you're testin' the water—or what?"

The shadow of a question clouded Frank's eyes, then moved on. "Why don't you sit tight for a minute? I want to have a word with Cole."

Starbuck's expression revealed nothing. Yet he was

astonished by the turn of events, searching for a reason where none seemed to exist. Frank rose, nodding to him, and walked to the bar. The conversation with Cole Younger was short, and heated.

"I sounded him out," Frank commenced guardedly, "and he strikes me as being on the level."

Cole nailed him with a sharp, sidelong look. "You're not serious—are you?"

"Why not?" Frank temporised. "He's smart and he's had experience dodging the law. And you saw for yourself, he's no tyro with a gun."

"Come off it!" Cole demanded churlishly. "The bastard's an outsider! I don't want no part of it."

"Then why are we here?"

" 'Cause I didn't want no trouble with Jesse! Besides, it gimme me a chance to get my wick dipped."

Frank's face grew overcast. "I think you're being shortsighted, Cole. We could use a good man on this job, and Hunnewell seems to fit the ticket."

"No sale!" Cole's headshake was emphatic. "I won't work with a stranger. You give him the nod and you can count me out! That goes for the boys, too."

Cole turned away, ending the discussion. He signalled Bob, and in short order they had each selected a girl. Without another word to Frank, they stalked from the parlour, trailed by a couple of blowzy whores, and mounted the stairs. Frank appeared slightly bemused, staring after them for several seconds. Then, with a hopeless shrug, he walked back to the sofa.

"Sorry, Hunnewell." He rocked his head from side to side. " 'The nature of bad news infects the teller.' "

"Come again?"

"A line from Shakespeare." Frank lifted his hands with a sallow smile. "I thought we could find a spot for you, but it seems I was mistaken. Maybe next time."

"Next time?" Starbuck repeated, genuinely confused. "What's that supposed to mean?"

"A figure of speech," Frank said evasively. "There's always a next time and a time after that. See you around."

On that cryptic note, Frank moved into the hallway and out the door. Starbuck simply sat there, stunned. He hadn't the least notion of what had transpired or why. Yet there was one thing about which he was utterly certain. He'd just been blackballed for membership in the James-Younger gang.

Late that night Alvina joined him in the parlour. The Younger brothers, drunk and raucous, had departed only a short while before. She looked some the worse for wear, sombre and somehow distracted. With a heavy sigh, she dropped beside him on the sofa.

"Well, lover." She smiled wanly. "How's things with you?"

"Slow." Starbuck's smile was equally bleak. "Mighty slow."

"Sorry," Alvina apologised. "I couldn't get rid of him. Usually he doesn't drink all that much; but there wasn't anything usual about tonight. He damn near killed that whole bottle."

"Forget it," Starbuck said darkly. "You got a job to do, and nobody's blamin' you for that."

Alvina studied his downcast face. "Aren't you going to ask me what happened?"

"Happened with what?"

"With Jim Younger," Alvina reminded him. "I was supposed to talk to him . . . remember?"

"Oh, yeah." Starbuck seemed to lose interest. "How'd it go?"

"It didn't! The bastard got drunk as a skunk and I never had a chance to sound him out."

"Don't matter," Starbuck said miserably. "Too late anyway."

"Too late?" Alvina parroted. "Too late for what?"

"Too late for me!" Starbuck's tone suddenly turned indignant. "Frank James halfway gave me an invite to join up with 'em. Then Cole Younger put the quietus on it so fast it'd make your head swim. I was in and out before I knew what hit me!"

"Jeezus!" Alvina murmured. "You've had yourself some night, honeybun!"

"I suppose you could say that."

"Well, at least I know why Cole nixed you."

"You do?"

Alvina gave him a bright nod. "They're planning a job. That's why I couldn't get a word in edgewise with Jim. He got drunk and bragged himself blue in the face." She hesitated, put a hand on his arm. "Don't blame yourself, lover. As big as this job sounds, Cole wouldn't risk breaking in a new man."

"Just my luck." Starbuck suppressed a sudden jolt of excitement. "How big . . . or didn't he say?"

"Oh, he said all right! To hear him tell it, they'll all retire when this one's over."

"Sounds like an express-car job."

"No, it's a bank. A real *big* bank."

"Wouldn't you know it!" Starbuck cursed, slumped back on the sofa. "Whereabouts? Not that it matters a whole helluva lot."

An indirection came into Alvina's eyes. "North-something-or-other. I think he said Northfield. Or maybe Northville. Tell you the truth, I wasn't listening too close. What a girl don't know can't hurt her."

Starbuck chanced one last question. "Northfield? Hell,

that don't sound so big to me. Where's it at?"

"Search me, lover. He didn't say and I didn't ask! All night he just kept saying it was going to surprise the living bejesus out of the Pinkertons."

"Wonder what he meant by that?"

"Who knows?" Alvina murmured wearily. "You'll pardon my French . . . but I really don't give a fuck anyhow."

Starbuck knew then he would learn no more. Yet, with luck, he thought perhaps he'd learned enough. The germ of an idea took shape in his mind, and his pulse quickened. A bank, more so than most places, would make a fitting stage. And a final curtain for Jesse James.

He wondered if there was a morning train to St. Louis.

CHAPTER 12

Starbuck revised his plan. After sleeping on it overnight, he decided the delay of another day was of no great consequence. Speed, in the overall scheme of things, was less essential than maintaining his cover story.

He had no clear idea when the robbery would occur. Yet it seemed unlikely the gang would ride out within the next couple of days. The Youngers, after their binge of last night, would need time to recuperate. Then, too, Frank James had evidenced no sense of urgency in either his attitude or his curious offer. All that indicated the holdup would not take place for at least three days, perhaps more. And since Starbuck's own plan was based largely on guesswork, he felt the need to copper his bet.

For Floyd Hunnewell to disappear mysteriously would almost certainly arouse suspicion. All the more so in the light of Alvina's thoughtless revelations the night before. A bit of insurance seemed in order, and for the simplest of reasons. There was an outside possibility that Floyd Hunnewell would, by necessity, return to Ma Ferguson's. To do so—without getting killed in the process—would require that his credentials as a horse thief withstand scrutiny. On balance, then, it seemed wise to enlarge the original cover story with still another tapestry of lies.

To that end, Starbuck improvised a tale designed to touch a whore's heart. He appeared disgruntled, thoroughly crestfallen that he'd muffed his chance to join the James-Younger gang. A change of scenery, he explained, along with a little action, was needed to restore his spirits. He'd decided to return to his old haunts—a horse-stealing foray into Kansas which would last a week, perhaps longer, depending on circumstances. Then, with his funds replenished, he would hightail it straightaway back to Ma Ferguson's. It wasn't goodbye, he told Alvina, but merely a pause in the festivities. Upon his return, the party would resume right where they'd left off.

Alvina accepted the story at face value. She was sad, even a bit misty-eyed, but not without hope. When he departed around midmorning, she was convinced their separation would be of short duration. She peppered him with kisses, hugging him fiercely, and let go only when he stepped through the front door. Waving, bravely snuffling back her tears, she watched as he rode away. For a whore, whose memories were generally bereft of sentiment, it was a moment to be treasured. She was overcome by the old sensation of a woman sending her man off to battle.

Starbuck turned his attention to the task ahead. Kansas City was less than twenty miles from Ma Ferguson's, and he arrived there early that afternoon. He left the gelding at a livery stable, paying a week's charges in advance, and emerged onto the street. For the next hour he circled through the downtown area, frequently doubling back, always looking over his shoulder. At last, satisfied he hadn't been followed, he went to the train station and collected a suitcase he'd checked the week before. A short while later he stepped into one of the town's busier hotels. There, registering under a false name, he took a room.

Upstairs, Starbuck paused only long enough to deposit the suitcase in his room. Then he quickly took possession of the bathroom at the end of the hall. With all the modern conveniences, including hot and cold running water, he set to work. Standing before the lavatory mirror, he peeled off the fake moustache and carefully scrubbed spirit gum from his upper lip. After undressing, he drew a scalding bath and lowered himself into the tub. The water slowly turned dark brown as he alternately lathered and rinsed his hair. A final washing, with his head directly under the tap, removed the last of the dye. When he inspected himself in the mirror, the transformation was complete. Floyd Hunnewell had been laid to rest.

Late that afternoon, Starbuck emerged from the hotel by a side exit. He caught a hansom cab and went straight to the train station. After dropping his bag at the checkroom, he purchased a ticket; then he swiftly mingled with the crowd. Only by a fluke would he have been recognised by anyone from Clay County; he was attired in his Denver clothes, and his hair was once again light chestnut in colour. Still, there was always that off chance, and he'd learned long ago that too much caution was far healthier than too little. By train time, he felt reasonably confident he was in the clear. On the stroke of six he boarded the evening eastbound for St. Louis.

At the first stop, an hour or so down the line, Starbuck hopped off the train. He collared the station agent, handing him a scribbled message and a ten-dollar bill. The agent, impressed by his generosity, promised to send the wire the moment the train was under way.

The message was addressed to Otis Tilford.

• • • •

Not long after sunrise the train pulled into St. Louis.
Starbuck left the depot on foot and headed uptown. A
walk in the brisk morning air took the kinks out of his
muscles and revived him from a long night in the chair
car. By the time he reached the corner of Olive and
Fourth, he'd worked up an appetite.

A café catering for the early-morning breakfast trade
caught his attention. He first used the washroom to
splash sleep out of his eyes and scrub his teeth with soap
and a thorny forefinger. Then he sat down to a plate of
ham and eggs, with a side order of flapjacks. He topped
off the meal with a cigarette and a steaming mug of
black coffee. On the street again, he went looking for a
barbershop.

By half past eight, he'd had a trim and a shave. He
reeked of talcum powder and bay rum, and he felt positively chipper as he walked along Fourth towards Delmar. At the corner, he entered the Merchants & Farmers
Bank Building. The elevator deposited him on the third
floor, and a moment later he pushed through the door of
the International Bankers Association. The receptionist,
still masquerading as a drill sergeant, evidenced no surprise at his arrival. His wire had been slipped under the
door early that morning and he was expected. She escorted him directly into Otis Tilford's office.

The banker was seated behind his desk. He smiled
and beckoned Starbuck forward. His eyes were strangely
alert and his handshake was cordial. He motioned to a
chair.

"I must say I'm delighted to see you, Mr. Starbuck.
There for a while I began to wonder if you had fallen
victim to foul play."

"Nothing like that," Starbuck said, seating himself.

"I've been on the go since I left here, and not a whole lot to report. Up till now anyway."

"You have news, then?" Tilford leaned forward eagerly. "A break in the case?"

"Maybe," Starbuck allowed. "Maybe not. All depends on the next turn of the cards."

"I don't believe I follow you."

"Suppose I fill you in on what's happened?"

"Yes, by all means! Please do, Mr. Starbuck."

Starbuck began with the tenuous leads he'd unearthed from the Pinkerton file. From there, he briefly recounted his trip to Indian Territory and the night with Belle Starr. Then, touching only on salient details, he related how he had infiltrated Ma Ferguson's bordello. Apart from the cover story, he made no mention of the disguise or the alias he'd assumed. As a matter of security, he never revealed professional secrets to anyone, not even a client. He went on to tell of Alvina and the Youngers, and his gradual acceptance as a regular at the brothel. Then, finally, he spoke of his strange conversation with Frank James.

"I got close," he concluded. "But close don't count except in horseshoes. One word from Cole Younger put a damper on the whole works."

"Good Lord!" Tilford said, visibly impressed. "You were actually face to face with Frank James!"

"Closer than I am to you right now. With a little luck, I could've killed him and the Youngers there and then. Course, I never tried for the obvious reason. I figured you wanted Jesse or nobody."

"Quite correct," Tilford said briskly. "Nevertheless, you are to be commended, Mr. Starbuck. To my knowledge, no one—certainly no Pinkerton—has ever made personal contact with Frank James. Not to mention the Younger brothers—and all of them in the same room!"

"All of them except the one we're after."

"A masterful piece of work, nonetheless! How on earth were you able to gain their confidence?"

"The girl," Starbuck told him. "She was the key. Once I got her on my side, the rest just fell into place."

"I marvel that the Pinkertons never considered such an approach."

Starbuck gave him a cynical smile. "I'd guess the Pinks wouldn't talk the same language as whores."

"Perhaps not." Tilford appeared nonplussed, and quickly dropped the topic. "Well, now, Mr. Starbuck! Where do we proceed from here?"

"I need some information, and I need it today."

"Exactly what sort of information?"

"Alvina—she's the girl I mentioned—let slip that the gang has a holdup planned. She wasn't certain, but she thought the name of the town was either Northfield or Northville. We've got to determine which it is—and where."

"Where?"

"What state."

"Are you telling me she gave no indication as to the state?"

"She couldn't," Starbuck replied. "She didn't know."

"And she wasn't precise as to whether it's Northfield or Northville?"

"She leaned towards Northfield. All the same, she wouldn't have sworn to it."

"So, then, we're faced with a conundrum of sorts, aren't we?"

"If that means a head scratcher, then I'll grant you it's a lulu."

Tilford steepled his fingers, thoughtful. "A possible solution occurs to me. The American Bankers Association publishes a booklet listing all member banks. I addition, when we were organising the International Association, we compiled a list of virtually every bank in the Midwest. Between the two lists, we might very well find the answer."

"Sounds good," Starbuck observed. "How long will it take?"

"I have no idea." Tilford rose from his chair. "However, I will attend to the search personally. I daresay that will speed things along."

"Need some help?"

"Thank you, no." Tilford moved around his desk. "I'll put every available clerk on it immediately. Please make yourself comfortable, Mr. Starbuck."

With that, Tilford hurried out of the office. Starbuck took out the makings and began building himself a smoke. He creased a rolling paper, holding it deftly between thumb and forefinger, and sprinkled tobacco into it. Then he licked, sealing the length of the paper, and twisted the ends. He struck a match on his boot sole and lit the cigarette. Exhaling smoke, he snuffed the match and tossed it into an ashtray. He settled down to wait.

Several times over the next hour Tilford's receptionist popped in to check on him. She offered coffee, which he accepted, and refilled his cup on each trip. At last, with his kidneys afloat, he declined the fourth refill. A cup of coffee was nothing without a smoke, and he put a dent in his tobacco sack during the prolonged wait. He was lighting yet another cigarette as Tilford bustled through the door. In his hand, the banker held a single sheet of foolscap.

"I fear we've somewhat compounded the problem, Mr. Starbuck."

"Oh, how so?"

"See for yourself." Tilford seated himself, and placed

the paper on the desk between them. I regret to say the prefix 'North' is not all that uncommon."

Starbuck pulled his chair closer and scanned the paper. On it, printed in neat capital letters, was a list of five towns: NORTHFIELD, ILLINOIS. NORTHFIELD, MINNESOTA. NORTHVILLE, MICHIGAN. NORTH-RIDGE, OHIO. NORTHWOOD, IOWA. His eye was drawn to the top of the list, and he briefly considered the two Northfields. Then he took a long, thoughtful draw on his cigarette.

"Illinois and Minnesota." The words came out in little spurts of smoke. "Guess we could toss a coin and hope for the best."

"Let me pose a question." Tilford studied his nails a moment. "Is it possible the girl was confused, somehow got the name of the town wrong?"

"Anything's possible," Starbuck remarked. "What makes you ask?"

"You will note"—Tilford tapped the paper—"there are five states listed there. Of those states, the James-Younger gang has been active in only one, that state being Iowa."

"You're saying there's a connection?"

"Precisely!" Tilford intoned. "For all his robberies Jesse James had limited himself to a very defined territory. If nothing else, the Pinkertons established that every robbery occurred either in Missouri or in a state contiguous to Missouri."

"I'm not much on four-bit words."

"Contiguous," Tilford elaborated, "simply means a bordering state. In short, the James-Younger gang had *never* been known to operate in a state which did no directly border Missouri."

Starbuck again scanned the list. "You're telling me we ought to forget Minnesota, Michigan, and Ohio?"

"I am indeed," Tilford affirmed. "I seriously question that Jesse James would cross Iowa to rob a bank in Minnesota. Nor would he cross Illinois and Indiana to rob a bank in Michigan. It flies in the face of a record established over a period of seventeen years."

Starbuck was silent for a time. "I take it you've got a theory all worked out?"

"Facts speak for themselves," Tilford said with exaggerated gravity. "I submit the robbery will take place in one of two towns. The logical choice—based on what the girl was told—is Northfield, Illinois. A distant second, at least in my opinion, would be Northwood, Iowa."

"Northwood's out," Starbuck said in a low voice. "She wasn't certain, but she only mentioned two names: Northfield and Northville." He paused, slowly stubbed out his cigarette in the ashtray. "Tell me about Northfield, Illinois. What size town is it?"

"Quite small. I believe the population is something less than five hundred."

"Which means the bank wouldn't be any great shakes. How about Northfield, Minnesota?"

"Considerably larger," Tilford admitted. "I would judge it at roughly five thousand."

"And the bank?"

"Old and very prosperous," Tilford said, frowning heavily. "One of the largest in the Midwest."

There was a moment of weighing and deliberation before Starbuck spoke. "Alvina told me it was a big job, bigger than anything the gang had ever pulled. So that pretty well eliminates the bank in Illinois. To my way of thinking, it narrows down to one candidate—Northfield, Minnesota."

"I strongly disagree," Tilford said sharply. "Why would Jesse James travel that far to rob a bank? There's no logic to it! Absolutely none!"

"Outlaws aren't noted for logic. Even if they were, I'd have to follow my hunch on this one. Jesse and his boys are out to make a killing, and it was Jim Younger himself who said so. That speaks lots louder to me than all your facts."

"Are you prepared to stake your reputation on a hunch, Mr. Starbuck?"

"Why not?" Starbuck said with sardonic amusement. "Except for hunches, I would've been dead a long time ago."

"And in the event logic prevails . . . what then?"

"Tell you what." Starbuck met his look squarely. "You alert the authorities at Northfield, Illinois. Meantime, I'll get myself on up to Minnesota. That way everybody's happy."

"Compromise was hardly what I had in mind."

"It's all you'll get," Starbuck said quietly. "I told you when I signed on . . . I do it my way or I don't do it at all."

There was an awkward pause. Tilford's features congested, and his mouth clamped in a bloodless line. "Very well," he conceded at length. "When will you leave?"

"First train out," Starbuck informed him. "I like to scout the terrain before I lay an ambush."

"Ambush!" Tilford looked upset. "Won't the authorities in Minnesota have something to say about that?"

"All depends."

"On what, may I ask?"

"On whether or not I tell them."

"Good God!" Tilford shook his head in stern disapproval. "Surely you don't intend to take on the entire gang—without assistance!"

"We'll see." Starbuck gave him a devil-may-care grin. "Sometimes it's easier to kill a man by operating alone. Northfield might be too civilised for *our* kind of justice."

Tilford could scarcely mistake the nature of the grin, or the words. He had, after all, hired a man to dispense summary justice. Northfield's wishes in the matter were wholly immaterial.

"Yes." His tone was severe. "You may very well have a point, Mr. Starbuck."

Starbuck unfolded slowly from his chair. He tugged his jacket smooth and walked to the door. Then, as he was about to step into the hall, he paused and looked back over his shoulder. A ghost of a smile touched his mouth.

"I'll let you know how it comes out."

CHAPTER 13

Starbuck stood on the veranda of the Dampier House Hotel. A cigar was wedged in the corner of his mouth and his hands were locked behind his back. Under a noonday sun, he puffed thick clouds of smoke and stared out across the square. His gaze was fixed on the First National Bank.

Only an hour before, upon arriving in town, Starbuck had checked into the hotel. He was posing as a sundries drummer, whose territory had recently been broadened to include Minnesota. Apart from the ubiquitous cigar, his attire was the uniform of virtually all travelling salesmen. He wore a derby hat and a snappy checkered suit with vest to match. A gold watch chain was draped across the vest, and a flashy diamond ring sparkled on his pinky. His physical appearance was unchanged, with the exception of an old standby.

A gold sleeve, crafted with uncanny workmanship, was fitted over his left front tooth. The overall effect, as with any subtle disguise, was principally one of misdirection. When he smiled, which was a drummer's stock in trade, people seldom saw his face. Their recollection was of a gold tooth and a steamy cigar. The man who called himself Homer Croydon was otherwise lost to memory.

Today, eyes squinted in concentration, Starbuck was performing a feat of mental gymnastics. A manhunter who survived soon acquired the knack of looking at things from an outlaw's perspective. Long ago, the trick had become second nature, and he was now able to step into the other fellow's boots almost at will. Visualising himself to be Jesse James, he pondered on a foolproof way to rob the bank.

Based on all he'd learned, Starbuck knew it would be a mistake to think in conventional terms. Jesse James, unlike most bank robbers, approached each job as though it were a military operation. The Pinkerton file rather conclusively demonstrated that the James-Younger gang was organised along the lines of a guerrilla band. Without exception, their holdups had been executed with a certain flair for hit-and-run. Surprise, as in any guerrilla raid, was the key element. Every step was orchestrated—planned with an eye to detail—and the gang generally made good their escape before anyone realised a robbery had occurred. That, too, indicated the meticulous preparation characteristic of each job. The retreat, and subsequent escape, was engineered with no less forethought than the holdup itself. And therein lay the mark of Jesse James' overall genius. In seventeen years, he had never been outfoxed. His trademark was a cold trail . . . leading nowhere.

Yet Northfield presented a unique tactical problem. Brooding on it, Starbuck slowly became aware that the situation was fraught with imponderables. The layout of the town did not lend itself to a hit-and-run raid. The square was open and broad, affording little in the way of concealment. On all sides, stores fronted the square; tradesmen and shopkeepers had a perfect view of the bank; any unusual activity would immediately draw their attention. The chances of discovery—before the job was completed—were therefore increased manyfold. In that event the odds also multiplied that the gang would be forced to fight its way out of Northfield. Because the river bisected the town, however, there were only two logical lines of retreat. One led eastward, along Division Street, which began on the corner where the bank was located. Yet, while Division Street was the quickest route of escape, any flight eastward would merely extend the line of retreat. Headed in the wrong direction, the gang would at some point be compelled to double back on a south-westernly course. For in the end, there was no question they would make a run for Indian Territory.

The other escape hole was westward, across the bridge. There, too, the tactical problem was apparent. To reach the bridge, the gang would have to traverse the entire length of the square. Should trouble arise, and the townspeople take arms, the outlaws would be forced to run a gauntlet of gunfire. At first glance, the hazards entailed seemed to rule out the bridge. Still, apart from surprise, the chief attribute of an experienced guerrilla leader was to do the unexpected when it was least expected. A calculated risk at best, the bridge might nonetheless offer the lesser of two evils. It led westward, the ultimate direction of escape, and it shortened the line of retreat by perhaps thirty or forty miles. On balance, then, the advantages might very well outweigh the hazards. No one would expect a gang of bank robbers to take the hard way out of town. Nor would they anticipate that the gang leader might deliberately—

Starbuck was rocked by a sudden premonition. He stepped off the veranda and crossed the block-long expanse of the square. At the bridge, he halted and stared for a moment at the houses on the opposite side of the

river. Then, on the verge of turning, his eyes were drawn
to the line of telegraph poles running north. His gaze
shifted south—no telegraph poles!—and any vestige of
doubt disappeared. Facing about, he subjected the square
to cold scrutiny. From a tactical outlook, the bridge instantly became a key vantage point. The entire square,
from end to end, was commanded by an unobstructed
field of fire. There was, moreover, the element of the
unexpected from where it was least expected. In the
event fighting broke out, the townspeople would be looking towards the bank, not the bridge. And the outcome
was easy to visualise.

Starbuck walked back to the hotel. Whether by deductive reasoning or swift-felt instinct, he knew he'd
doped out the plan. Some inner certainty told him the
holdup would proceed along the lines he'd envisioned.
All that remained was to decide his own course of action. As he saw it, there were two options, both of which
held merit. The critical factor was yet another of those
imponderables.

To kill Jesse James all he had to do was bide his time.
His room, which was on the second floor, fronted the
hotel and directly overlooked the square. The range,
from his window to the door of the bank, was roughly
forty yards. No easy shot with a pistol, it was nonetheless one he had made many times before. By placing his
gun hand on the windowsill—and holding high with the
sights—he felt entirely confident of a kill shot. When
the gang exited the bank, his shot was certain to go
unnoticed in the ensuing gunfire.

Then, still posing as a drummer, he need only check
out of the hotel and be on his way. Homer Croydon
would be remembered by no one. Nor would anyone
associate him with the death of Jesse James.

The alternative was to contact the town marshal.

However, that route would require discretion and an oath of silence. Should the marshal prove the talkative sort— and word of an impending robbery spread through Northfield—then any hope of trapping the gang would be gravely jeopardised. The risk was compounded by the fact that others, by necessity, would be drawn into the scheme. Quite properly, the marshal would insist on alerting some of the townsmen. Extra guns, and men willing to use them, would be needed against a band of killers. Still, by stressing the need for secrecy, there was every reason to believe the plan would work. The welfare of Northfield and its citizens would be at stake. And trustworthy men, committed to the common good, could be persuaded to hold their silence.

In the end, Starbuck's decision had little to do with Northfield. He was concerned for the lives of innocent bystanders, and he had no wish to see the square turned into a battleground. Yet, for all that, his decision was a matter of personal integrity. While he had killed many men, he was no assassin. To hide, and shoot down a man from his hotel window, somehow went against the grain. His code in such matters was simple and pragmatic. He always gave the other man a chance, but he tried never to give him the first shot.

On reflection, it was the way he preferred to kill Jesse James. No stealth or potshots from hotel windows. He would do it openly, face to face—on the street.

Shortly after the noon hour, Starbuck left the hotel and crossed the square. Opposite the bank, he rounded the corner and walked towards the marshal's office, which was one door down. Northfield appeared to be a peaceful town, with nothing more serious than an occasional fistfight or a rowdy drunk. Other than the marshal, he thought it unlikely the town would employ any full-time officers. When he entered the office, his judgement was confirmed. All the cell doors stood open, and except for the marshal, the place was deserted. Seated behind a battered desk, the lawman was idly cleaning his fingernails with a penknife.

"Afternoon."

"Yessir." The marshal gave his gold tooth and snappy outfit a quick once-over. "Do something for you?"

"Are you Marshal Wallace Murphy?"

"I am." Murphy closed the penknife and stuck it in his pocket. "What's the problem?"

"No problem, Marshal. I was instructed to call on you when I got into town."

"Don't say?" Murphy looked flattered. "Who by?"

"Mr. Otis Tilford," Starbuck lied. "President of the International Bankers Association."

"Oh, yeah! Now that you mention it, the name rings a bell. Formed not too long ago, wasn't it?"

"Last summer," Starbuck said with a note of pride. "We're headquartered in St. Louis."

"I take it you work for the association?"

"In a manner of speaking. I'm a private detective, Marshal." Starbuck grinned and tipped his derby. "This drummer's getup is strictly window dressing. I was hired as an undercover operative by Mr. Tilford."

"I don't believe I caught your name?"

"Luke Starbuck. Course, that's just between you and me. I'm registered at the hotel under the name of Homer Croydon."

Murphy was heavily built, with a square, thick-jowled face and a ruddy complexion. The chair squeaked under his weight as he leaned forward, elbows on the desk. He suddenly appeared attentive.

"Why all the secrecy?"

"Like I told you, I'm working undercover."

"So you did." Murphy eyed him with a puzzled frown. "What brings you to Northfield?"

"Well . . ." Starbuck let him hang a moment. "I need your word everything will be kept in the strictest confidence, Marshal. Otherwise I'm not at liberty to divulge the details of my assignment."

"I dunno." Murphy sounded uncertain. "If it's got to do with Northfield, that could put me in an awkward position."

Starbuck flashed his gold tooth. "I'd say it's more likely to make you the town hero. Hear me out and I think you'll agree I'm right."

Murphy nodded, digesting the thought. "Okay, fire away. Only I warn you—I won't be a party to anything that's not in the best interests of Northfield."

"Fair enough." Starbuck's expression turned solemn. "Sometime within the next week, the First National Bank will be robbed."

"Robbed!" Murphy stared at him, dumbstruck. "How the hell would you know a thing like that?"

"How I know isn't important—"

"Says you!" Murphy cut him short. "You walk in off the street and tell me the bank's about to be robbed? I'll have an explanation, mister. And I'll have it damned quick."

"Suit yourself." Starbuck read a certain disbelief in his face, and decided to embellish the truth. "I was hired to infiltrate a gang of bank robbers. I located their hangout—a whorehouse—and I managed to get on chummy terms with them. Three nights ago, one of them got drunk and spilled the beans. So I checked with Mr. Tilford and he ordered me to contact you on the double. Here I am."

Murphy looked at him with narrow suspicion. "How do I know you're on the level?"

"If you don't believe me," Starbuck said lightly, "then just hide and watch. They're on their way to Northfield right now."

"Who's they?"

"Jesse James and the Youngers."

Murphy's mouth popped open. "Did you say Jesse James—*the* Jesse James?"

"The one and only."

"That's impossible!" Murphy shook his head wildly. "Why would Jesse James come all the way to Minnesota to rob a bank? It doesn't make sense!"

"Pay close attention, Marshal." Starbuck's eyes went cold and impersonal. "I don't have time to waste arguing with you. They're headed in your direction and that's a rock-solid fact. Now, I can show you how to stop them from robbing the bank, not to mention covering yourself with glory." He paused, jerked a thumb over his shoulder. "Or I can walk out that door and leave you with egg on your face. I reckon it all depends on how much you like wearing a marshal's badge."

"What the hell do you mean by that?"

"Why, it's pretty simple," Starbuck said without expression. "The town fathers wouldn't look too kindly on a man who let Jesse James ride in here and empty out the bank. All the more so once they heard Mr. Otis Tilford sent a special representative to warn you in advance."

There was a stark silence. Wallace Murphy stared down at his hands, tight-lipped. He seemed to be struggling within himself, and several moments passed before he looked up. Then he dipped his head in affirmation.

"Go ahead, say your piece. I'm listening."

On impulse, Starbuck pressed the advantage. "One more thing. I call the shots from here on out. You can take all the credit, but I won't let you monkey with my plan. Understood?"

"Understood," Murphy agreed gingerly. "Only you better come up with something damn good."

"I already have," Starbuck said with an odd smile. "You see, Marshal—I know how they intend to pull the job."

"Big deal!" Murphy laughed uneasily. "What's to robbing a bank? You just walk in and pull a gun."

"Not Jesse James," Starbuck countered. "Him and his boys are old guerrilla fighters. So we're in for a military operation from start to finish."

"Would you care to spell that out?"

"For openers, a couple of the gang will post themselves somewhere near the bank door. They're the outside men, and their job is to keep the street clear. That way, there's less chance of trouble when it comes time for the getaway."

"In other words, they're the ones that'll show first?"

Starbuck nodded. "Once they're in position then Jesse and a couple more of the gang will enter the bank. We can depend on that. Jesse always handles the inside work himself."

"What's so unusual about that? Sounds fairly routine to me."

"There's an added touch," Starbuck said soberly. "At least two men, maybe more, will take control of the bridge. If trouble develops during the holdup, they'll keep everyone on the square pinned down with gunfire. Afterwards, they'll cover the withdrawal when the bunch at the bank starts back across the square. Their last job is to act as a rear guard; fight a holding action at the bridge. Once the others are across the river and in the clear, then they'll take off like scalded ducks."

"Damn!" Murphy suddenly grasped it. "That means

anybody who tangles with them would be caught in a crossfire. It'd be suicide to set foot on the square!"

"We'll let Jesse and his boys go right on thinking that. Meantime, we'll arrange a little surprise of our own."

"An ambush!" Murphy's eyes brightened. "By God, I like your style, Starbuck! How long you figure we've got?"

"Well, let's see." Starbuck pulled at his ear. "Tomorrow's Saturday, and they wouldn't risk it with the farm crowd in town. So I'd say the early part of the week, probably Monday."

"With seven or eight of them, we'll need some help with this ambush of yours."

"Not too many," Starbuck cautioned him. "The fewer involved, the less chance of word leaking out. Do you know three or four men who can be trusted to keep their mouths shut?"

"Oh, hell, yes!" Murphy chortled. "Half the men in Northfield would give their left nut for a crack at Jesse James."

"Hold it to three," Starbuck said firmly. "That's plenty for what I have in mind. And don't let the cat out of the bag! Arrange to get them together sometime tomorrow, and I'll explain the setup myself. I already know where I want them spotted."

"I guess that only leaves Fred Wilcox. He's the president of the bank. When do we give him the good news?"

"We don't."

"What?" Murphy went slack-jawed with amazement. "Fred's got to be warned! You can't let that gang of murderers walk in there cold!"

"I don't aim to." Starbuck regarded him with a level gaze. "But we can't risk a bunch of nervous Nellies tipping our hand. We'll hit the minute Jesse steps down out of the saddle. So don't work yourself into a sweat. He'll never make it inside the bank—I guarantee it."

"Kill him dead!" Murphy cackled. "Shoot him down like a mad dog! That's what you're saying, isn't it?"

Starbuck smiled. "If a man's worth shooting, then I reckon he's worth killing."

"Like I said, Starbuck." Murphy chuckled heartily. "I admire your style."

"One last thing," Starbuck advised him. "I fire the first shot. That'll be the signal for you and your men to cut loose; but I don't want anybody to get overeager. Agreed?"

"Agreed! You've got my word on it."

Wallace Murphy was tempted, but he let the question go unasked. He already knew the answer, and counted it no great surprise. Starbuck's presence in Northfield was explanation enough.

The first shot would be for Jesse James.

CHAPTER 14

On Monday morning, the First National Bank opened at the usual time. Fred Wilcox, the president and chief stockholder, arrived a minute or so before eight. Waiting for him were the bank tellers, Joseph Heywood and Alan Bunker. He unlocked the front door and the men filed inside. A moment later the shade snapped up on the wide plateglass window fronting the square.

Starbuck was seated on the veranda of the hotel. He pulled out his pocket watch and checked the time. The marshal had told him Wilcox was a punctual man, and he noted the window shade went up almost precisely on the stroke of eight. Around the square, following the banker's example, tradesmen began opening their doors. Northfield stirred and slowly came to life. To all appearances it was a typical Monday morning, unremarkable in any respect. The townspeople, suspecting nothing, went about the routine of another business day.

A cigar jutting from his mouth, Starbuck lazed back in the cane-bottomed rocker. His legs were outstretched, heels planted atop the veranda railing, and the derby was tipped low over his forehead. To passersby, he looked like a slothful drummer, sunning himself after a heavy breakfast. In truth, he was alert and observant, his eyes moving hawklike around the square. He set the rocker in motion, ticking off a mental checklist item by item.

The three men selected by Marshal Wallace Murphy were already in position. Their weapons were secreted, but close at hand, and there was nothing about them to draw undue attention. One, Arthur Manning, operated a dry-goods store, located two doors north of the bank. Another, Elias Stacey, was proprietor of the town pharmacy. His shop was on the southeast corner of the square, directly across Division Street from the bank. The third man, Dr. Henry Wheeler, was stationed in Starbuck's second-floor hotel room. A crack shot, widely known for his marksmanship, Doc Wheeler was armed with a breech-loading target rifle. The marshal, whose office was kitty-corner from the bank, kept a lookout from his window. His instructions were to stay off the street and out of sight.

Early Saturday morning, the three men had been summoned to the marshal's office. There, he had introduced them to Starbuck and briefed them on the forthcoming holdup attempt. The men had listened with dismay and shock, somewhat incredulous. Yet all three were veterans of the Civil War, and no strangers to bloodshed. Nor were they overawed that they were being asked to take arms against the James-Younger gang. They were, instead, filled with a sort of righteous indignation. Jesse James was vilified as a murderous blackguard, and each of them looked upon the defence of their town and their neighbours as a civic duty. To a man, they eagerly volunteered their services.

Starbuck had first sworn them to an oath of silence. He impressed on them the need for absolute secrecy, which included wives and friends and business acquaintances. Jesse James, he noted, would be on guard for anything out of the ordinary; it was entirely likely a member of the gang would reconnoitre the town one last time before the robbery. With the point made, Starbuck then went on to the ambush itself. Their primary objective was the group of robbers—four or five in number—who would assemble outside the bank. These men were to be killed on the spot, before they had time to react and turn the square into a battleground. The men at the bridge, so long as they made no attempt to cross the square, were secondary. By concentrating on the bank, a dual goal would be served. The majority of the gang would be wiped out and the robbery would be aborted on the instant.

From there, Starbuck had proceeded to the matter of individual assignments. Manning and Stacey, whose stores were in direct proximity to the bank, were to arm themselves with shotguns. Caught between them, the robbers would be neatly sandwiched in a crossfire; their shotguns would sweep the sidewalk immediately outside the bank with a barrage of lead. The marshal, armed with a repeating rifle, would fire from the doorway of his office. His principal concern would be the outside team of robbers; once the firing became general, however, he would be free to select targets of opportunity. Doc Wheeler, whose target rifle was equipped with peep sights, would be responsible for the bridge. The gang members there were to be killed or pinned down, and thus neutralised. In that manner, they would be effectively eliminated from the larger fight.

Starbuck next outlined his own role in the ambush. Several of the gang members—notably Frank James and the three Younger brothers—were known to him on sight. The odds dictated that one or more of these men would be part of the outside team, the first contingent to approach the bank. Upon spotting them, he would leave

the hotel veranda and cross to the south side of the
square. His movement would alert Manning, Stacey, and
Doc Wheeler that the holdup attempt was under way.
Once across the square, he would then turn east and
stroll towards the corner. By timing it properly, he would
arrive at the corner as the second contingent rode up to
the bank. One of these men was certain to be Jesse
James, and along with the inside team he would dismount at the hitch rack. The moment they were on the
sidewalk, and moving towards the door of the bank,
Starbuck would open fire. His shot would be the signal
for Marshal Murphy and the others to cut loose. With
luck, the whole affair would be concluded in a matter
of seconds.

Summing up, Starbuck had stressed the importance of
a dispassionate attitude. He reminded the men that the
James-Younger gang was a band of cold-blooded murderers, prone to acts of savagery. He urged them to shoot
to kill, and to continue firing until the last outlaw had
been taken out of action. Any hesitation, any show of
mercy, would only endanger innocent bystanders. To
save the lives of friends and neighbours required that
they kill quickly and efficiently. And with no regard for
the aftermath.

Arthur Manning, perhaps having second thoughts, had
then raised the issue of bystanders. In the event passersby happened along at the last moment or innocent
parties got in the line of fire, he wondered if it might
not be prudent to hold off, and let the gang rob the bank.
At that point, he observed, when they were once again
mounted and moving across the square, they could be
ambushed in a relatively open area. Starbuck assured
him that such a plan would result in random gunfire, and
imperil the lives of everyone on the square. By contain-
ing the shooting to a limited zone—the front of the

bank—there was less chance of someone catching a stray bullet. Doc Wheeler, whose usual business was saving lives, forcefully agreed. He advised Manning to leave tactics to Starbuck. The ambush, as laid out, was in his opinion their best hope. The others voiced assent, and the meeting had concluded on that note. Starbuck's plan would be followed to the letter.

To bolster their confidence, Starbuck had arranged a dry run later that afternoon. He waited until the farmers and their families began the trek homeward; with their departure, the Saturday crowds thinned out and the sidewalks became passable. Walking to the southwest corner of the square, he stopped and turned to face the bank. From there, he was in plain view of Doc Wheeler and the two tradesmen. He gave them the high sign, indicating he was satisfied with the arrangement. Then, cutting across the intersection on an oblique angle, he stepped off the distance to the bank entrance. By his stride, it was fourteen paces, roughly fifteen yards. He considered it an easy shot. One Jesse James would never hear.

Yet now, seated in the rocker, he wondered if today would be the day. Where Jesse James was concerned, there were few certainties, and a good deal of guesswork. Still, if a bank was to be robbed, then Monday was the ideal time. All morning, a steady stream of merchants and shopkeepers had trooped into the bank. Their receipts from Saturday's trade were heavy, and they were clearly anxious to get the money out of the stores and on deposit. Which made the bank a tempting target indeed. The vault would be stuffed with cash—and standing wide open.

As the noon hour approached, Starbuck experienced a moment of concern. If today was not the day, he knew he could expect problems with his squad of volunteers.

Wallace was a peace officer, and therefore somewhat accustomed to the vagaries of manhunting. The others, despite their wartime service, were newcomers to the game. A professional soon learned that patience and determination were essential in any match of wits with outlaws. Amateurs, on the other hand, were quick to lose their taste for killing. The excitement—that initial surge of blood lust—was short-lived. The longer the wait, the more time they had to think. And given enough time, most men would talk themselves out of the notion. Unless the gang struck today, that might easily happen in Northfield. For the three townsmen, the act of cold and premeditated killing would begin to weigh heavily. Tomorrow or the next day—

All at once Starbuck alerted. His pulse quickened as he spotted Cole Younger and the man named Clell Miller ride over the bridge. Unhurried, holding their horses to a walk, they proceeded on a direct line across the square. Their eyes moved constantly, searching the stores and the faces of people on the street. Anything out of the ordinary—empty stores or too few people abroad—would immediately put them on guard. For the job to go off as planned, the town had to appear normal, nothing unusual or out of kilter. Otherwise they would simply turn and ride back across the bridge.

Starbuck sat perfectly still. From beneath the brim of his derby, he watched them ride past and plod on in the direction of the bank. He casually stood, stretching himself, and yawned a wide, jaw-cracking yawn. Then he bit off the tip of a fresh cigar and lit it with the air of a man savouring a good smoke. Stuffing the cigar in his mouth, he went down the hotel steps and meandered across the square. On the sidewalk, he turned and strolled aimlessly towards the corner. Ahead, he saw the two outlaws rein to a halt before the bank and dismount.

Cole stooped down and pretended to tighten the saddle
girth on his horse. Miller circled the hitch rack and
stepped onto the sidewalk. With a look of bored indif-
ference, he stood gazing out at the square.

Approaching the corner, Starbuck slowed his pace.
Directly ahead, he spotted Stacey watching him through
the window of the pharmacy. Out of the corner of his
eye, he caught a glimpse of Manning leaning idly in the
doorway of the dry-goods store. He stopped before a
clothing emporium, playing for time, and made a show
of peering at the window display. The hotel, now diag-
onally behind him, was mirrored in the reflection of the
glass. He studied the window of his room, noting the
lower pane was raised; through the gauzy curtains, the
outline of Doc Wheeler was faintly visible. The men
were in place and ready to act the instant he gave the
signal. All that remained was for Jesse James to put in
an appearance.

Starbuck puffed his cigar and bent closer to the window. He checked the bank in the reflection, troubled by
what seemed an abnormal lapse of time. Cole and Clell
Miller, still loafing outside the bank, were staring in the
direction of the bridge. Starbuck turned his head slightly,
and took a quick peek. His expression darkened, oddly
bemused. Jim Younger, accompanied by two men unknown to him, cleared the east end of the bridge and
reined their horses off to one side. They dismounted,
reins gripped firmly, and stood as though waiting. Their
eyes were fixed on the bank.

A sudden chill settled over Starbuck. Something
about the setup was wrong, all turned around. The way
he'd figured it, occupying the bridge was to have been
the last step. Before then, both the outside team and the
inside team should have been in position. Yet the rear
guard had now taken control of the bridge and there were

no more riders in sight. No sign of the inside team!

Then, suddenly, a tight fist of apprehension gripped his stomach. He wheeled away from the store window and froze, turned to stone. Frank James and Bob Younger, led by a third man, rounded the corner of Division Street and entered the bank. The man in the lead, like Frank, wore a beard, and carried himself with austere assurance. His identity was all too apparent.

Starbuck spat a low curse and flung his cigar into the gutter. He saw their horses tied to the hitch rack on Division Street, and too late he realised his mistake. While he was watching the bridge, he'd been outsmarted and outmanoeuvred. Jesse James, foxy to the end, had circled Northfield and entered town from the east. A clever ruse, wholly unexpected, and timed precisely when it was least expected. The trademark of an old guerrilla fighter—and brilliantly executed.

Before Starbuck could react, the situation went from bad to worse. The proprietor of a hardware store next to the bank boldly approached Cole Younger and Clell Miller. He looked them over, openly curious, then walked on towards the bank entrance. Miller drew a gun and brusquely ordered him to move along. The store owner obeyed, rounding the corner onto Division Street. Then he took off running, shouting at the top of his lungs.

"Bank robbers! The bank's being robbed!"

With the element of surprise gone, the gang moved swiftly. Cole fired a shot to alert the men at the bridge. In turn, they began winging shots across the square, warning passersby off the street. A townsman, seemingly befuddled by the commotion, was too slow to move, and a bullet dropped him where he stood. Starbuck, with lead whizzing all around him, jerked his Colt and hurried to the corner. There he ducked behind a lamppost and waited. His pistol was trained on the bank entrance.

From the pharmacy, Stacey fired a shotgun blast across the street. Birdshot peppered Miller's face just as he started to mount his horse. At the same instant, the marshal cut loose from his office window and drilled a slug through Cole's thigh. Then, from the opposite direction, Manning stepped out the door of the dry-goods store and triggered both barrels on his shotgun. The impact of a double-load struck Miller in the chest, and knocked him raglike off his feet. He dropped dead in the street.

Doc Wheeler, firing from the hotel window, quickly routed the rear guard. His first shot, slightly low, killed a horse and sent the rider tumbling to the ground. His next shot went high and struck the bridge, exploding splinters directly over Jim Younger's head. On the third shot, the physician found the range. The remaining outlaw took a bullet through the heart, and pitched headlong off his horse.

A shot sounded from within the bank and one of the tellers stumbled through the door. He lost his footing and fell face first on the sidewalk. On his heels, the three inside men burst out the door and ran for their horses. Frank was in the lead, followed by Jesse, and last in line was Bob Younger. Bunched together, they dodged and weaved, snapping off wild shots as they headed for the hitch rack. The marshal and Elias Stacey opened up on them in a rolling barrage. The bank window shattered and bullets pocked the wall of the building all around them. Younger's horse reared backward and toppled dead as he grabbed for the reins. Beside him, still in the middle, Jesse bent low under the hitch rack.

Starbuck, tracking them in his sights, had not yet fired. From the moment they darted out of the bank, he'd waited for a clear shot. His concentration was on Jesse, but the other men were in the way, spoiling his aim.

Then, as Younger's horse fell dead, he saw an opening. He touched off the trigger as Jesse rose from beneath the hitch rack. Bob Younger, scrambling away from his plunging horse, stepped into the line of fire. The slug plowed through his arm from hand to elbow. Jesse vaulted into the saddle, and Starbuck fired a hurried shot. The slug, only inches off target, blew the saddlehorn apart.

Out of nowhere, Cole galloped into the mêlée and swung Bob aboard his own horse. Once again Starbuck was blocked, and he waited as they turned and thundered in a tight phalanx through the intersection. Standing, he moved from behind the lamppost and brought the Colt to shoulder level. He was vaguely aware of the marshal halting at the corner, and distantly he heard the boom of shotguns. Yet he closed his mind to all else, his attention zeroed on a lone figure within the pack of horsemen. He was determined to make the shot count.

The riders hurtled past him and his arm traversed in a smooth arc. From the rear, the horses were separated by wider gaps, and his sights locked on the bearded figure. The Colt roared and he saw Jesse's hat float skyward. He quickly thumbed the hammer back and once more brought the sights into line. Then, on the verge of firing, the horsemen drifted together in a jumbled wedge and he lost his target. There was no time for a last shot.

The outlaws pounded across the bridge and turned south along the Dundas road. A moment slipped past, then they disappeared from view on the opposite side of the river. A pall of eerie silence descended on Northfield.

Starbuck cursed savagely and slowly lowered the hammer on the Colt. His eyes were rimmed with disgust.

CHAPTER 15

A crowd of townspeople stood clotted together outside the bank. Unmoving, they seemed paralysed in a kind of stilled tableau. Their faces were set in a curious attitude of horror and sullen disbelief. All ears, they listened intently as Fred Wilcox vented his outrage.

Only in the aftermath of the shootout had the full carnage become obvious. One outlaw lay sprawled in a welter of blood on the sidewalk. Another, his eyes staring sightlessly into the noonday sun, was spread-eagled on the ground near the bridge. A townsman, killed when he failed to take cover, was crumpled in a ball on the north side of the square. One of the tellers, wounded when he attempted to flee the bank, was now being attended by Doc Wheeler. The other teller, Joseph Heywood, was less fortunate. His throat slashed, he lay dead beside the bank vault. The vault door was closed and locked.

Fred Wilcox, the bank president, was unharmed. A short, fat man, his visage was somewhat like that of a bellicose pig. His lips were white and all the blood had leeched out of his face. He was shouting at Wallace Murphy in a loud, hectoring voice.

"You're the marshal! You're paid to protect the town—not to get people killed!"

"I know that." Murphy looked wretched. "Things went haywire, Mr. Wilcox. We planned to get 'em before they got inside the bank—"

"Damn your plan!" Wilcox said furiously. "Your job is to prevent such things from happening!"

"We tried to," Murphy answered with defensive gruffness. "That's what I keep telling you. We had an ambush all laid out. Then Jack Allen walked out of his hardware store and spoiled the whole thing. If he hadn't got so curious, we would've mowed 'em down right where they stood."

"Don't blame Allen! The fault is yours, and yours alone! Poor Heywood would still be alive if it weren't for your bumbling."

Wilcox made an agitated gesture with both hands. His glance shuttled across the room, where the teller's body lay slumped beside the vault door. The stench of death was still strong, and a puddle of blood stained the floor dark brown. He suddenly looked queasy and his voice trembled.

"My God." He passed a hand across his eyes and swallowed hard. "I'll never forget Heywood's face. When they put that knife to his throat . . ."

His voice trailed off, and Murphy nodded dumbly. "How'd the vault door come to be locked?"

"I—" Wilcox tried to speak, choked on his own terror, then started again. "It was almost noon. I always lock the vault before I go to lunch. Merely a precautionary measure, nothing more."

"The robbers didn't get anything, then?"

"No," Wilcox said hollowly. "Not a dime."

Standing nearby, Starbuck listened without expression. Outwardly stony, he was seething inside. Within him the full impact of his failure smouldered corrosively, shadowing his every thought. An innocent bystander dead and a bank teller brutally murdered. And Jesse James unscathed, still very much alive. All in all, he reflected, it was a sorry performance. He'd made a monstrous gaffe, underestimating the outlaw leader and attaching far too much weight to his own assessment of the robbers' plans. In effect, he had second-guessed a tactical wizard, and he'd guessed wrong. The fault was his own, not Wallace Murphy's. Here today, men had died needlessly, and it left a leaden feeling in his chest. A feeling of abject loathing for himself. And a sense of homicidal rage towards the man who had outwitted him.

"The money," Wilcox went on bitterly, "has no bearing on what's happened. Joe Heywood is dead"—his finger stabbed accusingly at the marshal—"and I hold you personally responsible!"

Murphy looked at him with dulled eyes. "Nobody feels any worse about it than me, Mr. Wilcox. I was only trying to do my duty."

"Your duty!" Wilcox thundered righteously. "You chowderheaded ass! I'll have your job! Before I'm through, the people of Northfield will ride you out of town on a rail. Do you hear me—a rail!"

There was a harried sharpness in the banker's words. He was strung up an octave too high, and Starbuck brought him down. Stepping forward, he fixed Wilcox with an inquisitorial stare.

"Tell me something." His voice was pitched to reach the onlookers crowding the doorway. "Why did they cut Heywood's throat?"

"I—" Wilcox blinked several times. "I beg your pardon?"

"You heard me." Starbuck's eyes hooded. "There must've been a reason. It had to happen before all the shooting started; so it's pretty clear they used a knife to avoid attracting attention. What's the reason?"

"The vault." Wilcox looked ill, suddenly averted his gaze. "They wanted the combination to the vault. When I . . ."

"When you refused," Starbuck finished it for him, "that's when Heywood got the knife. Then they started for the other teller—now that you knew they weren't bluffing—and he bolted for the door. Have I got it straight?"

Wilcox blanched, mumbled an inaudible reply. Starbuck studied him a moment, then added a casual afterthought. "Who used the knife? Which robber?"

"Ooo God!" Tears welled up in Wilcox's eyes. "It . . . it was . . . one of the bearded men."

"Which one?" Starbuck persisted. "The one about my height, or the taller one?"

"Your height." Wilcox pulled out a handkerchief and loudly honked his nose. "The one who gave the orders."

"It figures." Starbuck turned away, motioning to the marshal. "C'mon, Wally. We'll leave Mr. Wilcox to count his money. Let's go catch ourselves some robbers."

Wallace Murphy thrust out his jaw and gave the banker an ugly stare. Then he let out his breath between clenched teeth, and followed Starbuck towards the door. On the steps they halted and stood looking at the upturned faces of the crowd. Murphy's chest swelled and he appeared to grow taller. His eyes blazed with authority.

"I'm forming a posse!" he rumbled in a gravelly voice. "That gang of murderers killed Joe Heywood and poor ol' Nick Gustavson! I give you my solemn oath the bastards will be caught and brought to justice! Any man jack that wants a hand in running 'em down—step forward!"

Several men moved to the front of the crowd. Murphy began ticking off names and issuing orders. The posse members were to provide their own guns and their own horses, and report back to the marshal's office on the double. They were advised to bring along blankets and enough rations to last at least two days. The chase would end when it ended, Murphy shouted. And not a moment before!

An hour later Starbuck and Murphy led six grim-faced men across the bridge. They rode south on the Dundas road.

A hunter's moon slipped out from behind the clouds. The posse was halted some ten miles southwest of Dundas. The men were dismounted at the side of the road, and no one spoke. Gathered around Murphy, they waited with an air of suppressed tension.

Starbuck was squatted down on his haunches. In the spectral moonlight, he slowly scrutinised a crazy quilt of hoofprints on the dirt road. After a time he stood and carefully followed a set of tracks that led west, into a stand of woods. There he knelt and once more studied the sign. He touched a spot of ground which glistened wetly in the light, and smelled his fingers. He allowed himself a satisfied grunt, and climbed to his feet. Then he walked back to where the men waited. He nodded to Murphy, gesturing along the road.

"Five horses, six riders," he remarked. "That means we're on the right trail. Bob Younger was riding double with Cole when they took off."

"What was it you found at the side of the road?"

"Blood." Starbuck rubbed his fingers together. "Still pretty fresh too. I know for a fact Bob Younger was wounded. So the way it figures—he passed out and fell off the horse not long after dark. I'd guess they had to let him rest a spell before they moved on."

"Sounds reasonable." Murphy pointed off into the woods. "We're in big trouble if they headed that way. There's nothing out there but swamps and heavy timber. Probably thirty miles of wilderness between here and the next farm road."

Starbuck's eyes narrowed. "Only three horses went that way, and one of them was carrying double. I'd say it was the Younger brothers and that fourth man. The one Doc Wheeler missed at the bridge."

"You mean to tell me they split up?"

"That's the way I read it. Looks to me like the Youngers took to the brush and the James boys stuck to the road."

"Hell of a note!" Murphy groaned. "They're forcing us to choose. We sure as the devil can't follow both trails!"

"Tell you what, Wally." Starbuck's expression was wooden. "Why don't you and your men stick with the Youngers? I'll tend to the James boys myself."

Murphy returned his gaze steadily. "I never asked, but I suppose I knew all along. You want Jesse real bad, don't you?"

"Yeah." There was a hard edge to Starbuck's tone. "I want him so bad it makes my teeth hurt."

"Any special reason? Or am I overstepping my bounds by asking?"

"No." Starbuck's voice took on a peculiar abstracted quality. "Some men need killing, and his name heads the list. I reckon that's reason enough."

"I'd sure as hell second that motion!"

"Lots of people already beat you to it."

Murphy took his arm and walked him off to one side.

"Just in case we shouldn't meet again, there's something I want you to know."

"Fire away."

"I owe you for the way you stepped in with Wilcox back there at the bank. Except for you, I would've been finished in Northfield. You pulled my fat out of the fire, and I'm obliged."

Starbuck smiled. "Catch the Youngers and we'll call it even." He offered his hand. "Good luck, Wally."

Their handshake was strong, and for a moment they stood grinning at each other in the pale moonlight. Then Starbuck walked to his horse and mounted. He nodded to the other men, reined sharply about, and rode off down the road.

Wallace Murphy watched until he disappeared into the night.

Events of subsequent days proved both frustrating and tantalising. Starbuck's manhunt took him on a tortuous path full of blind ends and false leads. Yet he never entirely lost the trail. Nor was he discouraged by the snaillike pace of the search.

The trail led him first to Mankato, some fifty miles southwest of Northfield. From there, always inquiring about two bearded men on horseback, he tracked the James brothers to Sioux City. Located on the Iowa-Nebraska border, the town represented a point of departure for either Indian Territory or Missouri. A major trade centre, the sheer size of the town also delayed his progress.

Finally, after several days of investigation, he discovered that a bearded man had swapped two saddle horses, along with a hundred dollars cash, for a wagon and team. The switch to a wagon left him puzzled; all the more so when he was unable to turn up a new trail. Exhaustive

inquiry at last provided the answer. A wagon, with one
clean-shaven man driving, and another on a pallet in the
back, had crossed the border into Nebraska. He concluded that one of the brothers, probably Frank James,
had been wounded in the shootout at Northfield. The
switch to a wagon indicated his condition had worsened
over the gruelling flight.

By shaving their beards, the outlaws had cost Starbuck precious time. Once he uncovered the ruse, he set
out in hot pursuit; but in the end, their lead was too great.
Some two weeks after the chase began, he rode into
Lincoln, Nebraska. There, in a maddening turnabout, the
trail simply petered out. A day was consumed before he
learned the wagon and team had been traded to a livestock dealer. The James boys had departed on horseback
three days before his arrival, and no clue to the direction
they'd taken. He was stymied.

There was, nonetheless, sensational news regarding
the Youngers. The governor of Minnesota had declared a
reward of $1,000 per man—dead or alive—and thereby
sparked the most massive manhunt in the state's history.
For the past two weeks, the outlaws had eluded capture
by hiding out in the wilderness maze of southern Minnesota. Then, trapped by a posse, they had taken refuge
in a dense swamp. The posse, led by Marshal Wallace
Murphy, surrounded them, and a furious gun battle ensued. When the smoke cleared, the Youngers had been
shot to ribbons. Bob had suffered three wounds, one of
which shattered his jaw. Jim, with a slug through his
right lung, had a total of five wounds. Cole, miracu-
lously, had survived eleven wounds, none of which
struck a vital organ. The fourth robber, identified as
Charlie Pitts, had been killed in the shootout. The
Younger brothers, after being loaded into farm wagons
had been carted to the town of Madelia. There, under a

doctor's care, they were sequestered in the local hotel.

Upon reading the account in a newspaper, Starbuck boarded the next northbound train out of Lincoln. The trip, with a brief layover in Sioux City, consumed the better part of forty-eight hours. On the evening of the second day, bone-weary and covered with train soot, he arrived in Madelia. He inquired at the depot and learned that the Youngers were being held under guard at the Flanders Hotel. A short walk uptown brought him to the hotel, which was located in the heart of a small business district. He found Wallace Murphy seated in the lobby.

The marshal let out a whoop, amazed to see him and clearly delighted. For the next few minutes they swapped stories, with Starbuck offering congratulations and Murphy extending words of encouragement. On that note, Starbuck asked to speak privately with Cole Younger. At a dead end, he was hopeful that Younger would provide a lead to the whereabouts of Jesse James. There was no love lost between the two outlaws, and with proper interrogation, he thought Younger might be persuaded to talk. Murphy quickly agreed, escorting him to a room upstairs. A deputy, seated inside with the wounded outlaw, was ordered to wait in the hall. Starbuck, prepared for a hostile reception, entered alone.

Cole Younger was swathed in bandages. Still in some pain, and doped up with laudanum, he was staring groggily at the ceiling. Approaching the bed, Starbuck thought he'd never seen a better example of death warmed over.

"Evening, Cole."

Younger rolled his head sideways on the pillow. He batted his eyes, trying to bring Starbuck into focus. Then, somewhere deep in his gaze, a pinpoint of recognition surfaced.

"I know you." His mouth lifted in an ashen grin. "You

was standin' on the corner . . . that day in Northfield. Saw you shootin' at Jesse and the other boys."

"Not the others," Starbuck said softly. "Just Jesse."

"Yeah?" Younger sounded pleased. "Well, I'm sorry to say you missed. The bastard leads a charmed life."

On impulse, Starbuck took a gamble. "I sort of guessed you two might've had a falling out."

"What makes you think that?"

"Easy to figure," Starbuck said with a shrug. "Bob was wounded and slowing you down. Jesse split up so him and Frank could make better time. Wasn't that how it happened?"

"Shit!" Cole said viciously. "You don't know the half of it. He wanted to kill Bob and leave him! I told him he'd have to kill me first."

"Wasn't Frank wounded too?"

"Yeah, but he was able to ride. After Jesse and me had words, they took off. Sonovabitch! All he ever cared about was savin' his own neck."

"You reckon he's headed for Belle's place . . . Younger's Bend?"

Younger peered at him, one eye sharp and gleaming. "Who the hell are you anyway? How'd you know about Belle?"

"Let's just say I've got a powerful urge to see Jesse dead."

"Join the club." Younger gave him a ghastly smile. "You ain't gonna find him at Belle's, though. She wouldn't give him the time of day—not without me along!"

"How about Ruston's spread?" Starbuck watched his eyes. "Down on the Pecos?"

"Ain't nothin' you don't know, is there? Only thing is, you're barkin' up the wrong tree. Tom Ruston swears by Frank, but he's like me when it comes to Jesse. He wouldn't piss on him if his guts was on fire!"

"You tell me, then. Where should I look?"

"Why should I?" Younger said hoarsely. "You got Pinkerton written all over you."

"Guess again," Starbuck said without guile. "I was hired by someone who wants a personal score settled. It's got nothing to do with you or your brothers . . . only Jesse."

Younger regarded him a moment, then nodded. "Without Belle, Jesse's got no place to run this time. So I'd say your best bet's Clay County. He's partial to his wife, and sooner or later he'll show." His lips curled in a cunning, wrinkled grin. "Watch the bitch and the dog won't be far behind."

Starbuck's instinct told him he'd heard the truth. He thanked the outlaw and wished him a speedy recovery. Then, as he turned towards the door, Younger stopped him with one last remark.

"Damnedest thing! You put me in mind of another feller I used to know. Met him once in a whorehouse!"

"Well, Cole, I guess that just goes to show you. It's a small world, after all."

The door opened and closed, and Starbuck was gone. Younger thought about it for a time, his brow screwed up in a frown. At last, no student of irony, he closed his eyes and surrendered to the laudanum.

CHAPTER 16

Starbuck's return from Minnesota was anything but triumphant. In a very real sense, he had travelled full circle, and the knowledge did little to improve his humour. Still, like a crucible enveloped in flame, Northfield had tested his character. He emerged with a kind of steely resolve.

Now, more than ever before, he was determined to kill Jesse James. No longer a job, it was a personal matter. A contest between hunter and hunted.

A day's layover in St. Louis merely strengthened his resolve. Covering all bets, he first sent a wire to the U.S. marshal in Forth Smith. He requested verification as to whether or not a pair of strangers, both white men, had been reported at Younger's Bend. The reply was prompt and unequivocal. Belle Starr and her husband had been arrested and tried for horse stealing. Found guilty, they had been sentenced by Judge Parker to one year in prison. Only yesterday, under heavy guard, the Starrs had entrained for the federal penitentiary in Detroit. Informants in the Cherokee Nation reported that Younger's Bend was now deserted.

Upon reflection, Starbuck decided to scratch Indian

Territory from his list. With Belle Starr in prison, there was small likelihood the James boys would seek refuge at Younger's Bend. The chance seemed even more remote considering the nature of Belle's in-laws. The reward for Jesse and Frank now totalled $10,000—and old Tom Starr might find the temptation too great to resist. Trusting no one, least of all a renegade Cherokee, Jesse would give Younger's Bend a wide berth. As for Belle, Starbuck was mildly amused. He thought the guards at the federal prison were in for a rough time. Where the lady bandit was concerned, anything that wore pants was fair game.

Otis Tilford was Starbuck's next stop. He gave the banker a blow-by-blow account of the Northfield raid and the ensuing manhunt. He made no attempt to spare himself, and freely admitted he'd been snookered by the outlaw leader. Oddly enough, Tilford seemed encouraged. The Northfield incident, he pointed out, had decimated the James-Younger gang. Which was a good deal more than either the law or the Pinkertons had ever accomplished. By virtue of that fact, Jesse James had lost his aura of invincibility. And that made him vulnerable as never before. Tilford heartily approved Starbuck's immediate plan. A staked-out goat, he observed, rarely ever failed to entice a man-eating tiger into the open. Zee James seemed the perfect bait.

After their meeting, Starbuck caught the next train for Kansas City. There he collected his suitcase from the depot storage room, and once more checked into a hotel. A dye job on his hair, added to the spit-curled moustache, turned the trick. He emerged from the hotel in the guise of Floyd Hunnewell. Then, stowing his suitcase once again, he reclaimed his horse from the livery stable. Late that evening, only three days after departing Minnesota, he entered Clay County. His destination was Ma Ferguson's bordello.

Alvina treated his arrival somewhat like a homecoming. After nearly a month's absence, she'd lost any hope he would ever return. She was both amazed and overjoyed, and she smothered him with a childlike affection that was almost embarrassing. Starbuck spun a windy tale which left even Ma Ferguson enthralled. Over the past several weeks, he related, he'd stolen a herd of horses in Kansas, trailed them to Montana, and sold the lot for top dollar. His bankroll was replenished—big enough to choke a horse, he told them with a wry grin— and he was ready to celebrate. Ma Ferguson beamed mightily and the party got under way. Like the prodigal son returned, nothing was too good for Floyd Hunnewell.

Somewhere in the course of the festivities, Alvina broke the sad news about the debacle at Northfield. Starbuck was properly stunned, expressing just the right touch of morbid curiosity and maudlin regret. All of Clay County, Alvina revealed, was in a state of mourning, absolutely devastated. With a shudder, almost weepy, she told him to thank his lucky stars. Had he been accepted into the gang, he too would have ridden hell-bent for Northfield. And got his ass shot off—just like the Youngers!

Starbuck thought it a damn fine joke. Yet he nodded solemnly, and agreed that he was indeed a mighty lucky fellow. He'd count his blessings, and stick to what he knew best, horse stealing. Alvina squealed with delight and made him cross his heart. So he did, and she sealed their pact with another syrupy kiss. Then she hauled him off to bed and welcomed him home in her own inimitable style.

That night, the waiting game began.

• • •

A month passed.

On occasion, Starbuck despaired and silently cursed what seemed an ill-fated venture. At other times, his hopes soared and he rode the intoxicating wind of renewed conviction. His spirits were up and down so often he felt like a broncbuster working a raw string of mustangs.

Towards the end of the second week of his wait, Cole Younger proved to be a swami. One whose crystal ball was not only unclouded, but unerringly accurate. Precisely as he'd predicted, the dog was indeed not far behind its mate. Zee James mysteriously disappeared from Clay County.

Starbuck learned the details from a new drinking crony. Alvina, who was herself a fund of information, had introduced him to Ed Miller. An aspiring bandit, Ed was a distant relation of Lamar Hudspeth, and claimed to have an inside track with the James boys. He was also the brother of Clell Miller, who had been blown to smithereens outside the Northfield bank. That, in itself, lent a certain credence to his gossipy boasting.

A minor celebrity himself, Starbuck traded on his credentials as a thief. He cultivated Miller's friendship by commiserating with him over the loss of his brother. Then, playing the big spender, he treated Miller to a nightly round of drinks. With practised ease, he quickly wormed his way into the man's confidence. And Miller, who was a talkative drunk, repaid his largesse manyfold. A question here and a question there elicited all there was to know about the clannish inner workings of Clay County. In short, Ed Miller and hard liquor were an unbeatable combination.

A couple of nights after Zee James vanished, the in-

vestment produced a windfall dividend. Sloshed to the
gills, Miller slyly unloaded the latest tidbit. Zee James,
he related with conspiratorial bonhomie, had slipped
away to join Jesse in Kansas City. Starbuck, who was a
master of subtle interrogation, plied him with drinks and
prompted him further. Before the night was out, Miller
had told all, impressing his friend with details known
only to trusted insiders. Later, when Miller staggered out
of the bordello, Starbuck acted quickly. Apologising to
Alvina, he complained of intestinal trouble, and begged
off for the night. Then he rode like the hounds of hell
for Kansas City.

Early the next morning, disguised as a rag-and-junk
man, Starbuck trundled a cart down Woodland Avenue.
Halfway along a quiet residential block, he stopped and
rapped on the door of a modest frame house. His hat
was doffed at waist level, and beneath it, his hand was
wrapped around the butt of his pistol. According to Ed
Miller, the master of the house went by the alias of T. J.
Jackson. His real name was Jesse James.

When there was no answer, Starbuck went next door.
He engaged the neighbour lady in conversation, and
soon had the full story. The Jacksons, she informed him,
had hastily packed and moved out late yesterday afternoon. She thought it a shame, for Mrs. Jackson, who had
arrived only the day before with their children, seemed
a perfect angel. As for T. J. Jackson, he'd always struck
her as a bit unsociable, somehow preoccupied. Still, in
all fairness, she had to admit he'd lived there not quite
two weeks, and spent a good deal of time away from
home. She surmised he was a travelling man, new to
Kansas City. She thought it a reasonable assumption, for
it was a furnished house. All of which reminded her to
tell the landlord his new tenants had decamped like a
band of gypsies. Without so much as a last goodbye.

Starbuck went away with his head buzzing. Everything fitted, down to the woman's physical description of T. J. Jackson. Yet the facts, like loose parts of a puzzle, made no sense. Assuming Miller had it correct—that Jackson was in truth Jesse James—then the sudden departure indicated panic. The natural question was why—after spiriting his wife and children into Kansas City—would the outlaw take flight. One day there, the next day gone, and seemingly without rhyme or reason. The whole thing beggared explanation.

That night, upon returning to Ma Ferguson's, Starbuck got both the explanation and the reason. Apparently Ed Miller had been wagging his tongue all over Clay County. A braggart, desperate to impress everyone he knew, he'd talked himself to death. Only that afternoon, Jesse James had called him out of his home and shot him down on his own doorstep. The killing, performed openly and in broad daylight, was a clear-cut warning. Those who spoke out of turn would speak no more— forever.

Starbuck found himself in the same old cul-de-sac. He'd been thwarted again—seemingly at the very last moment—by a queer juxtaposition of poor timing and bad luck. Worse, he'd lost his pipeline into the backwoodsy world of Clay County. Ed Miller, albeit unwittingly, had proved his most knowledgeable source to date. Now, with the pipeline shut off, he had no choice but to wait and keep his ear to the ground. Yet his patience was wearing thin, and the waiting sawed on his nerves.

For a week or so, Starbuck brooded around Ma Ferguson's. Alvina thought he was saddened by the death of Ed Miller, and he did nothing to dissuade her of the notion. In his view, no man was unkillable; though he was frank to admit some men possessed the proverbial longevity of a cat. Certainly Jesse James had expended nine lives and more over the years. Still, the outlaw was now encumbered by wife and children, a grave tactical error. A family reduced a man's mobility, and tended to anchor him closer to homeground. Some inner voice told Starbuck to sit tight. Clay County was the lodestone, and he felt reasonably confident Jesse James hadn't run far. Sooner or later, almost inevitably, the gossip mill would churn to life. And someone would talk.

The break virtually dropped into his lap. On a mild spring evening, a man unknown to Starbuck walked through the door of the bordello. He was big and fleshy, with the meaty nose and rheumy eyes of a hard drinker. Yet there was nothing to distinguish him from the other customers, and he normally wouldn't have rated a second glance. His furtive manner was the tip-off, and when he displayed no interest in the girls, that cinched it. Starbuck pegged him for a man on the dodge, with something or someone close on his back trail. And plainly terrified by the prospect.

After a couple of drinks, the man approached Ma Ferguson. She listened a moment, then levered herself out of her armchair and followed him into the hallway. A heated exchange ensued, with the man pleading and the madam of the house stubbornly shaking her head. An icy realist, Ma Ferguson was a woman of little charity. She provided a service, at a fair price, and studiously avoided any personal involvement with her clientele. The man was clearly asking a favour, and from Ma Ferguson's reaction, he'd picked the wrong whorehouse. His argument took on strength when he fished a wad of bills out of his pocket and pressed them into her hand. She wavered, locked in a struggle with avarice, and greed finally prevailed. The man was shown to a room

upstairs; but the price apparently included only lodging.
None of the girls was sent to join him.

Alvina, at Starbuck's request, soon pried the details
out of Ma Ferguson. The man's name was Jim Cummins. A first cousin of Lamar Hudspeth—who in turn
was related to the James boys—Cummins was privy to
all the family secrets. Yet he was also a close friend of
Ed Miller, and therefore guilty by association. Whether
he had or had not talked out of turn was a moot point.
Suspicion alone was enough to seal a man's death warrant, and he'd gotten the notice late that afternoon. Jesse
James had appeared at his sister's house, where he was
a full-time boarder and a sometime farmhand. The purpose of the visit was unmistakable.

His sister, when questioned, had denied any knowledge of his whereabouts. Understandably skeptical, the
outlaw had bullied and threatened, but he'd done her no
harm. Instead, he took her fourteen-year-old son into the
woods and attempted to beat the truth out of him. When
the boy refused to talk, Jesse James left him bloodied
and senseless, and rode off in disgust. That evening,
upon arriving home, Cummins realised he was in imminent danger. To run was an admission of guilt; to stay
put, on the other hand, would merely get him killed. He
needed refuge, and he needed it fast. He'd made a beeline for Ma Ferguson's place.

Starbuck sensed opportunity. Cummins' professed innocence had a false ring; anyone that close to the fire
had to come away singed. The great likelihood was that
Cummins knew too much for his own good, and the
good of Jesse James. Starbuck thought he might be persuaded to talk.

Late that night, with Alvina asleep, Starbuck eased
out of bed. He dressed in the dark and slipped quietly
from the room. All the girls had retired an hour or so

earlier, and the house was still. Fortunately, like all whorehouses, there were no locks on the doors, and that made his job simpler. He catfooted down the hall and let himself into Cummins' room. He waited a moment, listening to the even rise and fall of the man's breathing. Then he pulled his sixgun and crossed to the bed.

"Cummins." He stuck the snout of the pistol in Cummins' ear. "Wake up."

"What the hell!"

Cummins jerked and started to sit up. Starbuck pressed the muzzle deeper into his ear, forcing him down. His eyes were wide and white, bright ivory in the dark.

"Listen close," Starbuck said roughly. "I'm here to offer you a deal. So lay real still and pay attention."

"Who're you? How'd you know my name?"

"Who I am doesn't matter. The only thing that counts is what I've got to say."

"Awright," Cummins said stiffly. "I'm listenin'."

"You're going to tell me where Jesse's—"

"I ain't gonna tell you nothin'!"

"Shut up and listen!" Starbuck ordered. "You *will* tell me where Jesse's holed up. In return, I won't tell any of his kinfolks where you're hiding. That's the deal."

"I got no idea where Jesse's at! I swear it!"

"Too bad for you," Starbuck remarked. "That's the only thing that'll get you out of this fix alive."

"What d'you mean?"

"I mean you're no good to me unless you talk."

"You're bluffin'!" Cummins scoffed. "You wouldn't shoot a man just 'cause he don't know nothin'!"

"Think so?" Starbuck thumbed the hammer to full cock. "Try me and see."

Cummins took a deep breath, blew it out heavily. "Suppose I was to tell you? What happens then?"

"You go your way and I'll go mine. So far as anybody knows, we never met."

"Why you so set on findin' Jesse?"

"That's my business," Starbuck said deliberately. "Cough it up or get yourself a permanent earache. I'm fresh out of time."

"St. Joe," Cummins mumbled hastily. "Took Zee and the kids, and moved to St. Joseph. That's the straight goods!"

"What name's he going by?"

"Howard. Thomas Howard."

"Who told you so?"

"Lamar Hudspeth," Cummins said weakly. "He's my cousin, and he tried to do me a good turn. Jesse's puttin' a new gang together, and Lamar asked him to gimme a chance. I thought it was all set . . . up till today anyway."

"Who else got tapped to join?"

"Besides me, there's Dick Liddil, and Bob and Charley Ford. The Fords left for St. Joe yesterday. Liddil and me were supposed to leave tomorrow."

"What's he planning?" Starbuck pressed. "Another bank job?"

Cummins nodded. "Only nobody never told me when or where."

"St. Joe's a big place." Starbuck let the thought hang a moment. "Where would I find him . . . just exactly?"

"Search me," Cummins said lamely. "Lamar was gonna give me and Liddil the address just before we started out."

"One last thing," Starbuck said, his tone quizzical. "What made you think you'd be safe this close to home?"

"Hell, that's easy!" Cummins chuckled softly. "Jesse wouldn't be caught dead in a whorehouse, Safest place on earth!"

Starbuck marked again a phenomenon he'd noted before in certain outlaws. Family men, curiously God-fearing, they never blasphemed or cheated on their wives. Yet they thought nothing of robbery and cold-blooded murder. Their morality was not only selective, but took more twists than a pretzel. It was a paradox he'd never quite fathomed.

"You lay real still." Starbuck backed to the door. "One peep before I make it downstairs and you won't have to worry about Jesse. I'll fix your wagon myself."

"Wait a minute!" Cummins called out quickly. "Just for kicks, answer me a question. Who the hell are you, mister?"

"The name's Billy Pinkerton."

Starbuck smiled and stepped through the door.

CHAPTER 17

The train chugged into St. Joseph late the next afternoon. To the west, a brilliant orange sun dipped lower over the Missouri. The depot, which was situated above the waterfront, afforded a spectacular view of the river. Chuffing smoke, the locomotive rolled to a halt before the platform.

Starbuck stepped off the lead passenger coach. He was attired in a conservative grey suit and a dark fedora. His four-in-hand tie was funeral black, and a gold cross hung from the watch chain draped across his vest. He was clean-shaven, but his jaws were stuffed with large wads of cotton wool. The effect broke the hard line of his features and gave him the appearance of an amiable chipmunk. He was carrying a battered suitcase and a worn leather satchel. He looked very much like an itinerant preacher.

St. Joseph was located some forty miles northwest of Ma Ferguson's bordello. By horse, Starbuck could have ridden through the night and arrived early that morning. Yet he was confident that Jim Cummins—fearful of being branded a Judas—would reveal nothing of their conversation. With some leeway in time, he had walked from the bordello and ridden straight to Kansas City. There, in a whirlwind of activity, he had purchased all the paraphernalia necessary for a new disguise. Once more checking into a hotel, he'd rinsed the dye from his hair and temporarily laid Floyd Hunnewell to rest. By noontime, when he emerged onto the street, he was someone else entirely. After a quick lunch, he'd caught the afternoon train for St. Joseph. A milk run, the trip had consumed the better part of six hours.

Outside the depot, Starbuck paused and slowly inspected the town. A historic spot, St. Joseph was settled on the east bank of the Missouri River. Originally a trading post, it later became the jumping-off point for westward-bound settlers. Shortly before the Civil War, it served as the terminus for the Pony Express, with riders crisscrossing the continent between there and California. Following the war, it developed into a major rail centre, with one of the largest livestock and grain markets in Missouri. Now a hub of commerce, its population was approaching the thirty thousand mark. Which greatly compounded Starbuck's most immediate problem.

Before he could kill Jesse James, he must first locate a man named Thomas Howard. In a burgeoning metropolis the size of St. Joseph, that loomed as a task of no small dimensions.

All afternoon, staring out the train window, Starbuck had pondered the problem. However grudgingly, he'd felt a stirring of admiration for the outlaw. At best unpredictable, Jesse James had exhibited a whole new facet to his character. On the run, fresh from the defeat at Northfield, he'd performed a turnaround that was a marvel of ingenuity. By quitting the backwoods of Clay County, he had broken the pattern established over his long career of robbery and murder. And in the process he'd left no trail, no clue to his whereabouts. Instead, displaying both imagination and flexibility, he had taken up residence in Kansas City. A clever ruse, it had all but turned him invisible. He'd simply stepped into the crowd, joined the hustle and bustle of city dwellers. And vanished.

Yet, for all his cleverness, Jesse James had been unable to sever the cord. He was bound to wife and children, family and friends, and seemingly to the very earth of Clay County itself. In the end, those ties had proved his undoing. For no man disappears unless he cuts the knot with his past.

Still, given the nature of the man, Starbuck was not all that surprised. Apart from wife and children, Jesse James had been drawn back for perhaps the most elemental of reasons. He was a robber, and since early manhood he'd known no other livelihood. Northfield had destroyed his gang; the Younger brothers, following their capture, had quickly pleaded guilty in return for a life sentence. Then, too, the disaster at Northfield had left the outlaw leader virtually penniless. He desperately needed funds, and for that he had no choice but to form a new gang. Under the circumstances, it was only natural that he would return to Clay County. There, among family and friends, he could recruit men who were eager to ride with the notorious Jesse James. Untested but trustworthy, they would provide the cadre for a new guerrilla band. And above all else, because they were Clay County men, they would follow him with blind loyalty. His roots were their roots, and no stronger bond existed.

Even now, standing outside the depot, Starbuck had to give the devil his due. St. Joseph, although smaller than Kansas City, was yet another shrewd stroke. By not drawing attention to themselves, the gang could assemble anywhere in the town, and no one the wiser. The fact that he knew the names of the new members—Dick Liddil and the Ford brothers—was informative but of no great value. Today only one name counted—Thomas Howard.

Hefting his bags, Starbuck strolled away from the train station. On the walk uptown, he mentally conditioned himself to undertake a new role. From childhood he dredged up long-forgotten quotes from the Scriptures, and silently practiced the orotund cadence of a zealous Bible-thumper. By the time he bustled through the door of the town's largest hotel, he was wholly in character. He positively glowed with a sort of beatific serenity.

"Praise the Lord!" His voice boomed across the lobby with sepulchral enthusiasm. "And a good afternoon to you, brother!"

Halting before the registration desk, he dropped his bags on the floor. His face was fixed in a jaunty smile. The room clerk looked him over like something that had fallen out of a tree.

"May I help you, sir?"

"Indeed you may!" Starbuck said affably. "I wish to engage accommodations. Nothing elaborate, but something nonetheless commodious. A corner room would do nicely."

"How long will you be staying with us, Mr.—?"

"Joshua Thayer," Starbuck informed him grandly. "Western representative for the Holy Writ Foundation."

"Beg pardon?"

"The Good Book!" Starbuck struck a theatrical pose. " 'I am not come to call the righteous, but rather the sinners to repentance!' "

"Oh." The clerk seemed unimpressed. "A Bible salesman."

Starbuck looked wounded. "We all labour in the vineyards, brother. Each in our own way."

"I guess." The clerk turned towards a key rack. "Would you care to sign the register, Mr. Thayer?"

"Delighted!" Starbuck dipped the pen in the inkwell, scribbled with a flourish. "I plan to stay the week, perhaps longer. Your fair town looks hospitable, and promising. Very promising, indeed!"

"We're not shy on sinners." The clerk handed him a key. "Room two-o-four, Mr. Thayer. Up the stairs and turn right. The bellboy's out on an errand just now. He'll be back directly if you care to wait."

" 'Pride goeth before the fall,' " Starbuck intoned. "I can manage quite well, thank you."

"Suit yourself."

"By the way." Starbuck spread his hands on the counter, leaned closer. "An old acquaintance resides in St. Joseph. I haven't his address, but perhaps you might know him. His name is Thomas Howard."

"Sorry." The clerk shook his head. "Doesn't ring any bells."

"A pity," Starbuck observed. "But, then, 'the grains of sand are beyond counting,' are they not?"

The clerk gave him a blank stare. "I'll take your word for it."

"One last question." Starbuck lowered his voice. "Where might I find a peaceful spot for a mild libation?"

"A saloon?" The clerk eyed him with a smug grin. "I wouldn't have thought a man in your line of work would take to demon rum."

"On the contrary!" Starbuck beamed. " 'Let us do evil, that good may come.' Romans, Chapter three, Verse eight."

"Well, the quietest place in town is O'Malley's. Out the door and turn right. Couple of blocks down, on the corner."

"By that, I take it you mean a respectable clientele?"

"You might say that."

"I thank you kindly for the advice."

"Don't mention it."

"Peace be with you, brother!"

Starbuck collected his bags and crossed the lobby. As he mounted the stairs, his mind turned to the evening ahead. Saloons were the gossip mills of any river town, and he doubted St. Joseph would prove the exception. A question here and a question there, and anything was possible. Even the present whereabouts of one Thomas Howard.

He thought it looked to be a long night.

Starbuck rose early the next morning. His head thumped, and he regretted now what had seemed a workable idea last night. From the uptown saloons to the waterfront dives, he had toured St. Joseph until the early morning hours. He'd talked with a succession of bartenders and townsmen, and everywhere he had posed the same question. The sum of his efforts was zero.

No one had ever heard of Thomas Howard.

Through the window, a bright April sun flooded the room. One hand shielding his eyes, Starbuck rolled out of bed and padded to the washstand. He vigorously scrubbed his teeth and took a quick birdbath. After emptying the basin, he laid out a straight razor and mug, and poured tepid water from the pitcher. Then, with dulled concentration, he lathered his face and began shaving The image in the mirror was reflective, somehow far-away.

Somewhere in St. Joseph, he told himself, Jesse James was staring into a mirror and performing the same morning ritual. The outlaw, with his family to consider, would have rented a house in a quiet residential neighbourhood A newcomer to town, travelling light, he would have

likely rented a furnished house. His starting point would
have been—

The newspaper! The classified ads. Houses for rent!

Starbuck's hand paused in midstroke. Then, careful
not to nick himself, he finished shaving. Wiping his face
dry, he next stuffed his jaws with fresh wads of cotton
wool. Turning to the wardrobe, he dressed in his
preacher's suit and clapped the fedora on his head. The
Colt sixgun, fully loaded and riding snug in the crossdraw holster, was hidden by the drape of his jacket. A
last check in the wardrobe mirror satisfied him all was
in order. On his way out the door he collected the worn
leather satchel.

By eight o'clock, Starbuck was standing in front of
the St. Joseph *Herald*. He'd taken breakfast in a café
down the street, and casual inquiry had produced the
name of the newspaper's editor. Once inside, he bypassed a woman at the front counter with a chipper
wave. Several men, reporters and clerks, looked up from
their desks as he moved across the room. At the rear, he
halted before a glass-enclosed office and straightened his
tie. Then he plastered a grin on his face and barged
through the door.

"Good morning, Brother Williams!"

Edward Williams was a frail man, with moist eyes
and a sour, constipated expression. He laid a sheaf of
foolscap on his desk, and frowned.

"Who are you?"

"Joshua Thayer," Starbuck said in high good humour.
"I represent the Holy Writ Foundation, and discreet inquiry informs me that you are one of St. Joseph's more
upstanding Christian gentlemen."

Williams nodded wisely. "Bible peddler, huh?"

"No indeedee!" Starbuck trumpeted. " 'I give light to
them that sit in darkness.' "

"That a fact?"

"Allow me." Starbuck opened the satchel and took out a leather-bound, gilt-edged Bible. He placed it in front of Williams and stood back proudly. " 'Blessed are they which do hunger and thirst after righteousness!' Wouldn't you agree, Brother Williams?"

Williams studied the Bible. "If they do, I'll bet they pay an arm and a leg for it."

"According to Job," Starbuck said genially, " 'The price of wisdom is above rubies.' "

"Spare me the sermon." Williams tilted back in his chair. "What can I do for you, Mr. Thayer?"

"A small favour," Starbuck announced. "A good deed by which your fellow Christians will profit mightily."

"What sort of favour?"

"By chance, do you publish the names of newcomers to your fair city? A list—perhaps a column—devoted to some mention of those recently settled in St. Joseph?"

"Once a week," Williams replied. "People like to see their names in the paper; helps build circulation. We collect the information from realtors and landlords. Why would that interest you?"

Starbuck opened his hands in a pious gesture. "The lot of strangers in a strange city can oftentimes be lonesome. And I ask you, Brother Williams—what better solace for a troubled heart than the words of the Good Book?"

"In plain English," Williams said cynically, "you're drumming up a list of prospects to call on. Isn't that the idea?"

" 'Whatsoever a man soweth, that shall he also reap!' "

" 'Cast thy bread upon the waters, and wait for the fish to nibble.' Wouldn't that be more like it, Mr Thayer?"

"You are a man of rare perception, Brother Williams."

"Save it for the sinners." Williams leaned forward. "I take it you'd like to look over our back issues and copy down the names?"

"Precisely." Starbuck gave him a disarming smile. "The last couple of weeks should do very nicely. And needless to say, I shan't reveal how I came by the names."

"You do and I'll have your larcenous butt run out of town!"

"Never fear!" Starbuck struck a pose. " 'Wisdom excelleth folly!' So sayeth the travelling man's almanac."

Williams grunted. "The lady at the counter will dig out the files for you. Good day . . . Brother Thayer."

A short while later Starbuck walked from the *Herald*. In his pocket was a list of names and addresses, and a map of the city. One address—1318 Lafayette Street—was circled with a bold scrawl. The occupant was Thomas Howard.

Walking across town, Starbuck quickly formulated a plan. He would knock on the door, posing as a Bible salesman, and attempt to gain entry. From there, assuming he positively identified the outlaw, he would play it by ear. So early in the morning, there was every likelihood Zee James would be present. Even worse, it was possible the Ford brothers were being quartered at the house. In that event, he would simply make his sales pitch and depart without incident. Sooner or later, Jesse James would go out for a stroll, perhaps wander downtown on an errand. Time enough then to brace him on the street. Shout his name, let him make his move—and end it.

On the other hand, it was entirely conceivable he would find the outlaw home alone. All things considered, that would present the simplest, and the quickest, solution. By identifying himself, with the edge of surprise, he would force the gang leader into blind reaction. The outcome was foreordained. He would kill Jesse James on the spot.

The general neighbourhood was situated on a hill east of the business district. As Starbuck had suspected, it was quiet and respectable, modestly affluent. From downtown, he walked uphill, checking house numbers block by block. Some three-quarters of the way up the grade, he spotted the house on the opposite side of the street. A one-storey affair, with a picket fence out front, it stood on the corner of 13th and Lafayette. Halting at the corner, he pulled out his list and made a show of checking off names. Then he angled across the street with a jaunty stride.

A gunshot suddenly sounded from within the house. Starbuck stopped in his tracks, stock-still and watchful. An instant later he heard a woman's shrill, piercing scream. Then the door burst open and two men rushed outside. Jamming on their hats, they pushed through the fence gate, and turned downhill. The one in the lead darted a glance at Starbuck, but quickly looked away. The gate slammed shut and they hurried off in the direction of the business district.

Starbuck swore under his breath. He immediately pegged the men as the Ford brothers, and he had a sinking feeling about the gunshot. His nerves stretched tight, he walked to the fence and eased through the gate. Then he dropped the satchel and warily approached the house. His gun hand slipped beneath the front of his jacket.

The door was open, and from inside he heard a low keening moan. A step at a time, he edged slowly through the door. The children, a young boy and a little girl, were the first thing he saw. Across the parlour, standing frozen in the kitchen doorway, they stared with shocked round eyes. Their faces, like marble statuary, were drained of colour.

Starbuck's gaze shuttled from them to the woman. She was on her knees, caught in a shaft of sunlight from the front window. Her dress was splashed red with blood and her head arched back in a strangled sob. She cradled a man in her arms, rocking back and forth, holding him tightly to her breast. His feet were tangled in an overturned chair, and on a nearby sofa lay a double shoulder rig, pistol butts protruding from the holsters. His left eye was an oozing dot and the back of his skull was blown apart directly behind the right ear. A stench of death filled the parlour.

Starbuck saw then he was too late. The woman crouched on the floor was Zee James. Her blood-soaked dress and her wailing cry were stark testament to a grisly truth.

The dead man in her arms was Jesse James.

CHAPTER 18

The coroner's inquest began the next morning.

News of Jesse James' death had created a national sensation. Accounts of the killing rated banner headlines from New York to Los Angeles. The stories, based on hearsay and preliminary reports, were sparse on details. Yet the overall theme of the stories reflected a universal sentiment. The Robin Hood of American outlaws had been laid low by a hired assassin.

The hearing room was packed with an overflow crowd. Newspaper reporters from as far away as Kansas City and St. Louis were seated down front. Behind them, wedged together in a solid mass, was a throng of spectators. The majority, citizens of St. Joseph, were drawn by morbid curiosity. Farmers and people from outlying towns were drawn by grief, and a compelling sense of outrage. They were there to look upon the man who was already being labelled "the dirty little coward."

Starbuck was seated in the front row. Outwardly composed, he was still in the guise of the Bible salesman Joshua Thayer. Underneath, however, he was filled with a strange ambivalence. Jesse James was dead, and whether by his hand or that of Bob Ford, the result was the same. Yet he felt oddly cheated, almost bitter. Once again, as though some capricious power were at work, he had been thwarted at the very last moment. After months of investigation, added to the strain of operating undercover, the letdown was overwhelming. By his reasoning, he'd been robbed of a hard-won victory.

Still, for all that, his assignment was not yet completed. There was widespread speculation that Frank James would appear—at the risk of his own life—and take vengeance on his brother's killer. Starbuck considered it an improbable notion. Frank James, in his view, was too smart for such a dumb play. On the outside chance he was wrong, however, he waited. One day more hardly seemed to matter.

The inquest, thus far, had produced no startling revelations. Zee James, who was eight months pregnant, and reportedly still in a state of shock, had not been called to testify. Sheriff John Timberlake, summoned from Clay County, had earlier viewed the body in the town mortuary. Based on long personal acquaintance, he positively identified the dead man as Jesse James. Dick Liddil, collared at the last moment by Sheriff Timberlake, had been hauled along to St. Joseph. In corroborating the identification, he noted the deceased was missing a finger on the left hand. The outlaw leader was known to have suffered a similar loss during the Civil War.

Horace Heddens, the coroner, conducted the inquest like a ringmaster working a three-ring circus. He was on the sundown side of fifty, with thin hair and watery brown eyes. Yet his reedy voice was clipped with authority, and he brooked no nonsense from the spectators. When he called Bob Ford to the witness chair, the hearing room erupted in a gruff buzz of conversation. Heddens took up a gavel and quickly hammered the crowd into silence.

Starbuck, with clinical interest, studied the witness while he was being sworn. He thought he'd never seen a more unlikely looking killer. Under different circumstances, Bob Ford might have been a stage idol. He was painfully handsome, in his early twenties, with chiselled features and dark wavy hair. Only his eyes gave him away. He looked unsufferably taken with himself, somehow haughty. His demeanour was that of a celebrity.

The witness chair was centred between Heddens' desk and the jury box. As the coroner went through the preliminary questions, the jurors watched Ford with rapt attention. The effect was somewhat like people mesmerised by the snake rather than the snake charmer.

"Now, Mr. Ford." Heddens held up a long-barrelled revolver. "I direct your attention to this Smith & Wesson forty-four-calibre pistol. Do you recognise it?"

"I do," Ford said without hesitation. "It's the gun I used to kill Jesse James."

"For the record," Heddens said, placing the revolver on the desk. "You shot the deceased yesterday—April 3, 1882—at approximately nine o'clock in the morning. Is that correct?"

"Yessir," Ford smirked. "Shot him deader'n a doornail."

Heddens laced his fingers together. "For the benefit of the jurors, would you elaborate as to your motive?"

"The reward," Ford said simply. "I did it for the money—ten thousand dollars."

"Were you acting on your own, or at the behest of someone else?"

"Oh, it was official," Ford assured him. "I went to Sheriff Timberlake a couple of weeks ago. Told him I had a once-in-a-lifetime chance to get Jesse."

"Exactly how did this 'chance' come about?"

"Well, like I said, it started a couple of weeks ago. Jesse's gang was all broke up, and he come to Clay County lookin' for new men. I'd known him off and on, and he'd always treated me decent. So I told him me and Charley—that's my brother—wanted to join up and be outlaws. He took to the idea right off, and said I'd get instructions where to meet him. Course, he never had no idea we'd play him false."

"What happened next?"

"That's when I contacted Sheriff Timberlake." Ford's mouth lifted in a sly smile. "Told him I'd deliver Jesse for the reward and a promise of immunity. He went to see the governor, and by the end of the week we had ourselves a deal."

"Thomas Crittenden?" Heddens prompted. "The governor of Missouri?"

"The one and only," Ford said smugly. "He authorised me to go ahead and do it the best way I saw fit."

"There was never any question of taking Jesse James alive? The plan, as sanctioned by Governor Crittenden, was to kill him in the most expedient manner. Is that essentially correct?"

"Naturally." Ford grinned, and wagged his head. "Only a fool would try to take him prisoner. It was either kill him or chuck the whole idea."

"Proceed," Heddens said sternly. "What next transpired?"

"Jesse brought me and Charley here to St. Joe. He had a bank job lined up, and we was to stay with him till the time come. So we moved in with him."

"You refer to the deceased's place of residence, on Lafayette Street?"

"That's right."

"Continue."

"Well, it was touch and go for a while. Jesse was always on guard, real leery. Never once saw him go out of the house during the day. After dark he'd go downtown and get the newspapers, 'specially the Kansas City *Times*. But mostly that just put him in a bad frame of mind, and spoiled our chances all the more."

"Are you saying the newspapers affected his mood?"

"Yeah." Ford gestured with his hands. "A few days ago there was a piece in the *Times*. It went on about how he was all washed up, called him a has-been outlaw. He got awful mad, and said he'd show 'em Jesse James wasn't done yet. Things like that kept him edgy, and just made it harder for us."

"Harder in what way?"

"He always went armed, even in the house. Carried two guns, a Colt and a Smith & Wesson, both forty-fives. Wore 'em in shoulder holsters he'd had made special. So we just never had a chance to get the drop on him. Not till yesterday anyway."

Heddens addressed him directly. "Why was yesterday any different than normal?"

"Jesse was all fired up," Ford replied. "He'd decided to pull the bank job next Monday, and that put him in high spirits. After breakfast, me and Charley followed him into the parlour. He spotted some dust on a picture hanging by the front window, and darned if he didn't go get himself a feather duster."

"He was still armed at that point?"

"Yeah, he was." Ford's expression turned to mild wonder. "Then he says something about how the neighbours might spot him through the window, wearing them guns. So I'm blessed if he don't slip out of the shoulder rig and lay it across a divan. I like to swallowed my tongue."

"So he was then completely disarmed?"

"That's the size of it." Ford nervously licked his lips. "Next thing I know, he stepped up on a straight-backed chair and commenced to dust the picture. Charley and me looked at each other, and we figured it was now or never."

"For the record," Heddens asked with a note of asperity, "Jesse James was standing on a chair—with his back to you—and he was unarmed. Is that your testimony?"

"Yessir, it is."

"Proceed."

A vein pulsed in Ford's forehead. "Well, it all happened pretty quick. Charley and me pulled our guns, and I cocked mine. Jesse must've heard it, because he turned his head like lightning. I fired and the ball struck him square in the left eye. Not one of us ever spoke a word. I just fired and he dropped dead at Charley's feet."

The hearing room went deathly still. The jurors were immobile, staring at Ford with open revulsion. A woman's sob, muffled by a handkerchief, was the only sound from the spectators. At length, with a look of utter contempt, Heddens spoke to the witness.

"What were your actions immediately following the shooting?"

"We cleared out," Ford muttered, lowering his eyes. "We went down to the telegraph office, and I wired Governor Crittenden and Sheriff Timberlake what we'd done. Then we turned ourselves over to the St. Joe police. That was it."

"Indeed?" Heddens' nostrils flared. "And what was the gist of your message to the governor and Sheriff Timberlake?"

"Five words." Ford looked oddly crestfallen. "I have got my man. Wasn't no question what I meant."

"I daresay." Heddens was glaring at him now, face

masked by anger. "Allow me to summarise, Mr. Ford.
You capitalised on a man's trust in order to profit by his
death. He took you into his home—under the same roof
with his wife and family—and by your own admission,
he treated you fairly. In return, you waited until he was
defenceless, and then—with premeditation and in cold
blood—you shot him down. In short, you are nothing
more than a common assassin." He paused, drew a deep,
unsteady breath. "Have you anything further to add to
the record, Mr. Ford?"

"No, nothing," Ford said in a shaky voice. "Except I
ain't ashamed of what I done. Somebody had to kill—"

Heddens banged his gavel. "Witness is dismissed!"

Bob Ford rose from the witness chair and darted a
hangdog look at the jurors. Then two city policemen
stepped forward and led him out by a rear door. There
was a protracted interval of silence in the hearing room,
and all eyes seemed fixed on Heddens. Finally, with a
measure of composure, he consulted a list of names at
his elbow. He looked up, searching the front row.

"Joshua Thayer?"

Starbuck jumped. "Here!"

"Please take the witness chair."

Somewhat astounded, Starbuck stood and walked forward. Following the shooting, he had stayed with Zee
James and the children until the police arrived. Later,
after he'd made a statement at police headquarters, he
learned the Ford brothers had voluntarily surrendered.
With the killer in custody and the unsavoury details already leaked to the press, it never occurred to Starbuck
that he would be called to testify. Now, while the oath
was being administered, he prepared himself to continue
the charade. Any disclosure of his true identity would
merely serve to alert Frank James. And vastly compli-
cate his own life.

"Mr. Thayer." Heddens began, reading from an official document, "I have here your statement to the police. In it, you identify yourself as a Bible salesman. Is that correct?"

"Commissioned agent." Starbuck amended with an engaging smile. "The Holy Writ Foundation doesn't employ salesmen. The Good Book sells itself."

"I stand corrected," Heddens said with strained patience. "Nevertheless, while going about your duties, you were in the vicinity of the deceased's residence early yesterday morning. Would you please tell the jurors what you witnessed at that time?"

"A truly dreadful thing," Starbuck said with soft wonder. "I heard a gunshot, and then two men ran from the house and hurried off towards town. A woman was sobbing—most pitifully, I might add—so I took it upon myself to enter the house. I found a lady crouched over the man who had been shot. He was quite dead."

"At that time, you were unaware that the deceased was in fact Jesse James?"

"Oh, my, yes!" Starbuck's eyes widened in feigned astonishment. "I merely attempted to play the Good Samaritan."

"Very commendable," Heddens said dryly. "For the record, however, I wish to establish eyewitness identification. Do you now state that the men who ran from the house were in fact Charles and Robert Ford?"

"I do indeed," Starbuck affirmed. "Not one iota of doubt. I saw their faces quite clearly."

Heddens eyed him, considering. "One last question, Mr. Thayer. Did you attempt to stop these men from fleeing the scene?"

"Good heavens, no!"

"Did you order them to halt—call out for help from the neighbours—anything?"

"I would hardly have done that."

"Why not?"

" 'A living dog is better than a dead lion.' "

"I beg your pardon?"

"Ecclesiastes." Starbuck smiled in mock piety. "Chapter nine, Verse four."

"I see." Heddens frowned. "So you failed to act out of fear for your life. Is that it, Mr. Thayer?"

Starbuck gave him a sheepish look. "I am not a man of violence. 'Blessed are the meek; for they shall inherit—' "

"Very well, Mr. Thayer." Heddens rapped his gavel. "You're dismissed."

Starbuck nodded diffidently and returned to his seat. The inquest concluded with the testimony of Charley Ford. His story was a reprise of his brother's statement, and added nothing to the record. Late that afternoon the coroner's jury returned a verdict of justifiable homicide. Horace Heddens, in his closing remarks, laid the onus on Governor Thomas Crittenden. The Fords, however despicable their deed, were sanctioned by the highest authority of the state. The murder of Jesse James, he noted, was therefore a legal act. The verdict returned was the only verdict possible.

Then, ordering the Ford brothers released from custody, he adjourned the hearing. He refused all comment to reporters, and walked stiffly from the room.

The train bearing Jesse James' body departed St. Joseph that evening. The destination was Kearney, the slain outlaw's hometown. A short time later, Starbuck boarded a train bound for Kansas City. Upon arriving there, he immediately went through his chameleon routine. Joshua Thayer, Bible salesman, was quickly transformed into

Floyd Hunnewell, horse thief. By midnight, he was mounted and riding hard towards Clay County.

The following day he drifted into Kearney. The funeral was scheduled for late that afternoon, and by midmorning the town was swamped with several thousand people. Some were friends and neighbours, and many were heard to proclaim they had ridden with Jesse James during the war. But the majority were strangers, travelling great distances by wagon and horseback. They were brought there by some macabre compulsion, eager to look upon the casket of a man who had titillated them in life, and now in death. To the casual observer, there was something ghoulish in their manner. They had come not to mourn but rather to stare.

Starbuck, lost in the crowd, was there on business. With no great expectation, he was playing a long shot. He thought Frank James would be a fool to come anywhere near Kearney. Yet stranger things had happened. Grief was a powerful emotion, and it sometimes got the better of a man's judgement. He waited to see how it would affect the last of the James brothers.

A funeral service was held in the Baptist church. Afterwards, the casket was loaded onto a wagon, with the immediate family trailing behind in buggies. The cortege then proceeded to the family farm, some four miles outside town. Not all the crowd tagged along, but hundreds of spectators went to witness the burial. Beneath a large tree in the yard, the outlaw was laid to rest. Gathered around the grave were his wife and children, his mother and sister, and several close relatives. A last word was said by the preacher, then some of the men went to work with shovels. The women retreated to the house.

Frank James was not among the mourners.

The crowd slowly dispersed. Starbuck was among the

first to leave, and he passed through Kearney without stopping. All along, he'd somehow known Frank wouldn't show. As he rode south out of Kearney, he finally admitted what his instinct had told him in St. Joseph. Bob Ford, both at the police station and the inquest, had never mentioned the eldest James brother. And the obvious reason was at once the simplest explanation. Frank James was long gone to Texas.

By sundown, Starbuck arrived at Ma Ferguson's. The moment he walked through the door Alvina sensed something was wrong. He bought her a drink, and they sat for a while making small talk. She asked no questions, and he offered no explanation for his curious disappearance over the past four days. She appeared somewhat resigned, almost as though she had prepared herself for the inevitable. At last, with a look of genuine regret, Starbuck took her hand.

"Wish it wasn't so," he said quietly, "but it's time for me to move on."

"I know." She squeezed his hand. "You never was much of an actor, honeybunch. It's written all over your face."

Starbuck permitted himself a single ironic glance. "Guess some things are harder to hide than others."

Alvina gave him a fetching smile. "You're a sport, Floyd Hunnewell. I won't forget you—not anytime soon."

"That goes both ways."

Starbuck kissed her lightly on the mouth. Then, with an offhand salute, he rose and walked towards the door. Outside he stepped into the saddle and reined his horse out of the yard.

His thoughts turned to tomorrow, and St. Louis. And beyond that . . . Texas.

CHAPTER 19

"Good afternoon, Luke!"

"Mr. Tilford."

Otis Tilford rose from behind his desk. He was beaming like a mischievous leprechaun. His handshake was warm and cordial, and he appeared genuinely delighted to see Starbuck. He motioned to a chair.

"You made good time."

"Not too bad," Starbuck allowed, seating himself. "Caught the morning train out of Kansas City."

Tilford tapped a newspaper on his desk. "I've been reading about the funeral. I presume you were there?"

"You might say that."

"Of course!" Tilford chortled slyly. "Incognito, as it were! Hmmm?"

Starbuck shrugged. "Just a face in the crowd. Nothing worth talking about."

"The newspapers estimated the crowd at several thousand. Is that true?"

"Close enough." Starbuck took out the makings and began rolling a smoke. "It was sort of a cross between an anthill and a circus."

"Indeed!" Tilford snorted. "I must say I find it a rather

disgusting spectacle. All those people congregating to pay homage to a murderous killer! One wonders what the world is coming to."

"Folks need heroes." Starbuck lit his cigarette, exhaled slowly. "Jesse got canonised long before he died. Course, the way he died turned him into a regular martyr. I understand there's already a ballad out about how Bob Ford backshot him."

"Utter nonsense!" Tilford said angrily. "In my opinion, Ford richly deserves a medal."

"I got the impression he preferred the money."

"I was right, then." Tilford eyed him with a shrewd look. "You attended the inquest, didn't you?"

"What gave you that idea?"

"I read about a Bible salesman who testified. The news stories placed him on the scene immediately after the Ford brothers fled. I gather he was the first one inside the house . . . following the killing."

"You couldn't prove it by me."

"No?" Tilford searched his face. "Wouldn't you agree that it strains the laws of coincidence? A Johnny-on-the-spot Bible salesman—working that particular neighbourhood—on that particular morning?"

Starbuck took a long drag on his cigarette. "I wouldn't hazard a guess one way or the other."

"Good grief!" Tilford laughed. "I'm not asking you to compromise professional secrets. I simply wanted a firsthand account of what happened." He paused, watching Starbuck closely. "You were there—when Jesse James died—weren't you?"

"The Bible peddler was," Starbuck said evasively. "For the sake of argument, let's suppose I could tell you what he saw. Anything special you wanted to know?"

"I read an account of Ford's testimony at the inquest

Several newspapers, however, still claim he shot James in the back. Which version is true?"

"Half and half," Starbuck commented. "James turned his head just as Ford fired. So he got it straight on—clean through the eye."

"How can you be certain?"

"A gunshot wound pretty much tells its own story. In this case the eye was punched inward, like somebody had jabbed him with a sharp stick. The exit wound was bigger, and messier. Tore out the back of his skull and splattered brains all over the wall. No other way it could've happened."

"Then he died quickly?"

"Instantaneous," Starbuck explained. "Lights out before he knew what hit him."

"A pity." Tilford's mouth zigzagged in a cruel grimace. "He deserved to die harder."

Starbuck regarded him impassively. "Dead's dead."

"Perhaps," Tilford said without conviction. "On the other hand, a quick and painless death is no great punishment. A man with so many sins on his head should be made to suffer in *this* life."

"Nail him to the cross and let him die slow. That the general idea?"

"Precisely!" Tilford said with a clenched smile. "The Romans employed crucifixion to great effect. I daresay it was one of history's more lasting object lessons."

"I hear they also fed people to lions."

"Even better!" Tilford's eyes blazed. "I would have taken a front-row seat to watch Jesse James being devoured by a lion."

Starbuck examined the notion. "Some folks got stronger stomachs than others."

"Come now!" Tilford insisted. "Compassion hardly

seems your strong suit. Not after all of those men you've
. . . sent to the grave."

"You ever kill a man?"

"I—no, I haven't."

"Thought not." Starbuck fixed him with a pale stare.
"The killing's no problem. After the first couple of
times, you get used to it. But once you've shot a man
and watched him suffer, you sort of lose your taste for
slow death." His expression was stoic, and cold. "You
learn to kill them fast, *muy* goddamn *pronto*! Otherwise
you don't sleep so good at night."

Tilford looked at him, unable to guess what might lie
beneath the words. He sensed he'd somehow offended
Starbuck, yet the reason eluded him. He couldn't imagine that a manhunter would harbour ethics about killing.
Still, by reading between the lines, a rather primeval
code had been expressed. A code common to all the
great predators. Kill swiftly and cleanly, and do it well.
Sudden death.

"To be absolutely truthful," Tilford said at length, "I
haven't the stomach for it in any form or fashion. But
then, I suspect you knew that all along."

"I never gave it much thought."

"Well, now," Tilford said tactfully, "on to other
things. Where do we go from here?"

Starbuck stubbed out his cigarette in an ashtray. "I
just stopped off to say goodbye."

"Goodbye!" Surprise washed over Tilford's face.
"I'm afraid I don't understand."

"Simple enough," Starbuck remarked. "You hired me
to do a job, and I flubbed it up six ways to Sunday. So
I'm—"

"On the contrary," Tilford interrupted. "You've performed brilliantly, Luke! Without you, I daresay Jesse

James would not have been buried yesterday—or any other day!"

"No thanks to me," Starbuck reminded him. "Bob Ford's the one that got him. I was strictly a spectator."

"Nonsense!" Tilford scoffed. "You routed the gang! If it weren't for that, Ford would never have gotten anywhere near Jesse James. Perhaps you didn't fire the shot, but that's immaterial. Only the end result counts!"

"The fact remains, it was Ford who pulled the trigger. I don't take pay when somebody else does my job."

"That's absurd!" Tilford protested. "I'm the judge of what you did or did not do, and I say you earned the money. I won't hear of your returning one red cent!"

Starbuck gave him a tight, mirthless smile. "I never said anything about returning it."

"I fail to see the distinction."

"I'm trying to tell you I won't take any pay for Jesse."

"Then you're not quitting?"

"No." Starbuck grinned crookedly. "Not till the job's done."

"I see." Tilford looked relieved. "I take it you're referring to Frank James?"

"Only if you still want him."

"Indeed I do! He's no less guilty than his brother."

"Then I'll leave tonight. But I want it understood— you don't owe me another dime. I'll get Frank and then we're even steven. All accounts squared."

"Come now, Luke," Tilford admonished him. "That's carrying integrity a bit far, don't you think?"

"Take it or leave it," Starbuck countered. "I won't have it any other way."

"Very well," Tilford conceded. "Where will your search begin?"

"No search to it," Starbuck told him. "I know where he's hiding, and I'll be there by the end of the week. So you just go ahead and consider him dead."

"Luke, why do I get the impression I won't see you again?"

"No reason you should. Where I'm headed, I'll be closer to Denver than here. Once it's over, I reckon I'll head on home."

"Quite understandable," Tilford said, troubled. "But how will I know for certain Frank James is dead?"

"When it's done, I'll send you a wire."

"Oh?" Tilford pondered a moment. "I wouldn't have thought you'd put it in writing."

"Nothing fancy." Starbuck flipped a palm back and forth. "I'll just say 'assignment completed' and let it go at that."

"How will I know the wire was sent by you?"

"I'll sign it Floyd Hunnewell."

"Does that name have some special significance?"

Starbuck smiled. "Only to horse thieves and whores."

The trip south was long and boring. The train passed through Kansas and Indian Territory, and finally crossed into Texas. With nothing to do but stare out the window, Starbuck found that time weighed heavily. His thoughts, oddly enough, turned inward.

By nature, Starbuck was not given to introspection. He was at peace with himself, and he seldom examined his own motives. Sometimes too cynical, he tended to view the world through a prism of cold reality. Any illusions about other men—and their motives—were long since shattered. Saints and sinners, in his experience, all walked the same tightrope. None were perfect, and he often thought that blind luck, rather than circumstance, dictated which ones lost their balance. In the end, only a hairline's difference separated the upright from the downfallen. There was nothing charitable in his outlook,

for he'd discovered that rose-tinted glasses merely dis-
torted the truth. His cynicism was simply a by-product
of unclouded observation.

Yet, with time to reflect, he was struck by a queer
sentiment. The more he examined it, the more he realised it was wholly out of character. He survived at his
trade by virtue of the fact that he gave no man the benefit
of the doubt. Still, however sardonic his attitude, a worm
of doubt had begun gnawing at his certainty. He was
having second thoughts about Frank James.

Not at all comfortable with the feeling, he found it
growing more acute as the train rattled towards Fort
Worth. He ruminated on their one meeting, a brief
exchange of words at Ma Ferguson's whorehouse. He'd
sensed that Frank James was a man of some decency.
Even then, under the strained circumstances, the eldest
James brother had seemed curiously unlike the other
members of the gang. Some intangible quality—a mix
of honour and conscience—had shown through the hard
exterior. None of which fitted with the known facts. The
man was an outlaw and a killer, one who lived by the
gun. Quoting Shakespeare scarcely absolved him of his
crimes.

All the same, Starbuck had found him eminently likable. And that was perhaps the most troubling aspect of
the whole affair. His instincts told him Frank James
hadn't slipped off the tightrope. Instead, he'd been
pulled down by Jesse and the Youngers. Viewed from
that perspective, he was a victim of blood relations and
bad luck. Still, no man was victimised without his cooperation. Weakness of character was hardly an excuse
for murder. Nor was it sufficient reason to grant the murderer a reprieve. And Frank James was known to have
killed at least three men.

Stewing on it, Starbuck played the devil's advocate.

He argued both sides, and in the end he worked himself into a dicey position. On the one hand, the last survivor of the James-Younger gang most assuredly deserved killing. On the other, Starbuck was no longer certain he *wanted* to kill Frank James. His sense of duty was in sharp conflict with his personal feelings. Which was a pretty pickle for someone in the detective business. A manhunter with sentiment!

He finally laughed himself out of the notion. On the Pecos, there would be no time for such damn-fool non-sense. Otherwise the damn fool—not Frank James—would get himself killed. And that, indeed, was a personal sentiment.

With brief layovers in Fort Worth and San Angelo, Starbuck slowly worked his way westward. By the fifth day, he'd switched to horseback, and that evening he rode into Fort Stockton. There, posing as a saddletramp looking for work, he drifted into the local watering hole. His questions aroused no suspicions, and within the hour he struck pay dirt. Tom Ruston's ranch lay in the shadow of Table Top Mountain, along a winding stretch of the Pecos. He estimated it was less than a day's ride away.

By dusk the next evening, he had located the spread. Ruston used a Running R brand, and the cows on his range were easily spotted. The land was dotted with cholla cactus and prickly pear, and beyond the river a range of mountains jutted skyward like white-capped sentinels. Far to the northeast lay the Staked Plains, and some seventy miles south was the Rio Grande and the Mexican border. It was remote and isolated, literally out in the middle of nowhere. A perfect hideout for an outlaw from Missouri.

Starbuck camped that night within sight of the ranch compound. When dawn peeled back the darkness, he was squatted in an arroyo not thirty yards from the main house. Off to one side, purple blemishes in the gathering light, were a cook shack and a small bunkhouse. He watched, curbing his impatience, while the outfit slowly came to life. As the sun crested the distant mountains, a man emerged from the main house and walked towards the cook shack. He took the man to be Tom Ruston, and that assumption was borne out several minutes later. The rancher led a crew of cowhands from the cook shack, and moved directly to a large corral. There, the men roped ponies out of the remuda, and saddled up for the day's work. With Ruston at the head of the column, they mounted and rode south along the river. Apart from the cook, that left no one on the place except Ruston's wife. And Frank James.

Starbuck scrambled out of the arroyo and circled the house from the rear. At the corner, he paused, searching the compound one last time, and pulled his sixgun. Then he edged cautiously along the front wall, and halted beside the door. Inside, he saw a dark-haired woman washing dishes at the sink. Beyond the living area, there was a short hallway with doors opening onto two bedrooms. No one else was in sight.

One eye on the hall, Starbuck stepped through the door. He ghosted across the room, approaching the woman from behind. Suddenly she turned, reaching out for a dish towel, and saw him. She gasped, and her eyes went wide with terror. Her mouth ovaled, on the verge of a scream, and he had no choice. His left hand struck out in a shadowy movement and clouted her upside the jaw. She hit the sink, scattering dishes, and dropped to the floor. He wheeled and strode swiftly to the hallway entrance.

"Martha?"

A voice sounded from one of the bedrooms. Starbuck

stopped cold, hugging the wall. He thumbed the hammer on the Colt, and waited.

"Hey, Martha!" The voice was familiar, but strangely weak. "What's all the noise?"

Starbuck would later wonder what made him speak out. He could have waited until curiosity brought the outlaw through the door and ended it there. Instead, he called down the hallway. "Hello, Frank!"

There was a beat of hesitation. "Who's that?"

"The law," Starbuck answered. "I've come to take you in."

"You figure to manage that all by yourself?"

"No need to stall," Starbuck advised him. "Ruston and his boys already rode off. It's just you and me."

"What makes you think I'll go peaceable?"

"Because if you don't, I'll kill you."

"So what?" Frank shouted hoarsely. "I'd just as soon die here as get hung in Missouri!"

"Think on it a minute! With a slick lawyer—especially now that Jesse's dead—you might have a chance in court. With me, you've got no chance at all. It'll end here and now!"

"Mister, you're dreaming! I'd never make it to trial back home! Somebody would get me the same way they got Jesse—only easier!"

"No," Starbuck assured him earnestly. "I'll get you there in one piece, and I'll see to it you get a fair trial. You've got my word on it, Frank. No one will kill you!"

The intensity of Starbuck's voice gave his words a ring of prophecy. A leaden stillness descended over the house, and for a while he thought Frank wouldn't respond. Then, abruptly, a revolver sailed through the door and bounced across the floor.

"There's my gun! I've quit the fight!"

Starbuck eased down the hallway. He went to one

knee and took a quick peek through the door. Then he slowly rose and moved into the bedroom. He saw that his instinct hadn't played him false.

Frank James lay slack and unmoving on the bed. Ugly lines strained his face, and his eyes were oddly vacant. His breathing was laboured, lungs pumping like a bellows. He looked worn and haggard, older than his years.

"Frank." Starbuck nodded, quickly holstered the Colt. "What ails you? You look a little green around the gills."

"Don't worry." Frank tried to smile, a tortured smile. "I won't die on you. Got a touch of consumption, that's all."

"I'd say that's enough."

"Yeah, it wouldn't have been much of a fight, would it?"

Starbuck had a sudden vision of hell. He saw himself killing a bedridden invalid, not a bayed outlaw. The sight turned his guts to stone.

He silently blessed Frank James for throwing in the towel. And his gun.

CHAPTER 20

" 'Our virtues would be proud if our faults whipped them not.' "

Starbuck smiled. "Before we're finished, you'll have me spouting Shakespeare."

"It's like tobacco." Frank gestured with his pipe. "Once you've got the habit, it's hard to break."

"How'd you get the habit to start with?"

"Well, I never had much formal education. But I got a taste of Shakespeare in school, and I was always impressed by his eloquent way with words. He said things lots better than I ever could."

"Like the one you just quoted?"

"Yes." Frank stared out the train window, silent a moment. "Believe it or not, I've always considered myself a virtuous man. Does that sound strange, Luke?"

Starbuck considered the thought. Over the past month, he'd found Frank James to be a man of his word. After surrendering, the outlaw had convinced Tom Ruston to abide by his decision. The rancher acceded, and thereafter Starbuck had been treated like a guest. In time, Martha Ruston even forgave him the blow upside her jaw.

Their common concern was Frank James. For some
years, he had been afflicted with a mild case of tuberculosis. His condition worsened after Northfield, aggra-
vated by the desperate flight and a bullet wound in the
leg. When captured by Starbuck, he'd still been weak
and frail. Travel was out of the question, and Starbuck
had agreed to wait until he'd recuperated. Another
month of bed rest—and Martha Ruston's cooking—had
put him back on his feet. He was wasted and stooped, a
pale shadow of his former self; but he seemed somehow
relieved that the running was over at last. Four days ago
he had expressed the wish to get on with the business
of formal surrender. Starbuck readily approved, and they
had entrained for Missouri. Their destination was Jefferson City, the state capital.

Tonight, rattling across the Missouri countryside,
Frank James had turned reflective. Starbuck detected a
melancholy note in his voice, and sensed he was filled
with mixed emotions. With relief, there was also the
uncertainty of what lay ahead. Under the circumstances,
it seemed natural he would look backward in time. Tomorrow would mark the beginning of the end.

"Virtue's a funny thing," Starbuck said at length. "I
guess we all see something different when we look in a
mirror."

"No need to ask how a jury will see it."

"Don't sell yourself short. I'd say the odds are fifty-
fifty, maybe better."

Frank gave him a tired smile. "Well, however it works
out, I'm just glad it's over. I haven't known a day of
peace since the war ended. Always looking over my
shoulder, afraid to sleep without a gun close at hand. No
one could understand what that kind of life does to a
man. Not unless he'd lived it himself."

"I've got a fair idea," Starbuck said slowly. "Course,

I was on the other side of the fence. So it's not exactly the same thing."

"God!" Frank laughed suddenly. "When I think back to that night at Ma Ferguson's! It's still hard to believe you and that walleyed horse thief are one and the same."

Starbuck shrugged it off. "All part of working undercover . . . tricks of the trade."

"You fooled us good," Frank confessed. "After Northfield, Jesse knew we'd been euchred somehow. But I wouldn't have suspected you in a thousand years."

"No hard feelings?" Starbuck inquired. "I reckon you know by now there wasn't anything personal involved."

"Perish the thought," Frank said, grinning. "You were hired to do a job, and you did it. I'm just glad you never joined the Pinkertons."

"No chance of that," Starbuck chuckled. "I'm not much for crowds."

"I'd be the first to admit you did very well on your own. I swore I'd never be taken alive—and look at me now!"

Starbuck nodded, watching him. "You're reconciled to it, then? No regrets?"

"Only one."

"What's that?"

"The Bard said it best." Frank's eyes took on a distant look. " 'For mine own part, I could be well content to entertain the lag-end of my life with quiet hours.' "

"Like I told you, the odds are fifty-fifty."

"I wish I believed that as much as you do, Luke."

There seemed nothing more to say. Frank slumped lower in his seat and soon drifted off in an uneasy sleep. Starbuck sat for a long while staring out the window.

Early next morning the train pulled into Jefferson City.

From the depot, Starbuck and Frank James took a hansom cab to the state capitol. A domed structure, the building stood on a bluff overlooking the Missouri River. The view was panoramic, and under different circumstances would have rated a second look. Neither of them paid the slightest attention. Together, they mounted the marble steps and entered the main corridor.

A capitol guard directed them to the second floor. Upstairs, they circled the rotunda and walked directly to the governor's office. An appointments secretary, seated at a desk in the anteroom, looked up as they entered. His smile was at once pleasant and officious.

"Good morning, gentlemen."

"Morning," Starbuck said, removing his hat. "I'd like to see Governor Crittenden."

"And your name, sir?"

"Luke Starbuck."

The man consulted his appointment book. "I'm sorry, Mr. Starbuck. I don't seem to find your name on today's calendar."

"He'll see me," Starbuck said firmly. "Tell him I've brought Frank James here to surrender."

The man's eyes darted to Frank, then back to Starbuck. "Are you serious?"

"Dead serious," Starbuck said with a steely gaze. "So hop to it—now!"

The man bolted from his chair and hurried through the door to an inner office. Several minutes elapsed, then the door creaked open. The appointments secretary poked his head into the anteroom.

"Mr. Starbuck," he said weakly. "The governor wants to know if Mr. James is armed?"

"No." Starbuck fanned his coat aside, revealing the holstered Colt. "But I am, and I know how to use it. Tell the governor he's in no danger."

"Very well." The door swung open. "You may come in."

Governor Thomas Crittenden was seated behind a
massive walnut desk. A tall man, with glacial eyes and
a hawklike nose, he appraised them with a cool look.
Then he glanced past them, nodding to his appointments
secretary. The door closed, and he motioned them closer.

"You should be informed," he said curtly, "that I have
sent for the capitol guards. In the event you attempt violence, you will never leave this room alive."

Starbuck, with Frank at his side, halted in front of the
desk. He fixed the governor with a wintry smile. "You
can call off the dogs. Frank means you no harm."

"Are you a law officer, Mr. Starbuck?"

"Private detective," Starbuck said levelly. "I was
hired to locate Frank."

"Indeed?" Crittenden sized him up with a lengthy
stare. "By whom were you retained?"

"That's privileged information," Starbuck replied.
"Let's just say I'm here as an intermediary."

"An intermediary on whose behalf?"

"On behalf of my client—" Starbuck paused for emphasis. "And on behalf of Frank James."

"Oh?" A puzzled frown appeared on Crittenden's
face. "I understood you were here to effect a surrender."

"I am," Starbuck acknowledged. "So long as you
agree to certain conditions."

"Conditions!" Crittenden repeated with a sudden
glare. "What conditions?"

"For openers," Starbuck ventured, "you agree to announce that Frank surrendered voluntarily. I have his
gun in my possession, and you can say he handed it over
of his own free will. That ought to carry a little weight
when he goes before a jury."

Crittenden made an empty gesture. "Next?"

"You agree that he'll be tried on only one charge.
One murder, one bank job, or any combination thereof.

But it ends there, whatever the outcome. One trial—and that's it!"

"Anything else?"

"Nope." Starbuck dusted his hands. "Those are the conditions."

Crittenden shook his head from side to side. "Now tell me why I should honour your request?"

"I've got a better question." Starbuck gave him a straight hard look. "Why shouldn't you?"

"I don't bargain with murderers, Mr. Starbuck."

"You killed Jesse." Starbuck's voice was suddenly edged. "Don't you think the state's had its pound of flesh?"

"I killed no one!" Crittenden said abrasively. "Besides, I fail to see how that constitutes grounds for leniency."

"How about politics?" Starbuck suggested. "Would that get your attention?"

"Politics?" Crittenden appeared bewildered. "What earthly connection does that have with"—he flung out a hand at Frank—"a murderer?"

Starbuck eyed him with a steady, uncompromising gaze. "You lost lots of votes when you had Jesse assassinated. By giving Frank a square deal, it might just balance the ledger." He let the governor hang a moment, then went on. "Or aren't you interested in serving another term?"

Crittenden threw back his head and laughed. "Are you seriously suggesting that I would barter with a villainous killer merely to enhance my position at the polls?"

"Look at it this way, Governor. A practical man knows when to bend! Frank will be tried in a court of law, and a jury will decide his fate. Which means you've done your duty, and at the same time you've shown yourself to be a man of fairness and compassion. You'll come out smelling like a rose!"

There was no immediate reply. Starbuck sensed then he'd struck the right chord. Experience had taught him that all politicians justify unconscionable deeds in the name of noble ends. Thomas Crittenden was just such a man.

"Very well." Crittenden nodded with chill dignity. "I will instruct the attorney general to proceed accordingly."

"The people of Missouri won't forget you, Governor. It's a decision worthy of Solomon himself."

"One question, Mr. Starbuck." Crittenden studied him with a keen, sidewise scrutiny. "Why have you interceded on this man's behalf?"

Starbuck grinned ferociously. "I went out of my way to save his life. I figure it'd be a waste to let him hang now."

Words appeared to fail the governor. Starbuck turned and shook Frank James' hand with mock solemnity. He gave the outlaw a broad wink.

The charge was murder.

A trial date was set, with the proceedings to be held in the town of Gallatin. There, some thirteen years previously, the state alleged that Frank James had participated in looting the Gallatin Merchants' Bank. The actual date was December 7, 1869, and in the course of the robbery the bank cashier had been killed. Frank James was charged with having fired the fatal shot.

Missourians rallied to the cause. Though there was sharp disagreement about Jesse, the barometer of public opinion heavily favoured the elder brother. For an outlaw, Frank James was held in high regard and treated with singular respect. His mild manner and frail health evoked widespread sympathy, and there was an outcry to spare him the hangman's noose. Under the tightest security, he was taken by train from Jefferson City to Gallatin. Yet, at every stop along the way, the train was met by cheering crowds. The journey, duly reported by the press, was a triumph. The last of the James boys had come home.

Clay County led the way in establishing a defence fund. Contributions poured in from throughout the state, and the groundswell of support steadily gained momentum. Several attorneys volunteered their services; but Frank James shrewdly selected his own legal counsel. Heading the defence team was General Jo Shelby, a Confederate war hero reverently admired by all Missourians. The second member of the team, famed for both his courtroom oratory and his battlefield exploits, was Major John Edwards. The prosecutor, heavily outgunned, was Robert Spooner of Gallatin. His privately expressed opinion of Governor Thomas Crittenden was not fit for print. Publicly, he theorised that in the event of a conviction he himself might be lynched. The press agreed.

The case went to trial on a Monday morning. Prosecutor Spooner, vainly attempting to resurrect evidence, was handicapped from the outset. His only eyewitness to the killing was a former bank teller, William McDowell. Unfortunately for the state, McDowell had suffered a fatal stroke earlier in the year. By default, the star witness then became a local grocer, Fred Lewis. At the time of the robbery, Lewis was seventeen years old, and his memory had apparently dimmed with age. Upon hearing the gunshot, he testified, he had dashed into the bank and spotted two robbers exiting by the backdoor. Following close behind, he saw the men approach their horses, which were tethered in the alley. One robber was thrown to the ground when his horse bolted as he attempted to mount. He then swung up behind the other robber, and they galloped out of town on one horse. On direct examination, Lewis tentatively identified Frank James as the man who had taken the spill. On cross-examination, he admitted he'd been somewhat hysterical at the time of the holdup. He *thought* the robber was Frank James—but he couldn't be positive.

The second witness called to the stand was a farmer, Dan Smoot. On the morning of the holdup, he testified, he was riding into town as the robbers rode out. At gunpoint, they forced him to dismount and commandeered his horse. Then, with a polite goodbye, they thundered away and left him standing in the middle of the road. When asked to identify the accused, he squinted across the courtroom through store-bought spectacles. He finally muttered a reluctant "Maybe." On cross-examination, Major Edwards inquired whether he'd been wearing his glasses on the day of the robbery. With a look of profound relief, he admitted he hadn't. Major Edwards smiled knowingly at the jurors, and asked no further questions. On that note, the prosecution rested its case.

The defence called only two witnesses. The first was Frank James. He testified he'd taken no part in the robbery, and before being brought to Gallatin in irons, he had never set foot in the town. Prosecutor Spooner, attempting to rattle him on cross-examination, was unable to shake his testimony. Frank James left the witness stand to an ovation from the packed courtroom.

With order restored, Starbuck then took the stand Presented as a character witness, his testimony was compelling stuff. Counsel for the defense wisely allowed him to tell his story in his own words. He recounted the high lights of his undercover work and the results of his in

vestigation. He dwelled at length on the low morals of
the Younger brothers and their general disregard for human life. Then he went on to testify that, in his opinion,
Frank James was a man of high Christian principles and
the most unlikely outlaw he'd ever encountered. He
stated emphatically that Frank had welcomed the chance
to surrender, and had freely embraced the opportunity to
atone for his crimes. On cross-examination, he refused
to divulge the name of his client. He admitted, however,
that he had been hired to track down and kill the James
boys. When asked why he had spared the life of Frank
James, his reply left the spectators spellbound and all
but reduced the jurors to tears.

"I could have killed him several times over and in
each instance something stopped me. Some people
would call it divine intervention, mercy accorded a mer-
ciful man. I simply believe Frank James was meant to
live."

Final arguments produced the only real fireworks of
the trial. Jo Shelby and John Edwards, old soldiers that
they were, followed the maxim that the best defence is
a good offence. Instead of defending Frank James, they
attacked the state of Missouri. Their technique was to
raise the spectre of Jesse James. In summation, Major
Edwards addressed himself to the life and death of the
outlaw leader. His style of oratory was florid, and dev-
astatingly effective.

"There was never a more cowardly murder committed
in all America than the murder of Jesse James. Not one
among those on the hunt for blood money dared face
him until he had disarmed himself and turned his back
to his assassins!

"If Jesse James had been hunted down, and killed
while resisting arrest, not a word would have been said
to the contrary. In his death the majesty of the law would

have been vindicated. But here the law itself becomes a murderer! It leagues with murderers. It hires murderers. It promises immunity and protection to murderers. It aids and abets murderers. It is itself a murder!

"What a spectacle! Missouri, with a hundred and seventeen sheriffs! Missouri, with a watchful and vigilant marshal in all her principal towns and cities! Yet Missouri had to ally with cutthroats so that the good name of the state might be saved from further reproach. *Saved!* Why, the whole state reeks today of infamy!

"Tear the two bears from the flag of Missouri! Put thereon, in their place, a thief blowing out the brains of an unarmed victim, and a brazen harlot—naked to the waist—and splashed to the brows in blood!"

The jury deliberated ten minutes, and the verdict was unanimous. Frank James was acquitted.

Starbuck called on Frank early the next morning. Seated in the outlaw's hotel room, they rehashed the trial and chuckled at the devious ways of politicians. Governor Thomas Crittenden had indeed delivered on his promise. The Gallatin case, of all those on the books, was the weakest of the lot. Acquittal translated into votes, and for a politician there was no more compelling motive. Those who fed at the public trough understood the nature of the game. Or perhaps, as Starbuck labelled it, the world's second oldest profession.

"I never asked," Frank said after a time. "But now that it's over . . . who hired you?"

"When all's said and done, does it matter?"

"I guess not." Frank massaged his nose, thinking. "Only you'll have a devil of a time explaining why you didn't kill me."

Starbuck smiled a cryptic smile. "The way it work out, I reckon he'll get his money's worth."

"Well, all the same, I owe you more than—"

"Your credit's good." Starbuck extended his hand. "Stick to the straight and narrow, Frank."

Frank grinned like a possum. " 'Read not my blemishes in the world's report; I have not kept the square, but that to come shall all be done by the rule.' You can bank on it, Luke."

"I already did." Starbuck shook his hand hard. "Down on the Pecos."

Outside the hotel, Starbuck crossed the street and stepped into the post office. He bought stamps and pasted them onto a letter. The envelope was addressed to Otis Tilford, and inside was a bank draft for $10,000. The accompanying message was short and succinct: "No delivery, no charge. Refund enclosed."

He smiled and dropped the letter through the slot. Then, whistling softly to himself, he strolled down to the depot. He caught the morning train for Kansas City and points west.

His assignment in Missouri was complete.

CHAPTER 21

The Alcazar Variety Theater was hushed and still. Star-buck stopped just inside the bat-wing doors. All eyes were fixed on the stage and the crowd appeared hyp-notised. He joined them, thumbs hooked in his vest. A slow smile touched the corner of his mouth.

Lola Montana was bathed in the cider glow of a spot-light. She stood centre stage, her face lifted upward in a woeful expression. Her gown was teal blue and her hair was piled atop her head in golden ringlets. The overall effect was one of lost innocence, and smoky sensuality. Her clear alto voice filled the hall, pitched low and in-timate. She sang a heartrending ballad of unrequited love. And her eyes were misty.

Starbuck watched her with a look of warm approval. Her performance was flawless, utterly believable. She acted out the song with poignant emotion, and her sultry voice somehow gave the lyrics a haunting quality. The audience was captivated, caught up in a tearjerker that was all the more sorrowful because of her beauty. She had them in the palm of her hand, and she played it for all it was worth. There was hardly a dry eye in the house and even the pug-nosed bouncer looked a little weepy

She held them enthralled to the very last note.

A moment slipped past, frozen in time. Then the crowd roared to life, the theatre vibrating to thunderous applause and wild cheers. Lola took a bow, then another and another, and still the house rocked with ovation. At last, she signalled the maestro and the orchestra segued into a rousing dance number. A line of chorus girls exploded out of the wings and went high-stepping across the stage. Lola raised her skirts, revealing a shapely leg, and joined them in a prancing cakewalk. The girls squealed and Lola flashed her underdrawers and the tempo of the music quickened. The audience went mad with exuberance.

Jack Brady, proprietor of the Alcazar, suddenly spotted Starbuck. He bulled through a throng of regulars at the bar and hurried towards the door. His bustling manner attracted attention, and other men turned to look. A low murmur swept back over the crowd as they recognised the manhunter. The theatre owner, enthusiasm written across his face, stuck out his hand. He gave Starbuck a nutcracker grin, and began pumping his arm.

"Welcome home, Luke!"

"Hello, Jack."

"By God, you're a sight for sore eyes! When did you hit town?"

"Couple of hours ago," Starbuck said pleasantly. "Came in on the evening train."

"No need to ask where from!" Brady laughed. "The whole town's buzzing about you. Newspapers have been full of it for the last week!"

"Don't believe everything you read."

"Go on with you!" Brady hooted. "You made the front page, Luke! Headlines and a story as long as your arm. The whole ball of wax!"

Starbuck looked uncomfortable. "Well, I reckon it's yesterday's news now."

"In a pigs eye! Every son-of-a-bitch in Denver wants to buy you a drink. You wait and see!"

"I guess I'll pass," Starbuck said matter-of-factly. "Got a table for me, Jack?"

"You damn betcha I do! Best table in the house!"

Brady wheeled about and cleared a path through the crowd. Starbuck tagged along, not at all pleased by the attention. Westbound on the train, he'd read news stories of the trial, which had created a furor in the nation's press. Worse, he had found his photo prominently displayed in the papers, alongside that of Frank James. The publicity was unwanted, and the photo would definitely prove a liability on future undercover assignments. Still, despite the sensationalism, he'd thought his privacy would be respected in Denver. Jack Brady's ebullient greeting dispelled that notion. An unobtrusive personal life appeared to be a thing of the past.

A spate of jubilant shouts erupted all around him. Men jostled and shoved, pushing forward to slap him on the back or try for a quick handshake. There was a curious note to their congratulations and the general tenor of the reception. For all his reputation as a mankiller, they perceived no weakness in the fact he'd spared Frank James. Instead, they were all the more awed, oddly fascinated and unable to hide it. There was something godlike in possessing the power to kill—within the law— and choosing instead to grant clemency. The very idea of it was scary and admirable, all rolled into one. To the sporting crowd of the Alcazar, it gave Starbuck ever added stature. He was no longer merely a celebrity, the town's resident manhunter and detective. He was now a personage. A killer with class . . . and a touch of the invincible.

Onstage, Lola's attention was drawn to the commotion out front. She stared past the footlights and saw Jack Brady unctuously seating Starbuck at a ringside table. In the midst of the dance routine she waved and blew him a kiss. The crowd roared with delight, and Starbuck bobbed his head in an awkward nod. Then the orchestra thumped into the finale with a blare of trumpets and a clash of cymbals. The chorus line, in a swirl of flashing skirts and jiggling breasts, went cavorting into the wings. Lola bypassed the curtain call, moving directly to the side of the stage. She went down a short flight of steps and swiftly circled the orchestra pit.

Starbuck stood as she approached the table. Her china-blue eyes were fastened on him as if caught in something sweet and sticky. She threw herself into his arms and hugged him fiercely. Then, oblivious to the onlookers, she gave him a long and passionate kiss. Clapping and stamping their feet, the audience broke out in rowdy applause. For the first time in his life, Starbuck blushed. He finally got himself disengaged from her embrace, and managed to plant her in a chair. He sat down fast.

"Hello, lover," Lola said breathlessly. "Did I embarrass you?"

"Some," Starbuck replied with a shrug. "I'm not used to an audience."

"Who cares!" She wrinkled her nose with an impudent smile. "You looked too yummy to resist."

"Yeah." Starbuck's eyes dipped to the top of her peekaboo gown. "You might have a point there."

"Why, Mr. Starbuck!" She fluttered her eyelashes. "I do think you missed me . . . or did you?"

Starbuck chuckled. "You crossed my mind now and then. Couple of times, I even had trouble getting to sleep."

"I'll bet!" She sniffed, lifting her chin. "You probably tapped half the farm girls in Missouri!"

"Who, me?" Starbuck looked at her with mock indignation. "I was so busy chasing robbers it kept me worn down to the nubbin. Don't you read the papers?"

"Do I ever!" She threw her hand to her head with a theatrical shudder. "God, my heart was in my mouth when I read those stories. It's a wonder you weren't killed!"

"I can see you almost perished with worry."

"Well, seriously, lover." Her mood suddenly turned sombre. "Do me a favour and kill the bastard next time! I want you all in one piece."

"If it was anybody else—" Starbuck stopped, weighing his words. "Let's just say Frank James was a special case, and leave it at that."

A waiter appeared with a bottle of champagne. He poured, then tucked the bottle into an ice bucket and hurried off. Lola lifted her glass and leaned closer.

"A toast." Her voice went husky. "To you and me—and lots of long nights!"

"I'll drink to that." Starbuck sipped, then slowly lowered his glass. "Only we'll have to hold it to a couple of long nights."

"Ooo God!" She groaned. "Tell me it's not so!"

"Wouldn't lie to you," Starbuck said cheerily. " stopped by the office and there was an urgent message."

"Just my luck," she marvelled. "All right, break it to me gently. Where are you off to now, lover?"

"Wyoming," Starbuck confided. "Some payroll robber named Cassidy was kind enough to leave his calling card. A client wants me to . . . return the favour."

"It's the story of my life." She stuck out her lip in little-girl pout. "Here today, gone tomorrow."

"No," Starbuck said, a devilish glint in his eye. "Day after tomorrow."

"That's right!" She brightened, sat straighter. "You said a couple of nights—didn't you?"

"Play your cards right, and we might even squeeze in a matinée."

Lola Montana laughed a deep, throaty laugh. Starbuck poured champagne, and gave her a jolly wink. He thought it was good to be home.

EPILOGUE

New Orleans
May 14, 1903

Starbuck stepped off the trolley car on a warm spring evening. Crossing the street, he went through a turnstile and entered the fairgrounds. He walked towards a candy-striped circus tent.

The sticky humidity made him long for Denver. After two days in New Orleans, he was feeling a bit worn and frazzled. Age had begun to thicken his waistline, and he'd ruefully come to the conclusion that he no longer had much tolerance for heat. Yet, for all the passing years, he was nonetheless an imposing figure of a man. He was still sledge-shouldered, with solid features and the look of vigorous good health. His eyes were alert and quick, and the force of his pale blue gaze was undiminished by time. Nor had age dimmed his zest for his work and the challenge of the chase. He still hunted men.

These days, Starbuck seldom worked alone. Over the years, his reputation as a detective had brought him national attention. At last, with clients begging him to g on retainer, the caseload had become too much for one man. In 1890, he had begun an expansion programme, establishing branch agencies throughout the West. By the turn of the century, he had offices in Denver, San Francisco, Portland, and Tulsa. The agencies were staffed with former law officers, and he'd given each of the branch superintendents a high degree of autonomy. His own time was spent in the field, working directly with the operatives. No armchair general, he led by example and on-the-spot-training, rather than issuing directives. Sometimes, just for a change of pace, he took off on an assignment by himself. And that had brought him to New Orleans.

Last night, glancing through the newspaper, his eye had been drawn to an advertisement. The James-Younger Wild West Show was currently playing a limited engagement at the fairgrounds. Some months ago, he'd heard that Frank James and Cole Younger had formed a road company and were touring the country. Since the Gallatin trial in 1882, he and Frank had never crossed paths. Now, by happenstance, they were in New Orleans at the same time. His curiosity got the better of him.

Hopping a trolley, he'd gone to the evening performance. Like other Wild West extravaganzas, the show featured savage redskins and trick-shot artists and various specialty acts. The star attraction, however, was the two old outlaws. Between acts, they took turns lecturing the crowd. Frank spoke on the evils of crime, and recounted details of the life he'd led with his infamous brother. Cole spun windy tales about their outlaw days, and dwelled at length on the horrors of life in prison. The finale was a reenactment of the Northfield raid. Short on facts and long on melodrama, it dealt mainly with the bloody gun battle outside the bank. There were

running horses and an earsplitting barrage of blank gunfire and lots of dying men. The audience gave them a
standing ovation.

Watching from the bleachers, Starbuck was struck by
the men's general appearance. Neither of them had aged
well, and theatrical makeup did little to hide the ravages
of time. Frank was stooped and bony, almost cadaver-
ous, with the mark of years etched in his features. Cole
was little more than a bookmark of his former self. His
colour was jaundiced and his jowls hung like wattle
around his neck. Time lays scars on men, and in their
case the journey had been a cruel one. Both of them
looked long overdue for the old soldiers' home.

After the show, Starbuck went back to say hello.
Frank was genuinely delighted to see him, eager to re-
new an old friendship. Cole's greeting was civil but cool,
and he quickly excused himself. Later, seated in Frank's
dressing room, the reason became obvious. Cole's outlook, Frank explained, had been darkened by nearly
twenty years in prison. Then, too, he'd lost both his
brothers. Bob, after contracting tuberculosis, had died a
convict in 1889. Early in 1901, Cole and Jim had at last
been paroled. But the next year, despondent and unable
to find a job, Jim had locked himself in a hotel room
and committed suicide. Thereafter, Cole had worked as
a tombstone salesman and sold insurance, living from
hand to mouth. Not until they'd teamed up and formed
the Wild West Show had he begun to come out of his
shell. He still had a long way to go.

As for himself, Frank had no quarrel with life. His
wife had stuck by him, and he'd always managed to earn
an honest livelihood. His notoriety had made him an
attraction, and he'd had no qualms about cashing in on
the James name. Down through the years, he had worked
as a race starter at county fairs, lectured in theatres, and

even tried his hand as an actor in travelling stock companies. At times he felt himself an oddity—something on the order of a circus freak—but all in all he had no complaints. His only regret was that he'd never had the gumption to kill Bob Ford. Someone else had done the job—gunning down Ford in 1892—and his one consolation was that the "dirty little coward" had got it in the back. As for the future, Frank was relatively sanguine. The Wild West Show was booked into next year, and the money was good. When it finally folded, he thought he might try horse breeding, or perhaps go back to farming. He was now sixty years old, and sometimes felt a hundred. Clay County beckoned, and a rocker on the porch of the family farm had a certain appeal. There were worse ways for an old outlaw to end his days.

Starbuck considered the statement a small pearl of wisdom. Upon reflection, after returning to his hotel last night, he'd come to the conclusion it was typical of the man. Frank James was no phony, and he never tried to fool himself or anyone else. Even in the old days, he had possessed that quality so rare among gunmen. He saw things in the cold light of truth, without distortion or whitewash. And he never deluded himself about the romantic nonsense published in penny dreadfuls and dime novels. He was brutally honest about the life he'd led, and his statement summed it up in a nutshell. There were, indeed, worse ways for an outlaw to end his days.

Tonight, the thought was very much on Starbuck's mind. As he walked towards the rear of the circus tent, he marked again the wisdom of some men and the folly of others. Late that afternoon he had concluded his business in New Orleans, and the outcome was anything but satisfactory. He would have preferred a different ending altogether. Something more along the lines of that day, nearly twenty years ago, down on the Pecos. Yet some

men, unlike Frank James, were bound and determined
to go out the hard way. He took no pleasure in the fact
that he was still able to accommodate them. Dead or
alive somehow seemed an anachronism. Not at all suited
to the twentieth century.

Frank's dressing room was located directly behind the
bandstand. Starbuck found him seated before a mirror,
applying stage makeup. He looked up with a sheepish
grin.

"You caught me!" He gave his face one last dab with
a makeup sponge. "Hiding all these wrinkles takes considerable work."

"Near as I recollect," Starbuck said affably, "you always had a secret yearning to tread the boards. Looks
like you got your wish."

" 'All the world's a stage!' " Frank said with an eloquent gesture. " 'And one man in his time plays many
parts!' "

Starbuck's smile broadened. "I've played a few myself . . . here and there."

"A few!" Frank laughed. "Luke, you're a born actor!
You could've made it big in the theatre."

"Well, like you said, all the world's a stage."

Frank waved him to a chair. Starbuck seated himself
and took out a pack of cigarettes. Some years ago he
had switched from roll-your-owns to the new tailor
made variety. It was one of his few concessions to the
modern age; he still preferred, and used, ordinary kitchen
matches. He struck one on his thumbnail and lit the cigarette.

"Talking about rôles reminds me." Frank began stuffing an ancient briar pipe. "I meant to ask last night, and
it slipped my mind. You in town on business?"

"After a fashion." Starbuck took a long puff, and his
genial face toughened. "Fellow embezzled a bank out i

California. I got wind he was holed up somewhere in the French Quarter."

"Was?" Frank eyed him with a curious look. "You say that like he's not there anymore."

"Yeah, well—" Starbuck hesitated, a note of irritation in his voice. "I went to arrest him this afternoon. Damn fool decided to make a fight of it."

"He pulled on you?"

Starbuck nodded. "Had himself a little peashooter. One of those thirty-two-calibre jobs."

Frank regarded him sombrely. "So you killed him?"

"No choice," Starbuck explained. "I had the drop on him and he still went for his gun. A goddamn book-keeper, for Chrissake!"

Starbuck was not as sudden as he'd once been. Time had slowed his gun hand, but he now compensated by gaining the edge before he made his move. These days, the old .45 Colt, still carried in a crossdraw holster, was already in hand when the trouble commenced. If anything, he was more dangerous than ever.

"Too bad for him." Frank sucked on his pipe, his gaze speculative. "How many does that make? From what I've read, you must have better than thirty notches by now."

"Notches!" Starbuck repeated in a sardonic tone. "What a crock! Bat Masterson fed that hogwash to the papers and they swallowed it whole."

"I don't follow you."

"Well, last year he went to work as a sportswriter for the *Morning Telegraph* in New York. For my money, they ought to have him reporting on sporting houses. That and gambling was always his strong suit."

"Yeah?" Frank appeared puzzled. "So what's that got to do with this 'notches' business?"

"Once a tinhorn, always a tinhorn! He wanted to impress all his Eastern friends, and he needed an angle. So he bought himself an old Colt and cut notches in the handle. To be exact, twenty-six notches! Now he's got everybody convinced he tamed the West and killed all those badmen in gunfights. Spun himself a fairy tale and goddamn if they didn't buy it!"

"I take it you've got the straight goods on him?"

"For a fact!" Starbuck puffed smoke like an angry dragon. "I've known Masterson going on thirty years. He only killed one man in his whole life! And that was in a shootout over a whore. Course, nobody would believe the truth if you told them. He's set himself up as the he-wolf lawman of the frontier and it's all but carved in stone. I think back to marshals like Tilghman and Heck Thomas, and it flat turns my stomach. They're the ones that did the dirty work, and tinhorns like Masterson wind up with all the glory. Sorry bastard!"

"Life's funny." Frank wagged his head back and forth. "All this whiffledust about the old days ought to give people dizzy spells. Sometimes I think they prefer the lies—and the liars."

"Yeah, damned if they don't!" Starbuck considered a moment. "What's the reaction to these talks you and Cole give every night? Do the crowds believe you when you tell them how it really was with Jesse?"

"I tend to doubt it." Frank's eyes were suddenly faraway and clouded. "Legends die harder than men. Jesse was killed twenty-one years ago last month, and folks still believe what they want to believe. Hell, not long ago, even Teddy Roosevelt likened him to Robin Hood! And a president's never wrong. Anybody will tell you that."

"How about you?" Starbuck asked quietly. "When you look back . . . how do you see Jesse?"

Frank gave him a humourless smile. " 'Lord, Lord,

how subject we old men are to this vice of lying!' "

"Forget Shakespeare," Starbuck countered. "You're no liar, so tell me how Frank James feels."

"Luke, you heard my talk last night. I might have shaded the truth to add a touch of drama; but for the most part, it's what I say to every crowd, at every show. We robbed banks and trains because it was easy work. As for the poor and oppressed—we never robbed to help anybody but ourselves."

"And Jesse?"

"A hard man," Frank said with a distracted air. "Too hard for me to remember him with any real charity. I guess I just saw him kill too many people."

"I'd say that's epitaph enough."

"Let's turn it around," Frank said with a glint of amusement in his eyes. "How would you want your own epitaph to read?"

Starbuck looked stern, and then burst out laughing. "Tell you the truth, I don't give a good goddamn! I reckon I never did. Otherwise I would've chose a different line of work."

"You take that attitude and you'll wind up in the same boat with Tilghman and Heck Thomas. A hundred years from now nobody will know your name or anything about you. All they'll remember is Masterson and that crowd. The tinhorns who tooted their own trumpet!"

"No." Starbuck's weathered face split in a grin. "I'll be remembered. A whole crowd will turn out to greet me when I walk through the gates of hell."

"You call that an epitaph?"

"Why not?" Starbuck remarked softly. "I'm the one that sent them there."

"Do me a favour, will you?"

"Name it."

"When you get there"—Frank's mouth curled in an odd smile—"tell Jesse I said hello."

"Frank, you've got yourself a deal."

The old outlaw and the manhunter shook hands. Then Starbuck stood and walked to the door of the dressing room. There he turned, and gave the last of the James boys an offhand salute.

Outside the tent, a line was slowly gathering at the ticket booth. Starbuck skirted around them, idly wondering how large a crowd would attend the evening show. As he walked towards the fairgrounds entrance, it occurred to him that nothing had changed. Tonight merely confirmed what he'd always wanted to believe.

A lifetime ago he had followed his instincts and spared a wanted man. The gesture had cost him $10,000 and the everlasting enmity of a St. Louis banker. Now, looking back across the years, he thought he'd been repaid manyfold. Some men deserved to die and others deserved to live.

He was glad he hadn't killed Frank James.

READ THESE MASTERFUL WESTERNS BY MATT BRAUN

"Matt Braun is a master storyteller of frontier history."
—Elmer Kelton

THE KINCAIDS

Golden Spur Award-winner THE KINCAIDS tells the classic saga of America at its most adventurous through the eyes of three generations who made laws, broke laws, and became legends in their time.

GENTLEMAN ROGUE

Hell's Half Acre is Fort Worth's violent ghetto of whorehouses, gaming dives and whisky wells. And for shootist and gambler Luke Short, it's a place to make a stand. But he'll have to stake his claim from behind the barrel of a loaded gun . . .

RIO GRANDE

Tom Stuart, a hard-drinking, fast-talking steamboat captain, has a dream of building a shipping empire that will span the Gulf of Mexico to New Orleans. Now, Stuart is plunged into the fight of a lifetime—and to the winner will go the mighty Rio Grande . . .

THE BRANNOCKS

The three Brannock brothers were reunited in a boomtown called Denver. And on a frontier brimming with opportunity and exploding with danger, vicious enemies would test their courage—and three beautiful women would claim their love . . .

**AVAILABLE WHEREVER BOOKS ARE SOLD
FROM ST. MARTIN'S PAPERBACKS**

**Before the legend,
there was the man . . .**

And a powerful destiny to fulfill.

On October 26, 1881, three outlaws lay dead in a dusty vacant lot in Tombstone, Arizona. Standing over them—Colts smoking—were Wyatt Earp, his two brothers Morgan and Virgil, and a gun-slinging gambler named Doc Holliday. The shootout at the O.K. Corral was over—but for Earp, the fight had just begun . . .

WYATT EARP

MATT BRAUN